Julia James li[...]ceful verdant countr[...]wall. She also loves the Mediterra[...]yth and history, with its sunbaked landscapes and olive groves, ancient ruins and azure seas. 'The perfect setting for romance!' she says. 'Rivalled only by the lush tropical heat of the Caribbean—palms swaying by a silver sand beach lapped by turquoise water… What more could lovers want?'

USA TODAY bestselling author **Natalie Anderson** writes emotional contemporary romance full of sparkling banter, sizzling heat and uplifting endings—perfect for readers who love to escape with empowered heroines and arrogant alphas who are too sexy for their own good. When not writing you'll find her wrangling her four children, three cats, two goldish and one dog...and snuggled in a heap on the sofa with her husband at the end of the day. Follow her at natalie-anderson.com.

THE GREEK'S PENNILESS CINDERELLA

JULIA JAMES

SECRETS MADE IN PARADISE

NATALIE ANDERSON

MILLS & BOON

First Published in Great Britain 2020
by Mills & Boon, an imprint of HarperCollins*Publishers*
1 London Bridge Street, London, SE1 9GF

The Greek's Penniless Cinderella © 2020 Julia James

Secrets Made in Paradise © 2020 Natalie Anderson

ISBN: 978-0-263-27829-3

MIX
Paper from
responsible sources
FSC™ C007454

This book is produced from independently certified FSC™ paper
to ensure responsible forest management.
For more information visit www.harpercollins.co.uk/green.

Printed and bound in Spain
by CPI, Barcelona

THE GREEK'S PENNILESS CINDERELLA

JULIA JAMES

For Franny—my dearest friend. Always.

PROLOGUE

XANDROS LAKARIS TURNED ABRUPTLY, winged brows snapping together over his dark eyes, deepening the lines around his well-shaped mouth.

'Dammit! Just what do you suggest I do? Storm after her and drag her to the altar?' he demanded rhetorically.

The man he'd addressed, Stavros Coustakis, sat back in his chair, eyeing his visitor impassively. He had grey-green eyes, unusual for a Greek—but then—unlike Xandros, with his long and illustrious family history—Stavros Coustakis knew little about his antecedents.

'I'm a nobody,' he'd readily admitted, with the worldly cynicism Xandros was well used to in this man whose daughter he'd been engaged to marry, 'but I've made myself a very, very rich one.'

Those grey-green eyes hardened now at Xandros's outburst.

'No,' he retorted. 'It would do you no good. She has defied me and is therefore no longer my daughter.'

Xandros looked at him askance, his frown deepening. He knew Stavros was ruthless—a man few, if any, cared for—yet to hear him disown his daughter so casually was chilling. But he also knew that his own reaction to his former fiancée's flight was, in fact, predominantly relief.

He had been in no rush to abandon his carefree bachelor lifestyle, indulging in the easy-going short-term affairs which—thanks to his dark good looks, wealth and elevated social position in Athens society—had always come easily to him. Still only in his early thirties, he wanted a few more years of it before he tied himself down in marriage.

It was a preference which he knew warred with the dual

responsibility pressing heavily on his shoulders—not only to continue the ancient Lakaris family line, which could trace its heritage back to the imperial nobility of the long-vanished Byzantine empire, but also everything his father had impressed upon him all his life. That old money must continually be replenished with new or risk disappearing completely.

It was that necessity which had dominated Xandros's childhood. His grandfather had fatally combined lavish spending with rash investments, and the family had come dangerously near the point of complete ruin because of it.

Financial worries had been paramount in his boyhood years, with his father plagued by unpaid creditors and even impending bankruptcy, his mother fearful that their beautiful, gracious family home in the countryside beyond Athens would have to be sold. His father had driven himself relentlessly to restore the Lakaris fortunes and reverse his own father's unwise profligacy.

He had succeeded more than handsomely, restoring the Lakaris fortunes by the time his son had reached adulthood, but Xandros had grown up indelibly imprinted with the task of continuing his father's work and ensuring that never again would they want for money—that the family's wealth would never again be endangered, only enlarged.

An ideal opportunity to do just that—hugely—had presented itself in the prospect of undertaking a highly mutually lucrative merger with the Coustakis empire, its financial lines of business, from venture capital to insurance, that would fit ideally with the Lakaris portfolio.

Xandros's father, before his untimely death, had been keen to press ahead with it—and not just for financial reasons alone.

Xandros was well aware that his late father had been very keen on pointing out that their ties with Coustakis could, and indeed should, be even closer. And that Stavros's daughter Ariadne, despite her father's rough-and-ready self-made origins, would, in all respects, make Xandros a highly suitable wife...

He could see why. Ariadne, though perhaps a little young for him, being only in her early twenties, ticked all the boxes. A striking brunette, intelligent and cultured, she socialised in the same elite circles as he did, and they got on perfectly well together. From his parents' point of view Ariadne had the added advantage of not only being Stavros Coustakis's heir, but also the fact that her late mother had come from a very good family and had been best friends with Xandros's mother.

Moreover, Stavros Coustakis himself had become very keen on making the proposed business deal much more than a corporate merger.

'I've a mind to be father-in-law to a Lakaris and have a Lakaris grandchild,' he'd informed Xandros bluntly. *'Being a nobody myself.'*

For all his late father's enthusiasm, and his mother's urging, it had still not been an easy decision for Xandros to make, but in the end he'd gone for it.

And so, he'd thought, had Ariadne, who was keen to escape her domineering father as much as having any desire to marry. Okay, so neither of them was in love with the other, but they liked each other well enough, and he'd determined to do his best to be a loyal and supportive husband, and eventually a loving father to their children. That would have been enough, wouldn't it?

Except the text he'd received that afternoon, making him rush hotfoot here to Stavros's showy mansion in an exclusive suburb of Athens, had disabused him of that assumption.

Xandros—I can't marry you after all. I'm leaving Athens. I'm sorry—Ariadne.

The words echoed again in his head now—as did the covert tug of relief that had sprung up in him as he'd taken in the implications of her rejection. With Ariadne removing herself from the frame, he was now free to make what he'd preferred all along—a marriage-free merger with Coustakis Corp.

He'd said as much to the man who was not, after all, going to be his father-in-law.

'Very well,' he said coolly now, his voice clipped. 'Then that is that. Ariadne is no longer in the equation. However, as I have argued from the outset, marrying your daughter was never essential to our merger.'

He kept his eyes levelled on Stavros, seated at his heavily gilded desk, aware that he wanted out of this oppressively over-opulent mansion as soon as possible. His own taste was for minimalism, as in his own city apartment, or better still, the simplicity of his whitewashed, blue-shuttered villa on Kallistris.

Kallistris! The very name could lift his spirits! His own private island—his haven—a helicopter flight from Athens. The place he escaped to whenever his work or social life permitted. He had purchased it on attaining his majority, knowing that it would always be a safe haven for him, whatever life threw at him.

He would fly out there this very evening—spend the weekend, get away from all this. Away from a man he didn't like, whose daughter he hadn't really wanted to marry and now didn't have to, because it seemed she hadn't wanted to marry him either. Stavros Coustakis could forget about his ambitions for a Lakaris son-in-law and grandchild. It wasn't going to happen.

But first he wanted a definitive answer on the one thing he *did* want—the merger he sought. His eyes rested on Stavros Coustakis now, as he waited for his reaction. Was it go or no go with the merger? He disliked being played—

and with a party like Coustakis it was essential to meet hardball with hardball.

'You'll need to give me an agreement in principle,' he said now, 'or not.'

He glanced at his watch—a calculated hustle, as he well knew, and Coustakis would know, too, but that was the way the game was played.

'I'm flying out to Kallistris this evening.'

He wanted to be there in time to watch the sun set into the bay, the moon rise over the headland…

His mind snapped back to where he was now, and his gaze fixed on Stavros. Something was changing in those pouched grey-green eyes—they held a caustic gleam that Xandros suddenly did not like.

'I'm sorry to hear that,' Stavros was saying. His tone was smooth—too smooth. 'You see…'

There was a definite challenge in his voice now, which Xandros liked even less.

'Since you are so keen on this merger to take place, I had hoped that you would be flying to London instead.'

He smiled. Not a nice smile at all. And every particle of Xandros's consciousness went on high alert.

'In order to collect…' Stavros Coustakis's smile deepened, and the smile was indisputably a taunt, just as the now blatant cynical amusement in his eyes was overwhelmingly provocative '…my *other* daughter.'

Xandros froze.

CHAPTER ONE

ROSALIE SIGHED, CROUCHING down beside her bucket of soapy water, a heavy-duty scourer in her rubber-gloved hand, and poured bleach over the disgusting, greasy, trodden-in gunk on the cheap vinyl floor in front of the equally disgusting grease-splattered cooker.

The rest of the kitchen was just as disgusting. Whoever had rented this house had been a pig. The whole place was filthy, from top to bottom, and cleaning it was a pig as well. But it had to be done.

She sighed again. Her rent was due, and she also liked to eat.

She felt a familiar emotion burn in her.

One day I won't be doing this! One day I won't be cleaning up other people's filth and dirt! One day I won't be living in a total dive and paying a fortune for the privilege! One day I won't have a wardrobe consisting of clothes from charity shops! One day I won't be never going out and living on beans on toast...

One day she wouldn't be poor any more.

It was a poverty she'd grown up with. Her single mother, raising her daughter on benefits, had been plagued by life-long ill health, and Rosalie had been her carer both as a child and into her twenties. She had never been able to make a life of her own. It had just been her and her poor, frail mum, living in a shabby council flat in the East End of London.

As for her father—he didn't even know she existed. Her mother had told her as much, sighing over the one all too brief romance in her sad life.

'I knew him for such a short time! He was foreign—

so romantic!—working here in London on a construction site. Then I found I was pregnant, but he'd already left the country. I wrote to the construction company, to tell him you were on the way, but they couldn't have been able to trace him because I didn't hear back...'

And she never had either. Rosalie had written him off from an early age. All she and her mother had had was each other.

Rosalie's face shadowed. And now she did not even have her mother. Her poor unhappy mother had finally succumbed to chronic lung disease in the chill grip of last winter. With her death Rosalie had lost the council flat and lost the disability and carer's benefits she and her mother had lived on. But she had, she knew, gained her freedom.

Grieve though she did for her mother, she knew that finally, at twenty-six, she could belatedly start to make a life of her own. Make something of herself. Get qualifications, the ability to better herself, and escape from the poverty trap and the bleak, unlovely streets of her rundown part of the East End.

She sighed once more, scouring away at the filthy floor, feeling the small of her back aching. She'd been cleaning since eight in the morning, and now it was gone four. It would be another good hour's work on the kitchen before she could lock up, hand the key in to the agency, then get back to her poky bedsit and her crucial, all-important studies.

She'd signed up for online classes in accountancy, and getting those vital qualifications was her exit route out of poverty. To pay for them, and to pay for her dump of a bedsit and to keep body and soul together while she studied, she did cleaning work all day—however exhausting.

With a jerky movement she got to her feet, tipping the dirty water down the sink and setting it to refill, pouring in fresh bleach. She fetched the mop to clean the rest of the floor, then frowned suddenly, turning off the water as she hefted the full bucket.

What was that she'd heard?

The sound came again and she realised what it was. The doorbell was ringing.

Still frowning, and wary, for this low-rent house was not in the most salubrious area, she went into the entrance hall, setting down her bucket and opening the door cautiously. The view out to the nondescript street was almost completely blocked by the tall, male figure standing there.

Rosalie's eyes widened totally as impressions tumbled through her head. *Tall, dark hair, incredible eyes and face...*

Who on earth...?

She gulped silently, her gaze fastened on him helplessly. Then, abruptly, the man was speaking.

'I'm looking for Rosalie Jones,' he said, and his voice was deep and clipped and curt, with an accent she could not identify and had no time to think about.

Rosalie stared, still fixated on the overwhelming visual impact the man standing there was having on her. Then she realised what he'd just said.

'Who wants to know?' she asked sharply.

Apprehension spiked in her. No one who looked like the man standing there could possibly have the slightest business being in a rundown area like this! Everything about him was wrong here.

It wasn't his foreignness—that was commonplace in London. She gave a silent gulp. It was that air of being from a different world altogether—smooth, urbane, cosmopolitan, sophisticated. A world of luxury and wealth...

The flash suit, the silk tie, the polished shoes, the gold pin on his tie...all wrong for this part of London...

And most of all it was wrong—totally wrong—that a man like that should be asking for *her*...

His expression had tightened, as if he wasn't used to being challenged in any way.

'I need to talk to her.' His reply ignored her demand. He merely sounded impatient at her delaying tactic. 'Is she here?'

Rosalie's grip on the door tightened. 'I'm Rosalie Jones,' she said. She spoke reluctantly, and was about to repeat her question as to who wanted to know, but the expression on the man's face had changed.

'*You?*' he said.

There was total disbelief in his voice.

The dark eyes skewered hers. '*You* are Rosalie Jones?' His mouth tightened to a thin line. 'Impossible,' he said.

For a moment he just stared at her, that look of disbelief still upon his ludicrously good-looking face, and Rosalie found herself going ramrod stiff at the way he was looking at her. Because there was more than just disbelief in his face... There was something that suddenly made her burningly conscious of the way she was looking. Of what he was seeing.

Me, looking a total fright after cleaning this pigsty all day...

Then, suddenly, he stepped indoors, and another spike of apprehension shot through her, cutting off that burning self-consciousness.

'What the—?' she began indignantly.

But he had closed the front door, turning to her. That look of disbelief was still on his face, but he was modifying it, she could tell. Now it was a grim look, as though he were steeling himself to talk to her.

'*You* are Rosalie Jones?' he echoed. Incredulity flattened his voice.

She stared. Why did he sound disbelieving?

She tilted her face—he seemed very tall and overpowering in the small hallway, which was ill lit and shadowed now that the front door to the street was closed. It made her supremely conscious of the visceral impact of the man, from his immaculately cut sable hair to his polished hand-made shoes, via his planed and outrageously magnetic good looks and those amazing long-lashed dark eyes, which were raking over her as if he found her assertion outrageous.

'Yes,' she ground out again. And this time she got out the question *she* needed to ask—right now! 'Who are *you*, and what can you possibly want with me?' she threw at him.

With a visible tightening of his mouth, he answered her. 'My name is Alexandros Lakaris, and I am here because of your father,' he said.

Xandros saw the girl's expression go blank—and then pale with shock. His own feeling was not dissimilar, and had been ever since Stavros Coustakis had dropped his bomb-shell.

He could still hear the man's voice echoing in his head, and the exchange that had followed.

'Your other daughter?'

Xandros's stupefied repetition of what Stavros had an-nounced had fallen from his lips and the older man's ex-pression had not changed.

'Yes. I have another daughter. She lives in London. I am expecting you to go there and bring her here.'

He'd paused, and that unholy glint had come into his eyes again.

'Assuming, of course, you still wish to proceed with the merger you are so set on...'

Xandros's face had tightened, as if turning to set plaster.

'Tell me a little more, if you please, Stavros,' he'd re-plied.

His voice had been neutral...unlike the emotion scyth-ing in his chest. But he had determined he would deal with those emotions later. At that moment he'd simply needed information.

Stavros had supplied it, still speaking in that deliberately unconcerned way that Xandros had known was a wind-up—one he was equally determined not to react to.

'Her name is Rosalie Jones. She lives with her mother... or did until recently. I knew her mother...let me see, now... over twenty-five years ago, when I was working in the UK. It was a fleeting affair and we went our separate ways. However, I have always known of my daughter's existence, and now I think it is time she came here to Athens.'

He'd smiled, and Xandros had not cared for that smile with every atom of his being.

'In order to replace my errant former daughter, Ariadne.'

He had smiled again—that same mocking smile.

'I look forward to her arrival.'

And that had been all Xandros had got from the man. That and the knowledge, both galling and enraging, that he had been both outplayed and outmanoeuvred. Stavros Coustakis still, it seemed, had a mind to be father-in-law to a Lakaris...

Well, he would not succeed! Anger bit into Xandros hard, aggravating his ill humour. There was one reason and one reason only why he'd come to London. And that was to confront this hitherto totally unheard-of daughter of Stavros Coustakis and disabuse her of any expectations that her father might have put into her head.

Marrying Ariadne, whom he'd known for years, would have been one thing—marrying her unknown English half-sister was an absurdity he wouldn't even give the time of day to! The very last thing he wanted was for the wretched girl to turn up in Athens and plague him!

Just remembering Stavros's unholy taunt to go and fetch his 'other daughter' made anger spear through him. But now there was a different cause for it. A completely different one he could scarcely bring himself to credit.

His laser gaze rested on the female standing frozen in front of him. He was still unable to believe she was who she said she was. Because it was impossible—just impossible!

Whoever Stavros's hitherto totally unknown other daughter was, she just could *not* be the woman standing here!

However brief the liaison Stavros might have had with the girl's mother, his child would have been amply provided for. Stavros Coustakis was one of the richest men in Greece! So his daughter would obviously be the London equivalent of Ariadne, living somewhere appropriate for having so wealthy a father! Somewhere like Chelsea or Notting Hill or Hampstead—

But the contact address that had been supplied to him by Stavros at his hotel a short while ago had made him frown. What would Stavros Coustakis's daughter be doing in this tatty, rundown part of London? Was she into property redevelopment, perhaps? Seeing financial opportunities in clearing semi-derelict sites and here merely to scope out potential projects?

The actual truth, forcing itself upon him now as he stared incredulously at the figure in front of him, was... unbelievable.

He felt shock resonate through him again now, and his gaze skewered her, taking in every dire detail of her appearance—the stained tee, the baggy cotton trousers covered in damp patches, the hands in yellow rubber gloves, clutching a floor mop and a bucket reeking of disinfectant. Her hair was screwed up on top of her head in a kind of topknot from which messy tufts protruded. And as for her face—

His expression changed. He'd been so negatively impacted by the grim first impression she'd made that it had been all that had registered. But now...

His eyes narrowed in automatic male assessment. Okay, so her complexion was pallid and blotchy, lined with fatigue, and there was a streak of dirt across her cheek, but other than that...

Fine-boned features, a tender mouth, and beautiful eyes that, despite the dark hollows beneath them, are—

Grey-green.

Shock ripped through him again. For all his protest that this appallingly attired, rubber-gloved female with her mop and bucket just could *not* be Stavros Coustakis's daughter, those eyes—so incredibly distinctive—proved his denial and disbelief wrong.

Thee mou—she really is his daughter.

Shock stabbed him again—and he saw the same emotion intensify in her frozen face as well.

'My *father*?' she gasped.

The mop clattered from Rosalie's suddenly nerveless grip. Her vision seemed to be blurring, the world turning fuzzy...

She had heard the man who had just spoken say what surely to God he could not have said...

Because I don't have a father. I've never had a father... never...

He was saying something in a foreign language. She didn't know what—didn't know anything except that the world was still turning fuzzy and she seemed to be falling...

Then, like iron, his grip seized upon her arm and she was bodily steered into the kitchen, forcibly propelled down on to the chair by the rickety table. At last the falling sensation stopped, and the world became less fuzzy, and she found herself blinking blankly.

The man was now standing in front of her, towering over her, and she was staring at him with that weird, blurry gaze. He was speaking again, and she forced herself to hear him.

'Your father—Stavros Coustakis,' he was saying.

She mouthed groggily. 'Stavros Cous… Cous…?' She tried to say the foreign-sounding name, but couldn't make her throat muscles work properly.

The man was frowning down at her, and with a part of her brain that should not have been working she registered how the frown angled the sculpted planes of his face, darkening those incredible dark eyes of his to make him even more ludicrously good-looking than ever, doing things to her that were utterly irrelevant right now, at this moment when he had told her what she had never expected to hear in all her life…

'Stavros Coustakis.'

She heard him repeat the name in the accented voice which went, she realised, with the foreign-sounding name he'd said—just as it went with the air of foreignness about him.

She blinked again, staring at him. 'I've got a father?'

The question sounded stupid, because he'd just told her she had, but she could see it had an effect on the man, because his frown deepened even more, drawing together his arched brows and furrowing his broad brow, deepening the lines scored around his mouth.

'You didn't know? You didn't know Stavros Coustakis was your father?'

There was incredulity in the man's voice, and Rosalie looked at him blankly. 'No,' she said.

The man seemed to be staring down at her as if not believing anything about her. Not believing she was who she'd told him she was. And not believing she didn't know this Stavros Cous-something-or-other was her father.

Her *father*…

The word rang in her head. A word she never used—for what would have been the point? It was a word that was utterly nothing to do with her, because he didn't exist—hadn't existed except for those pathetically few short weeks in her poor mother's life, when he had seemed to bring romance before departing for ever.

But suddenly now, at this very moment, he *did* exist.

She felt shock ricochet through her at the realisation, and it made her voice thready as she asked the question burning fiercely in her head. 'How did he find me?'

It came out in a rush, a blurting question, and she gazed hungrily at this man who had come here and dropped this amazing, incredible, unbelievable bombshell into her life— a life that had suddenly, out of nowhere, changed for ever.

My father knows about me! He's sent someone to find me!

Emotion leapt within her, distracting her from the fact that the dark eyes looking down at her had suddenly veiled.

'That is something you must ask him yourself,' was his clipped reply, but she leapt onwards to the next question.

'Where is he?' Her voice was avid, hungry, the words tumbling from her.

'He lives in Athens.'

'Athens?' Rosalie's eyes widened. Her father was *Greek*? In her head her mother's voice echoed…

'He was foreign—so romantic!—working in London…'

'Yes.'

The man's voice was curt. She saw his face tighten, as if he were shutting her out of something.

'As for any other questions you may have, they can wait.' He glanced around himself. She could see his expression tighten even more. 'Get your things and we'll leave.'

Rosalie stared. 'What do you mean?'

That tight-lipped, angry look was back in his dark eyes.

'I'm taking you to Athens,' he said. 'To your father.'

Xandros glanced sideways at his passenger in the chauffeured car. She still had that blank expression on her face, as if she was not really taking in what was happening.

Make that two of us, Xandros thought grimly.

He'd come to London with no intention other than to warn Stavros's English daughter against her father's scheming. But now his anger at Stavros had found a new cause. Hell, he'd always known the man was ruthless—his disowning Ariadne was proof of that!—but what he'd done to this wretched other daughter of his was...unforgivable.

Keeping her in ignorance about her father—keeping her in abject poverty...

Emotion roiled in him, and there was a dark, angry glitter in his eyes. Stavros wanted his English daughter delivered to him in Athens? Well, Xandros would be glad to oblige! No way could he just walk away from her, leave her there in that slum...

She'd come eagerly enough—but then, why wouldn't she? She'd just discovered she had a father she'd never known about—of *course* she'd want to meet him! And why delay? There was obviously nothing for her here in London! Not if she was reduced to cleaning for a living!

So he'd waited as she abandoned her bucket and mop, shed her yellow rubber gloves, shrugged on a cheap, worn jacket, picked up a shabby tote bag and left with him—just like that. She'd put the house key back through the letterbox and climbed into Xandros's waiting car.

She hadn't asked any more questions and Xandros had been glad of it. Answering them would have been difficult—especially any about how her father had found out about her existence.

His mouth set again. *Let Stavros tell her that to her face.*

There had been practical issues about getting her to Athens that had required immediate intention. Most importantly, did she have a passport? The answer had been an affirmative, and she'd told him it was in her bedsit. The car had stopped there—on another rundown street not far from the place she'd been cleaning—and Xandros's frown had deepened. The terraced house was peeling, its railings broken and rusty. Empty bottles and litter lay on the steps, and there were sagging curtains at the window. A total dump.

She hadn't taken long, emerging ten minutes later lugging a battered suitcase and climbing back into the car.

His eyes flicked over her now. She was looking marginally better, having changed into cheap faded jeans and a sweatshirt. Her hair was neater, and she had a strong odour of deodorant now—not stale sweat from a day's cleaning. Her skin was still pallid and blotchy, though, her features tired and drawn. Only her luminous grey-green eyes gave her beauty...

He snapped his gaze away, getting out his phone. What was it to him what Stavros Coustakis's English daughter looked like? His impulsive decision to take her to Athens had been motivated solely by his anger at the callous way Stavros had so obviously abandoned her to abject poverty.

Maybe Stavros will be shamed into supporting her now! Or she can hire a lawyer to make a claim—even take her story to the tabloids. How one of Greece's richest men left his own flesh and blood to live in squalor...

One thing that would *not* be happening, though, was Stavros's crazy idea that he might actually substitute this wretched, ill-treated English daughter—a total stranger to him!—for the missing Ariadne.

Xandros's mouth tightened. And if that meant he had to walk away from any hopes of the business merger he wanted—well, damnable though it would be to abandon a project he'd been determined on, so be it.

No way would he consider saving the merger by marrying Rosalie Jones...

He wouldn't give the thought the time of day.

CHAPTER TWO

ROSALIE SAT CLUTCHING her worn tote bag, staring out of the tinted window. She'd never been in a car with tinted windows—never been in a chauffeur-driven car. And she'd never sat next to a man like the one she was sitting next to now.

She pulled as far away from him as she could. He was checking messages on his phone now—a seriously flash model, she could see—and paying her no attention at all. She didn't care. She didn't want his attention anyway.

Alexandros Lakaris. That was what he'd said his name was. But who he was was not important. Nor was the fact that he was the most fabulous-looking male she'd ever seen in her life, let alone that she'd been looking a total mess when he'd first set eyes on her.

Those incredible, dark, long-lashed eyes had looked at her so disdainfully...

But why should she care what he thought of her? All that was important was what he'd told her.

She felt excitement rush through her again.

My father—he exists! He's real! And he's found out about me! He wants to meet me! My father!

The words were running through her head, storming through her like a torrent, overwhelming her, and she was only hanging on by a thread.

Everything was a daze.

In a daze she'd rushed up to her dive of a bedsit, grabbing what clothes she could, stuffing them into her suitcase. She'd riffled through the room for her passport—acquired so hopefully, yet never had there been an opportunity to use it—then hastily stripped off, washing in cold water at the tiny sink in the rickety kitchenette in the corner. Her hair was filthy, but there had been nothing she could do about that—nor the fact that she badly needed a shower. All she'd been able to do was spray herself with deodorant and put on clean clothes.

She hadn't impressed Alexandros Lakaris much, she thought now, with a twist of her mouth. She'd still got that disdainful flicker from his eyes when she'd clambered back into the car, depositing her battered suitcase in the footwell.

Oh, who cared what he thought of her? He didn't matter. Nothing mattered except the amazing, fantastic thing that was happening to her.

She felt a tearing at her heart.

Oh, Mum! If only you could have lived to see this—to see the man you fell for finding me! How wonderful that would have been!

The car was stopping and she frowned. They were going down Piccadilly, nearing Hyde Park Corner, and she'd assumed they were heading out towards the M4 and Heathrow. But they were pulling up outside a flash hotel.

Alexandros Lakaris was putting away his phone.

'What's happening?' she asked. 'Aren't we going to the airport?'

'The flight is tomorrow,' came the answer. 'I only arrived in London this morning. You'll stay at my hotel tonight.'

'I can't afford this place!' she exclaimed, horrified.

'But your father can,' Alexandros Lakaris informed her.

Rosalie saw his mouth tighten in a fashion that was becoming familiar. And his eyes were raking over her again in that disparaging way of his.

'He can also afford some new clothes for you before you fly out.'

She thought she saw a sudden unholy glitter in those

incredible dark eyes she was so conscious of, try as she might not to be.

'You should go shopping,' he was saying, and there was a strange quality in his voice—a kind of smoothness that overlaid something quite jagged and pointed. 'There'll be time tomorrow morning before our flight.'

His eyes flickered over her, doing things to her they shouldn't but did all the same. Now they weren't disparaging. More like…assessing. She felt a sudden rush of ultra-self-consciousness that seemed to be heating her from the inside.

'And you might also want to take advantage of the facilities here at the hotel,' he went on in that same smooth voice. 'Hair salon, nail bar, beauty room—that sort of thing.'

Rosalie looked at him doubtfully. Surely that would be hideously expensive?

Alexandros Lakaris's expression had changed again. 'Charge it to the room,' he said now, as if seeing her reservations.

She swallowed. 'I don't want to cost my father too much,' she said.

That unholy glitter was there once more. As if something were amusing him. She didn't know what.

'Believe me…' his voice was as dry as desert sand '… he can afford it.'

Rosalie frowned. 'Are you sure?' she asked uncertainly. She could feel her stomach starting to churn. She pressed her hands together. 'Mr Lakaris, all I know about my father is what my mother told me—that he was foreign and was working on a construction site. A brickie—nothing more than that. So—'

He cut across her. 'Let's just say he's moved on since then. Now he has others to work for *him*.'

Her frown did not fade. Could what he was telling her be true? Belatedly she started to join up the dots she hadn't yet joined. Alexandros Lakaris—with his flash suit and gold tiepin, his polished handmade shoes and chauffeured car—was obviously a Mr Rich. And why would a Mr Rich have been sent as messenger boy to fetch her if not by another Mr Rich?

'How do you know my father?' she heard herself ask.

'We have a business association,' came his reply, said in an offhand fashion. 'I agreed to escort you to Athens for that reason.'

She opened her mouth to ask more questions, but he was opening his car door, getting out on his side. On her side a doorman came forward, opening her door and lifting out her suitcase as she stepped out on to the pavement.

Uncertainty still filled her—and confusion.

Could her father really afford all this? A hotel like this... new clothes for her? But it must be true—or why would she be here?

A wash of excitement swept over her. Had her life really been transformed like this—out of nowhere and so amazingly?

The doorman was holding a huge plate glass door open for her and Rosalie went into the hotel, staring around her. It was very modern, with a soaring glass atrium and miles of marble floor.

Alexandros Lakaris was striding past her, walking in as if he owned the place, going up to one of an array of reception desks, obviously as at home in this five-star hotel as he'd been out of place in that rundown house she'd been cleaning.

This was his world—the world of expensive luxury...

She hurried after him, staring about her, clutching her tote and knowing how totally underdressed she was for such a plush hotel. Swish, elegant people were everywhere and her gaze swept over them. For a moment she quailed. Then she rallied, her chin going up.

I hate being poor—but I'm not ashamed of it! Why should I be?

But maybe…maybe all that was over now.

Maybe I'm done with poverty! Done with it for ever!

Her eyes lit with excitement, anticipation and a pleasure and thrill she had never known in all her impoverished life. She looked around the spectacular atrium, drinking it in.

Oh, boy, was she going to enjoy this!

'Your room key—you're on floor five.'

Alexandros Lakaris was holding out a piece of folded card that contained a plastic key pass. The frown that was becoming so familiar to her was back on his face.

Well, what did she care about his disapproval? He was nothing to her—just her father's messenger boy.

She kept her voice cool as she took her key. 'Thanks,' she said in a careless fashion. 'Let me know when I need to be ready tomorrow.'

She didn't wait for an answer—surely he could relay it to her through the hotel staff—and sauntered off towards the elevator banks.

Whatever Mr Oh-So-Handsome-and-Rich Lakaris, with his disapproving frown whenever he looked at her, was going to be doing till tomorrow, she couldn't care less. As for herself—she knew *exactly* what she was going to be doing.

She stepped inside a waiting elevator, and jabbed the number five, rolling her shoulders. They were stiff from her day's hard work. The overused muscles in her arms and legs were tired, and her hands felt like soggy sandpaper. The small of her back was aching, her knees knobbly from kneeling.

The elevator slowed, its doors slid open, and she stepped out into a lushly carpeted corridor, heading down towards her room on feet that were as tired and aching as the rest of her, but suddenly light as air.

Her drab and dreary life had been utterly transformed!

Tomorrow she'd be flying to Athens—her first ever trip abroad!—to meet the father she had never known, who had now, like a miracle, discovered her existence! How fantastic was that? And for today—tonight—she was here in this amazing hotel and she was going to have a fabulous time, enjoying every last bit of what was happening to her!

Totally!

She couldn't wait…

Xandros checked his appearance in the en suite bathroom's mirror, minutely adjusting his bow tie. He was dressed for a formal dinner at one of the City's livery companies which he'd decided to attend that evening while he was here in London. It might prove a useful occasion to start what he would now, inevitably and annoyingly, have to undertake: prospecting for an alternative merger target.

His mouth thinned with displeasure and exasperation. His hopes for the Coustakis merger looked to be totally scuppered by his point-blank refusal to give the slightest attention to Stavros's outrageous scheming.

Did the man really think I would just swap from Ariadne to this other, totally unknown daughter?

It was ludicrously unrealistic—distasteful, even, for both himself and her—for Stavros to think that either of them would go along with it.

His thoughts strayed to the fifth floor…to Stavros's worn-down, shamefully neglected English daughter whom he'd so impulsively brought here. He knew what was behind that impulse—and it wasn't just his anger at Stavros. His face shadowed. Poverty was always frightening—even just the thought of it.

Memories from his own precarious childhood plucked at him. His parents, talking to each other in low voices, their expressions tense, talking about what further economies might next be made. His mother bewailing the fact that they might even lose the Lakaris family home. His father working long, punishing hours at the office, trying to salvage the wealth his own father had squandered.

The fact that he had done so—triumphantly—could not take away the stress and uncertainty—and outright fear—that had dominated his youth and childhood even all these years later. So much so that the luxury he now enjoyed—and enjoy it he did—was appreciated to the hilt. It might so easily have been otherwise...

And hopefully now Stavros's English daughter, having known nothing but poverty all her life, condemned to cleaning filthy houses for a living, could look forward to an easier life, too.

He was glad he'd recommended that she do herself up, get some beauty treatments, buy some decent clothes, before she flew to Athens. After all, she was the daughter of one of the richest men in Greece—she should start looking as if she was!

What will she look like when she's dressed properly? Groomed properly?

He felt his masculine interest pique, a memory flickering of those hints of potential beauty behind her drab appearance, her luminous grey-green eyes. Her figure was good, even in the cheap jeans and sweatshirt...enticingly slender, yet full-breasted...

He snapped his thoughts away. They were inappropriate. He felt sorry for her—that was all. Nothing else.

He headed off for his dinner, resolutely putting her out of his mind.

Rosalie sighed luxuriously. This was bliss—bliss! And it had been ever since she'd slid the key card down the lock and stepped inside her hotel room.

What a room!

A vast bed, satin curtains, an armchair and a table, a

massive wall-hung TV—and an en suite bathroom to die for! She'd tossed her bag down on the bed, kicked off her worn trainers and danced around in sheer glee. Then she'd sunk down on the huge soft bed and opened the leather brochure describing the hotel's facilities.

Moments later she'd been lifting the house phone…making a lengthy—a *very* lengthy—booking in the spa, to be cleansed and pampered to within an inch of her life! Wraps, facials, manicure, pedicure, haircut, massage…the lot!

Now, hours later, with all the fatigue and the aches and pains of her overworked body vanished, her skin like satin and her hair like silk, she was propped up against the pillows on her huge bed, idly surfing her way through the vast array of channels on the TV. She was replete from the gourmet meal delivered by Room Service, picking at delicious chocolates and polishing off a half-bottle of white wine from the minibar.

Heaven—just heaven!

To think that this morning I woke and had no idea at all I'd be ending the day like this!

And she'd be flying off tomorrow to meet the father she had never known…

Wonder and joy flooded through her—and then a twist of grief.

Oh, Mum—if only you could have lived to enjoy this, too! To know that the man you fell for so many years ago finally discovered us again…

She lifted her glass, emotions full within her. As she set it back on the bedside table a rap on the door sounded. She started, then realised it must be Room Service, back to collect the dinner trolley.

Levering herself off the bed, she padded to the door in her complimentary bathrobe and slippers, opening it without thinking.

It wasn't Room Service. It was Alexandros Lakaris.

* * *

Xandros had been in two minds as to whether to check on Stavros's daughter on his return from his dinner or just leave her be. A reluctantly acknowledged sense of responsibility had led him to do the former. However much the girl was nothing to do with him, he'd plucked her out of her familiar surroundings and deposited her here, in what was obviously a totally alien environment for her. He'd better just make sure she was okay, and not doing anything stupid.

Like opening her hotel room door to anyone who knocked.

'You should have checked who it was before opening the door,' he reprimanded her.

For a second he thought he saw her eyes widen at seeing him. Then it was gone.

'I thought you were Room Service,' came the unconcerned answer. 'Anyway, what do you want?'

She sounded offhand, as if she couldn't care less.

'I wanted to make sure you were all right,' he replied evenly, keeping a tight rein on his annoyance at this indifference to his concern for her.

'I'm fine,' she answered. 'In fact—*blissful*!'

Her offhand manner vanished as she said the word, her face lighting in a smile for which there was only one word.

Radiant.

Xandros's breath caught. His eyes focussed sharply as he realised it was not just her smile that was making his breath catch. She had quite definitely undergone a whole bunch of beauty treatments…

The formerly pallid, blotchy skin was now clear and glowing, the lines of ingrained fatigue vanished, and there were no dark hollows underneath her distinctive grey-green eyes any more—eyes that were wide-set and luminous under finely arched brows. Her hair had obviously been washed, cut and styled, and was pinned up loosely, with delicate tendrils framing her face. She'd had a manicure, too. He could see the now smooth, long-fingered hand holding together the edges of her towelling robe, which was doing nothing to conceal the deep vee of smooth, pale flesh and the long line of her slender throat…

Without the slightest effort on his part, Xandros felt the start of a low, purring reaction stirring in him that came out of pure, unadulterated, raw masculine instinct.

Because there was something about talking at this late hour of the night to a woman standing in a hotel doorway wearing only a towelling robe and looking the way she was looking now. He had spent the evening dining well and drinking some very tolerable wines, with vintage port to follow, and something about the moment was really very…

Tempting.

Tempting, indeed…

The low purr intensified and he almost—*almost*—reached out his hand to draw a slow, exploring finger down that deep vee of her robe…almost let his other hand lift to her face, cup the delicate line of her jaw, tilt up her chin so that he could close in on her and lower his mouth to hers… to touch and taste those silken parted lips…

Thee mou! Am I insane?

He hauled his wayward thoughts away.

It's out of the question—totally out of the question!

Having anything to do with Stavros's English daughter other than the barest minimum was unthinkable.

'Good,' he said briskly, and continued in the same manner. 'I stopped by to tell you that we'll need to head for the airport after lunch. So you can have the morning for shopping. The concierge will book a personal shopper for you at one of the department stores to speed things up. Don't worry about how to pay. I'll cover it with the store directly for now and sort it with your father later.'

He would take a particular pleasure in sending a hefty

bill to Stavros—and not just because the man owed his shamefully neglected daughter big-time. He was pretty damn sure that Stavros had known he'd be dismayed to see how unlike Ariadne his older daughter was. Ariadne—cultured and couture-clad—had been eminently suitable as a Lakaris bride...unlike her ill-dressed, downtrodden, impoverished London-born half-sister.

It would have amused Stavros, Xandros strongly suspected, envisaging Xandros's predicted discomfiture at the prospect of taking so unlikely a bride in order to achieve the merger he wanted.

His mouth tightened. Yes, well, not only had he no intention whatsoever of matrimony now—with either sister!—but he could also play games of his own. It would amuse *him* to deliver Rosalie Jones to Stavros looking the way the daughter of one of Greece's richest men *should* look. Deliver her—and walk away.

Because Stavros Coustakis was not going to game-play with him one single time more. He was done with it. *Done.*

He snapped his mind back to the present moment, keeping his voice and manner businesslike. 'When you've finished shopping I'll meet you in the hotel lobby and we'll head to the airport.' He gave her another brisk nod, keeping everything neutrally impersonal. 'So, until tomorrow, goodnight.'

He turned away, heading back to his own room.

Best not to think of Stavros Coustakis's English daughter.

However radiant her smile...

CHAPTER THREE

ROSALIE SANK INTO the hotel car that had been sent to collect her—and her treasure trove of purchases—from the very upmarket department store in Knightsbridge where she had just spent three fabulous hours in the hands of a personal shopper.

It had been heaven—a fantasy come to life!—to try on garment after garment, each and every one of them so incredibly beyond her normal clothes budget, which had been focussed all her life on the cheapest of chain stores and charity shops.

It had been beyond her wildest dreams. And it was all thanks to her father! The father she had never known—who had never known about *her*!

And now they were to meet—this very evening!

Excitement and happiness filled her to the core.

Back at the hotel, the myriad bags full of her purchases were whisked away to be packed into the new suitcases she'd also bought. Her battered old case, full of her battered old clothes, would be held in storage for the time being. It was all being taken care of.

Now all she had to do was have lunch in the hotel restaurant and be ready, as instructed, for departure for the airport at two thirty.

Her expression changed. Alexandros Lakaris had made it crystal clear that she was nothing more than a chore to him. It was just as well she'd resolved to treat him as nothing more than her father's messenger boy. Even if last night, when he'd turned up at her room door in that tailored tux of his, looking even more incredibly drop-dead fantastic than he had in a zillion-dollar business suit, she'd had to physically stop herself gawping at him and remember that he was nothing and nobody to her...

Well, it was obvious, wasn't it? She was equally nothing and nobody to him. So she would match his manner with hers—brisk and impersonal.

An hour later, with another heavenly gourmet meal inside her, she was enjoying to the hilt the knowledge that today, in one of her umpteen fabulous new outfits, unlike on her arrival yesterday, she looked exactly the part for a swish hotel like this.

She sailed out of the restaurant into the lobby.

Xandros glanced towards the entrance to the hotel restaurant where, so the reception clerk had informed him, Stavros's daughter was lunching. He had had a business lunch in the City, and now he wanted to head for the airport.

A woman was emerging from the restaurant, sashaying forward on high heels, her tall, elegant, long-legged figure cinched by a royal-blue waist-hugging fitted jacket with bracelet sleeves, and a narrow knee-length skirt. A pale blue silk chiffon scarf flowed behind her as she walked and her slender throat was adorned with a double rope of pale blue crystal beads. Long, lush blonde tresses waved back from her face...her perfectly made-up, beautiful face.

Stavros's daughter.

Rosalie Jones.

Shock jarred Xandros—the same level of shock he'd felt yesterday, when she'd announced her name to him, but for the totally opposite reason now.

Because now, as she sailed up to him, there was only one word to describe her.

Stunning. Just...*stunning*.

Unbelievably so.

His eyes raked over her, taking in every detail of her amazingly displayed beauty. Oh, he'd got hints of it last night, but now…in all her new finery, with her face perfectly made up, her hair fabulous, her figure fully revealed in that close-fitting outfit and her legs lengthened with those four-inch heels…now she was a revelation.

A stunning revelation.

Deep inside, he felt that same low, insistent purr that had come from nowhere last night when he'd seen her in her towelling robe. It was starting up in him again. Much more strongly… But this time, in the face of that incredible full-on beauty of hers, there was no chance of silencing it. Nor, he realised, did he want to. What he wanted was to enjoy the sheer, raw masculine pleasure of watching this totally stunning female walk up to him. Around her, he could see other male heads turning, and a primeval satisfaction filled him. Of all the men present in the hotel lobby, whether guest or staff, it was *him* whom she was heading towards…

It felt good. And he didn't care why.

She stopped in front of him. 'So, are we off?' she enquired briskly.

He gave a start, realising that he must stop just gazing fixedly at her.

'To the airport?' she prompted. She glanced towards the reception desk. 'I checked out before lunch,' she went on. 'The concierge has taken my old suitcase into storage. I'd better get the new ones,' she said.

She sashayed off to the concierge's desk, and Xandros paused for a moment to revel in the sight of her rear view. Her perfectly formed rear view…

He kept it in sight as they left the hotel and she got into the waiting car. Inside, as he took his place beside her, he let his gaze go to her face.

'So, you went shopping, I see?' he said, his voice dry. It would be sensible, he told himself, to stay low-key about this.

She turned towards him, and a waft of expensive perfume came his way as she did so. 'Oh, *yes*! It was *fabulous*!'

Just as it had the previous night, a showstopping smile lit up her face. And, just as it had last night, Xandros's breath caught.

'The personal shopper was brilliant—she knew exactly what would suit me and saved me a ton of time!' Rosalie Jones was enthusing.

Xandros allowed his glance to wash over her. It was enjoyable to let it do so. 'You look,' he said, 'very good.'

He felt a wash of pleasure go through him at the fact that he had ensured she had at least been able to indulge her a little after what had been, till now, a punishingly deprived life.

'I want to look my best for my father,' she was saying now, in answer to his compliment.

Her expression wavered for a moment, and there was a show of anxiety in it.

'I want him to be proud of me,' she said. 'To be pleased he's discovered I exist after all these years of not knowing. I only wish my poor mother had lived to see this day. How thrilled she'd have been!'

With an effort, dragging his attention away from her, taking in what she'd just said, Xandros kept his expression neutral. It was hard to hear her getting it so pitifully wrong about the callous and neglectful man who had fathered her. Hard to hear just how tough her life had been.

'Poor Mum!' she went on now, sadness in her voice. 'She only knew my father for such a short while and then he was gone. She couldn't trace him, so he never knew about me.'

She bit her lip again, her hands twisting over her brand-new elegant leather handbag.

'Knowing now that he's been successful in his life, it seems so dreadful that he didn't know about us before now. My mother's health was never good, and we had to survive on state benefits because she wasn't well enough to work, and I had to look after her… It was always a struggle. Always—'

She broke off, glancing at him.

'It meant I couldn't get a job either, or even any college education.' She gave a half-defiant shrug, 'That's why I have to do the work I'm doing. I'm living as cheaply as I can, saving as much money as I can. I've started evening classes…an online course—'

She broke off again, her expression changing.

'But now everything's changed! Now everything's going to be *wonderful*!'

The sadness had vanished from her voice and her face had brightened. She rested her gaze on Xandros, looking at him expectantly. Ruthlessly, he kept his own gaze inexpressive by sheer effort of will, though her sorry tale of all she'd been through had stung him.

I should tell her what Stavros is like! I should tell her not to push her hopes too high! Not to pin them on him at all!

But he could not bring himself to see her crash down so brutally.

And she's not my problem—not my concern!

That was what he had to remember. He slammed the stern instruction into himself. Just as he had to remember that, however amazing she looked—and he had not expected her to look anything like that—he should keep his instinctive male reaction to her firmly checked. It was at the very least…irrelevant.

I'm just taking her to Stavros—that's all.

And as for that—well, however much of a crushing disappointment Stavros Coustakis would turn out to be, even having a father like Stavros was better than the life she'd been leading up till now, wasn't it?

She'll get something from him, surely? Even if it takes lawyers or the tabloids to screw it out of him!

She was speaking again now, and he realised she'd asked a question. A question he didn't want to answer.

'So, how *did* he find out about me?'

Xandros's expression shuttered even more. 'Like I said yesterday, that's a discussion for you to have with him.'

To his relief, she only nodded, and moved on to another question.

'What else can you tell me about him? You said he's been successful in life, but in what way?'

'Construction, mostly,' Xandros answered, relieved the topic had moved on. 'But he's branched out since—insurance, financing…that kind of thing. He's a very shrewd businessman.'

'I'm glad for him,' she said. Then she paused, her expression changing, her manicured hands playing with the strap of her soft leather bag. She frowned. 'What about… well, his personal life? You see,' she went on in a rush, 'it's dawned on me that…that I might not be his only offspring!'

She lifted her eyes to Xandros—Stavros's distinctive grey-green eyes.

'Is he married?' she asked. There was a nervousness in her voice that he could actually hear.

He shook his head. 'He's widowed. His wife died some years ago. But…' He paused. 'But they had a daughter. A few years younger than you. Ariadne.'

He saw her eyes widen.

'Oh, that's wonderful! I have a sister! Oh, you don't know how wonderful that sounds! Will I meet her?'

Xandros shook his head again. 'She's abroad at the moment.' He tried not to sound evasive.

'Oh, that's a shame! I hope… I hope she won't mind having a sister…'

Xandros's expression tightened. Who knew what Ariadne would think about this unknown daughter of her father arriving out of nowhere?

'Do you know her? My sister?'

The artless question was unanswerable. Not without explanations he had no intention of giving. So he only nodded, and to his relief realised his phone was ringing.

With a murmured 'Excuse me…' he answered it, grateful for the reprieve.

It was a reprieve he kept going till they arrived at Heathrow. Wading into the grim details of Stavros Coustakis's Machiavellian machinations was not something he was prepared to do.

He glanced sideways at the daughter Stavros had summoned to take the place of the daughter he'd disowned.

She'll cope with the situation when she discovers it—she'll have to!

And whether she would cope or not—whichever it was—it was not his problem and not his business. Because, for all his impulsive decision to take Rosalie Jones out to Greece to claim what she could of the heritage she'd been denied all her life, on one thing he remained adamant. Nothing—absolutely nothing—would induce him to fall in with her father's ludicrous plan for him to marry Ariadne's sister just to achieve the merger he was set on.

However stunningly beautiful she'd turned out to be… and however hard it was to drag his eyes from her…

Tiredness was lapping at Rosalie. Though it had been absolutely fantastic to enjoy her very first plane flight in first class, where champagne and a gourmet dinner had been served, and she'd loved nestling into her soft, capacious leather seat, flicking through complimentary high-fashion magazines as if to the manor born, the flight had been long and they'd landed in near darkness.

Greece, she'd discovered, was two hours ahead of the UK, and it would be nearly another hour before they arrived at her father's. He lived, so Alexandros Lakaris had informed her when she'd asked, in one of the most exclusive suburbs of Athens.

She couldn't wait to get there! To finally meet her father! But even all her excited anticipation couldn't stop her energy levels dropping away as they drove away from the airport. She felt flat, suddenly, and out of nowhere apprehensive.

'We're nearly there now.'

The voice at her side made her turn her head from peering out of the car window, though there wasn't much to be seen outside. It was so strange to think that she was in a foreign land.

But it isn't foreign! That's the whole point! It's the land of my father, and I'm as much Greek as I am British!

Yet as she made out the road signs in Greek lettering, and all the shopfronts, the traffic driving on the 'wrong' side of the road, it all seemed very alien.

The car was turning off the busy main road now, nosing down quieter roads that became spacious and tree-lined and less brightly lit by street lamps. At either side high walls girded the mansions hidden behind them, glimpsed only through steel gates. The car turned again, down yet another wide avenue, and then slowed in front of a pair of steel electronic gates. The driver spoke into a grille, and the gates swung open.

Rosalie felt her nerves tauten, her hands clutching at her handbag on her lap. The car moved slowly forward, over a crunching gravel carriage sweep, to pull up at the entrance to a white-fronted mansion, with wide steps leading up to huge double doors. The driver was getting out, opening her door.

She turned to the man who had brought her here, lifting her out of her grim, grinding, cheerless life in the East End of London to deposit her here at her father's house.

'Thank you for bringing me,' she said.

She made her voice bright, though she didn't feel bright. She felt nervous, but she wouldn't let it show.

Just like I didn't let it show that I could see, when I sailed out of the restaurant at the hotel, that he was finally changing his mind about me! That I finally wasn't invisible to him!

It had been a good moment, a gratifying one, and she had relished it. But it seemed a long time ago now.

Besides, what does it matter whether I'm invisible to him or not? Or that he's so incredible-looking? So what? It's my father I've come here for.

With a movement as graceful as she could make it, she got out of the car, gazing up at the imposing frontage of the house.

My father's home.

She tried to feel the excitement she should be feeling, but the nervous flatness that had come over her since landing was still paramount. She could hear the driver extracting the suitcases with all her expensive new clothes in them. The front door was opening—was this her father coming out to greet her? The father whom she had never known, who had never known about her...

But it was just a manservant in a white jacket, ushering her indoors with a murmur in Greek she didn't understand. Rosalie cast a look back at the car, where the driver was resuming his seat, and raised a brief hand in farewell to the man who had brought her here... Alexandros Lakaris.

Did he respond? The tinted windows made it impossible to know. And then the car was moving off around the carriage sweep, disappearing through the gates.

She turned and went inside her father's house.

She felt suddenly very alone.

Xandros sat back in his seat. For a moment, just before she'd walked up the steps, he'd had to suppress an impulse to get out and go in with her. Not to let that hapless girl face Stavros Coustakis all on her own.

He drew a breath. She wasn't his concern, and she certainly wasn't his responsibility. Rosalie Jones had entered his life briefly and now she had left it again. He would keep it that way and get back to his own life.

He lightened his expression determinedly. After Ariadne's rejection he'd felt a sense of freedom. He should heed it. He hadn't wanted to tie himself down—not in his heart of hearts—and now he wasn't going to.

As the car headed back into central Athens he let his mind play with pleasurable anticipation upon just how... and with whom!...he would celebrate this happy new freedom, enjoying the kind of affairs he was used to enjoying—the kind that never lasted and never led to anything longer than a few months.

His mind drifted over various females of his acquaintance, each of them a beauty, each of them, he knew from long experience, not averse to any sign of interest from him.

He felt an unwelcome frown form on his forehead, and his fingers started to tap impatiently on the armrest. There was one problem he was encountering in his mental parade of willing beauties. Not a single one of them held any allure for him whatsoever. And into his mind's eye was intruding one that did.

A showstopping figure, a cinched-in waist, endless legs, long, waving blonde hair...and grey-green eyes.

He slammed his thoughts shut. No—that was not going to happen...

Definitely, *definitely* not.

CHAPTER FOUR

ROSALIE LOOKED ABOUT HERSELF. It was a bedroom. She'd been shown up to it by the manservant, followed by two maids who'd started to unpack her suitcases until Rosalie had halted them. She was not comfortable with people waiting on her hand and foot.

She turned now to the manservant. 'When will I be seeing my father?' she asked in what she hoped was a casual fashion, hoping he spoke English.

He did, with a strong accent, but his words filled Rosalie with surprise and dismay.

'Kyrios Coustakis is out this evening,' he informed her in lofty tones. 'You will see him in the morning.'

She opened her mouth to speak, but now more maids were coming in, bringing in a dinner tray and coffee. The manservant bowed, and took his leave along with all the maids.

Rosalie stared at the door he'd shut behind him and felt a headache coming on. Tiredness snapped at her. Maybe, she thought, it was better that she postpone her all-important first encounter with her father till the morning, when she'd be fresher.

But the flatness that had assailed her since landing did not abate, even after she went to have a shower in what proved to be a highly opulent en suite bathroom, with gold taps and shower fittings and patterned marble on the walls.

Padding out into the bedroom, wrapped in a bath towel, she could see the room's opulence was just as lavish—there was gilding everywhere, from the bedframe and bedside table lamps to the gold-threaded drapes and massive chandelier.

The effect was… She puckered her brow. *Oppressive.*

With a sigh she sat herself down to pick at the food on an equally gilded tray. Lifting the silver dome revealed chicken in a very rich sauce, fried potatoes and beans. Though she felt bad about it, she couldn't face any of it, and soon replaced the dome, settling for just a bread roll and some strange-tasting butter. The coffee was strange, too—very thick, full of grounds, and there wasn't enough milk.

A wave of homesickness swept over her. Not for the festering bedsit she'd lived in till yesterday, but for the council flat where she'd grown up, where it had been just the two of them—she and her poor, frail, ill mum, all that each other had had, the two of them against the world, alone in the little flat. It had been small and shabby, and paying the bills and putting food on the table had always been a grim challenge, where every penny had done the work of two, but it had been *home*…

But this is home now. My father's home. My home.

The word hung strangely in the centre of her consciousness. Home? Was that what this huge, over-opulent, servant-staffed house was to be for her now?

She felt a heavy sigh escape her. One that should not have. For surely coming here, to her father, would be the best thing that had ever happened to her?

As she went to climb into the huge too-soft bed, with its satin sheets that were too slippery, she made herself imagine their meeting tomorrow. Made it vivid in her mind.

He'll sweep me into his arms! Hug me close! Tears in his eyes and mine! And it will be wonderful! Oh, so wonderful!

As sleep closed over her she wanted to dream of it—dream of the magical meeting that awaited her. But the dreams that came were not of her unknown father. They were of the man he'd sent to fetch her. Who meant nothing to her—nothing at all.

He was only a handsome stranger who had delivered

her here and then driven off again into the night, job done. Disposing of her like an unwanted parcel.

No one worth dreaming about.

'Kyrios Coustakis will see you now.'

The stately manservant was standing at Rosalie's open bedroom door. She turned from the window. Strong sunlight was shafting across what the morning light showed to be a manicured garden, with fountains, gravelled paths and close-clipped topiary. A garden that looked impressive from the house.

But she wasn't here to think about ornamental gardens. She was here to go downstairs and finally meet the man who, over a quarter of a century ago, had encountered her mother and brought her into existence.

Emotion knifed in her, but she controlled it. So much was welling up in her, but she dared not let it out. Yet.

Her heart was thumping as she followed the manservant downstairs. She'd dressed with extreme care, wanting to give her father no cause for disappointment or disapproval. Her smart yellow shift dress was knee-length, with cap sleeves and a round neckline, her hair was drawn back into a neat chignon, and she wore minimal make up. Her heels were low, and they clicked as she went down the sweeping marble stairs and across the imposing entrance hallway.

The manservant knocked discreetly at a pair of double doors set opposite, and Rosalie heard a voice say sharply in Greek, what she supposed was 'Enter' or 'Come in.'

The manservant opened the door and Rosalie walked in. Her heart was thumping like a jackhammer with anticipation. With hope.

The man who must be her father was seated at a desk across an expanse of tapestried carpet, and the whole room was lined with floor-to-ceiling bookcases filled with books. It was at once impressive and intimidating, Rosalie registered, with the part of her brain that was not focussed on the man watching her approach.

But her eyes were only for her father—fixed on him. She reached the desk, expecting him to stand up, come to greet her. Embrace her. Welcome her to his life.

But he did not. He simply sat back in his chair. Looking her over.

'So,' he announced, 'you are here.'

His gaze was like a gimlet and then he made a sudden gesture with his hand. 'Turn around.'

Rosalie stared, eyes widening. Suddenly it was as if there was sand in her throat. Why wasn't he getting up and coming to her, greeting her, hugging her?

'I said turn around.'

Her father's voice, strongly accented, had sharpened, as though he disliked not being obeyed immediately.

A frown creased Rosalie's brow. 'What for?' She heard the words come from her without her volition, in an automatic response to an order.

Something snapped in his eyes. 'Because I tell you to!'

'You *tell* me to?' There was disbelief in her voice.

She saw his eyes snap again.

Grey-green eyes, like mine.

The thought flitted across her brain, but she had no time for it. He was speaking again.

'If you want what I can give you, you will do what I tell you!' Something changed in his voice—something that made it not sharp, but as if something were twisting it out of true. 'And I can see from your expensive get-up that you *do*, indeed, want what I can give you. *If* I choose to do so!'

He sat back in his chair, steepling his fingers.

'Do you understand the situation now?'

Rosalie shook her head. No, she did not understand the situation. She did not understand it at all. This was her *father*. And yet he was speaking to her as if she were a...a servant! A lowly employee… Not as his long-lost daughter at all…

She felt something stab inside her—a pain so sharp that she felt it pierce to her core. But she also felt the force of what he'd just said. She'd rushed out to buy designer clothes the moment she knew she could.

'I… I'm sorry…' The words stumbled from her. 'I… I bought nice clothes because I thought…thought you would like me to look…nice…for you. I wanted to please you—' She could hear her voice catch as she spoke, but couldn't prevent it. 'I didn't mean to waste your money!' she finished in a rush of apology.

Her father's expression changed. Sharpened almost to the point of glinting.

'You won't—be assured of that,' he retorted. 'And if you wish to please me do as I tell you. Turn around!'

Tautly, Rosalie did what he bade. As she came full circle he was nodding, his expression less sharp.

'That's better,' he informed her. His gimlet eyes rested on her face assessingly, his hands still steepled. 'You have my eyes—good. The rest must come from your mother. I remember very little about her.'

'She remembered you!' Rosalie cried out before she could stop herself. 'She told me everything she could—'

Her father's expression changed again. There was a cynical light in his eyes now. 'I made sure there wasn't much to know. And I kept it that way.'

A frown furrowed Rosalie's brow. She could feel her emotions tightening within her, still feel that pain inside—because this wasn't right… This wasn't right at all. This wasn't the way it was supposed to be…

'So…so how did you find out about me? My mother told me that she tried to get in touch when she learnt she was pregnant, by writing to the construction company, but you must have left the country already because she never heard back. Her letter must never have reached you—'

'Of *course* it reached me!'

A gasp broke from Rosalie and she stared at the man across the desk from her.

An impatient look crossed his face. 'I've always known of your existence.'

Rosalie stared on. Inside her, a stone seemed to be occupying her entire lung capacity.

'You've *always known*?' The words forced themselves past the stone that was choking her.

'Of course!'

'You've *known* and never got in touch?'

'Why should I have?'

'*Why?* Because I am your *daughter*!'

A sneer had formed on his face—Rosalie could see it. Was appalled by it. Appalled by everything that was happening…

'What was that to *me*?' he retorted. 'Nothing! What possible interest could I have had in you, or your fool of a mother?' His face tightened, an expression of angry displeasure forming. 'You have been of no use to me until now. Which is why I sent for you.'

Emotion was storming in Rosalie, hard and angry and desperately painful.

'You knew about me and did *nothing*? Nothing to *help*? Did you *know* how ill my mother was?'

The grey-green eyes so hideously like her own flashed again.

'She was a fool, like I said! A clinging, feeble-minded fool! As for you—the state looked after you as a child… Your mother got child support, a flat to live in. Why would I waste *my* money on you?'

The harsh, cruel words about her hapless mother struck her like blows and she flinched to hear them. Protest rose in her, and she sent an arm flying out to encompass the opulence of the room she stood in, the grandeur of this mansion her father lived in.

'You're *rich*! We were so poor—grindingly poor! Mum was so ill she couldn't work, and I couldn't either because I had to look after her—'

A hand slammed down on the desk's tooled surface with heavy force. 'Be silent! Don't come crying to me! My money is *mine*—do you understand? Mine to do with *exactly* as I like!' His face hardened. 'And if you want to enjoy a single cent of it you'll change your attitude, my girl!'

Rosalie's face froze. She'd heard the last of his outburst—*'my girl!'*—and it was as if the words were acid on her skin.

But I'm not his girl—I'm no more his daughter than a block of wood! He knew... He knew about me and never cared at all...

The words tumbled through her stricken brain like spiked wheels, each one inflicting stab after stab of pain.

As if through a mist she saw her father get to his feet, come around the desk. For a moment, a wild, last frantic flare of the pitiful emotion that had been filling her ever since Alexandros Lakaris had made that astounding announcement leapt within her as for the briefest space of time she thought he was coming to her now, to embrace her in a crushing, paternal, loving embrace...

Her father, after all these long, empty years...

But he simply reached out to take her elbow and steer her bodily towards a pair of ornate chairs a little way from the desk.

'Sit,' he instructed, and lowered himself heavily on to the other chair.

Like a dummy, she did so, her legs suddenly weak.

He nodded. 'Now that you have divested yourself of

whatever sentimental rubbish was in your head, you can listen to me.'

His eyes rested on her like heavy weights. They were puffy eyes, she found herself registering abstractedly, irrelevantly, and there were deep lines scored around his mouth, which was thin and tightly set.

'You need not think that you won't come out of this a great deal better off than you have been all your life,' he continued, and there was less harshness in his voice now, as if he were adapting it to what he was saying. 'On the contrary. This is your lucky day indeed, I promise you! You will be able to live up to the clothes you have so eagerly rushed out to acquire! You'll be able to buy ten times that number! Live a life of idle luxury! Buy anything you want! Have anything you want!'

His voice altered again, the expression in his eyes changing, and Rosalie sat there numbed, yet with her mind filled with knives, her lungs choked.

'Tell me,' she heard him say, as if from far, far away, as if she weren't really sitting there, unable to move, filled with horror and disbelief at the ugly truth of the dream she had so stupidly woven in her head, 'what did you make of our handsome Alexandros, eh?'

She stared…swallowed. 'Alexandros Lakaris?' she echoed, as if she had not heard aright. Why was this man who was her father but not her father—no, never her father—saying the name of the man he had sent to bring her here?

'Yes, the handsome and oh, so well-born Alexandros Lakaris! So eager to go and find you and bring you to Athens!'

There was a twist in his voice, and Rosalie could hear amusement—a cruel amusement.

'So eager to do what is necessary to achieve what he wants. Tell me,' he said again, and the thin mouth twisted, and there was a glint in the grey-green eyes as if he took pleasure in what he was saying, 'just how disappointed *was* he when he found you? My daughter—charring for a living! Hah! How that must have galled him!'

His thin mouth set. 'So, was it he who had you cleaned up and dressed to come here?' A harsh laugh broke from him and his hands clenched the arms of his chair. 'Not that it would have mattered a jot to *him*! It's just a bonus that you've turned out to be a looker, despite your origins, if enough money is spent on you! He can thank his lucky stars for that—and so can you! You'll enjoy your luxury lifestyle *and* Alexandros Lakaris as well! Every woman in Athens will envy you!'

The grey-green eyes sparked again, with gratified relish.

'And I will get exactly what I want, as I always do! A lordly Lakaris for a son-in-law!'

Rosalie stared at him, as if from a long, long way away.

'Son-in-law?' The syllables dropped from her mouth uncomprehendingly.

She saw the man who was her father and yet would never, *never* be her father lift his hand in a swift, impatient gesture.

'Of *course* my son-in-law! Why else do you imagine I have had you brought here? To marry Alexandros Lakaris, of course!'

She heard him say it, and yet did not hear him. Her mind was reeling, as if she were in a car crash that was going on and on and on, and she could not get out of it, could not escape it…

'You're mad…'

The blunt words were hollow as she spoke them. And she saw the face of the man who'd just told her the most impossible, insane thing in the world—the man who had only moments earlier smashed to pieces the idiocy she'd conjured up in her stupid, *stupid* brain—twist with anger at her retort.

'Do *not* try my patience! It is all arranged—all agreed. Alexandros Lakaris wants to merge his business with mine, and it is an excellent financial prospect for both of us. But I will only let him do so for a price. The price is you. *Thee mou*, what is there for you to look like that for? You've seen the man! I tell you again, every woman in Athens will envy you!'

'You're mad...' She said the words again, but this time, finding some last vestige of strength in her boneless limbs, she forced herself to her feet. She was in a nightmare—a living nightmare.

She turned away, wanting only to get out of there—get out of the room, get out...

Her father's harsh, ugly voice slashed through the air.

'Walk away from me now and you walk away completely! You can go back to the slums of London! Back to the gutter! You will get nothing—*nothing* from me!'

She turned. Her face was like stone. 'Go to hell!' she said.

And she left the room, tears and misery choking her throat at the ruination of all her dreams.

Xandros sat at his desk, unable to concentrate on what he should be doing—going about the daily routine of his business life. Instead an image was playing in his head. Tugging at his conscience...

The way he'd just driven off last night as Stavros's unwitting daughter had been swallowed up into her father's oppressive mansion... Walking in there with all her dreams about some fairy-tale reunion with a father who would embrace her lovingly and welcome her into his life.

His mouth set. Well, she'd have been disabused of *that* by now. Presumably they'd met, and she'd realised just what kind of a man Stavros was.

She'll be devastated...

The words were in his head and he could not stop them. Nor could he stop himself suddenly pushing back his chair and getting to his feet. He flicked the intercom and told his secretary he was heading out for a while, that she should cancel his scheduled meeting with his finance director.

Reluctance warred with his conscience. No, he did *not* want to have anything more to do with that toxic set-up, and, no, Stavros Coustakis's English daughter was *not* his concern, let alone his responsibility, but for all that...

I can't just abandon her like that.

That was the brute truth of it. Like it or not, he should have given her some warning of what to expect, and not let her indulge herself in illusions of some kind of heavenly reunion. He should at least check that she was...well, *coping* with the situation.

Ten minutes later he was in his car and heading out of central Athens. His plan was vague, but it focussed on calling at the Coustakis mansion...enquiring after the girl. Just checking that she was okay...salving his conscience.

And most definitely he would not let his eyes rest once more on the astonishingly revealed beauty that had so unexpectedly emerged from behind that wretched bucket and mop image of his first sight of her. He crushed the thought instantly, before it could take any shape at all.

No, that was *not* the reason he was checking up on Rosalie Jones. Not at all...

Rosalie was walking. Rapidly, blindly and with one purpose only: to find some kind of public transport—a bus, a tram, a train...she didn't care what—to get her to the airport. Where she would raid her meagre savings to buy the cheapest possible ticket back to the UK.

Because anything else was impossible. Just impossible!

Emotions knifed in her, anger and misery, both of them stabbing and slicing away at her. Hot tears stung her eyes as she hurried, head down, clutching the handbag that held her precious passport and wallet. She was oblivious to everything except her need to reach the main road. Oblivious to the low, lean car suddenly pulling up beside her at the kerb.

She saw it only when a figure suddenly vaulted in front of her, tall and blocking out the morning sunshine. She stopped dead, her head jerking up.

Alexandros Lakaris was striding towards her, catching her arm.

'What's happened?'

His voice was sharp and she stared blindly at him, the hot, stinging tears in her eyes making him misty. She saw him frown, heard him say something in Greek just as sharp.

'I'm going back to England!' she bit out. 'I need to get to the airport! There has to be a bus, or a tram, or—'

He cut across her. His expression was grim. 'We need to talk,' he said.

Violently she yanked her arm free. 'No, we do *not* need to talk! I've *had* my talk! And my *father*—' she said the word with a twist in her voice that was like swallowing acid '—has explained *everything* to me! So, Mr Alexandros Lakaris, we do *not* need to talk! I am having *nothing* to do with my father's total *insanity*! And nothing to do with *him*!'

She heard Alexandros Lakaris take a harshly incised breath. Alexandros Lakaris—the man who, so her monstrous father had just informed her, had brought her to Athens solely and specifically for the purpose of marrying her, so he could do some kind of lucrative business deal with the foul, despicable man who had said such cruel things about her poor mother, who had treated her so callously—the vile pig of a man who she was now ashamed to call her father.

'Just what has he said to you?' Alexandros Lakaris bit

out, his face dark, his eyes darker. He took another heavy breath, his mouth tightening, shaking his head. 'I should have warned you—prepared you—'

Words burst from Rosalie, exploding from her. 'He said he's always known about me! He's known about me from the very start! He's known about me and he has done nothing! Nothing at all! He left my poor, poor mother to cope all on her own! He didn't lift a finger! Just left us to *rot*!'

Her voice was broken, choking on what she was saying, facing up to. It was as if she couldn't stop the words pouring from her—couldn't stop the hot, stinging tears streaming down her face.

'He let her live on child benefit, grateful for a council flat! He *let* her and he didn't care! Not even when he got rich! He could have sent money, made some maintenance payments for me—he could have *helped* her!' The sobs were tearing from her now, and her voice was choking and broken. 'He has so *much* and we had *nothing*! But he didn't care—he just didn't *care*!'

She couldn't say any more. Her face was convulsing, her shoulders shaking with emotion. All those years of struggling and making do, of her poor, sick mother coughing up her lungs in their damp flat, eking out every last penny, dreading every bill that arrived until finally the end had come and she had died in poverty and bleakness. And she herself, homeless after the flat had been repossessed by the council, reduced to living in that stinking dive of a bedsit, working every hour of the day cleaning up other people's filth, studying into the small hours of the night to get the qualifications she'd need to lift herself out of the grinding poverty she'd lived in all her life.

And her father had known and done nothing—*nothing*— to lift a finger to help either of them!

It burned in her like acid and she could not bear it—she just could not bear it.

She was shaking like a leaf, choking and trembling, sobbing out hot tears…

CHAPTER FIVE

AND THEN ARMS were coming around her. Arms that were holding her, cradling her, letting her sob and sob for all the sadness and bleakness of her mother's life, of her own... sob for the cruelty and callousness of the man she had to call her father when she would have torn every shred of his DNA from her body if she could.

She sobbed until there were no more tears in her, barely conscious of the hard chest she was collapsed against, of the strong arms around her, holding her. The same hands that were now carefully, slowly, setting her back on her feet as her anguished sobs died finally away. A handkerchief was being handed to her, fine cotton and huge, and she took it, blowing her nose and wiping away the remnants of her tears, blinking to clear her blurred vision.

Alexandros Lakaris was speaking, and his voice held something she'd never heard in it before. It was the last thing she'd expected from him after the impersonal brusqueness he'd treated her with in London.

Kindness.

'Come, let me give you a lift—it's the least I can do.'

He ushered her towards the car and she sank down into the low leather seat, her legs weak suddenly, her whole body exhausted. She was drained of all emotion. Barely aware of what was happening.

He got into the driver's seat, pulled her seat belt across and fastened it. Then he turned to her. When he spoke the kindness was there in his voice again, but now she could also hear apology.

'I'm sorry,' he said. 'Sorry that I didn't warn you. Sorry that I just left you there last night.' He took a heavy breath.

'I'm sorry that you had to find out just what sort of man your father is.'

She saw his expression alter, his face set. Absently, with a part of her brain that was working even though it shouldn't be, because it was quite irrelevant, she was aware all over again of just how incredibly good-looking he was, with his deep-set, long-lashed, dark, dark eyes and his sculpted mouth, and his chiselled jawline and sable hair.

Unwillingly, in her head, she heard her father's hateful words score into her. *'Every woman in Athens will envy you—'*

She tore them from her. Tore away everything else he'd said. Every outrageous, appalling word...

How could he even think it—let alone assume it?

But she wouldn't think about what he'd said. Wouldn't give it the time of day.

The man sitting beside her—the man her despicable, monstrous father had said such things about—was speaking again, his voice sombre and heavy.

'Stavros Coustakis is not known for caring about other people,' he said tersely. 'But he *is* known for manipulating people for his own ends.'

Rosalie felt his gaze on her, as if he was assessing how she was going to take what he was telling her. She stilled. Heard him go on.

'That's what he's been trying to do with me—and...' He paused, his dark eyes now holding hers quite deliberately. 'It's what he's tried to do with you.'

His mouth thinned again, and he drummed his fingers on the dashboard.

'Look, like it or not, we do need to talk. There are things I need to explain to you. Things you need to know. But not in this cramped car.' He suddenly gunned the engine, which made a low, throaty noise. 'I'll take you to lunch.'

He held up a hand, as if she were going to protest. 'Then afterwards I'll get you to the airport, okay?'

Rosalie's face worked. He was being different, somehow. It was as if he were speaking to her for the first time. Speaking honestly—not concealing anything. And that, she realised slowly, was why he'd been so brusque with her in London.

Because he knew all along what I'd be facing when I met my father.

Well, now she knew, too—and it had devastated her. Repulsed her.

She nodded numbly. 'Okay,' she said, her voice low. She was not able to summon the energy to say anything else.

In her lap she twisted his handkerchief, then busied herself stuffing it into her handbag. He would hardly want it now, all soggy and used.

She sat back, exhausted suddenly. It had all been too much. Much too much. Too much for anything except sitting here, staring out of the window, saying nothing, letting Alexandros Lakaris drive her wherever it was he was taking her.

Where it was was the seaside.

She surfaced from the numbness in her head sometime later, and stared through the windscreen at the expanse of bright blue sunlit sea appearing as they reached the coast.

'Welcome to the Aegean,' said Alexandros Lakaris.

He pulled up outside a swish-looking restaurant on the seafront, flanking an even swisher-looking marina, where swisher yet yachts bobbed at their moorings.

He got out, and Rosalie found herself doing likewise—found herself breathing in the warm, fresh, salty air, lifting her face to the bright sunshine as it shone down on that blue, blue sea. Out of nowhere she felt the oppression and misery encompassing her lift a fraction.

She looked about her. There was a promenade opposite

the restaurant and people were sauntering along. There was a pebbly, shingly beach beyond, and an air of leisure and relaxation.

'This is where Athenians come to get out of the city,' Alexandros Lakaris was saying.

'It's lovely,' Rosalie heard herself reply, and she heard her voice warming, in spite of all the misery still locked inside her.

'It's not the best the Aegean has to offer, but it's good for somewhere so close to Athens. Anyway, let's get some lunch.'

He steered her into the restaurant, which wasn't too busy, and they were soon seated at a table that was indoors, but open to the pavement seating area of the restaurant. Menus were set in front of them, and with a start Rosalie realised she was hungry.

After the emotions of the morning it seemed like a balm to her to be doing something so simple as sitting here, ordering lunch. Even though she still seemed to be drained dry, incapable of thought or decision.

I'll just go with what's happening at the moment. I can't do anything else—not now.

The food appeared swiftly. They'd both ordered fish, and it was served grilled, with rice and fresh salad, and it was, Rosalie discovered, extremely tasty.

Alexandros Lakaris didn't make conversation, just let her eat in silence. But it was a silence she could cope with, even welcome. The warm breeze off the sea caught at the tablecloth, fluttered the flags on the yachts, and the sun was still dancing off the little waves on the sea. It was calm, peaceful, and she was grateful for it. Glad of it.

She pushed her empty plate away. Her misery felt less now.

'Better?' Alexandros Lakaris asked.

She nodded. He was still being different from the way

he'd been with her in London. It was as if something were changing between them, though she didn't quite know what. He beckoned to the waiter to remove their plates, ordered coffee, looked back at Rosalie.

'Then I think it's time we talked,' he said.

Xandros sat back, his eyes resting on the face of Stavros Coustakis's daughter, who had just had had her hopeless dreams about her father ripped from her and the ugly truth shoved in her face. He gave an inward sigh, compunction smiting him. Yes, he should have warned her—but he hadn't, and now he must make up for that omission.

She was looking a little better than she had when he'd found her storming away from the Coustakis mansion— that, at least, was something.

He felt emotion pluck at him. Taking her into his arms as she'd sobbed out her rage and misery had been an instinctive gesture. But it had felt good to hold her in his arms... good to feel her soft, slender body folded against his. Good to let his gaze rest on her.

Okay, any make-up she might have been wearing had been washed off in her flood of understandable tears, but her beauty was undimmed for all that.

He felt thoughts flickering somewhere deep in his brain—thoughts he shouldn't grant admittance, but which went on flickering all the same.

He did his best to ignore them.

'Whatever your father may have told you, this is what you need to know,' he began.

He reached for his coffee, took a large mouthful, needing the caffeine. He would keep this as simple as possible.

'The reason I am involved with your father is that I am keen to pursue a business merger with him. Not the construction side—that isn't my thing—but in his investment- and finance-based operations. They would fit perfectly with my own business enterprises and add considerable value to both of us. Your father knows that as well as I do. However—' he took a breath '—your father is also entertaining other ideas. He wants more than a mere business merger.'

He eyed Rosalie carefully. Her expression had been changing as he'd spoken—and not for the better.

'He wants,' he said, 'to merge our families.'

There—he'd said it. And it was like setting a match to dry tinder.

The grey-green eyes—her undeniable heritage from Stavros—flashed like knives.

'He *informed* me—' she bit out every word '—that *apparently* every woman in Athens would envy me when I became your wife.'

The deep, vicious sarcasm in her voice was coruscating.

Beneath his breath Xandros cursed fluently and expressively.

Stavros's daughter ploughed on. 'And he told me that if I did *not* choose to arouse that envy in the breast of every woman in Athens I could take myself back to my London slum and I would never see a single cent of his precious bloody money!'

He saw her jaw set like iron, her eyes stony.

'Which is exactly what I am doing,' she finished bleakly. 'I wish to God you had never found me!' There was a tearing sound in her voice now. Her features twisted. 'Why didn't you *tell* me that was the only reason you'd trekked to London? To bring me here so you and he could cook up some *insane* way to seal a business deal?'

There was incredulity in her voice, as well as anger.

'It wasn't like that,' Xandros said, his voice tight. 'Your father wanted that, but I...' he took a heavy in-breath '... I never had the slightest intention of doing what Stavros wanted! My sole aim in going to London at his bidding was to make it clear to you that whatever your father might have told you about his ambitions for a marriage-based merger I, for one, would not be cooperating!'

He paused again, and then went on. He had to say this next bit…

'As for why I ended up bringing you out here after all,' he went on, hardening his voice automatically, 'bear in mind that I'd naturally assumed that, as Stavros's daughter, you would be living the kind of affluent life similar to your sister's here in Athens.' His expression darkened. 'Once I'd seen—to my absolute shock and disbelief—that the daughter of one of Greece's richest men was living in the kind of poverty she should never have had to endure, how could I leave you there?'

He took another breath.

'So I resolved to bring you to Athens,' he went on. 'In the hope that once you knew the truth about your father, just how rich he is, you might…well…' he gave a shrug '…if not shame him into providing for you, at least you get *something* out of the brutal fact that Stavros Coustakis is your biological father! As for the merger… *All* I want is a business merger. Believe me!' he finished feelingly.

He glanced away, out over the promenade to the sea beyond, then looked back at her again. He had to say the rest of this now. She deserved as much.

'The reason your father wanted you brought from London,' he said, 'was because your half-sister also refused to go along with his scheme.'

He saw her eyes widen in shock.

'He wanted you to marry *Ariadne*?'

He nodded. He would keep this as brief as possible. 'She refused. Left the country.' He watched her expression change. Become bitter.

'So, after ignoring my existence all my life, he found I

was suddenly useful to him…' Her voice was hollow, and the bleakness was back in it.

Xandros reached for his coffee, which he needed now more than ever. 'That's about it,' he agreed tightly.

He found himself thinking that Stavros would have assumed that, unlike Ariadne, who had her mother's family to turn to, this East End daughter he'd knowingly and deliberately kept poor would be open to both his bribery and his threats.

Well, Rosalie Jones had rejected both all the same. She was, or so it seemed, prepared to return to her grim, impoverished life rather than be subject to her father's machinations in exchange for a life of ease. He felt admiration for her resolve fill him. Yet he knew it was a resolve that would cost her dearly.

He set his drained coffee cup back on the table. 'Are you really set on going back to London?' he asked.

She nodded, her mouth set, her expression bleak at the prospect—and who could blame her?

The image of how he'd found her, looking exhausted and worn down, reeking of bleach and worse, that mop and bucket in her rubber-gloved hands, was suddenly and vividly—unacceptably—in his head.

I can't let her go back to that!

'No.'

The word fell from his lips, instinctive and automatic. Adamant. A frown flashed across his face. No, she would *not* go back to that appalling, poverty-stricken life! It was unthinkable—unthinkable for the daughter of one of Greece's richest men! Surely he could help her get *some* degree of recompense from her father—find her a lawyer ready to take up her cause? Or a tabloid journalist? Or both?

Her outburst cut across his cogitations.

'I don't have a *choice*!' she threw back at him, her voice

bitter. 'I refuse to have *anything* to do with a man who has said such vile, cruel things about my poor mother! Who knew he'd got her pregnant and then deserted her anyway, condemning her to a misery she endured for the rest of her tormented life without lifting a finger to help her—let alone the daughter he knew perfectly well he had! He can rot in hell for that! And for thinking he could *buy* me with his bloody money and that I'd *crawl* to him for it so I wouldn't have to go back to the poverty he deliberately kept me in, hoping it would make me malleable and desperate!'

Xandros could see her face working again, could hear the rage in her voice mounting once more. The fire in her eyes was making them more luminous than ever...her fury was animating her features...intensifying her beauty...

From somewhere deep in that part of his brain he'd had to silence before, the part that he had refused to pay any attention to, came a thought that was so outrageous he tried to stifle it at birth.

But it would not be stifled. Would not be silenced.

Because there was another way she could avoid being condemned to a life of grinding poverty. His mind raced. A way that would simultaneously do *him* some good as well. A considerable amount of good.

As his eyes rested on her agitated, stricken face, which for all the emotion working in it was still not diminished in its effect, on the emotion flashing in her eyes, lighting them into a blaze, he heard words rise up in his throat. Insane, surely, as it would be to say them...

And then he said them anyway.

'What if there was a different alternative?'

His eyes held hers, holding them by the sheer power of the will that was welling up in him from that deep, impossible place in his brain.

She stared. Blankness was in her face.

'What alternative?'

He held her eyes still—those beautiful, expressive eyes of hers—masking his own expression. But beneath the mask his thoughts were churning wildly. Was he really going to say what he was about to say? Could he mean it?

Then there was no more time for questioning himself, for he could hear himself speak. Saying the words.

'You marry me after all.'

She was staring at him. The blankness on her face was gone. And her expression now was one of total rejection.

'Hear me out,' Xandros urged. He was marshalling his own thoughts, moving them rapidly across his consciousness as they formed. 'You marry me—just as your father wants,' he repeated. *'But—'* and the emphasis was absolute '—you do so on *your* terms—not his.'

Her grey-green eyes were still stony with repudiation so he went on, hearing his own thoughts springing into being.

This will work! And it will work infinitely better than the marriage I was prepared to undertake with Ariadne! Because what made me so reluctant about Ariadne was the prospect of a permanent marriage! Of tying myself to her...having children! Losing my freedom.

But the marriage that was racing through his head now would be quite different! It would be win-win both for him *and* Stavros's downtrodden English daughter!

He set it out rapidly and concisely—frankly—in a cool, clear, businesslike manner.

'We marry—without delay—so your father will finally give the go-ahead I'm seeking and commit to the merger. Thereafter it will take about half a year for the merger to be completed. There are legal aspects, financial checks, due diligence, staffing issues, regulatory conditions that must be met.' He reeled off the list. 'As well as organisational conditions that I want to put in place. These things are seldom simple and never speedy. So we stay married for the duration and then—and *only* then—when the merger is irreversible, and I have what I want…'

His expression changed.

'Then we simply divorce and go our separate ways. The payoff for me is that I get the merger I want—it's ideal for my business—and you…' He drew a breath. 'You get a handsome divorce settlement from me by way of a thank-you for enabling me to get my business merger. You can pick up your life again—go back to England, do whatever you want.'

He took another breath, levelling his eyes intently on her, making her understand what he was promising her.

'You will never know poverty again.'

His eyes didn't let hers go. He was willing her to see what he was seeing. Willing her to agree. To say yes.

And even as he waited for her reaction he knew, with a searing awareness that he had been trying to silence ever since his car had glided to a halt beside her bowed figure, storming away from the Coustakis mansion with her hopeless dreams in tatters, that there was a whole other reason why he had proposed what he had.

His eyes rested on her…on the beauty that had been revealed to him…the beauty he could not now forget. Could not pass by…

There was a truth about her he could not deny—a truth that had been blazing in him like a fire that could not be quenched. It was flaring again now, as she sat opposite him, gazing at him incredulously with those luminous wide-set grey-green eyes, so incredibly beautiful…

I want her—I desire her. Since the moment she revealed her amazing beauty to me in all its radiance I have known that. I thought I had to ignore it, suppress it, because I refused to play Stavros's infernal games! But if she can be persuaded to what I am urging her now… I can indulge in my desire for her! She can be mine!

Six months, he'd said. Well, that was all his amours ever lasted anyway. After that they always burned out, became stale and tedious. No woman he'd desired had ever lasted longer and he preferred it that way—he freely admitted that.

Six months would get him everything he wanted! It would guarantee a business merger that would double the Lakaris fortune, just as his father had intended, and, as a sweetener like no other, this stunningly beautiful woman he could not take his eyes from would be his for the duration.

What more could he possibly want?

The question was rhetorical—the answer was blazing in his head.

All he needed was her agreement, and his eyes willed her to give him the answer he sought...

Rosalie heard what he was saying—heard his words, though she could scarcely credit them—but it was the last of them that was echoing in her head as he fell silent.

'You will never know poverty again.'

She swallowed. Looked about her. The swish restaurant they were lunching at was filled now with diners, all well heeled. Waiters hovered discreetly, taking orders for the delicious gourmet food that was the everyday fare of those who frequented places like this.

She shifted position in her chair, feeling the soft fabric of the outfit she was wearing—remembered the price tag that had been on it. It would have been as impossible for her to buy on her cleaning wages as buying a villa in the Caribbean...

Memory plunged through her of the last two days...the night she'd spent at that five-star London hotel, the luxury and the lavishness of it all. The fortune it had cost.

Her eyes went back to the man sitting opposite her with his unreadable expression, waiting for her response.

She looked at the superb cut of his business suit easing across his broad shoulders, the silk tie, the gold tiepin, the svelte look of sleek, expensive grooming about him… thought back to the low, lean car he'd driven her here in, with its famous logo on the bonnet and the deep soft leather bucket seats she'd sunk into. Thought back to the flight in first class she'd taken to Athens, the non-stop champagne, the hovering flight attendants, the very lap of luxury…

She'd tasted that world—that luxury—glimpsed like a tantalising marsh-light what might have been hers had her father been the kind of father she'd woven such futile hopes and longings around…

But because those hopes and longings had crashed and burned, all she could do now was go back to London—back to the life she had there…all she'd ever have.

A sick feeling of dread and deep reluctance filled her.

Can I face it? Can I truly face it? Once my anger and my hurt and my outrage have worn off? Once I'm back in that dump of a bedsit, listening to the addicts and the drunks in the other bedsits? Hearing the endless traffic in the street, smelling the damp in the walls…spending my days slogging to clean up other people's filth and my nights trying to stay awake to study, because study is the only hope I have of escaping from the life my father's callousness has condemned me to…

The grim, bleak life she would be condemned to again.

Unless…

CHAPTER SIX

SHE FELT HER hands clench in her lap. Made herself look at the man who had just said what he had said. His eyes were resting on her, his expression veiled. He was waiting for her to answer him.

'So,' Alexandros Lakaris said, his voice level, eyes resting on her still, 'what do you say?'

She couldn't answer him. Not yet. Too much was in her head. He seemed to realise that, because his expression changed, became less intent. He was backing off. Giving her space.

She saw him sit back, pour himself more coffee.

'It's a lot to take in—for both of us.'

There was a smoothness in his voice now, and the slightest masking of the expression in his amazingly dark deep eyes. Eyes which she was all too aware she just wanted to go on gazing into, despite all the tumult in her beleaguered mind.

How easy it would be, she found herself thinking, just to go on looking into them…letting all the stormy emotions twisting inside her subside, letting herself just fall into that dark, gold-flecked gaze…

How tempting…

But he was continuing, easing his shoulders, reaching for his refilled coffee cup. 'So what I suggest is this. Don't rush back to London just yet. Stay tonight, at the very least, in Athens. I'll book you into a hotel at *my* expense,' he emphasised, 'because it's only fair that you have enough time to think about your answer.'

He drained his coffee and got to his feet, holding out his hand to her. 'Come—let's get some fresh air. A stroll by the sea will do us both good.' His mouth twisted wryly. 'It's been a strenuous two days—and an emotional roller coaster for you.'

She let him draw her up, because it seemed easier to do so, let him fold her hand into the crook of his arm and pat it with brief reassurance. He led her out of the restaurant, pausing only to settle the bill with a flick of a gold-trimmed credit card. Then they were out on the pavement, and he was guiding her across the road to the seafront.

The warm sun was like a blessing on her, and she felt its benediction on her confused, exhausted emotions as they strolled along.

Alexandros Lakaris was pointing out a couple of islands visible out to sea, mentioning how the bay had once, in Athens's Classical Golden Age, been the scene of the famous battle of Salamis against Persian invaders, telling her about Greece's struggles so long ago.

Rosalie listened, glad of the diversion from her turbid thoughts and emotions, finding herself interested in what he was saying. She knew so little about Greece, ancient or modern...

But it's my heritage—just as much as my English heritage! A heritage I've been denied. And even if my father is a man to deplore and be ashamed of, that doesn't mean I have to reject everything about this side of me!

She felt her gaze flick from the seascape to the man at her side, as they strolled along the promenade in the afternoon warmth. Strolling along as if they were already a couple...

But it's absurd what he's suggested, isn't it? Surely it is?

Her thoughts swirled within her, impossible to make sense of. All she knew right now was that somehow, and she did not know how, it seemed to be so very easy, so very relaxed, to be walking along like this, in a leisurely fashion, with his tall figure beside her matching his steps to hers.

He took them to the start of the marina.

'Do you have a yacht?' Rosalie heard herself asking, looking at all the boats bobbing on the water.

He shook his head. 'A dinghy,' he said. 'I keep it moored at Kallistris.'

'Kallistris?'

'My island.'

Rosalie's eyes widened. 'Your *island*? You have an *island*? A whole island to yourself?'

He looked amused. 'It's a very small island,' he said. 'But it is my favourite place on earth.'

His expression changed and she lifted her eyes to his. There had been emotion in his voice—deep emotion.

'Tell me about it,' she heard herself say.

They resumed their stroll, walking along the edge of the quay on old cobbles, near the water lapping and slapping against the hulls of the moored yachts.

'It's reachable by helicopter and I go there whenever I can,' Alexandros Lakaris was saying.

His voice warmed with fond affection—she could hear it. 'There's very little on it. Goats, mostly! And an old fisherman's cottage by the beach, done up as a villa now. There's a smallholding inland, where Panos and Maria live—they look after the place for me. It's very peaceful.'

'It sounds lovely,' Rosalie said wistfully.

A whole island all to yourself, set in this azure sea, beneath this golden sun... A world, a universe away from the squalid back streets of the East End.

'So, what would you like to do now?' Alexandros Lakaris was asking her as they reached the far side of the quay. 'Shall we go for a drive? And then back into Athens?'

She gave a nod. It was easier to let him make the decisions, easier to go with the flow.

Maybe it would be sensible to spend one more night here. To at least think over what he's thrown at me.

Was it really as absurd as it sounded? When the alternative was so grim… When she'd had a brief, tantalising taste of the kind of luxurious life she could enjoy for months and months if she went with what he'd so extraordinarily suggested.

And at the end of those months she could go back to England with the divorce settlement he was promising her after he'd got the merger he wanted.

Into her head sprang visions of the kind of life she could lead if she did not have to go back to the bleak, exhausting slog she'd come from.

I could get out of London! Move to the country or a beautiful cathedral town! Or even the seaside. Make a completely new life for myself! A life of my own choosing.

The vision hovered in her head. So incredibly tempting…

They reached the car and he opened the passenger door for her. As he did so, he paused, frowning, as if something had just struck him.

'Where is your luggage? All the clothes you bought?'

Rosalie's face hardened as she got into her seat and he did likewise, gunning the powerful engine.

'I left them,' she said. 'And I wish to God I didn't have to wear this outfit either! I'll be sending it back to him from London.'

She heard Alexandros Lakaris say something in Greek. She thought he must be swearing, so perhaps that was just as well.

'I'll have them fetched for you,' he said, his face grim with displeasure as he moved off into the roadway. He turned to her. 'Would it persuade you to keep them if you knew that in fact it was me who paid for them? I was going to charge them to your father, but in the circumstances…'

'I can't accept them from you either!' Rosalie exclaimed hotly. 'How could you think I would?'

'If you accept my proposal, then of course you can,' he replied. 'In fact,' he went on, 'you'll need many more.' He glanced across at her and there was that glint in his eye again. It did things to her that it shouldn't. 'As my wife,' he said, 'you would be superbly dressed...'

She made a face, trying not to see herself let loose in yet more gorgeous designer departments. 'Is that supposed to persuade me?' she posed.

'Will it?' he countered.

She shook her head. 'I mustn't let it,' she answered in a low voice, looking down at her lap. She gave a sigh, then looked at him straight, took a breath. 'Mr Lakaris, if—'

He cut her off with a frown. 'I think we have gone long beyond the stage of formal address,' he said wryly. 'My friends,' he went on, 'call me Xandros.'

'Well, whatever I call you,' she persisted, 'I have to be absolutely sure that I'm not...not...letting you buy me things. Expensive clothes. Expensive hotel rooms. Expensive meals, come to that...'

He frowned. 'You were happy enough to buy clothes when you thought your father was paying.'

'That's different—he's my father. But you'd be—'

'Your husband,' he supplied. 'And you, as I set out at lunchtime, would be my wife,' he went on, and there was a crispness in his voice that she could hear clearly. 'A wife who is enabling me to make a *lot* of money, thanks to this merger!' He glanced at her briefly. 'Does that reassure you at all?'

'I suppose so,' she said uneasily.

'Good,' he replied decisively. 'And now...' he changed gear and the powerful car shot forward, before settling into a fast cruising speed along the highway '...let's put all that aside for the time being. Tell me—how do you fancy driving out to Sounion? There's an ancient temple there, and a dramatic headland. Let me show you something of Greece.

If a couture wardrobe can't tempt you to marry me, maybe Greece will!'

She heard humour in his voice, and he threw her a slanting smile.

His eyes went back to the road ahead, but Rosalie's did not do likewise. That brief smile, crinkling his eyes and curving his sculpted mouth, had made her stomach flip.

Her gaze focussed on his strong, perfectly carved profile, the fine blade of his nose, the chiselled jaw, the faint furrow of concentration on his broad brow as he overtook a lorry and then eased his square long-fingered hands on the steering wheel again. She took in the breadth of his shoulders, the long, lean length of him—the whole incredible package of honed masculinity that was Alexandros Lakaris—and she was unable to tear her gaze away.

She was helpless to stop her father's jibing words echoing in her head.

'You'd be the envy of every woman in Athens!'

Galling though it was, how could she deny the truth of that jibing taunt her father had lanced at her? For she knew, with a burning consciousness, that when it came to temptation Alexandros Lakaris, all six feet of drop-dead gorgeousness, was in a league of his own...

She dragged her thoughts away, her eyes away.

If they married on the terms he'd set out—*if!*—then that factor, above all, was not a good reason.

In her head his words hovered again—his promise to her.

'You will never know poverty again...'

Temptation like an overpowering wave swept over her. She could marry this incredible-looking man, enjoy his wealth, revel in the lifestyle that would have been hers had her father not been as callous, as heartless, as despicable as he was. And she could walk away at the end of it all with a passport to a better life for herself.

I could do it! I really could do it!

But would she? That was the question she must answer. And it hung in her head like a burning brand.

Xandros glanced expectantly towards the entrance to the hotel's rooftop restaurant. He'd phoned through to Rosalie's room and she was on her way. He was glad she had accepted his suggestion that they have dinner together tonight, glad she'd let him book her into this hotel in central Athens, and glad that she hadn't insisted, after all, on him driving her to the airport so she could fly back to London.

And he was glad, above all, that at least she hadn't blown his proposal out of the water.

Because the more he considered it, the more ideal it became. In his head he ran through all the reasons why one more time as he took a sip from the gin-based cocktail he'd been served as he waited for Rosalie.

Just as he'd told her that afternoon, all the financial reasons stacked up irrefutably. And so did his own personal reasons. Reasons that, as he caught sight of her hovering a little hesitantly at the restaurant entrance, seared across his retinas.

His gaze was riveted on her as she walked towards him, guided by the maître d'.

A swift phone call to the Coustakis mansion as they'd headed back from Sounion at the end of the afternoon had resulted in her two new suitcases full of designer clothes being delivered to the hotel by the time they reached it. And clearly, in the hours since she'd checked in, she'd taken her pick of the contents.

To very good effect.

His eyes swept over her, warming with rich appreciation. An LBD—classic style—skimmed her tall, slender body flawlessly. She wore it with an evening jacket lightly embroidered in silver thread, adorned with a long silver necklace and matching bracelets. Her hair was upswept, which lengthened her graceful neck, enhancing an elegance that was rounded off by high heels that gave her an amazing sashaying walk as she approached.

Thee mou, but she was beautiful! To think she had clutched that damnable bucket and mop and scrubbed filthy floors!

Even as he thought about it, another thought gelled in his mind.

She never will again—never!

Whatever it took to convince her to accept his proposal, he would do it. She deserved no less.

And nor do I.

He felt that low-frequency purring start inside him as she came up to him. This beautiful woman, whose existence he had known of for only four days, had blown him away.

He got to his feet, greeting her warmly, letting the glow in his eyes show his appreciation of her.

It was having an effect, he could see—the very effect he wanted.

She wasn't impervious to him—he knew that with absolute certainty. He'd seen that revealing flare in her eyes, try to conceal it as she might. And when they'd been in London he had sensed, with his very well-honed male instinct and his considerable experience of her sex, that she was as appreciative of him as he was of her, however offhand her manner had been.

But that initial deliberate indifference to him—caused, he thought ruefully, by his own guarded behaviour towards her, because he'd been unwilling to disabuse her about her father and unwilling to admit to himself how drawn he was to her—was all gone now. There was no longer any need for it.

He felt the purring inside him heighten. Now they could give their sensual awareness of each other full rein.

It was there right now—he could tell—in that flaring of

her pupils as he smiled in welcome. In the flaring that was echoed in his own eyes. In the quickening of his pulse...

Impulse took over. An unstoppable urge. Without full consciousness of what he was doing, only male instinct possessing him, he caught her hand, rested his other hand lightly on her slender waist.

'You look fantastic!' he breathed. His voice was husky, again unconsciously—he couldn't help it. His eyes moved over her face, taking in just how exquisitely lovely she looked, gazing at him now, wide-eyed, unconsciously inviting...

That low-frequency purr intensified. Became irresistible...

His mouth dipped to hers...

It was the lightest of kisses—the softest brushing of his mouth on hers, lasting only seconds. The merest fleeting sensation...the merest sip of the honey of her silken lips... The kind of kiss any man could greet any woman with in public.

And yet he had to use every ounce of his self-control to draw back from her, to smile down at her and release her hand, her waist, help her to take a seat. He could see that her face had flushed, her colour heightened and the low purring inside him was glad of this visible evidence of her response to him.

Of his to her he needed no second proof. Desire rushed through him. And an absolute certainty that the half-crazy idea he had blurted out to her that afternoon to stop her fleeing back to London, to the grim, bleak life she lived there—the impulsive offer that, despite his original determination to have nothing to do whatsoever with Stavros's English daughter, had seemed the most obvious thing to make—was, in fact, the one idea he longed to make happen... He wanted to make her his.

He resumed his own seat, his eyes never leaving her. Her

gaze had dipped and she was busying herself smoothing a napkin over her lap, the colour gradually subsiding from her flushed cheeks. Xandros knew he needed to put her at ease with him. There would be time enough to make clear to her just how he felt...

'I thought it best to dine here at the hotel,' he opened. 'The food is excellent and I thought you might like the view.'

He gestured to the picture windows, which opened on to a terrace beyond. He heard her breath catch with delight as she looked past him to see what he was indicating: the ultimate symbol of Athens, spotlit as it always was by night.

'The Acropolis!' she breathed, with wonder in her voice, leaning forward to maximise her view.

'And the Parthenon on top of it,' he supplied.

Her face had lit up, enhancing her beauty, and as she gazed at the vista Xandros gazed at her face. One thought only blazed in him: whatever it took to convince her to accept his proposal, he must do it.

He could tell that her presence here with him was drawing eyes. Not because he was dining with a beautiful woman—Athens society was well used to that—but because up until recently the woman he'd been dining with had been Ariadne Coustakis.

And that, he realised, thinking it through rapidly, was yet another bonus to be gained from going through with the plan that he'd put to Stavros's English daughter that afternoon.

It will give me a highly acceptable explanation for why my relationship with Ariadne is no more. A totally unexpected coup de foudre when I met her half-sister led her to release me from our engagement.

The tale would play well, and it would silence any speculation arising from his precipitate marriage to another woman. He did not want Rosalie to be the butt of gossip.

He realised she was talking.

'It looks so close...the Acropolis!'

'It's quite some distance away, really—it looks close because there are no high-rise buildings between here and it,' he replied. 'Many buildings have a view over it—my apartment does,' he said.

He started to tell her about the extensive ruins of classical times, both on the Acropolis and at its base, and then went on to describe some of the geography of the city itself—the different areas from Plaka to Syntagma Square.

She listened with interest, asking questions, increasingly relaxed as their dinner arrived, sipping at her wine.

'I must buy myself a guide book,' she said. A shadow crossed her face. 'It seems sad that I know absolutely nothing about a city that I should have known all my life—'

She broke off, took another mouthful of her wine.

'It isn't too late to learn to love your Greek heritage,' Xandros said quietly.

He left it at that—let the thought gel, take root. He left unspoken, for now, the corollary... *If you marry me...*

Throughout dinner he kept the conversation and the mood casual, easily friendly, and it served his purpose well. For all the privations of her deprived upbringing she was obviously not unintelligent—just ignorant of a great deal of what he took for granted. But she held her own, asked good questions, showed a sensitivity that he appreciated.

'I know there's a fuss about the Elgin Marbles being in the British Museum,' she ventured, 'but I don't really understand why.'

'Because,' Xandros informed her sternly, 'they are not the "Elgin" Marbles at all—they are the *Parthenon* Marbles! The problem is,' he went on, 'that Lord Elgin acquired them in good faith—but from an authority that did not own them in the first place. From the Ottoman government of Greece at the time.'

She wrinkled her brow. 'Ottoman…?'

'The foreign empire from Asia Minor that conquered the Middle East and the ancient Byzantine Empire in the fifteenth century—and ruled Greece for four hundred years until we finally shook them off! It was a dark time for Greece. A dark time,' he added, 'for my family.'

She looked at him questioningly.

'My family goes back a long way,' he supplied. 'Back to the Byzantine Empire itself—the empire that succeeded the Roman Empire at the start of the Dark Ages for Western Europe. Here in the east the light of civilisation continued to burn, and the Byzantine capital, Constantinople—modern-day Istanbul—was one of the greatest cities on earth!'

She frowned, and he realised he needed to explain something more to her.

'It's because my family can trace its roots so far back,' he said, choosing his words carefully, 'that your father—who, by his own admission, is a completely self-made man—is so keen on marrying *his* family into it.'

He saw Rosalie's expression change.

'He threw it at me,' she said. 'The fact that I would be marrying "a lordly Lakaris".'

Xandros's mouth twisted. 'Was that before or after he threatened to throw you out, still as penniless as he'd deliberately kept you all your life, if you didn't do what he wanted?'

He shook his head, dismissing his own question. If Stavros's daughter married him it would not be at her father's bidding—let alone because of his financial blackmail.

'But we don't need to consider your father at all,' he said with a dismissive shrug. 'After the despicable way he's treated you he deserves no consideration! What we do is our business—not his.'

He saw Rosalie's expression flicker momentarily, and then a questioning look in her eye.

'Are you really "lordly"?' she asked.

Did her question indicate reservations? Xandros shook his head again. 'Not for centuries!' he said lightly. 'The Byzantine Empire ceased to exist over five hundred years ago!'

She frowned again. 'I thought there was a king of Greece at some time. Isn't there a royal family somewhere?'

'In exile,' Xandros explained. 'But it was never actually Greek. The family is an offshoot of the Danish royal family, installed when Greece got its freedom from the Ottomans in the nineteenth century. There are links to the last of the Byzantine imperial dynasties, but very distant. Not involving my family at all.'

It seemed irrelevant to add that during the era of the Greek monarchy his forebears had been courtiers—those times were long gone now. His thoughts darkened. Besides, it had been during the final post-war phase of the monarchy that his grandfather, with close personal links to the royals, had lived so extravagantly and recklessly, creating a financial precipice that had nearly bankrupted the family.

As his grandson, he was still intent on ensuring such danger would never again threaten the Lakaris fortunes. And it was that intention that was the driver for this Coustakis merger that his father had recommended as the best way forward. The lucrative merger to which the exquisitely beautiful woman opposite him was now key.

It will work—the plan that I have come up with! It will placate Stavros, convince him to agree to the merger. It won't tie me permanently in marriage, and yet it will give me all the time I want with this most desirable of women...

Now all he had to do was convince her to accept him and claim her for his own...

CHAPTER SEVEN

ROSALIE STIRRED, STRETCHING her limbs in the wide bed, waking slowly. She had slept so much better than on that night of nerve-racked tossing and turning she had spent in that over-gilded bed in her father's over-gilded mansion. Then, her dreams had been fitful, filled with seesawing hopes and apprehension. But last night they had been very different.

They had been filled not with anxious imaginings of her forthcoming encounter with her long-lost father, which bitter reality had sent crashing and burning into oblivion, but with memories of the afternoon she had spent with Alexandros Lakaris.

And their evening together.

And his kiss on greeting her…

She felt a melting within her as memory replayed that moment—how his mouth had dipped to hers, brushing with exquisite lightness the tender swell of her lips.

So brief…so magical…

And so entirely unexpected.

Because nothing in his behaviour towards her till that moment had given her cause to think that he was thinking of her in those terms.

Oh, she'd seen the stunned expression on his face when she'd sailed out of that hotel restaurant in London, glitzed to the hilt after her shopping spree. And it had been gratifying not to be Little Miss Invisible to him any more, after his obvious disdain for the way she'd looked when he'd found her.

But after complimenting her on her improved appearance—it would have been difficult for him to have ignored the difference all those beauty treatments and a designer outfit had made to her!—he'd reverted to his earlier attitude: impersonal to the point of indifferent. And he'd clearly been glad to be shot of her when he'd dropped her off at her father's house and driven off immediately.

But she'd been wrong about him. Quite wrong.

More memory pushed into her head. How she'd sobbed all over him in her rage and misery when he'd found her fleeing her father's house the next day…how comforting he'd been. How kind and sympathetic. She heard his words again, as he explained to her just why he'd brought her to Athens, how shocked he'd been to find her living the way she'd had to in London.

'How could I leave you there like that?' he'd said.

She felt her throat tighten.

I thought him brusque and uncaring—but he isn't! He isn't at all.

There was a warmth in him she had never suspected. Just as she had never expected that kiss last evening.

Memory came full circle and it played again in her head, tantalising and beguiling…

But had it meant anything?

It was just a kiss in public. He probably kisses every woman he dines with. Especially a woman he wants to persuade to marry him.

And there it was—centre-stage in her head—the one thing she had to think about. Marrying Alexandros Lakaris for six months to their mutual financial benefit.

Emotions, thoughts, churned inside her. Could she really do it? Do what Xandros was urging her to do?

She lay there, staring up at the ceiling, thinking through the implications. For six months she would be Alexandros Lakaris's wife—dressed up to the nines, enjoying the kind of luxury she had never dreamt would come her way in all her life! She would be living here in Greece, exploring the heritage she had never known.

Suddenly there was a bleakness in her eyes. She would not have a chance to get to know that heritage if she went back to her poverty-stricken life in London. How long would it take her to earn enough money to come back to Athens? Even when she eventually got a half-decent job once she had some qualifications?

Her expression shadowed. This time yesterday she had thought it would be through her father that she would experience her Greek heritage. Now it might be through Xandros.

And would that be unwelcome?

The answer was there as soon as she asked the question. Of course not! How could it be?

She knew now that he was far kinder than she'd originally thought him, and angered on her behalf by her father's callousness. That must surely warm her towards him. Plus, she knew simply from the time she'd spent with him so far that he was easy to be with, interesting to talk to, good-humoured and well-informed—without being in the least patronising about her lack of knowledge in things he took for granted thanks to his privileged background.

And then, of course, there was the most obvious, inescapable fact of all about how it would be if she accepted the extraordinary proposal he'd made to her.

The fact that a single glance from those incredible, dark, gold-flecked, long-lashed eyes of his could make her pulse race in ways she had never known... The fact that she just wanted to gaze and gaze at his absolute male perfection... drink in everything about him...

And how could she not be smitten with her limited experience? It had always been difficult, even impossible, looking after her poor, frail mother as she had, to have any kind of social life...any kind of romance... How could anyone compare with Xandros?

From the very first she had acknowledged his searing

impact on her. How could it be otherwise? He was the stuff of dreams, of fantasies... But could she—would she—make them real?

And would *he*?

If she were really to go ahead and marry him, then what would he expect? Or want...? What would *she* want?

Even as she formed the questions the answers were there, in the quickening of her blood as she replayed, yet again, the soft, sensuous touch of his mouth on hers. It had engendered within her an ache, a yearning for something more... Oh, so much more!

The phone beside her bed started to ring, interrupting her hectic thoughts. She picked it up. It was Xandros.

'Hi,' he said.

His voice was warm and friendly. And good to hear.

'Have you had breakfast yet? If not, how about brunch by the hotel pool? In half an hour?'

'So...' Xandros eyed her carefully as they sat at a table in the poolside bistro. 'Do you think you've reached a decision yet?'

He didn't want to pressurise her, but...

I want her to say yes.

Watching her, he was glad he was wearing sunglasses, for it gave him the opportunity to study her without her being aware of it. He was even more sure of what he wanted. He hadn't seen her yet in leisurewear, and now that he was it was every bit as rewarding as seeing her in more formal daywear and evening wear.

The short, above-the-knee sundress in a swirling pattern of yellow and blue, its halter neck exposing her graceful shoulders, looked good on her. More than good. Her hair was not upswept this morning, but pulled back into a simple ponytail, and the long, lush sweep of it curved over her bare shoulder. She was wearing make-up, but minimal—

just mascara, a trace of eyeliner and lip gloss. She looked fresh, natural…and breathtakingly lovely.

His mind went back to the way she'd looked that first day—with dirt smeared on her face and hollows under her eyes, fatigue in every line of her body.

Never again—never!

She hadn't answered him and he stilled, watching her. He could see the expressions moving in her eyes, her lips pressing together as if she were nerving herself to speak. He saw her swallow.

'Do *you* still want to go ahead?' she asked. Her voice was low—diffident, even.

'If you're asking if I've changed my mind, the answer is no,' Xandros said firmly. He paused, then said what he thought she needed to hear right now, softening his voice, seeking to reassure her. 'It will work out. I promise you. You won't regret it. I'll make sure of that.'

He gave a wry, quirking smile, wondering off-hand how many other women of his acquaintance would have been so hesitant about accepting an invitation to marry him…

Then he sobered. Yes, well… Rosalie's half-sister hadn't been that keen, had she?

Even thinking about Ariadne made him feel all over again that underlying sense of relief he'd experienced when he'd read her text. His eyes rested now on her half-sister. He wondered how he could ever have truly imagined himself capable of marrying Ariadne…

She was beautiful, yes, but never—not once—had he felt that low purring desire go through him the way it was doing now, yet again, as he sat eating brunch with Rosalie.

She was who he desired… And if she said yes now—as he hoped beyond hope she was about to do—then his desire would be richly fulfilled…

He let his gaze continue to rest on her, waiting to see

what she would say. 'Do you need more time?' he asked, searching her face.

She gave a quick shake of her head. 'No—no, that wouldn't help. I... I've thought it all through. I can't really think more than I've thought already.'

Was there a slight flush to her cheeks as she spoke? A momentary dip in her gaze? His eyes stayed on her. He was waiting for her next words. Urging her to say them, and for them to be the ones he wanted to hear.

'So?' he prompted.

He felt the world was holding its breath. *He* was holding his breath. He saw her swallow again, inhale. Lift her chin. Look right at him. Give him a quick, decisive nod.

'Let's do it!' she said.

The words rushed from her, as if she might suddenly change her mind. But he would give her no chance to do so—*none*.

He reached for her hand, took it in his. Held it fast. 'Good call,' he said.

Satisfaction rushed through him, his mood soaring. And why should it not? He was getting what he wanted—*everything* he wanted! She was his. Life had never seemed better, nor the bright sun brighter.

He couldn't wait to make her his wife...

'Do you like it?' Xandros's voice was enquiring.

Rosalie stared at the ring on her finger, glittering with diamonds.

Was this real? Had she really said yes to the idea Alexandros Lakaris had put to her less than twenty-four hours ago?

Should I have taken more time to give him my answer?

But she'd thought it through, and through, and through. Either she said yes or she went back to her grim, bleak, poverty-stricken life in the East End of London. And she couldn't face that—not now! Not when she'd had a glimpse of escape from it, a taste of what luxury felt like. It might be venal to look at it like that, but that was easy to say if you were rich…

The diamonds scintillated in the lights of the very exclusive jewellers she and Xandros were in. Emotion caught at her.

Mum would have loved to see this day! See this ring on my finger! She would be glad for me—thrilled for me!

That was what she must think. No one—not even her monstrous father!—would be harmed by what she was going to do. Both he and Xandros would be richer and so, in six months' time, would she. Oh, not rich like them, but rich enough to escape for ever from the bleakness of her London life.

Mum would want that for me—I know she would!

'If you don't like this ring there are plenty more to choose from,' Xandros was saying now.

She looked up at him. 'It's fabulous!' she said. 'If you think it's necessary?' she added doubtfully, knowing how horrendously expensive a ring like this must be.

'Yes, it is,' Xandros replied firmly. 'People will expect it.' He gave her a pointed look. 'Rosalie, this marriage has to look genuine. I mean, it *will* be genuine, but there can't be any questions about it, okay? So, like it or not, you'll have to endure wearing it!'

His tone was light, good humoured, but she got the message. Kyria Lakaris-to-be had to look the part—right down to the priceless engagement ring now weighing upon her finger.

She felt its weight as they made their next stop—the register office—to set in motion the process of enabling them to marry. She would need her birth certificate, she discovered, and Xandros undertook to have it couriered out to Athens. The wedding would take place as soon as possible and Xandros—thankfully—had allayed the chief of her alarms.

'We'll keep it completely private—no guests. Not even family, okay?'

She was relieved. Having her father present would have been unendurable. Xandros had already told her that *he* would deal with him—she would not have to see him or have anything to do with him.

'I'll let him think that after throwing your tantrum yesterday—because that's the way he'll see it!—I've prevailed upon you to see the sense of what he said.' Xandros had told her over brunch, his expression taut. 'The rest is true enough—that I've whisked you away, put you up in a hotel and am now planning our wedding with all speed. As for my own interests in this...' His tone had taken on an edge that had been audible. 'I'll be making it crystal clear to him that the wedding *only* goes ahead once I have his commitment—in writing—to the merger, and a promise that active negotiations to that end will start immediately. He will give me leave to proceed with due diligence and all the other matters the merger will require, and he will co-operate fully with all the legal processes.'

There were 'legal processes' between her and Xandros, too, that had to be addressed. Their next port of call was his private lawyer's office, where Rosalie's only protest was at how much money Xandros had stipulated in the pre-nup was to be paid in the event of their divorce—a divorce that was not going to be an 'if' but a 'when'.

'It's far too much!' she protested as they left.

He looked across at her. 'Rosalie, don't argue. If you want me to show you just how much my annual profits are projected to increase once the merger with your father goes ahead, then I shall. I am going to be a much richer man than I am now! Your payoff is worth every penny, I promise you!'

She subsided, but with an uneasy sigh. So much money…
When she had been so poor…

She felt his hand take hers, as if he sensed her unease.

'It will be okay,' he said.

The warmth in his voice was reassuring, and reassurance, Rosalie discovered, was what she needed over the coming days.

She was to go on staying at the hotel until they married, when she would move in with Xandros. He took her to see his apartment, so she could get used to it, and she gazed about her at the spacious expanse and clean lines.

'Not too minimalist?' he asked.

She shook her head. It seemed very…*intimate*…to be here with him, alone in his apartment. Yet his manner towards her was exactly as it was in public—friendly and easy-going. Just that. She was glad, because it made her comfortable to be with him, but at the same time…

She watched him pick up a pile of personal post and leaf through it, busying himself opening an array of envelopes. She wandered off, not wanting to distract him, glancing into the formidably equipped kitchen before discovering the bedrooms. There were three—two guests and a clear master. She stood in the doorway for a moment, her expression uncertain.

Would it be her bedroom as well as his?

A quiver of uncertainty went through her. Since that first evening when they'd dined together he had not kissed her again—not even a peck on the cheek to say hello or farewell. She felt a strange little tug around her heart. Part of her wanted to ask him just what kind of marriage theirs was going to be, however brief—but part of her could not bring herself to do so.

Because in the end did it matter? Did it matter that he was the most fantastic-looking man she'd ever set eyes on? That since that kiss at the restaurant she had felt an ache, a yearning, that he had awoken in her with that brief touch of his lips on hers?

That wasn't the reason they were marrying! That was what she had to remember. The reasons they were going to marry were financial—nothing more than that. And if that was all Xandros wanted of their brief marriage then she must accept it.

Except that strange little tug around her heart came again... No man, she knew, would ever set her pulse racing, bring the colour to her cheeks, make her so blazingly aware of her own body...of his...

Her eyes went to the huge double bed in the master bedroom. Wide enough for two...wide and inviting... But would she ever be invited into it...? Uncertainty mixed within her with yearning...longing...

'Here you are!'

Xandros's voice was warm as it sounded behind her. Rosalie turned.

'Seen everything?' he asked.

For a second his eyes rested on her with an expression she could not quite make out. Then it was gone. He was speaking again.

'I've been going through the post—mostly invitations! But we'll ignore them all until we're safely married. Then,' he said, and his eyes washed over her, 'I'll start showing you off. I'm looking forward to it!'

Rosalie felt herself colouring, confusion filling her again. Was it just that he wanted her to look her best for his friends and acquaintances? To show the world—and convince her father—how real their marriage was? He could afford no hint that it would be over and done with before the year was out, leaving Xandros with what he wanted—the merger with her father—and herself with a hefty divorce payout?

Is that all our marriage is going to be about?

She turned away, feeling that strange tug of emotion coming again, and stepped back into the wide corridor, then into the triple-aspect reception room, her feet taking her towards the view of the Parthenon on the Acropolis. She paused to gaze out over it, still feeling that strange tug of emotion.

Hands closed lightly over her shoulders and she felt Xandros behind her, his breath warm on her neck. Her own breath caught, feeling him so close, catching the spiced scent of his aftershave... She wanted to lean back into him, feel his arms go around her waist to embrace her, but she was too unsure to move.

'It's a good sight, isn't it?' he murmured softly.

She gave a slow nod, conscious not of the ancient monument but only of his hands upon her. For a moment—just a moment—she felt his touch tighten, as if he would turn her to him. As if he would take her into his arms...

Then, instead, he merely grazed the top of her head with the lightest and most fraternal of kisses, his hands dropping away.

'I'll run you back to your hotel,' he said.

There was nothing in his voice but his usual easy-going manner.

With a flickering smile of acquiescence Rosalie let him usher her out of his apartment, outwardly serene. But inside, she knew, she was conscious of a sense of disappointment. Of a creeping melancholy.

She had no business feeling that way. No right at all.

But she did, all the same.

Xandros was visiting his mother. He didn't want to, but he owed her that at least. He'd had to make a difficult phone call to her before he'd flown to London, telling her as carefully as he could that Ariadne had pulled out of their engagement.

'But *why*?' his mother had cried, dismayed. 'I thought it was all agreed!'

'So did I,' he'd said. 'But there it is. I have to respect her decision.'

He knew his mother was upset. She had wanted him to marry Ariadne, the daughter of her childhood friend—to marry her and achieve the merger her husband had urged his son to make as a sure way to increase the Lakaris fortunes he had worked so hard to rescue. She had wanted him to marry and give her grandchildren, to cheer her widowhood and to continue the ancient line to which he had been born, of which he was now the sole representative since the untimely death of his father three years ago.

And if Ariadne had been the perfect bride for him in his mother's eyes, Xandros knew with foreboding that she would deplore his sudden decision to marry Ariadne's illegitimate English half-sister instead.

Which was why he had to visit her in person—to explain the precise reasons for his precipitate action.

As he had expected, she did deplore it—and vocally.

'Xandros, who *is* this girl? Nobody! You can't possibly be thinking that she can be a substitute for Ariadne!'

'That is precisely what I *don't* think!' he answered. He took a breath and looked into his mother's eyes, which held a troubled expression. 'She understands my reasons and agrees it will only be a temporary arrangement. And...' he took another breath '...this won't just be for my benefit. I want to do this for *her*,' he said feelingly. 'She's had a wretched life. Coustakis never acknowledged her existence. He condemned both her and her mother to lifelong poverty. She deserves better!'

His mother looked at him, her expression still troubled. 'Are you sure?' she asked slowly. 'Are you sure that you know what you're doing, Xandros?'

He looked at her straight. 'Yes,' he said. 'And it is very, very simple, I promise you.'

She looked as if she was going to say something more, but he forestalled her. He did not want their conversation moving on to any other aspect of just why he was going through with this marriage—that it was precisely *because* it was going to be temporary that it appealed to him, and that as soon as he was free of it, his desire for Rosalie slaked, he would resume the carefree, unattached bachelor lifestyle his mother considered a waste of his time.

He changed the subject away from marrying Rosalie and the reasons he was doing so.

'Tell me, have you heard anything from Ariadne? Her mobile phone isn't working. Coustakis must have cancelled it—he's vindictive enough to do that, after disowning her as he has! My guess is she's gone to stay with her maternal grandmother's relatives in Scotland. But I don't know their whereabouts, or even their name.'

His mother shook her head. 'I have heard nothing from Ariadne either. I try not to worry, but—'

Xandros gave her what reassurance he could. 'Well, she has a mind of her own—she'll turn up when she wants to.'

It was the best he could say. No point giving voice to his own growing suspicions of just why Ariadne had bolted, or where she might be now... She was no longer his concern.

Only her half-sister was. The half-sister who held a sensual allure for him that Ariadne had never had, for all her dark beauty. The half-sister he was due to marry in a handful of days, as soon as the paperwork permitted.

His mother would not come—it would be easier that way, both for her and for his bride. After all, theirs was not going to be a *real* marriage—not by anything other than legal definition. It was simply a means to an end. Two ends. Business, yes. And also pleasure...

The low purring started up along with the powerful engine of his car as he headed back to Athens. Oh, yes…very, very decided pleasure. Pleasure that he was having to exercise all his self-control not to start indulging in before the knot was tied.

That tantalising but fleeting kiss in the hotel restaurant was a torment to remember, and when she'd come to see his apartment he'd had to busy himself with his mail in order to keep his hands off her. Especially when he'd found her gazing at his bed…as if she were already envisaging them there together.

He'd so very nearly obliged her… But he'd drawn back, permitting himself only that light, brief touch on her shoulders—and even that had been a torment before he'd released her again…

It was a torment he was schooling himself to endure. A rushed seduction in a hotel room, or even at his apartment, was not what he wanted. No, there was only one place he wanted to make Rosalie his own…

One perfect place he yearned to be with her…

CHAPTER EIGHT

THEY WERE DINING out the night before their wedding. Not at the hotel this time, but at what was obviously a very exclusive restaurant. Rosalie was thankful that it wasn't crowded or noisy. Nor was it, as far as she could tell, a fashionable watering hole for their generation.

'I thought you might like somewhere quiet,' Xandros said as they sat down at their table. 'This place is one of my mother's favourites when she's in town, for that very reason.'

Rosalie looked at him. 'Your mother?' Her brow furrowed and she spoke hesitantly. 'I… I didn't realise that she was still…well, still alive.'

'Very much so,' Xandros answered drily. 'She doesn't live in Athens, but out in the country. I'll take you to meet her sometime after our wedding.' He paused, and then he said, quite deliberately, 'She understands about our marriage.'

He didn't say any more, and Rosalie didn't probe. After all, did it really matter if Xandros's mother existed? It wasn't as if she was going to be a *real* mother-in-law any more than Xandros was going to be a real husband. And not just because their marriage was going to be so brief…

Her eyes went to him as he consulted the waiter about tonight's menu choices, taking in, as she always did, the sable feathering of his hair, the curve of his sensual mouth, the dark, long-lashed expressive eyes. She felt her senses heighten, wanting only to gaze at him, at just how incredibly, fatally attractive he was…

She remembered how she'd gazed at him that very first time, open-mouthed, when she'd opened the door of that rundown rental property to see him, unable to tear her eyes away from him.

And she still couldn't.

The same feeling of regretful melancholy went through her as she'd felt in his apartment. She must learn to subdue her growing longings. She must accept that she had read too much into that brief, fleeting and unrepeated kiss of greeting at the hotel restaurant that first night. For him it had been nothing more than a casual public salutation. It had meant nothing more than that.

'Pre-wedding nerves?' he asked.

He'd caught her expression and misinterpreted it, and she was glad he had—because there was no point him thinking anything else.

'There truly is no need for them,' he said. His dark eyes held hers. 'Rosalie, I want you to enjoy the kind of life you've never had before.'

His eyes washed over her and she felt their force—impossible not to. Any woman would feel it. Especially one so starved of romance as she was...

But Xandros was making it clear that he didn't want romance to be a part of their marriage. So, although his eyes were warm upon her, although he always complimented her on her appearance, his attitude towards her was nothing more than friendly, easy-going and companionable.

She must be glad of that—grateful. Grateful that her life of hardship and endless penny-pinching was done with. That, after all, was why she was marrying Xandros. For nothing more.

She must remember that.

Or else torment herself with yearning for what was not going to happen...

So stop mooning over him! Don't long for what he isn't interested in! Just match his own attitude towards you—it's all he wants.

And that was what she did determinedly as they dined—on yet another exquisite gourmet meal of the kind that was now her daily diet.

She would be grateful for that, too—every day—and never take it or anything else about this luxurious life she was living for granted!

Afterwards, he took her back to her hotel, insisting cheerfully that he would see her to her room.

The thickly carpeted corridor leading to Rosalie's room was hushed and quiet and deserted.

'You don't have to walk me to my room!' she protested good-humouredly. 'I won't get lost!'

'You might totter off down the wrong corridor on those towering high heels,' he replied at her mild protest.

She gave a light laugh, and acquiesced, yet she was conscious of the empty length of corridor stretching ahead of them and of being alone with Xandros. It made her ultra-aware of him...of his presence at her side. It would have been easier, she thought ruefully, to say goodnight in the lobby.

They reached her door and she fumbled in her bag for her key, nerves jangling out of nowhere. She turned, the key card in hand, ready to say a bright goodnight, but the word died on her lips.

He was standing close to her—too close—but she couldn't back away. The door was behind her. She was conscious—suddenly, burningly—not just of how close he was, but how she could catch the faint scent of his after-shave, see in the dim light of the empty corridor how his strong jaw was already faintly etched with regrowth, giving him a seductively raffish look in his dark lounge suit.

She felt a flush of heat go through her and was suddenly conscious, too, of how the dress she was wearing—a close-fitting, beautifully tailored cocktail dress—was moulding her body, her breasts and her hips. Conscious, above all, of how breathless she was…

He was smiling down at her—but not with the familiar, nothing more than friendly smile he usually gave her. This was a different smile. One she had seen only once before… That first evening they had dined together…

Her breath caught and she could do nothing at all except let his smile wash over her, his eyes holding hers even as she felt him take her key card from her nerveless fingers and slide it down the lock, pressing the door open with a splay of his hand.

That smile tugged at his mouth…his sensual, sculpted mouth.

'This time tomorrow,' he said, his voice low, 'we shall be married. And it will be fine, Rosalie, I promise you. It will bring us everything we want.'

She could only gaze at him, saying nothing at all. She could hear her heart thudding in her chest and there was not a scrap of air in her lungs. Her eyes were widening… pupils dilating…

She saw something change in his eyes, intensify, and heard him say something in Greek…something that sounded rasping. Then he was speaking in English.

'You know…' he said softly.

And out of nowhere she felt the timbre in his voice doing things to her, sending her blood pulsing through her veins in a hot, hectic throb that she could not stop—could not stop at all.

'You really shouldn't look at me like that…'

'Like what…?'

The words were faint on her breath—the breath that was not in her lungs. That throbbing pulse was at her throat, at her temple, in the deep core of her body—the body that was now yearning infinitesimally towards him, her face lifted to his, gazing up at him with wide eyes.

And in his eyes she could see, in the dark, sweeping depths, a glint of pure gold. The tug at his mouth deepened, half-rueful, half-anticipatory.

'Like you want me to do…this…' he said.

And as he spoke, in that low, soft voice, she saw his lashes sweep down over his eyes, his face lower to hers.

His lips touched hers and his kiss was velvet silk, brushing slowly, seductively across her mouth, easing her own lips apart, softly and surely, deepening his slow, leisurely tasting of her until he was taking his fill…

Bliss went through her, pure and exquisite, and she gave her mouth to him, let him taste and take her, explore and possess…

She felt her body sway towards his, her eyes flutter shut as she gave herself to what was happening.

Xandros was kissing her…

Kissing her in a way that made that earlier, brief, fleeting kiss seem nothing more than the merest promise of what a kiss could be…

Kissing her as she had never thought it possible for a kiss to be!

And she was melting into it, drowning in it, this the softest, most sensuous sensation in the entire universe, this the exquisite honeyed feathering of his mouth on hers.

It seemed to go on and on, and she was weak with it, faint with it…

And she wanted more…oh, so much more…

A low, helpless moan sounded in her throat, and as if with an instinct of their own her hands reached around him to draw his body to hers, to feel the hard, strong column of his back beneath her fingers—

At her touch he pulled away from her in sharp withdrawal, his mouth releasing hers abruptly, his hand moving away from the door.

Her eyes flew open.

He was looking down at her with an expression that was closed—shuttered, even—and she gazed at him in a helpless haze, lips still parted...

She saw him take a breath. A ragged inhalation. Saw him take a step backwards.

He shook his head. 'This was a mistake,' he said.

There was a blankness in his voice, and he took another breath, deeper than the first, his expression changing again.

'It's late. You should get some sleep. I must go.' He reached past her to push her door open wider. 'Go in, Rosalie,' he said. His voice was firm and his mouth tightened. 'You need to get to bed. We have to be with the registrar by eleven.'

She felt his hand on the small of her back. Broad and impersonal. Turning her towards her room.

She caught the edge of the door, instinctively resisting. Trying to turn back to him.

'I...'

The pulse at her throat was throbbing, and there was a flush of heat across her cheeks. Her lips were still parted. Still yearning for his...

And as her eyes lifted to his she knew yearning filled them. A yearning she could not crush, or halt, or do anything about. For the blood was still beating in her veins, blinding her to everything but the kiss they had shared.

'No.'

There was harshness in his voice. Rejection.

'Rosalie—*goodnight*!'

He turned away, and then he was striding down the hushed and deserted corridor, his gait rapid, gaining the end in moments, turning towards the elevator, lost to her sight.

She felt emptiness, desolation, as she went into her room. He had kissed her in a way she had never known a kiss could be. A kiss to melt her to her very core. And then he had set her aside.

His rejection echoed in her head.

'This was a mistake.'

A cry broke from her.

Xandros stood out on his apartment's balcony, staring at the floodlit Acropolis, not seeing it. He was hearing his own words echo in his head.

'This was a mistake.'

His hands tightened over the railing. *Thee mou*, one hell of a mistake! It had taken all his strength to push her inside—keeping himself on the outside—and to turn and walk away, with every step wanting to turn around and stride back to her, to step inside her room and—

No! Don't go there! Not even in imagination! Least of all that...

He took a shuddering breath. He'd been a rash and reckless fool to walk her back to her room—he should have resisted the temptation. But he hadn't wanted to say goodnight quite yet. Had wanted to prolong the evening with her. Prolong it in a much more intimate way...

No! He was heading down dangerous paths again.

He clenched his jaw, exerting control over himself just as he had since that evening he'd allowed himself the sweet pleasure of greeting her with that all too brief and fleeting kiss. It had taught him that any contact with her would be like a match to tinder. That he must control himself, deny himself, until he had her all to himself.

As he would tomorrow.

Tomorrow night...the start of their honeymoon. The start of their marriage, when she would be his...

That low purring started up in him, so familiar to him now whenever he thought of the breathtakingly alluring woman who would soon—oh, so achingly soon now—be his entirely...

And until then...

He turned away, clicking shut the balcony doors and striding into his bedroom, stripping off his tie as he did so, slipping his cufflinks.

His eyes glinted. Until then the traditional remedy for thwarted passion was going to be very necessary.

He headed for the en-suite bathroom. Time for a cold shower. A *very* cold one...

Rosalie gazed, enthralled, as the helicopter started its descent, feeling again the leap of pleasure she'd felt when Xandros had announced, just after their wedding that morning, that he was taking her to his private island for their honeymoon.

She hadn't thought they would have a honeymoon at all—not in a marriage like theirs. But then she had realised that, just as he wanted her to wear the fabulous diamond engagement ring and also, since the simple brief ceremony that morning, which had passed in a blur of Greek with an English translation for herself in a room at the town hall, her new wedding ring, so a honeymoon would be expected as well. To show the world—show her father—that theirs was a proper marriage.

And she knew she could be glad that it was to be on Kallistris. On Xandros's private island they wouldn't be on view for anyone else to think it odd they weren't all loved-up...

Her eyes shadowed momentarily but she banished her thoughts. Last night had been...*difficult*. The understatement rang hollow. But in the sleepless hours that had followed she had come to terms with it. She'd had to.

Xandros had kissed her—she'd all but begged him to, and mortification burned in her as she remembered what he'd said to her—and promptly regretted it. Well, she had learnt her lesson. From now on she would be only what he wanted her to be—bright, cheerful, friendly, appreciative, enthusiastic...

She ran out of adjectives to describe the way she would need to be with this man who had called kissing her a mistake, and went back to gazing, rapt, as the little island—the smallest of a small cluster set in the azure Aegean—loomed closer and closer. And then they had landed, setting down on a small helipad by the sea's edge.

Xandros vaulted out, thanking the pilot, and Rosalie, glad she'd changed out of her tailored wedding outfit into cotton trousers and top at the hotel before setting off, jumped down lightly. Xandros, too, had changed out of his customary business suit into chinos and an open-necked shirt—looking just as drop-dead gorgeous as he always looked.

Rosalie sighed inwardly.

'Mind the downdraft!' he warned, and hurried her to the edge of the helipad as the helicopter took off again in a whirl of rotors.

As it disappeared, Xandros turned to her. 'Welcome to Kallistris,' he said.

His eyes were warm, his smile warmer. She felt her insides give a little skip, but she only smiled back, and then both of them turned as a Jeep came rattling along the coastal track towards them.

'Ah,' said Xandros, looking pleased. 'Panos.'

The weather-beaten face of his island's caretaker broke into a huge smile as Xandros introduced him, warning Rosalie that Panos spoke little English, but that his wife, Maria, was more fluent.

'*Kalimera,*' said Rosalie, gingerly trying out her highly limited Greek.

Her hand was taken in a bear grip, and shaken vigorously.

'Kyria Lakaris!' exclaimed Panos, and it gave Rosalie a start to hear her married name.

I'll have to get used to it, she thought to herself.

Just as she would have to get used to living with Xandros…but as friends, nothing more than that.

She dragged her eyes away from him, hoping forlornly that perhaps with time she would stop wanting to gaze endlessly at him, because now they were married she was going to have to inure herself to his constant presence. She swallowed.

They set off in the Jeep. Xandros chatted in Greek to Panos and Rosalie hung tightly to the window frame as they bumped rapidly along the unmetalled track.

They rounded a rocky promontory, and she gave an exclamation of spontaneous delight. 'Oh, how beautiful!'

They were looking down on to a small but perfectly formed bay, its furthest end bounded by another promontory. Between the two stretched a pristine pebbled beach lapped by the azure sea that girded the whole island. Nestled in the centre, just above the beach, was a small one-storey villa, framed by a mix of silvery olive trees and pink-flowered oleanders.

It was like something on a picture postcard, whitewashed, with a blue door and matching blue window shutters, the whole house festooned with vivid, crimson bougainvilleas.

'Do you like it?' Xandros turned to her.

'It's perfect!' she enthused.

She felt her mood lift. However difficult it was going to be to be here, alone with Xandros, having to conceal her hopeless susceptibility to him, surely the opportunity to be in this beautiful place would make it worthwhile! Never again in her life would she have a chance to holiday on a private Aegean island.

Xandros gave a slashing grin as Panos screeched to a halt in a cloud of white dust and helped her down as a stout, middle-aged woman bustled out through the blue door.

'Welcome, welcome!' Panos's wife greeted them, and then embraced Xandros in a bear hug, chattering away to him in Greek, before guiding Rosalie inside the little villa, saying, 'Come! Come!' in enthusiastic tones.

Inside it was much cooler, and Maria led the way off to the left, down a tiled corridor and into a room that was, Rosalie surmised, going to be her bedroom. Xandros's must be the one beyond.

Did Maria and Panos realise that she was not a true bride in any sense? What had Xandros told them about their marriage?

She gave a mental shrug—that was his concern, not hers.

Panos delivered her suitcase and Maria hefted it on to the bed to start unpacking. Rosalie moved to help, but was waved away.

'Go! Go to your husband!' Maria ordered her.

Giving in, Rosalie ventured out into the corridor, making her way outdoors. The heat of the afternoon hit her immediately, and the crystal-clear sea lapping the pebbled beach beckoned. She kicked off her sandals, turned up her trouser hems, then waded ankle-deep into the cool water.

'This is joyous!' she exclaimed.

Footsteps crunched on the pebbles behind her.

'I'm glad you think so.'

Xandros's voice sounded warm, and Rosalie turned. He'd swapped his chinos for denim shorts, his open-necked shirt for a pristine white tee, and Rosalie was instantly and vividly aware of how the tee moulded his muscled torso, how the denim cut-offs revealed his lithe and powerful bare legs.

She snapped her gaze away, looking instead at his face— which wasn't much help, for he was sporting aviator sunglasses. The breeze was lightly ruffling his dark hair, and he looked just ludicrously, jaw-droppingly attractive.

She gave a gulp.

Sexy—the overused word was impossible to dismiss. Impossible to deny. It described him totally. Even though it was a completely pointless way of describing him…given the nature of their marriage…

She gulped again, trying to sound normal as she answered. 'Who wouldn't?' she returned with a half-laugh. 'Everyone who comes here must think so!'

'No one comes here,' Xandros said.

Rosalie's expression altered and she looked at him, puzzled.

'This is my sanctuary,' Xandros was saying now. 'I don't bring anyone here.'

Except a wife who isn't a real wife on a honeymoon that isn't a real honeymoon…

The words hung in her head, unsaid. Impossible to say. Unnecessary.

He went on speaking, changing the subject, and she was glad.

'Maria's just serving some refreshments. You must be thirsty, I'm sure.'

She followed him up the beach into the welcome cool under a huge cantilevered parasol that shaded a table and chairs in front of the villa, where Maria was setting down a tray laden with coffee, fruit juice, water and a plate of syrupy nut-strewn pastries.

'Eat,' she instructed, and bustled off.

Rosalie gratefully poured herself a glass of juice, cut it with iced water, and knocked it back appreciatively.

'Are you going to mortally offend Maria and not eat one of her pastries?'

Xandros's laconic question interrupted her train of thought.

'They look delicious, but I've been eating like a pig since…well, since I was let loose on gourmet food!' Rosalie answered lightly. 'I'll be as fat as one too if I keep going the same way!'

Dark eyes washed over her assessingly. 'I think that unlikely.'

Xandros's voice was dry, and there was something about it that made her own mouth suddenly dry. She wished he hadn't looked at her the way he had.

He doesn't understand the impact he has—even just saying things like that.

The trouble was, it didn't help her that he didn't…

I have to make myself not react! I have to! Or I'll never survive this honeymoon, never mind six months of being married to him…

In her head she heard yet again the brief, stark words he'd said to her last night before he'd walked away.

'This was a mistake.'

Those were the words she had to remember.

The only words.

CHAPTER NINE

'So, do you fancy a swim?' Xandros pushed his empty coffee cup aside, drained his iced water and looked across at Rosalie. His breath caught silently. In formal daywear and nightwear she looked breathtaking, but in casual gear she looked every bit as stunning...

He got to his feet. A swim would be good for more than just cooling off and freshening up. It would take his mind off what he would like to do right now. Sweep her off her feet and into his bedroom—his bed.

But she wasn't ready for that yet, and he was no clumsy teen, wanting to rush his fences. Their wedding night would come—but not now.

'How about it?' he asked, looking down at her.

She smiled and stood up. 'Sounds wonderful,' she said. 'I'll go and get changed.'

He did likewise, and five minutes later was at the water's edge. He watched her come out of the villa, in a one-piece swimsuit covered in a beach wrap, her hair pinned up on top of her head. His breath caught again—she looked so lovely...

She also looked self-conscious, and with a gallantry he hadn't known he possessed he gave her a half-wave, then waded into the water, executing a duck dive and surfacing into a powerful freestyle, heading out to sea.

Far enough out, he turned, treading water. She'd discarded her wrap and was knee-high in the water. 'Come on in! It's not cold!' he called to her.

'It's gorgeous!' she called back, and went on wading in, to chest height.

Then, lifting her arms, she plunged into a breaststroke

and headed out towards him. When she was near she halted, rolling on to her back, slowly extending her legs and arms to keep herself afloat, closing her eyes against the brightness of the sun.

Xandros watched her offering her fabulous body to the sun, with nothing but the material of the turquoise one-piece between it and her nakedness...

Something quickened inside him and moved—something he had not felt before—as she floated, so still...so achingly beautiful.

His gaze feasted upon her.

I could kiss her now, as she floats on the water, eyes closed, lips parted...

Almost he succumbed to the temptation welling up in him. But wiser counsel prevailed. They were out of their depth at this distance, and any kind of kiss would soon find them both under the surface and flailing for air. No, there would be time enough for kisses. Kisses and so much more...

'You look like a basking mermaid,' he said instead, a smile in his voice.

She did not open her eyes. 'I feel like one,' she answered. 'This is absolute bliss.'

He turned on his back and floated wide himself. 'It is,' he confirmed.

He went on floating beside her peacefully for a while, bobbing in the gentle swell, keeping his eyes shut against the bright sunshine. He was conscious that they were drifting further out to sea. He said as much to Rosalie, turning himself over to check their distance from the shore. She did likewise.

'But the Mediterranean is tideless, isn't it?' she asked.

'There's a slight tide—and definitely currents—but nothing like what you're used to in Britain,' he answered, and they both started to make their way with a slow breast-stroke back towards the beach.

'I'm not used to the seaside anywhere,' she replied. 'I've never been till now.'

Xandros's expression changed. 'You've *never* been to the seaside?' His voice was disbelieving.

'Not even Southend!' she exclaimed, half-humorously, half-sadly. 'That's the closest seaside for East Enders, but Mum was never well enough to go. Never well enough for anything, really—not that there was any money for holidays anyway,' she finished.

Now he could hear more sadness in her voice than humour. Pity for her filled him, and resolve, too—to do whatever he could to compensate her for the deprivations of her impoverished life. Even in the darkest days of his childhood, when money worries for his parents had been at their height, he had enjoyed an affluence way beyond Rosalie's.

Well, now she would enjoy not only mere affluence, but luxury—all that he could provide for her. Every luxury—and every pleasure.

He felt his brow furrowing as he swam. It was new to him to entertain such an impulse. All the women he'd been involved with had come from his own world, used to luxury and expensive living—Ariadne included. And for none of them—not even Ariadne—had he felt this overwhelming desire to provide for them. Make them happy.

His eyes went to her now as she swam beside him, her gaze focussed on the approaching beach.

I want to make her happy! That's exactly what I want to do!

It was a strange feeling. A novel feeling. A good feeling.

And it was a feeling he went on feeling, bringing to him an inner warm glow as they waded ashore.

'If you've any energy left, let's go for a walk. I'll show you something of the island. Nothing too strenuous, I promise.'

Nor was it.

Showered and dressed again, he led the way up a narrow path through the thickly growing oleander bushes on the far side of the beach.

As they reached the clifftop, and the vista of the rugged coastline and the wild, maquis-covered terrain opened up before them, Rosalie gave a smile of pleasure at his side.

'Oh, it's beautiful!' she said enthusiastically.

Xandros looked at her, smiling himself. She was wearing sunglasses, and her hair was caught back with a barrette. But it was being winnowed by the wind spilling off the clifftop. She pushed it back with her hand, taking in the view. Her beauty was natural, unforced. He wanted to do nothing but gaze at her and drink it in.

Then, abruptly, she started. A goat, followed by several more, leapt from behind some low bushes, disturbed by their presence, bounding away inland.

'They're supposed to be feral,' Xandros told her, 'But Maria feeds them if she thinks they look hungry. In exchange, she milks them and makes cheese. I expect we'll sample some tonight at dinner. Speaking of which,' he went on, 'we'd better head back. We'll come up another day— bring a picnic lunch with us. It's a great spot for watching the sunset, too—though tonight it's going to be the Champagne Sunset Show, down on the beach.'

She smiled. 'Sounds good,' she answered.

'And we must brace ourselves,' he said, humour in his voice, 'for Maria will have excelled herself with dinner. She's been cooking all day, Panos told me.'

A wedding feast. A wedding feast to fill them both up. Give them energy for the night ahead.

Their wedding night...

Rosalie glanced at her reflection in the long mirror on the wall in her bedroom. Her brushed cotton dress fell in soft butter-yellow folds to her ankles from a high waistline. The slight bodice was ruched over her breasts, skimming her shoulders. She'd draped a creamy embroidered shawl around her, held her hair back with a narrow headband. Her make-up was minimal—some mascara and lip gloss—and her fragrance was a light floral scent, not the heavier perfume she had indulged in in Athens.

She frowned uncertainly. Though she wasn't in the least glitzed up, as she had been in Athens, should she have dressed up at all? Would Xandros think she was trying to send a message he did not wish to hear, as he had made so clear last night?

Well, her behaviour towards him must show him otherwise, that was all. She had managed it so far—that walk up to the clifftop had gone okay, and all she had to do was keep that going. Be interested in what he said, be cheerful and friendly and easy-going.

And not look at him too often…

She made her way outside to the beach, to find Xandros already there, relaxing back in a canvas chair, long legs outstretched. The sun was low on the horizon, bathing the scene in rich red gold.

'Come and sit down.' He got to his feet. 'The sunset show is about to begin.'

There was an ice bucket on a table, and in it an open bottle of champagne. Rosalie took her seat and Xandros resumed his, pouring a flute for each of them.

She took hers from him, conscious of the slight brush of his fingers as she did so. Now, in profile against the lowering sun, she saw his eyes resting on her. Saw the warm glow on her.

'To our marriage,' he said, and lifted his glass to tilt it against hers. 'May it bring everything to us that we want.'

It was something she could drink to, and did, but even

as she did so she was conscious of the tug of that strange melancholy again.

But what if I want more from it than you do?

It was a dangerous thought, and a useless thought, for she knew perfectly well why they had married and what it would give them. A great deal.

But not each other.

That was not what their marriage was about and she must remember it. Remember it with piercing purpose now, as she took a sip of the beautifully beading liquid, felt its bouquet shimmer in her mouth.

For a moment—just a moment—their eyes met over the flutes and she felt something shimmer deep inside her along with the champagne's bouquet…

She turned her head away, lest her eyes reveal it. Gazed out over the water, shading from azure to gold as the sun lowered. Neither talked, as if by mutual consent, just watched quietly, the only sound that of the wavelets lapping onto the pebbles.

Moment by moment the sun pooled into the waiting Aegean.

And was gone.

Xandros pushed back his chair, getting to his feet. 'I can smell the fruits of Maria's labours. It would not do to be late for them!'

They strolled back to the villa, Xandros taking the champagne with him, and made their way round to the gable end of the house, beyond their bedrooms. There was a pretty little stone-flagged terrace, girded by a low wall on which sat pots of red and white geraniums. A vine-covered pergola arched over it, threaded with fairy-lights which also wound around the wooden supports of the pergola.

A table was set with a white linen tablecloth, a centrepiece of fragrant white flowers and a huge candle in a glass holder which gave a soft glow to the whole scene.

Rosalie's face broke into a rapturous smile. It was all so enchantingly beautiful.

She exclaimed and said as much, and Xandros smiled, ushering her to the table, refilling their champagne flutes.

Then Maria was bustling out to the terrace, emerging from somewhere at the back of the villa where, Rosalie presumed, the kitchen was situated.

'Welcome! Welcome!' She beamed. Then, 'Eat, eat!' she instructed, depositing upon the table a vast platter groaning with food.

Mounds of delicious-smelling slices of slow-cooked lamb were layered over fragrant rice and roasted potatoes, lapped with green beans and fried tomatoes… There was enough to feed way more than just themselves.

'I did warn you,' Xandros said, catching Rosalie's eye, his mouth tugging in a smile.

'Where are the dozen other dinner guests?' she responded humorously.

He laughed, and began to serve up.

Rosalie gave a moan of appreciation. It all tasted incredible. The herb-crusted lamb melted in her mouth—it had been slow roasting over charcoal for hours, Xandros told her—and the accompaniments, hearty as they were, tasted, to her mind, better than all the gourmet food she'd been revelling in since Xandros had lifted her of the poverty she'd known all her life.

'This is so *good*!' she enthused.

Maria emerged yet again, this time bringing an open bottle of red wine, depositing that, too, on the table with a flourish.

Rosalie ventured another line of phrasebook Greek, trying to saying how good the food was, and acquired a volley of approving speech in return.

Xandros translated for her. 'She says you need to be strong for your wedding night,' he told her.

In the candlelight there was a knowing glint in his eyes that Rosalie found difficult to cope with. But then reason came to the rescue.

He knows the irony of that. That's what that glint is for.

A shadow fluttered over her and she reached for her flute again, to banish it. But as the meal progressed it was hard to keep to her resolve not to be beguiled by everything about Xandros.

He'd always been attentive to her when they'd dined together in Athens, but this evening, under the fairy-lights woven into the vines, in the soft, flickering candlelight, she could see his eyes constantly on her. Warm...glinting...

She tried to ward it off.

He doesn't realise the effect he's having! That's the thing—he doesn't mean it...doesn't intend it. It just comes naturally to him. It's part of who he is.

The most intensely attractive male she could imagine, let alone have set eyes on in real life.

She fought it—she had to—but it was getting harder by the minute.

He'd poured a full glass of red wine for her, and its heady strength could not be denied. Perhaps it was not wise of her to imbibe so freely, but it washed the rich lamb down so perfectly it was hard to refrain.

Her plate was empty now, finally, but then there was a smaller second helping for them both, because it was so good it was impossible to refrain from that.

But when Maria re-emerged, whisking away the remnants and then replacing the lamb with another platter groaning with pastries, Rosalie gave an echoing groan.

She sat back, shaking her head. 'I couldn't! Not a thing!'

Across the table from her, Xandros laughed, picking up his wine glass and draining it. 'These are different from this afternoon. Lighter. Filled with curd cheese and honey. Try one. You'll like it, I promise you.'

Tempted, she did just that, and he was right—it was delicious.

'Is this the goat's cheese you told me about?' she asked Xandros brightly. That was better, surely? Asking about goats and cheese…anything that wasn't about the way his dark, long-lashed eyes were resting on her…

He nodded, helping himself to several of the pastries and starting to demolish them. Where they all went, Rosalie wasn't sure—certainly not into body fat.

Memory leapt in her—seeing him stripped down to swim shorts had been even more disturbing than seeing him when he'd been wearing that moulding white tee. In the sea she'd been able to see what it had been moulding. A perfectly honed torso, with smooth, golden pecs, and ripped and rippling abs…

She banished the memory. Definitely not a safe one. Not when she had a glass of champagne and nearly two of red wine inside her.

A sense of danger caught at her. She must not succumb—*must not!*—to the seductive aura all around her. Xandros opposite her, the gold-flecked glint of his eyes resting on her, lounging back, looking so lithe, so fabulous, so incredibly tempting…

I have to resist it! Resist him! Resist everything about him—everything he does to me when I'm gazing at him like this…

Because he didn't want her—not in that way.

Into her head came the words he'd thrown at her last night as he'd broken away from their kiss.

'This was a mistake.'

And it *would* be a mistake—*her* mistake this time!—for her to carry on indulging in gazing at him the way she wanted to. Indulging herself in anything about him at all. What did she know of men? Her romance-starved, constricted life had given her no experience—let alone of a man like Xandros.

He'd finished his pastries and was pushing his empty plate away from him, his gaze resting on her with half-closed eyes. She tried to drop her own gaze because she knew she should…must…but found she couldn't. She tried not to be aware of how she could feel her pulse beating at her throat—but she couldn't ignore it. It was impossible… just impossible.

He leaned forward suddenly, reaching out with his napkin in his hand. 'You've got a pastry crumb caught on your lip,' he said.

His voice was husky as he dabbed at the offending particle, his fingers just brushing the soft curve of her mouth.

She felt the pulse at her throat surge, her breath go still in her lungs. Her eyes held his, helpless to do anything else.

The candle was burning low in its glass case, starting to gutter, and the heady scent of the white flowers in the centrepiece—jasmine, Xandros had told her earlier, when she'd asked—caught at her senses.

He caught at her senses.

Xandros—the man she had married. Married that morning, making her his wife. A wife who was not a wife—not the way real wives were—for that was not why they had married. Not to sit here with him at this candlelit table, under fairy-lights that echoed the stars blazing in the heavens far above them, while soft waves lapped on the beach and a choir of cicadas chorused in the unseen vegetation beyond the little terrace. Not to see the eyes of the man she had married that morning resting on her with a gaze that was turning her slowly and unstoppably into liquid mush…

He was getting to his feet. She heard the scrape of his chair on the stone paving, and then he was beside her.

'Shall we skip coffee?' he said.

He was smiling down at her, a half-smile through half-closed eyes that were resting on her upturned face. The smile deepened, curving the edges of his mouth—his perfect, sculpted mouth—indenting lines around it that shadowed the planes of his face in the soft, low light. His eyes washed over her again, and in their depths she could see that dark gold seductive glint again. No hint of irony in it now...

She felt the breath leave her body.

'There's an age-old custom I want to try out,' he said, and his voice was husky again.

She didn't see it coming—was incapable of doing so. She could only give a breathless gasp as he scooped her bodily into his arms, striding with her into the villa.

He gave a laugh of triumph and possession. 'Carrying my bride over the threshold!'

She could say nothing, do nothing, could only gasp again, her arm automatically hooking around his neck, feeling the strength of his shoulders, feeling her body cradled against his.

'Xandros!' she cried out, half in consternation, half in bewilderment.

She was utterly overcome.

Overcome by being in his arms, lifted by him, her body caught against his strong muscled torso, his grip encompassing her totally.

He strode along the short length of the corridor, swept her into a bedroom.

Not hers, but his.

He laid her down upon his bed, flicked on the bedside light, came down beside her. Propped himself up to gaze down at her.

She could not breathe...could not speak. Blood was drumming in her veins, her eyes, and she could only stare up at him, gaze helplessly. His eyes were pouring into hers, and now they were not half closed at all, but blazing with a gold that was not a glint but a molten pool.

'I have been waiting for this moment all day,' he said, and there was a rasp in his voice. *'All day.* Waiting...' He took a ragged breath. 'Waiting since I saw you sashay out of that restaurant in London before we flew out to Athens. And now, finally, my wait is over.'

His head lowered, his mouth dipping to hers. And she was lost. Lost utterly in a bliss she could not stop because it was him kissing her. Xandros kissing her with a slow, feathered touch that was deepening all the time, parting her lips, reaching within, purposeful, tasting, seeking... finding. Melding.

It was a kiss as devastating to her as the kiss he had given her last night at her hotel room doorway. A hundred times more devastating! A thousand—

She could not stop him. Did not want to. Wanted only to let her eyes flutter shut and give herself to the exquisite feathering of his lips on hers, the soft, persuasive caress of his mouth as he eased hers open, deepening the kiss.

Bliss took over—sheer, gorgeous, unalloyed, insistent bliss. Bliss that went on and on as his hands tightened on her, as his mouth drew from hers yet more response.

A sense of sweeping oblivion overcame her as everything, in the entire universe ceased to exist except this moment, now, this moment that went on and on.

Until, as if he were pulling away under the strongest duress, he lifted his mouth from hers. His gaze was a wash of desire that blazed from him like the sun.

'Welcome to our wedding night,' he said.

CHAPTER TEN

ROSALIE STILLED, HIS words echoed, lifting her from the pool of sensual oblivion in which she had been drowning with his kiss.

Confusion filled her. 'I… I don't understand.' The words fell from her, summing up the whirlpool of confusion inside her.

How could this be happening—*how*?

Xandros's brow furrowed as he drew back from her a little. 'Don't understand what?'

Then his brow cleared, a smile starting to play about his mouth, and she could see even in the dim lamplight those deep flecks of gold in his eyes that somehow made her feel breathless all over again.

'Isn't it very simple?' he asked.

'But…' She swallowed. 'You said it was a mistake. Last night… That kiss… At my room in the hotel—'

He stared down at her. Then a wry, rueful laugh broke from him. 'Do you have *any* idea how hard it was for me to walk away from your room last night?' he asked, and she could hear the husk beneath the rueful tone. '*That* was why kissing you was a mistake!'

He took a ragged breath.

'Do you have *any* idea how hard it has been to keep my hands off you this entire time? That first evening at the hotel…at least we were in public—but when you came to my apartment, looked into my bedroom at my bed…'

Greek words broke from him, and then he was back to English.

'I've been in torment! Waiting to have you here all to myself…'

She gazed up at him, taking in his words. Taking in the implication of them. Something was soaring in her, taking flight, lifting her up and up and up…

'But now… Ah, now…' he went on, and his voice was husky again, with a sensual twist to it that set in motion inside her a vibration that seemed to be in every cell of her body. 'Now the time is right. Now,' he said, 'the time is perfect…'

He brushed his lips to hers again, softly, fleetingly. Arousingly. She gave herself to it, gave herself to *him*, to all that he was drawing from her, arousing in her—to the sense of wonder filling her, the wonderful, wondrous release of all that she had been trying so hard to keep in check, to stamp out of herself…

And now—like a fantasy made real, a dream come true—she did not have to! Because she had been so wrong about him! The truth was wonderful, glorious, like the blaze of desire that she could see in his eyes, pouring into hers now as his mouth lifted from her.

He wants me! He wants me as I have come to want him! And he can have everything he wants of me—everything…

She could feel her heart start to slug in slow, heavy beats, a throbbing deep inside her. Her senses were dizzy, hyper-aware and yet dazed and dreamlike. The wine sang in her blood, but she was not intoxicated…not by wine.

He kissed her again, and now she was kissing him back, opening her mouth to his, letting him feast upon her as she did on him. She was taking his mouth with hers and then his mouth was lifting from hers again. And as he gazed down at her his dark eyes were pools of sensual desire that sent a thrill through her, a heady quickening of her pulse that was like nothing she had ever felt or known in all her life.

His hand was moving along her hair like a soft caress, the tips of his fingers touching her cheek, drawing along the contour of her cheekbone, tracing her jaw, lingering over her mouth, shaping it with his touch. His eyes poured over her and she could see those gold flecks, the lush, smoky lashes dipping down as he explored her parting lips yet again with his delicate, sensual touch.

His fingers trailed own the exposed column of her throat, slowly, deliberately. Oh, it was so achingly arousing. She could only gaze up at him, feeling every sense come vividly alive, twisting her fingers to catch at the soft pillow beneath her head.

His hand smoothed lower and her breath caught. Though he said not a word she knew what he intended—oh, she knew with an ache inside her…

'So very, very beautiful…'

The husk in his voice was a rasp now, and as he murmured the words his hand rounded over the sweet swell of her breast. Beneath his palm, through the thin material of her dress, the lacy fabric of her bra, her breast engorged, its peak flowering at his enfolding touch.

A groan broke from her, soft and low, and he gave an answering laugh, moving his mouth to take the place of his moulding palm. Another groan broke from her at this renewed and oh, so exquisitely delicious onslaught on her body. And even as his lips teased her through the thin fabric of her garments his hand was sliding the strap of the dress from her shoulder, taking with it her bra strap as well.

She was hardly conscious of it, her whole focus only on the sensations he was arousing in her with his sensuous ministrations to her peaking breast. Only when his hand cupped her did she realise, with a startled little intake of breath, that her breast was now exposed to his view—and to his touch.

Oh, his touch…!

Wonder filled her, and a sense of amazement, and along with that a growing, irresistible sense of arousal, of a sensual sexual excitement that was firing within her like a slow-burning flame that suffused her whole body, making a sudden restlessness fill her, so that every nerve ending seemed hyper-aroused and she was ultra aware of her own body…ultra aware of a growing, insistent need…a need for the blissful, arousing touch of his hands, his mouth, to intensify, to be everywhere, to stroke and caress and explore…

She felt her spine arching of its own accord, as if her body were inviting more of what his mouth and hand were doing at her breast. Another groan broke from her, in a kind of helpless surrender to what was happening to her—a surrender she was making with her own desire…

For a new hunger was building in her now—a new need not just to lie there, her hands flexing in the pillow, her eyes fluttering shut at the exquisite sensations his ministrations to her bared, exposed and achingly cresting breasts. He had bared both now to his touch and his mouth, and his lips were laving her peaked nipple, his sensitive fingers skilfully squeezing and scissoring.

This new hunger was moving her limbs restlessly, searchingly, and her seeking hand soon found what it wanted, snaking around the strong column of his neck, her fingers playing in his hair, while her other hand girdled the lean circuit of his waist, as if of its own volition pushing the material of his shirt free from his waistband, sliding across the warm, strong contours of his back.

It felt glorious, wonderful, exhilarating! And then her legs were sliding sideways, for suddenly she was aching to feel the full length of his body on hers, wanting to feel his hips against hers, his thighs lying within the cradle of hers, to feel—with shock, and amazement, and a catching of her breath in realisation—just what the full weight of his body on hers entailed…

Did he hear the revealing catching of her breath? He must have, for his mouth lifted from her breast and his eyes were pouring into hers now, those gold flecks burning to molten flame.

'Do you not know how much I desire you?' There was humour in his voice, but promise, too... His long eyelashes dipped over his molten gaze and his mouth lowered to hers. 'How very, very much...'

And suddenly the tenor of his embrace changed. Its slow sensuality quickened, and it was with an abrupt movement that he was pulling his shirt over his head, not bothering with anything so delaying as buttons, before coming down on her again, kissing her again, warmly, persuasively, ardently.

Then, briskly, he had rolled her over on to her front and was smoothing the material of her dress upwards, lifting her hips and waist, ridding her of all that was not necessary as he turned her back to face him, her long hair tangling around her throat, cascading over her naked breasts.

For a moment, endless and timeless, he gazed down at her. She heard Greek words breaking from him, and then English, as his gaze devoured her.

'You are so beautiful. Perfect...'

Then, with another sudden movement he stood up.

'Don't move.'

His voice was a growl, and in the dim light he towered over her, his golden torso bronze in the light from the lamps as she gazed upon the perfection she had known that baring would reveal to her.

And not just the perfection of his torso.

With a widening of her eyes she realised why he had stood up, for with brisk haste he was casting aside his chinos and the last remaining barrier between them...

She shut her eyes. It was instinctive, immediate, and even as she did it she heard him laugh. As if in triumph and satisfaction.

And then she felt his weight beside her on the bed, lying

beside her. Felt his hand smooth her hair from her face as she dared to open her eyes again.

His gaze was pouring down on her once more, desire blazing...

Then his mouth lowering to hers again. And with bemused wonder she gave herself to every exquisite, sensual caress—for what did she know of how a couple made love, except what she had read or fantasised about in the long, lonely, empty years of her youth?

And now it was happening. Desire and growing passion were sweeping her away, unleashed kiss by kiss, touch by touch, caress by caress. Caresses that now, emboldened, she was seeking for herself, revelling in the muscled sinews and the warmth of his smooth skin, the contours and sculpting of his spine and hips and broad shoulders as an instinct as old as time urged her on.

Her spine arched, her breasts pressed against the wall of his chest and her hips crushed his. And then came the shock, the wonder of his arousal for her, his blatant desire, and, oh, the quickening of her own flesh, so that the hunger within her was growing, and mounting.

She wanted him—dear God, she wanted him... She wanted all of him, wanted his complete possession, wanted to give herself to him as a woman gave herself to a man... totally and all-consuming...

Her urgency and her hunger were his, answering his. He was cupping her shoulders, rearing up over her only to swoop down on her mouth with one last arousing full-throated kiss...and then he was plunging deep, deep within her as her thighs parted to receive him and her body opened to him...

Pain knifed through her and a piercing cry was torn from her throat. Her body froze.

Greek broke from him. Disbelief was in his eyes as he pulled away from her, staring down at her.

She could not move—could only feel the pain echoing still in her body…the body that was instinctively closing against him now. As it did so he was immediately freeing her, rolling sideways, lifting his weight from her.

His head whipped towards her and there was still that stunned disbelief in his face. 'Rosalie! *Thee mou*—why did you not *tell* me?'

Her body had curled instinctively into a foetal position, her thighs pressed close together, her arms, without his body to hold, fallen slackly to her sides.

She turned her head to him, her expression working, her body and her head a tumult. 'I… I…'

She could get no further. And suddenly, out of nowhere—out of the mountainous tower of her emotions and the overwhelming confusion of her mind and body over all that had swept over her—another tearing cry broke from her and she burst into tears. Tears for all that had happened…that had *not* happened.

Immediately, with an oath, he brought his arms around her—arms that held her, drew her towards him, rocked her in his embrace, cradling her like a child.

His voice was no longer shocked, but concerned—comforting. Cherishing. He spoke to her in Greek, soft and mellifluous, and she couldn't understand a word, nor hear it properly either, through the muffled sobs she stifled on his chest as her face pressed against it, her shoulders convulsing with her tears, her body shaking.

How long she wept, she didn't know, but she felt the tears easing from her, felt a kind of washed-out, exhausted calm overcoming her. And still he talked to her, softly and gently, his hand smoothing her back, comforting and reassuring her, holding her close and closer still against him as her body ceased its shaking, started to slacken in his arms.

Exhaustion washed over her, thickening the air, her breath. Her tear-filled eyes were stinging, her eyelids drooping. Her eyes were heavy, so very heavy…her breathing was slowing, easing…

And then sleep—sweet, sweet sleep—folded over her.

Xandros stood by the sea's edge, where the morning sun was bright on the water, his thoughts on the woman he had left sleeping in his bed—and not just any woman, not just one of his amours.

My wife. My bride. My virgin bride…

He felt his breath catch, felt the contours of his life changing, reshaping themselves. It felt strange. And strangely wonderful…

Footsteps crunching on the pebbled beach behind him made him turn. His face lit with a warm smile.

'Kalimera,' he said softly.

But his new wife—his bride—did not return his smile. Instead she paused in her hesitant approach towards him. He went to her, took her hands in his. She had put on a pair of turquoise shorts, a pink tee. Her hair was loose, she wore not a scrap of make-up—and she looked the most beautiful he had ever seen her…

He felt something turn over inside him.

But her expression was troubled.

He pressed her hands with his, compunction filling him. 'How are you?' he asked, with concern in his voice. 'I am so, so sorry if I… If I hurt you last night. But…' he took a rueful breath '… I simply didn't realise…'

He saw colour fill her cheeks, flushing them, watched her gaze drop. Compunction smote him again. He drew her closer to him, dropped a kiss as light as a feather upon her forehead. Her eyes flew up to his again. Their expression was still troubled.

'It's *me* who should be apologising!' The words broke from her. 'For…for disappointing you!'

Xandros could only stare at her. Could she really mean

that? He kissed her again, on the mouth this time, swiftly, but without passion—only with reassurance.

'*Never* think that,' he said firmly His eyes held hers, intent with meaning. 'Never. From now on we will take things at the pace *you* set. And when the time is right— when you are ready—then everything will be all right.' He smiled down at her, his expression warm, his voice husky as he spoke. 'I promise you, my beautiful virgin bride, that when you cry out in my arms again it will only be from ecstasy...'

For a moment that was timeless, endless, his eyes held hers, infusing that promise deep into her. Then, knowing he had said enough for now—knowing, too, that if he held her this close any longer he would not be able to resist kissing her with passion—he gave her hands one last squeeze and let them go. He knew with every male instinct in him that a passionate kiss was not, alas, something she could cope with right now.

In quite a different voice, light and cheerful, he said, 'Time for breakfast. And today,' he added, 'we will simply—enjoy!'

Rosalie sat herself down at the table set at the front of the little villa. Maria bustled out with a tray piled high with breakfast.

'As ever, enough for half a dozen,' Xandros murmured good-humouredly as Maria disappeared again.

Rosalie gave a flickering smile. Xandros was being so *nice*—as cheerful and easy-going as he had been yesterday. Gratefully, she went with it. A sense of emotional exhaustion over anything else had taken her over, as if she just couldn't cope with anything else right now.

Besides, the scent of new-baked bread and the rich aroma of freshly brewed coffee plucked at her senses.

'Tuck in,' Xandros urged with a wide smile, passing her the butter and a pot of golden honey.

She felt her anxious thoughts ease a fraction. He was showing her a way to cope with them, to cope with the tumult of feelings inside her. And she would follow the lead he was setting for her, would find her own way, her own path. Take her time. She would feel only the ease of being here, in this beautiful place, and enjoy all it brought.

She would enjoy her breakfast, enjoy the loveliness of this beautiful island, and enjoy the sheer pleasure of eating *al fresco* like this, with the sun sparkling on the azure sea.

It was so infinitely distant from the life she had known till now, from the mean streets and ugliness of London—even from the busy bustle of Athens. This, here, now, was peace—absolute peace. Absolute beauty.

And Xandros was smiling at her—there was warmth in his voice, in his eyes... He was being so kind, so considerate.

Memory plucked at her of how kind he'd been that dreadful morning when she'd fled her father's house with all her stupid hopes smashed to pieces, when she'd sobbed all over Xandros... She'd done the same last night and he'd been just as kind...

She felt her heart swell and emotions swirled in her again. Quite what they were, she did not know—she knew only that it was Xandros at their centre... Only Xandros.

'So, what would you like to do today?' he was asking now.

He was giving her, she knew with a little pang, a timely interruption to her thoughts...to emotions she could not yet make sense of.

'We could take a dip in the sea again, and then catch some rays before the sun gets too high. And then maybe, if you feel up to it, we could take the dinghy out later? How does that sound?'

She gave a flickering smile again, nodded. Letting him take the lead, guide her forward.

He wanted her to enjoy the day and she found that she did. It would have been impossible not to.

She swam, the cool salt water easing her body and the low ache between her legs dissipating, and then she let the sun warm her, giving herself to its golden balm. Then there was a leisurely *al fresco* lunch—more fresh bread, Maria's goat's cheese, sweet tomatoes and succulent home-grown olives. And afterwards, as he had promised, Xandros took her out on his dinghy, skimming them peacefully across the sun-drenched bay, back and forth, not talking while she leaned back, feeling the breeze fill her hair as well as the sail. Feeling a sense of peace fill her.

On their return, Maria attempted to feed them again, but Xandros took her for a walk—not up the cliffs this time, but inland, to Maria and Panos's home.

Panos proudly showed her his vegetable garden, groaning with produce, and his fruit-laden peach and lemon trees, and his olive grove, and his well-fed chickens and his stout pigs, and his two very fine-looking mules. She admired all of them unstintingly, and then he sat them down and plied them with almond biscuits washed down with a glass of his lethal home-distilled peach brandy, while his two deceptively fierce-looking dogs leaned heavily against Rosalie's legs, panting gently in the heat and inviting her to pet them, which she smilingly did.

Before they left Panos pressed a huge watermelon into Xandros's hands, and a basket of sun-warmed tomatoes into Rosalie's.

'Epharisto poli...nostimo!' she ventured, trying out her phrasebook Greek. She thought it meant 'Thank you... delicious!'

Panos's weathered face split into a huge grin, and with some voluble Greek he promptly added a pair of ripe peaches to the basket.

'We must make our getaway before we empty their

larder!' Xandros murmured with a laugh, and they did just that.

They set off back to the villa, accompanied by Panos's dogs until he called them with a piercing whistle, whereupon they padded back to him.

'They have a good life, Panos and Maria,' Rosalie heard herself say. 'Simple, but good.'

'They do.' Xandros nodded. 'But you know…' his tone was thoughtful '… I sometimes wonder whether, if I tried to live like Maria and Panos, Kallistris would lose its magic. Sometimes when you have too much of something you enjoy, it palls.'

She glanced out to sea, thinking about what he'd said.

But I've had so little all my life! So little of anything, really—except my mother's love. In that, I have been rich indeed.

But of everything else she'd had so little as she'd grown up—even in comparison with her contemporaries. They had had girlfriends, boyfriends, romance in their lives…

Her eyes flickered back to the man walking along beside her, who could melt her with a single glance, a single touch, a single kiss. Who had revealed to her, last night, a desire that had swept her away into a sea of searing passion…until her inexperienced body had confused and confounded her.

But now he was promising her not shock and tears, but ecstasy in his arms…promising to make her truly his as she had never thought she would be.

He will be my lover—and I his…

She had not thought this strange, brief marriage would bring her that—had not looked for it or allowed herself to dream of it—but if it did, why be shy of it? Why refuse what she had never thought would be hers?

He wants me as I want him!

And why should that not be something to rejoice in? Even for the short duration of their time together? Her life had changed utterly in so short a time, all thanks to Xandros. She would be grateful to him for ever. Grateful for all he was making possible. Grateful that he desired her as she did him.

And it will be good—oh, so good! For he is everything I could ever dream about in a man! Everything!

The wonder of it filled her. She felt a warm rush around her heart and lifted her eyes to his. He caught them, smiling down at her, warm and caring.

For her and her alone.

For the night to come—when she would give herself to him and take all that he was offering her.

For all their time together.

In the dark of the night, in the warmth of his bed, she lay in his arms, filled with a golden incandescent glow. How was it possible to have felt such bliss, to have responded to his skilled, but oh, so gentle possession?

She had cried out—not in pain this time, but in wonder, just as he had promised her—and joy had flooded through her, along with a pleasure, an ecstasy so intense her spine had arched like a bow, her limbs straining, her hands clutching at the strong, straining sinews of his back. And he had thrown his head back as he, too, had reached that same peak of absolute union.

And now she lay in his arms, with an exhaustion so profound and a wonder so deep binding her to him as her hectic heart rate eased. She felt her breath, warm upon his strong, supporting chest, felt her eyelids close, sleep washing over her in the cradle of his arms.

In all the world this was the only place she wanted to be.

As he felt the soft, trembling body in his arms lapse into restful slumber Xandros slackened his hold. His own body was succumbing to the torpor of satiation, but before the last of his conscious thoughts ebbed from him he knew that one was uppermost. The one he treasured most.

Just as he had promised her he would, he had made it wonderful for her... And for himself as well.

Like I've never known it.

But why...? Why should that be?

Like feathers on a stream, thoughts drifted through his mind. Never before had he been a woman's first lover—and never before had a woman been his wife...nor shared his haven on Kallistris...

Were they the reasons it had seemed so...*so special*... with Rosalie?

The question hovered like a drop of rain held in the still air...and as sleep finally flowed over him it dissolved like mist. Yielding no answer.

Rosalie lay in the sun, offering her body to its warm caress. Her skin was no longer pale. The passing days had turned it to golden honey...

Five blissful, sun-kissed days!

Five even more blissful nights...

Nights of giving herself entirely to Xandros—to what they had together.

She felt her breath catch in wonder and delight.

Xandros—oh, Xandros!

She cried out his name in her head and felt her heart glow as warmly as her body.

How was it possible to be so happy?

How impossible was it not to be?

Day after day they had taken their leisure—swimming, sailing, paddleboarding, snorkelling, taking picnics up to the headland, going for easy walks amongst the wild goats through the herb-scented maquis, drinking cocktails on the beach, watching the sunset and the moonrise, feasting every evening on Maria's groaning banquets to give them strength for the long, long nights when they burned with passion and desire…finding ecstasy in each other's arms…

She felt heat beat up in her cheeks. Was it because he was her first lover that it was so good? So special? Was that the reason?

Or was it because she had taken one look at him as she'd opened the door of that rundown rental house she'd been cleaning and known he was the most fantastic-looking male she'd ever seen in her life?

Or was it because he had swept her out of her grim, grinding poverty to bring her here, to the land of her forebears, showering upon her this amazing life of wealth and luxury, promising her that never again would she know hardship and deprivation?

She did not know why—she knew only that it was so, and that in Xandros's arms she knew a bliss that she had never imagined possible.

Why it was, she left unspoken.

Unanswered.

Xandros crunched across the pebbles, his eyes going immediately to Rosalie, sweeping over her dozing form. He felt desire quicken, as it always did, and he hunkered down beside her, indulging himself in softly brushing his hand over the soft swell of her midriff, exposed by her brief bikini.

Her eyelids fluttered open and her face broke into a smile.

He brushed her mouth with his. 'Can I tempt you to a swim before lunch?' he asked, and smiled, drawing back.

'You can tempt me to anything.' She gave an answering smile.

'Now, there's an offer!'

There was a glint in his eye as she sat up.

Today was their last day on Kallistris—they would be heading back to Athens first thing tomorrow morning. He wasn't looking forward to it. He never liked to leave Kallistris anyway, but now his reluctance was even more marked. He'd happily spend more time here, lotus-eating with Rosalie, rather than go back in Athens, plunging head-first into all the work that making his merger with Coustakis a reality entailed.

He was conscious of the irony—after all, he had only married Rosalie to achieve the merger he wanted, and yet here he was wishing he could have more time with her here. Back in Athens he'd be putting in long days at the office and would only see her in the evenings.

Well, he would strive to make it possible to get back here as much as he could. Even a weekend would be better than nothing.

He helped her stand up now, and then stripped off to his swim shorts. Both of them waded into the waiting sea.

His thoughts went back to that first swim they'd had together. Before he had made her his own. Was it really only five days ago? They seemed to have been lovers for so much longer. It was as if they'd always been together. As if they always would be.

He frowned, wondering where that thought had come from, and dismissed it immediately as he launched into a powerful freestyle, ploughing out to sea. It was Kallistris, he thought, increasing his speed. It had that effect on him… making him forget about anywhere else. An island, indeed, of lotus-eating, where time stopped and there was neither past nor future, only an endless blissful present.

But time didn't stop in the world beyond, and back in Athens his time would be busy. His agenda non-stop. Maybe the enchantment he was feeling with Rosalie would start to wear off there. Perhaps here, on Kallistris, where he'd never brought his amours, she seemed more special than she really was.

He left it at that, focussing on exerting his every muscle

to accelerate and maintain his speed, then curving around to head back to shallower waters, where Rosalie was sedately criss-crossing the bay in a gentle breaststroke.

He dived under the water, surfacing beside her in a shower of diamond water drops, and she gave a start of surprise. He grinned, and caught her for a kiss.

'I wonder,' he said wickedly, 'what making love in the water might be like?'

She gave a gurgle of laughter. 'Leave it to the dolphins!' she quipped.

He laughed in answer, wading ashore with her.

'Okay, I'll trade it for a leisurely siesta instead,' he promised her, with a knowing glint in his eye.

Sleep would not be on the agenda…

Tomorrow morning they might be back in Athens, but for today, at least, lotus-eating and lovemaking were all he would allow.

All he wanted.

Rosalie stood gazing at her reflection. She had dressed with particular care, wanting to look her most beautiful for Xandros this evening.

Our last evening here…

A pang smote her. She was not looking forward to returning to Athens, but she knew they must. Xandros needed to get on with all the work that making his merger with her father's business entailed. That was what they had married for.

Their marriage was a means to an end—nothing more than that.

The fact that she and Xandros had become lovers was irrelevant to achieving that goal.

That is what I have to remember and never forget. The day the merger is accomplished is the day our marriage ends and we go our separate ways.

She turned away from her reflection, not wanting to see the woman there—the woman whose life had been transformed in ways she had never realised it would be when she had first landed on this beautiful enchanted island. Tomorrow they would be leaving, but she would arrive back in Athens a different person. There could be no going back to the one she had been.

She felt emotion catch at her, but let it slip away. It was best that it did. Best to simply pick up her flowered shawl and make her way out to the walled terrace. Maria, she knew, had prepared a farewell feast for them, and Xandros would be waiting for her. She must make the very most of this last evening here.

In Athens it would be…different.

She would not have his constant company…would need to be self-reliant. Already she had resolved to fill her days productively. Exploring Athens, learning Greek, and even, she had decided, picking up her online studies. Qualifications were never wasted, and when she was back in England they would come in useful even with the incredibly generous divorce settlement Xandros was promising her.

She might start her own business…make investments… after all, she had the rest of her life ahead of her. Her life beyond Xandros…

She felt a chill strike her and pulled her shawl a little closer around her shoulders.

Yet it did not seem to warm her.

CHAPTER ELEVEN

DESPITE HER RESOLVE to be self-reliant when they were back in Athens, and not expect Xandros to dance attendance on her, Rosalie found she had to keep reminding herself that his priority was not her—it was making the merger he had married her to achieve a reality. It meant he spent long days at his office—long days in which she had to occupy herself.

She did just as she had resolved to do—assiduously exploring the city and its cornucopia of ancient treasures, attempting to learn the language as she'd told herself she would and picking up her online studies again, courtesy of the brand-new laptop Xandros had presented her with. She also, at Xandros's behest, sampled the many upmarket fashion shops in Athens in order to extend her designer wardrobe yet further—it was frivolous, but wonderful to be able to indulge herself as a budding fashionista...

After the grim, exhausting slog of her London life she knew she should only be grateful that her days now were this easy, and if her evenings alone in his apartment stretched, with Xandros often not home till late, and working weekends as well, she refused to let herself feel neglected.

She had no right to feel that way.

No right to miss him or to miss the leisurely pace they'd enjoyed on Kallistris.

On Kallistris, by day and by night, they had made slow, lingering love, with Xandros's skilled mouth and fingertips drawing from her such sensual bliss that it had been a white-out of the mind. Now there was only urgent passion, swiftly sated. When she awoke he was already up and getting ready for the office, leaving her with a brief kiss and nothing more.

She sighed, feeling guilty. She should not let herself be like this. She had so *much*! A life of ease and luxury. She had no right to feel so down. No right to want yet more.

To want Xandros to herself while she had him.

She frowned—where had *that* come from? That reminder of their time being limited. Of course it was— she'd known that from the very start! Neither of them was committed to the other except for the time they had allotted to stay together in this brief, temporary marriage.

You knew that from the start! And you knew that his focus was going to be on getting the merger done! You've no business to feel neglected or feel sorry for yourself!

But as she heard his key in the lock—early for him on this Friday evening—she felt her spirits life instantly and her mood soar. She'd seem almost nothing of him these last two weekends since returning to Athens.

Tossing his briefcase down on the sofa, Xandros swept her up into his arms. 'At last! A weekend *not* in the office!' He kissed her, and set her back, resting his hands on her shoulders. 'Time to party!' he told her.

He took a deep breath before speaking again, his words sounding heartfelt.

'I've slogged long enough—I want a break. So how about it? Let's rig ourselves up and head out! It's the birthday party of a friend of mine and I don't want to miss it— *and…*' he nodded at her and his expression was telling '… it's high time I showed you off! But first…'

His grip on her shoulders changed, becoming a caress. The expression in his face changed, too, and gold glinted in his eyes.

'But first,' he said again, 'I want to make up for all my neglect of you—'

With a catch of her breath and a quickening of her veins Rosalie realised what he intended.

His long lashes swept down over his eyes. 'Kallistris,' he said huskily, 'was far too long ago...'

His kiss was slow and sensual and melted the very bones of her. With a low laugh of triumph he surfaced, effortlessly scooping her up into his arms and carrying her through into his bedroom to lower her down upon the bed, coming down beside her.

His hand smoothed her hair from her forehead. 'Have I told you recently how very, very beautiful you are, Kyria Lakaris?'

The husk in his voice was deeper...the gold glints in his eyes more molten.

'Not recently,' she said, and sighed in warm anticipation. Gladness was filling her, arousal was beckoning, and there was another emotion, too. Relief.

He still wants me.

Had that been her fear, these last weeks? Had she thought that Xandros was turning into a workaholic not just because he had to run a multi-million-pound business doing whatever it was that he did *and* overseeing a complex and demanding merger as well? Had she not wanted to admit that she feared his attraction to her had palled?

But now, as his mouth began to glide down her throat, his fingers deftly slipping open the buttons of her shirt, of his shirt as well, his thighs moving across hers so that she felt their strength, she knew, with another sigh of pleasurable arousal, just how very keen he was to get her naked. And, beneath him, she could cast all those fears aside and glory in what came next.

A burning fusion that made her cry out again, and again as his body took her to an ecstasy that had not been hers since their last night on Kallistris.

She clung to him, shuddering in the aftermath, feeling

his heart hammering as fiercely as her own, knowing his limbs were exhausted, the bedclothes in a tangled turmoil.

He pulled her tight against him. 'I must have been mad to work so hard,' he breathed. He levered himself up on his elbow. 'I'm going to take a break—for the whole weekend!' He dropped a slow kiss on her mouth. 'But tonight—tonight, Kyria Lakaris—I want you to put on the gladdest of your glad rags and make me the envy of all Athens!'

The envy of all Athens? Into her head came the jibing words her father had thrown at her when she'd defied him. It was *she* who was supposed to be the envy of all Athens...

And later, as they joined Xandros's friends in the *salon privé* at the exclusive restaurant where they were gathering, she could see that the jibe had held some truth in it. His friends were welcoming, though she found herself feeling shy, hanging on to Xandros's supporting arm, and they were happy to talk to her in English, though most of their lively conversation was conducted, understandably in Greek, but two of the most elegant women there made a beeline for her.

'We are in mourning!' they teased her. 'Xandros has been captured at last!'

'We all wanted to marry him—but he evaded us!' The nearest woman's dark eyes gleamed. 'So what is your secret?'

The other woman gave a laugh. 'The same as Ariadne's!' she exclaimed.

She seemed about to say more, but Xandros had turned away from the man whose birthday it was to drape an arm around Rosalie's shoulder.

'Come and meet the birthday boy,' he said, drawing her away. 'I want to see the envy in his eyes!'

His friend certainly showed his admiration, and Rosalie could not help but be glad she had made such an effort tonight, knowing that in such company she must do Xandros justice. Her newly purchased cocktail dress, in hues of peacock and royal blue, was, she knew, stunning in its design.

'Don't leave me alone with your wife for a second, old friend,' the birthday boy teased openly, 'or I will steal her away from you! She is ravishing!'

She smiled, knowing it for the laddish joshing that it was, but was glad of Xandros's possessive arm around her.

They took their seats for dinner at a long, formally set table laden with silverware and crystal glasses. Conversation reverted to Greek, and became very lively and good-humoured, with Xandros clearly a key player.

Part of Rosalie warmed to see him relaxed and convivial—and yet part of her ached, too, and she did not know why. And although his arm was draped around her shoulder, showing the world they were an item, she felt a distance from him.

I'm just passing through his life…and he through mine. By winter all this will be over. I'll be back in London. He'll be part of my past—nothing more than that…

She felt her throat tighten, felt memory burn. She remembered how their bodies had clung to each other in throbbing passion just a few brief hours ago…how close they'd seemed. As if nothing could part them. But time would do just that—part them in a matter of months. Just as they'd planned from the outset.

Her throat tightened again, and she felt that strange melancholy assail her as it had in his apartment, before they had married.

On Kallistris it had vanished.

Now she felt it again. More poignant.

Xandros sat back in his chair at the desk in his office and frowned. Some critical financial documentation that Stavros Coustakis should have made available to him by now had still not been sent over.

His mouth thinned. Was this the man playing yet more of his damn games? If so, his only purpose could be to flex his power just for the sake of it. After all, he'd got exactly what he'd held out for—a Lakaris son-in-law—so why the delay now? At this rate getting the merger pulled together would take irritatingly longer than Xandros had wanted it to take.

On the other hand... His expression changed. It was an ill wind that blew no one any good at all.

A delay will give me longer with Rosalie.

His dark eyes glinted appreciatively. That would definitely be a bonus—no doubt about it.

One of the things that was exacerbating his frustration with his father-in-law's dilatory co-operation over expediting the merger between them was the fact that all the demands of making it happen were keeping him in the office for far longer than he wanted.

Increasingly, he wanted to be spending time with Rosalie. Making the most of her while he had her—before they had to part company and go their own ways.

The frown was back in his eyes again. That was a pretty negative way of putting it...

And why be negative about something that's a positive?

Because of course it was *entirely* a positive that theirs was to be a temporary marriage, existing only for the purpose of making the Lakaris-Coustakis merger a reality.

It was a positive that when that happened he and Rosalie would dissolve their marriage and she would return to England, to a comfortable life of financial security. Leaving him in Greece to resume his carefree bachelor lifestyle again.

Except... His frown deepened as he sat at his desk, staring blankly at his computer screen. Except he had to admit that thought held little appeal.

Instead, his thoughts went back to the previous weekend. It had been good to take Rosalie to that birthday celebration—surprisingly good to realise that he, too, was now one of the many married couples of his acquaintance and no longer a singleton. Rosalie had seemed to enjoy herself, which was important, and though he'd heard her half-sister's name mentioned he had forestalled any deterioration of the conversation into potentially tactless discussion of Ariadne.

Anyway, it hadn't needed his arm possessively around Rosalie to show all his friends the convincing proof that Ariadne was history and why. They'd all been able to see how blown away he was by Rosalie—and not just because of her stunning beauty, or the way he only had to look at her to want to sweep her off to bed.

I enjoy her company.

He'd known that from the start, he realised—even before he'd claimed her for his own. She was easy to be with... enjoyable to be with. *Good* to be with. Good to spend time with.

They'd done a lot of that over the weekend. Spending time together. On the Saturday, the day after the birthday bash, they'd piled into his car and taken off across the Corinth Canal into the Peloponnese, down past the ancient sites of Mycenae and Epidarus.

Rosalie's eyes had widened as he'd told her the tales and the history he'd grown up with, which she hungered for to make up for her missing birthright.

They'd spent the night in Naphlion, Greece's first capital after regaining its modern independence, and Rosalie had been enchanted by the graceful old houses and peaceful squares there. It had been good—very good—to wander with her, hand in hand, exploring the narrow streets and byways, taking their time, taking their ease, enjoying it all...

He wished he could look forward to taking her sightseeing the whole of the coming weekend. But that wasn't going to be possible. Not because he would be tied to his desk, working on the merger, but because his mother had invited them to lunch on Saturday.

He knew he couldn't get out of it. His mother needed to meet Rosalie—if for no other reason than to forestall any potential gossip that she was ostracising her new daughter-in-law. To stop any rumours that she wasn't meeting Rosalie because she expected the marriage to be of short duration. *That* must definitely not get back to Stavros!

Xandros gave a resigned sigh. He hoped his mother would go easy on Rosalie...not make her preference for Ariadne too obvious. Had she heard from Rosalie's sister yet? he wondered, and then put the question aside. Ariadne would surface when she was good and ready, and he wished her well. But between her and Rosalie there was no comparison. None at all.

How could he ever have seriously contemplated marrying Ariadne? It seemed absurd now. Now that he had Rosalie...

While he had her...

Without his being aware of it, the frown had come back to his eyes...even before his secretary had put her head around his door to tell him that the Coustakis accounts he'd been so impatient for had still not arrived.

Stavros's delays were not all that displeased him...

Rosalie's eyes widened as Xandros nosed his car down the long drive and his mother's home came into sight. This was not a house—it was a mansion! More like the Greek equivalent of an English stately home. The large three-storey edifice was set in equally spacious grounds, deep in the countryside to the north of Athens. Tall cypresses flanked it on either side, and a large stone ornamental pond with a trickling fountain fronted it as they crunched along the gravel drive.

'It was built in the nineteenth century,' Xandros was telling her, 'by my great-great-grandfather, after the creation of the modern Greek state. I grew up here.' He paused. 'I was very fortunate to be able to do so,' he went on.

His voice had changed, Rosalie could hear, and she looked at him questioningly.

He caught her look and gave her a faint smile as he drew up in front of the grand front entrance. 'It very nearly had to be sold,' he said. He switched off the car's engine, looking at her. 'My grandfather lived very extravagantly, and it was my father who had to battle to save the family fortune. It was touch-and-go all my boyhood. He succeeded, but…' His expression tightened. 'It shortened his life…all the stress he was under for so long. That is why, you see, I'm so very keen on making this merger with your father happen. I never want the kind of financial worry I grew up with to affect my family again.'

His expression changed again, and his voice became apologetic.

'I know that probably sounds…well, *insulting* to you, given what you and your poor mother had to put up with all your lives—'

She shook her head. 'No…' she answered slowly. 'I think it explains why you've been so kind to me—why you don't want me to be poor again.'

It did, she realised. In his own way he felt a degree of similarity between them, vastly different though their backgrounds had been. And, she thought—and it was a strange thought, given that vast difference—it also made her understand how similarly driven he was, how dogged his determination to achieve the merger he sought by whatever means necessary.

Just as I was determined to lift myself out of poverty by whatever means necessary. Whether that was by working my guts out as a cleaner to fund my studies or by marrying…

Her expression flickered. Was that why she'd married Xandros? The only reason? Truly the only reason…?

The question hovered and she was unwilling to seek an answer. Was grateful that he was now giving a rueful smile to her response.

'Well, it is kind of you to say so,' he replied. 'And I hope you can be as forbearing with my mother.' His mouth tightened. 'I need to tell you that Ariadne's mother was a good friend of hers, and for that reason my mother shared your father's enthusiasm for my marrying your half-sister. She accepts that Ariadne did not share that enthusiasm, but—'

He broke off. The grand front door was opening, and a butler—or so Rosalie surmised—was emerging. Xandros got out, greeted the stately personage and came round to open Rosalie's door.

She got out, nerves pinching. This was an ancestral home, by any standards, but it was strange to think of what Xandros had just disclosed—that the wealth he so obviously enjoyed had not always been guaranteed. Strange, too—and more disturbing—to think that Xandros's mother had wanted Xandros to marry Ariadne, just as her father had, even though Xandros and Ariadne had clearly had no intention of going along with either parent's wishes.

Butterflies fluttered in her stomach. It wasn't going to make it any easier to cope with the forthcoming meeting. But at least she had the comfort of knowing that Xandros's mother knew just how artificial their marriage was.

She was glad she had dressed with extreme care, in a modestly styled dress, and had applied equally modest make-up. And she was glad when Xandros gave her hand a reassuring squeeze as the stately butler showed them in to a drawing room whose elegance matched the grand house.

The woman greeting them was equally elegant.

'My dear…' Kyria Lakaris said faintly, her smile even

fainter, and then she smiled far more warmly at her son when Xandros kissed her cheek.

He made most of the conversation during the visit, sticking to anodyne subjects such as their recent venture into the Peloponnese, and Rosalie was thankful. Though he kept mostly to English, his mother very often replied in Greek.

Is she trying to shut me out, or am I being oversensitive?

She gave a mental shrug, because in the end what did it matter whether Xandros's mother disapproved of her? Disapproved of her son marrying her? She would be gone out of his life soon enough.

Several times during the laborious luncheon they sat through, in a dining room as elegant as the drawing room, she heard her half-sister's name from her mother-in-law, and she could tell by his tone of his voice, even in Greek, that Xandros's replies were terse. He always pointedly reverted to English, making some remark about his boyhood.

It was the only subject that drew a response from his mother—the first sign of animation Rosalie had seen in her yet.

'This is a wonderful place for a child to grow up—so much space to run around in! And for the next generation, too. I so look forward to seeing my grandchildren here,' his mother commented, looking at Rosalie. 'Of course, had Xandros married Ariadne—'

Xandros's voice cut across her, saying something repressive in Greek. His mother's mouth tightened, but she did not continue.

Rosalie had got the message, though. Well, Xandros's mother would have to wait for her grandchildren—wait until her son was free of his current marriage.

Wait until he marries again. To a real wife this time, so they can make a life together...have children... Xandros's children...

She snapped her mind away. Xandros's future children were nothing to do with her. There was no point, was there, in her sudden vision of a pair of toddlers running about in the sun-drenched gardens beyond the dining room windows…?

She would be gone from his life by then…

Long gone.

Her gaze flickered out to the gardens again, and she felt an inexplicable tightening of her throat assail her.

She longed for the lunch to be over, and finally it was. It was with a real sense of relief that she drove off with Xandros.

'Thank you,' he said, 'for coping with my mother.'

His expression was speaking volumes, and Rosalie was appreciative.

'She's bound to be concerned by the nature of our marriage,' she answered generously. 'She's protective of you. It's understandable.'

He cast her a glance. 'Thank you for that,' he said. 'You see,' he went on, and Rosalie could hear the constraint in his voice, 'she is very fond of Ariadne, and she's worried by her continued silence. I've told her your half-sister will surface when she is good and ready to do so.'

'I hope she does.' Rosalie's voice was warm. 'I long to meet her! It would be lovely to do so before I leave Greece!'

She turned away, looking out over the countryside, at the fields and the ubiquitous olive groves baking in the afternoon sun. It was high summer now. Time was passing. The inevitable date of her departure was that much closer.

'How is the merger coming along?' she heard herself ask, looking back at Xandros.

That, after all, was setting the timetable for the duration of their marriage. Like a ticking clock, counting down the hours…the days…the weeks and months…until there was no further need for them to be married.

No reason for them to be together…

He changed gear, revving the engine and picking up speed. His expression tightened.

'Not as fast as I'd hoped. Your father isn't exactly rushing to complete it. He keeps me waiting for essential information and so on.'

She saw him give a shrug, and was aware, though she knew she shouldn't be, that there was an upside to any delay. An upside for *her*, at least…

It put back, just a little, the ticking clock of their marriage…

Xandros was still speaking, and she shook the forbidden thought from her head.

'Doubtless it's all just one of his power plays—he likes to stay in control of things…and people.' A sympathetic glance came her way. 'As you know to your cost.' He changed gear again, speeding up even more. 'But we'll get there.' His expression lightened. 'Anyway, let's not waste what's left of the weekend dwelling on it! We'll take the scenic route back to the city—I can show you some more sights.'

They did just that, taking in the ancient sites of Eleusis and Megaris, and Rosalie enjoyed every minute. But then, she thought wryly, she would enjoy going round an industrial estate if it was with Xandros…

I just like being with him—anywhere, any time…

But nowhere he had yet taken her, either now or on the previous weekend, however glorious and spectacular in terms of sightseeing, could compare with Kallistris.

Will we ever get back there?

Yearning filled her. A yearning that maybe he picked up on telepathically, because when they stopped for coffee, midafternoon, he glanced at her and said, 'Let's try and get away to Kallistris before much longer, shall we? Get in a weekend there? Would that be good?'

Rosalie's face lit, and she answered enthusiastically.

* * *

In the end it was another fortnight before they could get back to Kallistris, but when they did it was every bit as good as she remembered. The island was as beautiful as ever, the little beach was as beautiful as ever, the simple whitewashed villa as beautiful as ever, the sea was as crystal clear as ever, the sun as hot as ever.

The two days passed in a flash—not nearly long enough—though they did nothing except swim and sail and sun themselves and be fed gargantuan meals by Maria.

I want more—so much more! And not just of Kallistris. Of Xandros. For much, much longer...

She knew she shouldn't feel that way, but she could not stop herself.

I don't want this time with Xandros to end! I want it to go on and on!

But how could she want that when it had been no part of their agreement? When the clock was ticking inexorably towards the time when there would be no purpose to their marriage any more.

Yet she could not deny the truth of it to herself. And it was a truth that continued to pluck at her on their return to Athens, when she resumed the life she'd got used to there.

Days passed into weeks, with Xandros again putting in long hours at work, interspersing them with short, intense periods of being with her.

Sometimes they managed to get to Kallistris at the weekend; more often, though, it was just driving out to explore yet more of Greece with him—up to Delphi, famed for its oracle, and out to the long island of Euboea, across the dramatic Gulf of Corinth bridge to visit the site of the ancient Olympic games.

Sometimes they stayed in Athens, taking it easy in the apartment, with long lie-ins and vegging in front of the TV, tuned to an English-language channel or watching online movies. Or dining out *à deux* in beautiful restaurants. Or socialising at a dinner dance, or another grand and glittering affair.

And, although it was a thrill to dress up so finely, she knew that it was because she was with Xandros that she enjoyed them so much.

Her days were still solitary, but she didn't mind. Some of Xandros's female friends had asked her to lunch, but she'd never gone. She didn't want to be stand-offish, but she was worried that without Xandros to shelter her she might let it slip that she would not be making her life with him.

It was safer to keep her own company. Just as she was today, settling down at her favourite pavement café for lunch.

She was making dogged progress with her self-taught Greek-language lessons, aided by books and podcasts, and she tried it out assiduously as she went around Athens, or even on Xandros himself. Now she unfolded the easy-read tabloid newspaper she'd just bought, a dictionary to hand, to see what she could manage of its articles.

A shadow fell across her as she pursed her lips, making out an unfamiliar word in the headline. She assumed it was the waiter, coming to take her order, and looked up with a smile.

It froze on her face.

It was her father.

CHAPTER TWELVE

SHOCK AND DISMAY jolted through her. She had not set eyes on him since she had stormed out that hideous morning after he'd ripped all her stupid dreams to pieces.

Without asking, he sat himself down.

'So,' he said, his English strong and accented, 'my dutiful daughter.'

His voice was as unmelodious as she recalled, and there was a mocking look in his pouched eyes. Rosalie could say nothing, could only feel the mix of shock and dismay possessing her.

'What? No kiss for your devoted father? The father who got you such a rich and handsome husband?' The mockery came again, along with a jibing twist to his voice. 'I *knew* you'd see sense and marry him—I didn't keep you in poverty so you wouldn't know what side your bread's buttered on! You like the luxury life, just like everyone does,' he sneered.

'What do you want?' Her voice was terse and tight. She could feel her heart starting to hammer in her chest.

His heavy eyebrows rose. 'Want? What do you *think* I want?'

His grey-green eyes, so like hers though he himself was nothing like her—*nothing*—bored into her.

'I want what I have told you I want. I've got half of it—my fancy Lakaris son-in-law. Now I want the rest.'

He leaned forward, his piercing gaze working over her, resting on her abdomen assessingly before coming back to her still-frozen expressionless face.

'I want my Lakaris grandson,' he said. His eyes narrowed. 'Are you breeding yet? You've had long enough for that fine husband of yours to play the ram!'

Rosalie gasped—not at his crudeness, but at what he'd said.

He gave a coarse laugh. 'Did you think I'd be content with him just putting a ring on your finger? He'll have to put a baby in your belly, too! So,' he repeated, 'are you breeding yet? It's a simple question and a crucial one.' There was a look of relish in his face now, as if he were enjoying what he was telling her. 'Crucial for that handsome husband of yours, that is!'

She swallowed. Her heart was still hammering in her chest. 'What…what do you mean?'

'Crucial,' her father answered, 'if he wants to complete this precious merger he's after.' He cocked his head, surveying her with his heavy-lidded gaze as if he were a snake and she a cornered mouse. 'No baby, no completion,' he spelt out.

He got to his feet, looking down at her as icy water pooled in her stomach.

'Tell him that!' His mouth gave that cruel twist again. 'And as for you—how long do you think you'll last as his dressed-up doll of a wife if you can't bring him the one thing he married you for? Getting his hands on my business! And don't think to come running to *me* if he discards you. I won't lift a finger. You can get back to your London slum and starve again! So,' he finished, turning away, 'get yourself pregnant, my girl—if you want to stay in the lap of this luxury you've grabbed with both hands.'

He walked away. Climbed into the tinted-windowed car idling at the kerb, which drove off.

Leaving Rosalie sick with dismay.

Across the ancient city the floodlit Parthenon blazed on the Acropolis. But Rosalie, standing on the balcony of

Xandros's apartment, her hands clutching the railing, was blind to it. Blind and deaf to everything except the thought pounding in her head like a merciless drum.

You have to tell him—you have to tell him.

She had to tell Xandros what her father had said. Threatened. Because it had been a threat—a stark and ruthless threat. No baby—no merger.

She felt her stomach clench.

We thought we were outmanoeuvring him...turning the tables on him. Now he's turned them back on us!

The feeling of sick dismay that had filled her at her father's words was there again, and she could not rid herself of it. How could she not dread having to tell Xandros...? Tell him that their marriage had been pointless all along. That the merger he wanted so badly was going to be impossible to achieve.

I have to tell him! But I can't—not yet! Not tonight!

She wanted—craved—a little longer with him before she had to shatter his hopes. Just a little longer...

With a smothered cry, she wrenched herself away, hurrying indoors. Xandros would be home soon, and she had to change for the dinner dance they were going to tonight. She had another new evening gown to show off to him. She must look as beautiful as she always strove to look for him—had to see his eyes light and glint with admiration and desire...

Just give me tonight with him! I'll tell him tomorrow—in the morning...

As though it might be easier then... When it was going to be the hardest thing in the world.

Xandros was leading her out onto the dance floor, taking her into his arms. Rosalie's eyes clung to him. He was looking as superb as he always looked in black tie, and she knew by the expression in his eyes as he gazed down at her that she was spectacular, in a sumptuous off-the-shoulder gown in champagne satin, with diamond drops at her ears, her hair upswept into an elaborate style, her make-up full and dramatic.

All around were couples equally resplendent, and chandeliers glittered above them as Xandros swept her away into the dance. Rosalie clung to him as he whirled her around— a former Cinderella at yet another lavish ball, dancing the night away with the most handsome man in the room. Her very own prince… Living the high life. Living the dream…

But what was the dream? What would it be worth to me, all this lavish luxury, if I wasn't here with Xandros?

She heard the question in her head as her gaze drank him in. Her fingers tightened on his sleeve as she leaned into his tall, hard body with unconscious closeness. She knew, without any shadow of a doubt, and with a catch in her heart that tightened the vice that had been squeezing around her ever since that ugly confrontation with her father, that without Xandros none of this glitter and glitz and luxury and wealth would be anything at all!

It's Xandros I want—and I would want him even if we were living as simply as Maria and Panos do. It would be paradise enough because I would be with Xandros.

But what use was it, that searing self-knowledge?

It was true for *her*, not him!

She might want Xandros only for himself—not for the freedom from poverty he promised her, not for the taste of luxury she was enjoying in this time she had with him— but he saw it very differently.

The vice tightened around her heart again.

He wants me only as a gateway to his merger with my father's business.

And if that gateway slammed shut Xandros would end their marriage. There would be no reason to continue it. Unless…

As she gazed up at Xandros in the whirl of the dance she felt a rush of emotion so intense she could not bear it. Felt a temptation she could hardly dare give thought to. Yet it burned in her head…

What if I don't tell Xandros? If I never tell him my father's impossible demand?

The thought swirled through her as the music whirled them about—a thought that stung her conscience like a wasp.

I could do what my father wants—it would be so easy…

Since their honeymoon she had taken responsibility for contraception by going on the Pill. All she had to do was stop taking it…

Yearning filled her. Oh, to have Xandros's baby! To know that she could stay with him for ever! Make a family with him!

Longing possessed her, fierce and urgent—urging.

You could do it—it would be easy…so easy…

And totally unforgivable.

Xandros grinned at the antics of Panos and Maria's young grandchildren, who were visiting with their mother. It had been an impulsive notion for him and Rosalie to head to Kallistris this morning, after last night's dinner-dance, but well worth it—as it always was.

His eyes went to her now, warming as they did so. She, like him, was smiling at the two toddlers, the older one petting Panos's dogs, the younger stalking a chicken. Xandros made an admiring comment to the doting grandparents, and offered his congratulations on being informed that their daughter was expecting once again.

His glance went to the children's mother, now rescuing the chicken from her daughter's attentions. Her pregnancy didn't show yet, but then Maria's daughter had inherited her mother's fuller figure. His glance travelled on to Rosalie. *She* was so slender that pregnancy would show immediately…

He caught his thoughts. The very idea of Rosalie pregnant—

'Shall we head down to the beach for a swim?' he asked her, to push away a thought that had no business being there.

They took their leave and padded down the trackway to the villa companionably, hand in hand. He'd half expected Rosalie to make some comment about the cuteness of Maria and Panos's grandchildren, but she was silent. He glanced at her sideways. Her face was slightly drawn…as if she were lost in thought. Perhaps she wasn't making any remark about the toddlers for the same reason as he. Because pregnancy, babies, children were absolutely nothing to do with themselves…

He felt the thought move in his head, found himself squeezing her hand more tightly, as if not to let her go.

But I'm going to have to let her go sometime, aren't I? Once the merger is done.

A frown formed on his brow and his glance went to her again. From Panos and Maria's smallholding he could still hear the gleeful laughter of the toddlers. The sound tugged at him. Thoughts came unbidden…

What if they were ours? Mine and Rosalie's? What if we were making our lives together, making a family together for ever?

The questions hung in his head. Motionless. Unanswerable.

His gaze slipped across to the blue horizon over the sea. Gulls were swooping and hovering, borne aloft on the air currents. Suddenly, one folded its wings and dived, plunging down into the water as if it had seen something it wanted. Something invisible to Xandros but there beneath the surface.

All he had to do was do as the gull had done and find what he was seeking. The answer to his wondering question...

Rosalie was staring into thin air, her hands clenched in her lap. Tonight—she must tell Xandros what her father had said tonight! She *must*. Before the unforgivable temptation that had swept over her as she'd danced in his arms and that had kept on coming back over and over again all through the weekend became too overwhelming to resist. A temptation made even more powerful by seeing Maria and Panos's grandchildren...so adorable, so enviable!

He has to know! He has to!

But, oh, she did not want to tell him! She wanted to go on as they were for just a little longer...a *little* longer...

One more weekend on Kallistris...and another...and another...

How can I bear to ruin what we have? To end it so much sooner than it has to end by telling him how impossible it is to complete the merger he's set his heart on? The merger we married to achieve. The sole purpose of our marriage...

Unless...

The word hung in her head again, testing her to the utmost—tempting her to the utmost. She felt anguish fill her, her hands clenching again in her lap.

A sudden sound distracted her hopeless thoughts. The phone was ringing. The apartment's landline, not her mobile.

She frowned. If it was Xandros, he'd use her mobile number. He'd flown up to Thessaloniki for the day, to meet with some of her father's senior managers based there to discuss the staffing implications of the merger when it happened.

But it can't happen, can it? Not now.

Everything Xandros was doing was a waste of his time. *I have to tell him—I just have to...*

The landline went on ringing, despite her nerve-racking thoughts, and she got up reluctantly to answer it.

'Parakelo?' she said, hoping she would not get a volley of Greek beyond her capabilities from someone wanting to speak to Xandros.

But the call was for her.

'Rosalie?'

The voice was female—and recognisable. It was Xandros's mother.

Surprise filled Rosalie—and a sudden apprehension. 'Kyria Lakaris?'

'Yes. My dear…'

There was a slight pause, as if Xandros's mother was deciding what to say, and that bite of apprehension came again. Never before had Xandros's mother phoned her, so why…?

Something's happened to Xandros!

Apprehension sharpened to fear…

'I am in the lobby. May I come up?' asked Xandros's mother.

Fear subsided into wariness.

'Yes—yes, of course,' she replied.

The line went dead, and Rosalie opened the apartment door just as the lift doors opened to reveal Xandros's mother.

Politely she stood aside, to let her enter her son's apartment. Her mother-in-law—the very last person Rosalie had expected to see—seemed agitated. Apprehension bit at Rosalie again.

'My dear, I need to speak to you,' Xandros's mother said.

She sat herself down on one of the sofas, and Rosalie lowered herself tensely to the other.

'Has something happened?' she heard herself ask, not able to keep the alarm out of her voice. 'To Xandros?'

The older Kyria Lakaris shook her head. 'No,' she said quickly.

Too quickly, Rosalie thought. Something *had* happened—something that was not good.

Yet what her mother-in-law said next reversed that thought instantly.

'My dear, Ariadne has returned!'

Rosalie's face lit. 'Oh, I'm so glad! I know you were very worried about her.'

Xandros's mother nodded. But her demeanour was still agitated, and she went on speaking rapidly. 'Yes…yes, I *was* worried indeed. But she has been, as Xandros thought, with her relatives in Scotland. Now, though, she is back in Greece—she arrived at the weekend. She came to me because of her…estrangement…from her father—' She broke off.

'He has behaved very badly towards her,' Rosalie said, wanting to make it clear where her sympathies lay. Her face lit again. 'I do hope so very much, though, that Ariadne will want to meet me. I've been longing to meet *her*—'

Xandros's mother cut across her, her expression constrained. 'That would not be…advisable,' she said, as if searching for the right word. 'You see…' The expression of constraint deepened and she pressed her lips tightly for a moment. 'Ariadne is pregnant.'

Rosalie stared. She could not think of anything to say except, 'That's wonderful!'

Xandros's mother was looking at her strangely. 'That's a very generous thing to say…' she said slowly.

Rosalie stared. 'I don't understand. Why is it generous?'

'You are generous,' said Xandros's mother, 'to be so understanding of the predicament your predecessor finds herself in.'

'My…my predecessor?' Rosalie's voice was hollow.

'Of course,' Kyria Lakaris was saying. 'Ariadne was engaged to my son until the moment she disappeared.'

The world seemed to tip on its axis, dislodging everything in it. Everything except one single word.

'Engaged?'

It fell like a ton weight from Rosalie's lips. She stared at Xandros's mother. Shock was knifing through her.

Kyria Lakaris looked at her frowningly. 'Did you not know?' she was saying. 'The wedding was all set—it was a great blow to him when she ran away...broke off the engagement.'

'They were *engaged*?' Rosalie could only echo the word again. Inside, shock was detonating, reaching all her limbs so that she was weak from it. 'He...he told me that Ariadne refused point-blank to entertain our father's obsession—'

But Kyria Lakaris was shaking her head in negation. 'My dear—no. Just the opposite. She was perfectly willing to marry Xandros.'

'But Xandros... Xandros said he would never be manipulated by my father! He came to London to tell me so!' Rosalie was gasping, snatching at all the things Xandros had said to her.

His mother was shaking her head again, contradicting her with the gesture. 'That was after Ariadne panicked. Pre-wedding nerves—I'm sure it was only that! Had Xandros not gone chasing to London, I am quite, quite sure Ariadne would have seen sense and come home.' Regret was audible in the older woman's voice as she went on, 'They were ideally suited to each other, your half-sister and my son.'

Then, in front of Rosalie's stricken eyes, Kyria Lakaris's face brightened.

'And now they can be once more!' she exclaimed.

Rosalie stared. 'I don't understand...' she said slowly, each word dragged from her. 'You...you've just told me that Ariadne is…is pregnant. So how can she and Xandros ever…ever get back together?'

His mother's expression had changed. It was filled now with a new emotion. It was pity. Chilling Rosalie to the core.

And a moment later she knew why.

'You have been married to Xandros for less than three months,' Xandros's mother said. 'And Ariadne…' She paused for a moment, her eyes holding Rosalie's with a painful expression. 'Ariadne has had her first trimester confirmed. So you see…' she took a breath '…there can be no question about it—your half-sister carries my son's child.'

CHAPTER THIRTEEN

XANDROS THREW HIMSELF down on the hotel bed in Thessaloniki. He'd just had a brilliant idea. He would phone Rosalie, explain that he needed to spend another day here at the Coustakis offices—the managers there had been only just briefed by Stavros, in another damn delaying tactic of the man!—and suggest she fly up here tomorrow to join him. Then, his meetings over, he would hire a car and take off with her to explore the countryside of northeastern Greece.

Hell, if Stavros was in no rush to get the merger done, why should he be?

It would give him yet more time with Rosalie—taking the next few days to show her the resorts of the trident-shaped Halkidiki, with the extraordinary monastery atop Mount Athos. Even get to Macedonia and show her the fabulous tomb of Alexander the Great's father, with its treasure trove of gold filigree ornaments.

He smiled at the prospect. Two days—maybe more if they felt like it!—of the non-stop company of the one person he wanted to be with!

Rosalie.

Rosalie, Rosalie, Rosalie—her very name was a delight! Just as *she* was a delight! All of her—all the time. In every way...

He felt emotion well up in him. The same emotion he'd felt last Sunday afternoon, when he'd imagined what it would be like if it were Rosalie who was pregnant, not Maria's daughter. Say, just by chance...

Or even not by chance...

What then...?

The implications hovered in his head, spreading out through his consciousness, filling his mind.

We'd stay together, obviously—keep our marriage going...

Okay, that wasn't what they'd originally planned—not what he'd intended or wanted—but that had been then... not now.

His expression changed. Now things were different. His time with Rosalie had changed him.

Had it changed his plans, his intentions as well?

Changed what he felt about marriage?

About Rosalie?

Into his head came what he'd said to her when she'd praised the lifestyle Panos and Maria enjoyed.

'Sometimes when you have too much of something you enjoy it palls...'

He frowned. Was that true of his time with Rosalie? Would the time come when he had had too much of her, so that being with her palled?

It seemed an absurd question!

Do I really want our marriage to end when the merger is done?

His eyes flickered.

A baby would keep us together...

A child with Rosalie...

He turned over the thought in his mind.

Enticing. Appealing...

Perhaps, he mused, gazing up at the ceiling, lost in this strangely beguiling thought, when she joined him here he would draw her out on the subject... On the subject of not rushing to end their marriage. At all.

I need to know! To know what she feels—what she wants.

Surely he was not hoping in vain?

Memory was full within him—of the passion and desire in their lovemaking, the way her beautiful body clung to his, the heights they reached together every time! And it was more than when they were in bed—in and out of bed it was the same. Her smiles, her laughter, her kisses and her conversation… Surely it all pointed to the same thoughts, the same feelings, that were filling him more and more with every passing day…every passionate night…?

I want her with me all the time! Every day and every night! And I want her to want the same!

It was as though a light had gone on in his head, showing him things he'd never seen before…things that were now illuminated in a brilliant golden light. He reached for his phone to call her, to hear her voice, ask her to fly up here.

Before he could pick it up, it started to ring. He grinned. Was Rosalie telepathic as well as all her other manifold charms?

But as he answered, and heard the voice of his caller, his smile was wiped from his face.

'Ariadne?'

He jackknifed upright.

Her voice came clear over the ether. Sounding fraught.

'Xandros! I've got something to tell you. And it can't wait. It just can't!'

Everything in him froze.

Rosalie squirted cleaning fluid into the bathtub, and started to scrub the inside, her movements as automatic as they were familiar. Anguish filled her—and not just because she was right back where she'd started: in London, broke and cleaning for a living. Just the way Xandros had first found her.

That was her anguish—that single word, his name.

Xandros—the man she loved.

That was the truth of it—bitter now as gall. With every golden day she had spent with Xandros—every passion-fuelled night—the truth had been coming to her. Deny it as she had—suppress it as she'd had to.

We married to make the merger happen. But for me it became more—so much more.

How could it not? Pain shot through her. How could she *not* have done what she had, day after day, night after night? How could she *not* have fallen in love with Xandros? Weaving dreams that their brief marriage might last instead of ending?

That we might make our whole lives together—have children, a future... It was a dream I longed for so much that the temptation to make it happen was almost impossible to resist!

Cold shivered through her. Her punishment for so very nearly yielding to the unforgivable temptation to let herself get pregnant…have Xandros's baby, bind him to her for ever…was unbearable.

It would be her half-sister who would have his baby now.

The half-sister who, far from refusing outright even to countenance marrying Xandros, had in fact been willing—as willing as Xandros had been to take Ariadne to his bed as his fiancée…

A corrosive sickness filled Rosalie, as if she had swallowed the bleach she was cleaning the bathtub with, and into her aching head came his mother's oft-repeated words: *'They were ideally suited to each other...'* And now they could be again. *I must hope with all my heart that whatever made Ariadne run away, reject Xandros, she can now find happiness with him! The happiness they must have felt when they agreed to marry. Why should they not be happy? They will have everything—each other, their baby, even the merger...*

Because her father would have got what he wanted: a Lakaris son-in-law and a Lakaris grandchild—with the daughter he'd originally wanted to have them.

Pain smote her yet again.

Ariadne would have everything.

And I will have nothing.

Only her memories. Her broken dreams. Her broken heart.

Useless tears smarted in her eyes and she rubbed them away with the back of her rubber-gloved hand. Went on with her cleaning.

After all, there was nothing else for her to do now...

The phone was ringing on his desk, and Xandros snatched it up on its first ring. It was his lawyer. The last person to have seen Rosalie the day she'd disappeared—saying she was filing for divorce.

The word still bit like a shark and he could not shake it off. Its jaws were clamped around him, drawing blood...

'Any news?' he demanded.

His adrenaline levels were sky-high—had been ever since Ariadne had phoned him in Thessaloniki, two weeks ago now. Ever since he'd received Rosalie's text shortly thereafter.

Xandros, your mother has told me about Ariadne, so I'm going back to London today.

Emotion convulsed in him. It was like some bitterly ironic replay. Ariadne had texted to say she was fleeing from him. Now Rosalie had done the same.

Except that it isn't the same at all! Not by a million miles—not by all the distance between the galaxies!

When Ariadne had fled all he had felt was relief.

With Rosalie it was...

Desperation.

As brutal as that.

Clutching him, crushing him.

He took a ragged breath now, the phone clamped to his ear.

'We have received a contact address,' came the reply.

'Finally!' breathed Xandros, relief flooding through him.

Five minutes later he'd booked a flight to London—into whose anonymous millions Rosalie had simply…disappeared.

Despite his urgent efforts there had been no trace of her. Not at the dive she'd used to live in, nor at the cleaning agency she'd worked for. She'd just…vanished.

But now—at last—she'd shown up!

He punched in the number for Ariadne and she answered immediately, anxious to hear from him.

'She's got in touch! Told the lawyer how to reach her,' he announced. 'So I'm flying straight off to London now.'

But his buoyant relief did not last beyond his hot-footed arrival at the hotel she'd given as her contact address. Where she awaited the paperwork that she expected him to send her so as to expedite the divorce she was initiating.

He stared disbelievingly at the reception desk clerk.

'But she *must* be staying here—she's given this hotel as her address!'

It wasn't the same hotel he'd taken her to that first night he'd found her, because he'd already checked there. And now she didn't seem to be at this one either.

Frustration knifed in him—and anxiety, too. The credit card he'd given her when they'd married hadn't been used—so how was she paying for whatever accommodation she was in? The last thing he wanted was her resorting to her own meagre finances… Especially after what she'd told his lawyer—

He snapped his mind away—back to what the hotel clerk was repeating to him.

'I am so sorry, Mr Lakaris, but there is absolutely no record of Mrs Lakaris as a current or recent guest.'

Nor had she booked in under her maiden name—or the Coustakis name.

Grim-faced, he checked into the hotel himself, going up to his room with a heavy frown. He shrugged off his jacket, threw himself down on the bed.

Where is she?

The question burned in him, finding no answer.

Where to look next?

She could be anywhere! Anywhere at all!

A discreet knock sounded on the door. Irritated at the disturbance, he got up, strode to the door and yanked it open. It was Housekeeping. The turn-down service.

Except the chambermaid who stood there gasped in shocked dismay.

It was Rosalie.

The blood was draining from Rosalie's face, and faintness drummed in her ears.

She could not move…was frozen to the spot with shock.

With dismay.

With something that was the very opposite of dismay…

And then Xandros was seizing her, dragging her into the room, holding her by her shoulders.

'Rosalie? What the *hell*?'

She heard words breaking from him.

'So that's why there's no trace of you here as a *guest*!' He was staring at her, shock in his face. 'How can you possibly be working *here*?' he demanded.

'They…they provide accommodation for housekeeping staff,' she said falteringly. 'I gave up my old bedsit when—'

He cut across her, an expletive breaking from him and then a volley of vehement Greek.

'We have to talk,' he said grimly.

He propelled her to the room's armchair, pressing her

down into it. Her legs were like jelly and she sank down heavily. It was as if a storm was breaking out in her head.

Xandros towered over her.

'Why the *hell* did you leave Athens like that? Without talking to me first?' he demanded.

His eyes were like black pits, his face stark.

'To say *what*, Xandros?' she cried in reply.

Her heart was hammering, each beat a blow hard enough to crush her to the ground.

It was unbearable to see him.

I thought I would never set eyes on him again.

Pain clutched at her at the thought—and at the reality of seeing him. Because there was no reason for him to have sought her! No point—no purpose.

No purpose in anything now except what she had to do now—what she was telling him, the words tearing from her.

'It was obvious what I had to do. I had to set you free!' She swallowed, and there was a razor blade in her throat, drawing blood. 'Free to marry Ariadne.' Her voice changed. 'As you always wanted to.'

He was staring at her, his brows snapping together in an uncomprehending black frown. He lowered himself to the bed, leaning forward. In the low light his features seemed gaunt and strained, and tension racked his jacket-less shoulders.

Helplessly, she let her eyes rest on the way his powerful chest moulded the fine material of his shirt… Then she dragged her pointless gaze away. He was gone from her—as distant as the stars in the sky. All she had to do now was tell him that she knew that, accepted it…

'Your mother told me, Xandros!' she said, her voice twisting painfully. 'Told me what I had absolutely no idea of! That you and Ariadne were once *engaged*!'

'My mother—' His voice was bitter.

'Xandros! Don't blame her! I'm grateful to her—incredibly grateful! She was as kind as she could possibly have been about it! She was upset—I could see she was. Upset for me as well as upset because obviously the whole situation is a mess! An unholy, hideous mess!' A cry broke from her. 'If *only* you hadn't given up on Ariadne! She'd have come back to you—as she has now—and then…then everything would have been all right.'

She took a gulping breath, leaning forward, willing him to hear her out. To know she was doing all she could to clear up that unholy, hideous mess. The mess that had Xandros married to one woman while another carried his child. The woman he had wanted to marry all along…

'But it still will be all right,' she said urgently now. 'I'll do everything I can to get our divorce through as fast as it can be done, I promise! And as for the pre-nup—of course I won't be taking a penny from you!' She swallowed. 'Not now you don't need me to get your merger with my father.'

Her face worked. She knew she had to say this, too. That it would make it easier for him in the long run.

'There's something I haven't told you. I was… I was going to steel myself to do it, but I didn't want to spoil that last weekend on Kallistris. My father cornered me in a café the day before and he told me…' Her voice faltered, but she forced herself on. 'He told me that he would not progress the merger until—' Her voice cracked with the pain of it all and the bitter, bitter irony. 'Until he knew that I was pregnant.'

She clenched her hands together, twisting her fingers tightly in her misery. She made herself meet those blank dark eyes that were resting on her with a weight she could not bear. Crushing the air in her lungs, making it impossible to speak. Yet speak she must. Her eyes were huge, imploring him to understand.

'So, you see, Xandros…' She faltered once more, and then went on—because what else was there to do now but play it out to the bitter end? Even though it was tearing her into ragged shreds. 'When your mother told me about Ariadne... Well, it's all worked out for the best, hasn't it?' Her voice flattened, and she forced herself on. 'Everything has come together just the way you originally wanted! And for my father, too—so he won't delay things any more. You'll get your merger and you'll get the wife you always planned to have—the one your mother wanted for you, who she said was ideally suited to you—and my father will get his Lakaris grandson. And you will also get the next Lakaris heir to continue your bloodline.'

She swallowed again, felt razors in her throat.

'It's a happy ending all round,' she said.

Except for me.

She felt herself give a silent cry of anguish. But then it had never been going to be a happy ending for her, had it? And not just because of her father's ultimatum.

Because even with the merger Xandros would have terminated our marriage after six months. I would have lost him anyway. So what's the difference if that loss has happened sooner and I have to bear seeing my half-sister get the life that I would give everything to have...?

The pain was just the same.

She took another razored breath, feeling the torment of seeing Xandros again—parting from him again—knife through her.

Xandros was looking at her, his dark eyes holding hers. Yet suddenly they were veiled. Unreadable.

'The next Lakaris heir...'

His deep voice echoed hers. Something shifted in his eyes, in those dark, lambent depths. Something she could not recognise. She saw him take a breath, heavy and incised, and then he spoke again, his shoulders flexing minutely.

'Yes, well...' he said, and there was a heaviness in his voice that made no sense. 'That won't exactly be the case.'

Rosalie swallowed. 'I suppose Ariadne's baby might be a girl,' she heard herself reply—as if discussing its gender were just a passing topic of conversation, instead of a nail in the lid of the coffin of her stupid and pathetic hopes, a nail driven into her breaking heart.

'It can be anything it likes!' Xandros retorted.

Something shifted in his eyes again—something that seemed to ignite in them.

'Because it isn't mine.'

Rosalie could only stare, uncomprehending, feeling a flame deep within her that was like a searing point of light...a laser that shot with blinding brilliance.

She was staring at him, her face blank. It took all Xandros's strength to hold her gaze to tell her what she needed to hear.

'It would be a biological impossibility for it to be so,' he went on, his eyes never leaving her gaunt, strained face.

He saw her face work.

'But the timing—your mother told me. Ariadne's into her second trimester, so her pregnancy must have begun while she was still...still engaged to you...'

His jaw steeled. 'Rosalie, why do you think Ariadne refused to marry me? I thought it was simply because she balked at doing her father's bidding. But there was another reason.' He took an incising breath, his mouth pressed tight. 'A reason I had already started to suspect, and which she has now confirmed to me. She met someone else. Someone who fathered her baby. There can be no doubt about it! Her baby *cannot* be mine, because the most I ever shared with your half-sister was a goodnight kiss!'

He looked at her. Her grey-green eyes were distended. Those eyes that had captivated him from the first—that still did. That always would...

'So now it's *you* who must see, Rosalie.'

But what *did* she see? What did this woman who had fled from him really see?

Too much and not enough.

He felt emotion crush his lungs. Emotion he needed to hold back.

'My mother got it wrong,' he said. 'Ariadne arrived out of the blue at the house, her pregnancy showing, and my mother jumped to what to her was the obvious conclusion. The *wrong* conclusion! When Ariadne realised what my mother had assumed she phoned me straight away. But it was too late.' His voice changed. 'You'd gone. Disappeared to London. Filed for divorce.'

He got up suddenly, striding restlessly to the window and back again, wheeling around to look down on her where she was sitting limply, immobile, white as a sheet.

'A completely unnecessary divorce,' he said quietly.

He saw the expression in her eyes change, saw something moving in them. And for the first time since Ariadne had phoned him at the airport in Thessaloniki he felt hope.

But then it was gone. And her voice, when she spoke, was as strained as it had been before, stumbling over her words.

'But it is still going to be necessary,' she said heavily. 'Our divorce. Because of what my father threw at me. His impossible demand that unless… Until…until I'm pregnant the merger you married me to get will never happen.'

He plunged his hands into his pockets. Steeled his jaw. Took a breath before saying what he had to say now.

'There won't be a merger,' he said. 'I'm pulling out of it.'

Xandros was looking at her. He was silhouetted against the drawn window drapes, hands plunged into his trouser pockets, his stance stiff, face expressionless. And yet in his eyes…

Rosalie felt a pulse start to thump in her throat. Hammering in her veins.

'You're pulling out?' she echoed, her voice as blank as her face. 'But *why*?'

'Why? Because I never...*never*...want you to doubt the reason I say this to you now.'

Something flashed across his face and the pulse at her throat thumped more strongly yet. The set of his broad shoulders seemed different, somehow, but still tense.

'Why,' he asked slowly, his eyes never leaving her, 'do you call your father's demand "impossible"?'

She swallowed. There were still razor blades in her throat, drawing blood...

'Because...because...we were only meant to be married for half a year! My getting pregnant would have been a disaster!'

His eyes were resting on her...so dark. So unreadable.

'Would it?'

She stared. 'I don't understand...'

His expression changed. In place of that unreadable mask something moved in his eyes. Something it was impossible for her to read. Then the faintest smile hovered fleetingly at his mouth. The mouth that had once kissed her into senseless bliss but would never do so again.

Pain like an arrow across her cheek scathed her heart.

'Perhaps,' he was saying now, still speaking slowly, with the same strange expression in his face, 'I would have welcomed it.'

There was still the same tension across the broad sweep of his shoulders, in the motionless poise of his stance.

She felt her face pucker. 'Don't say that, Xandros—'

Her voice was broken. *She* was broken. Broken into tiny fragments that she could not hold together.

He stood looking down at her, that expression she could not read—dared not read—still in his eyes.

He was speaking to her again.

'Don't say it because the thought of bearing my child appals you? Don't say it because a child would bind us, one to the other, for all our days…all our lives? Don't say it because that would be a fate that would horrify you?'

She felt her throat twist, those razor blades embedded in it agonising. She could not stop them. Could not stop anything at all. Could not stop his voice—could not stop him starting towards her, hunkering down, taking her trembling hands in his. He was looking into her eyes, from which tears were starting to spill. Tears she could not bear to shed but could not stop.

'*Does* it appal you?'

His voice had changed, and she could not bear that either. Could not bear what it held…what it was asking of her.

'Don't tell me that it does! Don't tell me that!'

His eyes were holding hers now, and she could not stop that either—they were pouring into her.

'Because I won't believe you. Call me arrogant, conceited and presumptuous, but I won't believe you! I won't believe you, Rosalie, because my head is full of memories that give the lie to that! Memories that burn and scorch within me. Memories of the nights we have spent in each other's arms! Memories that glow with all the warmth and radiance of the summer sun. Memories of the days we have spent in each other's company. *Good* days…precious to me—so precious.' And now his voice was ragged with the emotion he was no longer trying to hold in check. 'Days I never want to end. Nights I never want to lose.'

His hands closed around hers, so warm, so strong, so comforting and protective. So possessive.

'You told me that you wanted to set me free,' he was saying now. 'But I don't *want* to be free of you! I don't *ever* want to be free of you!'

Her face was working, and inside her heart was working,

too. 'You…you said… We agreed…when we married…six months…to get the merger done…'

He crushed her hands with his. Strong and warm and enclosing.

'I've told you—to hell with the merger! I don't want it any more!' His voice was vehement, then urgent. 'Because there is only one thing I *do* want.'

He lifted her hands to his mouth and kissed them, one after another, his gaze pouring into her like velvet.

'I wanted to tell you before you fled back to London. To tell you that our time together has changed me—changed me completely!' He made a face, half-rueful, half-wry. 'Rosalie, I freely confess that one of the main attractions of keeping our marriage temporary—of keeping *you* temporary—was the fact that it had been the way I'd always lived my life. It suited me.'

The rueful expression deepened.

'It suited me very well. So well it made me reluctant to agree to marry Ariadne, even though—as my mother and your father were so keen to point out—it would have been so "suitable". The relief I felt when she jilted me only confirmed that I was not ready to settle down. But what I was too blind to realise—' and now there was more than ruefulness in his voice…there was a twist of pain and remorse that caught at her as he spoke '—was how everything would change…with *you*! With *you* in my life! Day after day. Night after night. Just *being* with you.' His expression changed again, and now there was a blaze in his eyes. 'Just you…making everything *wonderful*!' he said.

He kissed her hands again, keeping them fast in his as if he would never let them go again. His face was blurring in her vision now, and she could not breathe…dared not… could only gaze at him, listen to him speak…her heart so full she thought it must overflow with hope, with longing to hear what he was telling her…confessing…

He was speaking again now, and she clung to his words…to the hands holding hers so close, so fast…

'I was starting to feel it more and more. I was even welcoming the delays your father was putting in my way because they would give me more time with you! But I still never realised *why* I was feeling it—or what it was that I was feeling! It took that last weekend on Kallistris, seeing Maria and Panos's grandchildren, to open my eyes to what I truly wanted. Not the promise of my old freedom! What use would that be to me when my old life had gone for ever? I didn't want it back! What I wanted…' his voice softened '…was what I already had—with you. *Only* with you. You in my life, just as we were—for always. And more.' He took a breath. 'Children. A family…' He paused. 'A wife to love and be loved by…' He paused again. '*You*, Rosalie. Only you.'

Her tears were falling openly now, sliding down her paper-white cheeks. He brushed them away with his mouth softly, like velvet, and then his lips found hers, soft and quivering, and he kissed them, too.

'Only you,' he said again.

He drew back, his eyes full with all that he had said.

'I wanted you to come and join me in Thessaloniki—wanted you to start to discover *your* feelings just as I was discovering mine. I was starting to think about not wanting our marriage to end—wanting to make it permanent in the most binding way of all. Then Ariadne phoned, telling me that of all bitter ironies you believed she carried my baby—her, the very last person I would want to be the mother of my child now that I'd realised there was only one woman I could ever think to have a child with, to spend my life with! And everything exploded in my face!'

He gave a shudder, his face convulsing.

'Being without you these two endless weeks has been agony!' He shook his head, his eyes filled with remembered pain. 'Proving to me just how much you've come to mean to me! I've been *desperate* for you, Rosalie! Desperate to find you—desperate to tell you the truth. Not only the truth that my mother had got it so wrong about Ariadne, but the most important truth to me of all! That I love you and want you, beyond all things, to come back to me. To make our marriage real—and for ever.'

His gaze was pouring into hers again, his dark eyes turning to liquid gold. Turning her to liquid gold as well.

'Can you…? Will you…?' His voice was husky. 'Do you want that, too? Can you love me as I have come to love you? I won't give up hope, Rosalie! Ask of me anything but that!'

He gazed at her, drinking her in. His expression had changed again. Intensity and ardour softened it now, making it tender. Cherishing. Loving…

'The fact that you are sitting here with tears pouring down your face from those eyes that have beguiled me since I first beheld them, and that you have let me kiss you as I have, and that your hands, Rosalie, are clutching mine as if you would never let them go… All that, my dearest heart, gives me cause to hope…'

She gave a choke—a cry from her throat. 'I didn't mean to fall in love with you, Xandros! Because I knew that wasn't what you wanted! It was no part of why we married. We were always destined to part! So…' She took a ragged breath, so much emotion inside her. 'Do you really mean what you have just said?'

His hands tightened on hers and he gave her an old-fashioned look before getting to his feet, retaining her hands, which he lifted with his.

'There may be only one way to prove myself,' he said, and the glint in his eyes was pure gold.

He drew her to her feet, her limbs unresisting. Her tears were drying on her cheeks and her vision was clearing. She was focussing on the one man alone she would ever want. The man who was now lowering his mouth to hers…

His kiss was everything she remembered—everything she would remember all her days for the searing joy that filled her as his mouth claimed hers. As his heart claimed hers. As *he* claimed her.

'My for ever wife,' he said, breathing in the sweet breath of her honeyed mouth. 'My for ever love.'

She gave herself to his kiss, long and sweet and deep, and her hands slipped from his to wind about his neck as his hands clasped her waist, holding her so close against him that nothing could ever part them again…

Except the buzzing in her apron pocket.

He pulled back. 'What the—?'

Rosalie gave a shaky laugh. 'It's my manager—wanting to know why I'm taking so long to turn down the bed in this room.'

Xandros yanked the phone from her pocket and answered it.

'This is Xandros Lakaris in Room 504. Mrs Rosalie Jones Lakaris is otherwise engaged right now. And for the next fifty years and more! Oh, and by the way, she's just handed in her notice. Effective immediately.'

He chucked the phone on the desk. Turned back to her. Took her into his arms again.

'I think,' he said, and there was a gleam in the liquid gold of his eyes that melted her, 'we can turn down this bed perfectly well together…'

He drew her down with him and she gave a sigh of bliss.

Of radiant, everlasting love and perfect, perfect happiness.

EPILOGUE

ROSALIE SMILINGLY ACCEPTED the glass of champagne that her mother-in-law's stately butler was offering to her from a silver platter before discreetly withdrawing. She and Xandros had just arrived from yet another sojourn on Kallistris, where they loved to spend all the time they could. But this was an occasion she would not have missed for all the world.

She raised her flute to the young woman sitting opposite her in the beautifully appointed drawing room, tenderly holding her newly christened baby in her arms.

It was Xandros who gave the toast, standing beside Rosalie's silk-upholstered armchair.

'To my sister-in-law and her beautiful daughter,' he said, raising his glass.

His words were echoed by his wife and his mother.

'To dear Ariadne,' his mother said fulsomely.

'To my wonderful sister!' Rosalie exclaimed warmly.

Her eyes met Ariadne's. In the months since she had returned to Athens, her heart soaring with happiness, so much had happened—and everything was wonderful... beyond wonderful!

Xandros's mother had greeted her with tears, asking forgiveness for having caused so much grief, so unintentionally.

'I did not know you loved my son,' she had said. 'Or he you. I did what I thought I had to do—had no choice but to do—but I *never* meant you any harm, nor the grief I caused you! And now, if you can forgive me, I welcome you to our family as I should have done from the beginning—for you are a part of us for all time. You have made my beloved son the happiest of men, and for that you will always be precious to me.'

And it was her mother-in-law who had overseen the meeting between the two half-sisters. Rosalie had been full of trepidation, lest her hopes not be matched, but her fears had been unnecessary.

So like herself—yet so unlike—Ariadne had been eager in her greeting.

'You can't know how wonderful it is to have a sister!' she had exclaimed.

For a few moments Rosalie let her thoughts go to the man who had brought about the two half-sisters in their very different lives. Then she left him where he was—in his callous, uncaring existence. He had given love to neither of his daughters and neither of their mothers—he deserved nothing.

Her mouth twisted. For all that, her father would now get the only thing he seemed to want. Which, in turn, would give Xandros the merger which she had persuaded him not to withdraw from after all.

She needed no proof that Xandros wanted what she herself so longed for, for no other reason than the one they shared. A baby to bless their marriage and fill their cup of happiness to the brim.

Her eyes went now to Xandros, exchanging a secret glance with him. They would not steal Ariadne's moment now, but very soon her own pregnancy would start to show, and then it would be a time for family rejoicing.

So she raised her glass again, her expression warm, and felt Xandros's hand on her shoulder warm upon her, cherishing and loving. How blessed she was to have so much!

Oh, Mum, you're the only one I miss who should be here—but you will be in my heart always, and in my memories. And if my baby is a girl I will give her your name—and all the love you gave to me.

Then her gaze went to her husband's once again, her heart overflowing as their eyes wound into each other's. Unconsciously her hand slipped to her stomach, fingers splaying in a protective gesture.

A little gasp came from her half-sister. Ariadne's eyes widened.

'Rosalie! Can it be…? I know that gesture! Are you—?' Her voice was breathless, excited.

Rosalie gave a helpless laugh, exchanging a rueful glance with Xandros. So much for secrecy!

Her mother-in-law had gone very still, her champagne flute poised halfway to her mouth, eyes only on Rosalie, bright with eager hope.

'Shall we?' Xandros asked of Rosalie, with resigned humour in his voice.

She gave a nod. Too late now for prevarication.

Xandros duly raised his glass again. 'I think,' he said, taking a breath, 'we have another toast to make… To the next Lakaris!'

There was a cry of delight from her mother-in-law, of excited glee from Ariadne, and then Xandros's smiling mouth was swooping down on hers in celebration, in joy, and in endless love.

As it always would be between them.

For all time. And way beyond.

* * * * *

SECRETS MADE
IN PARADISE

NATALIE ANDERSON

For my Friday Coffee Crew—love you guys :)

CHAPTER ONE

JAVIER TORRES IGNORED the paperwork strewn across his lap and gazed out of the tinted window of the SUV, absently watching his driver walk into the small store to stock up on refreshments. It was late afternoon, the weather was glorious, and he ought to feel like a king. He was back on the threshold of paradise—Santa Cruz, the most populated of the Galapagos islands and arguably one of the planet's most isolated and fascinating places. He was here to oversee the start of the hotel rebuild he'd recently invested in. Yet instead of feeling satisfied, he was distracted by an uneasy, prickling sensation. No matter how hard he tried, he couldn't shake the recollection of the last time he'd been here. More precisely, the redhead he'd ravished. There really wasn't any other word for what had transpired between them. But she'd ravished him right back—with such rare intensity that she'd haunted his dreams every night of the eighteen months since.

It wasn't as if he'd never had a one-night stand before. It was pretty much all he had. *She* hadn't though. A wisp of wicked amusement flickered through him as he remembered there'd been a number of firsts for her that night. She'd been travelling, all the way from Australia, and who knew where in the world she was now? Certainly not Javier. She'd not been there when he'd woken the next morning and he'd had to return to mainland Ecuador that evening in time to catch his flight home to New York.

It wasn't supposed to matter. He'd not meant to care. Only he'd been unable to forget. Searing memories tormented his nights and teased in unwanted, unsummoned daydreams. Javier had rarely daydreamed before meeting her. And the impact she'd had on his sex life was frankly appalling. He was stuck in the longest ever stretch of abstinence. He told himself it was because he was busy with work projects and plans. In reality no woman he'd met since had aroused him. It was infuriating. He could do with a fantastic, physical night of unfettered pleasure; the stress release would be good and being back on this island only brought those memories to the fore even more.

And just like that she appeared—walking out of the shop—an erotic vision with her stunning solar-flare-red hair and fantastically generous curves. Javier groaned. Of course his tormented mind would conjure her here. It was the ultimate in wishful thinking and the craving was so strong he simply sank back into the seat, helpless to do anything other than enjoy the mirage. His skin tightened as his muscles surged at the sight of her lush body. That first night he'd seen her before she'd seen him and the artless confidence with which she'd walked from the water, bold in her bright green bikini and owning her space, had made her the sexiest thing he'd ever seen. Now she turned as a young couple followed her out of the store. She pointed something out down the road and the other woman handed her a phone. The couple posed beside the store sign while the redhead took their picture. Then the redhead turned as Javier's driver emerged from the shop. He sent her a massive smile. Of course he did, who wouldn't when passing a woman that stunning? But all this interaction meant she wasn't a hallucination.

The universe went mute. Javier didn't blink or breathe. His heart didn't beat. He stared intently, watching her walk in those slightly too snug jeans that strained to contain her gorgeously shapely hips and thighs. His mouth dried. Her loose khaki linen shirt was unbuttoned, revealing a white tank top beneath, giving the merest, most tantalising glimpse of her other blessedly bountiful curves. And that glorious riot of red was barely holding up in a half-tumbling topknot, revealing her high cheekbones and freckled skin. Every muscle clenched at the sight of her intensely feminine frame while the memory of her soft, silken heat consumed him.

His driver opened the door.

'Wait a moment, please,' Javier instructed hoarsely.

The redhead's smile had just gone nuclear. Javier's tension sky-rocketed and he turned to see who warranted such a warm welcome. His burst of strain was soothed as he saw an elderly woman slowly walking along the path. She was carrying a baby—a dark-haired, smiling bundle who stretched his tiny arms out and wriggled impatiently as he saw the redhead run towards them.

Noise returned in a jangling cacophony, pummelling Javier as he watched the reunion. He drew a sharp breath while his brain whirred—registering that relationship, calculating the passage of time with precision, computing the shocking combination of facts in a nanosecond and coming up with a conclusion that was utterly appalling.

Cold panic clashed with wild horror. Because he knew with absolute certainty that the redhead *was* the woman he'd seduced all those months ago—Emerald, the sweet siren from that beautiful beach. And that baby was definitely her child. And with equal unequivocal, icy conviction, he knew her child was also *his*.

An awful crevasse opened within, rapidly filling with a hot lava of guilt. She'd had his baby and he'd not known. Because she'd not been able to contact him. Because that night he'd been careless and he'd not told her his true name.

Now he studied her again—not seeing the sexy curves of her body and the striking colour of her hair this time, but the frayed, faded edges of her shirt, the worn patches of her jeans, the strain around her eyes. At the signs of her struggle, that guilt within him grew, as did utter regret for her and for her child.

Children had never been on Javier's *to do* list and, frankly, would never be. As for marriage? Well hell, no. He'd not just witnessed the worst of those intimate wars, he'd been collateral damage. So no, his life was rich enough with work, any instinctive need to leave a mark sated by the creation of his own little business empire, any inner restlessness soothed by travel. He had no need and no desire for deep relationships or emotional responsibilities. The concept of fatherhood was so far from his realm of knowledge it was like a bad joke—how could he possibly do a decent job of parenting when he'd had such a rubbish example in his own life? Well, not a rubbish example, more like *no* example at all.

He'd never wanted some other poor kid to be rejected and neglected the way he had. Yet—albeit inadvertently—he'd done exactly that to his own for months. Anger surged at his incompetence, but so did something primal. The need to protect. And the need to make things right. But that sense of duty wasn't backed up by paternal knowledge or skill. He clenched his jaw, biting back his disappointment in his own failings. He was no hero, but he'd provide what he could, as soon as he could. He just had to figure out the best way how.

* * *

Emerald Jones glanced at her watch. Less than twenty minutes and she'd have Luke back. It had only been an hour but she missed him already. Such long shifts at the small store were hard, but she was incredibly grateful for the chance to keep her dignity and her boss, Connie, adored spending some time with Luke in the afternoons. The rest of the time Emmy was able to keep him occupied in a little playpen behind the counter, though she worried she wouldn't be able to for much longer given how adventurous and alarmingly mobile her curious little boy was becoming. That was a problem she was too tired to think of a solution to yet. Honestly? She was surviving one day to the next.

She glanced up as a tall figure stepped through the shadowed doorway. As he moved into the light a hit of pure exhilaration soared, a leap of joy so powerful she almost cried out with delight. Instead she froze—that sound trapped in her throat.

Eighteen months ago the world had tilted, never returning to rights. Now it tilted again, taking another rotation and rendering everything upside down.

'Ramon?' she breathed.

Dark brown eyes—a decadent mix of cocoa and coffee—stared into her soul. Vaguely she absorbed details—the charcoal linen trousers, the white shirt, the sleeves rolled to three-quarters, revealing tanned, strong forearms—but it was those eyes that stunned her. She trembled from tip to toe with a powerful whole-body reaction. She'd suffered this shudder of raw recognition that first night too. He'd captured every iota of her attention in a way no other person ever had. And look what had happened.

Hormones. Her own chemistry had failed her. Because

with another micro blink of time she'd remembered. He wasn't 'Ramon'. He'd deceived her, he'd lied about his identity and his reason for being on the island. *Nothing* had been real. He'd used her so completely. She'd shown him the most perfect place and then he'd stolen it. She hated him for that.

But at the same time, more memories stirred—those secret ones she'd tried to bury. Because while he'd taken the place she loved, she had to admit he hadn't *stolen* that other deeply personal thing from her. She'd given him her body, her virginity, more than freely. In that moment she'd been so willing, and it had been so magical she could never brand it a mistake, despite discovering his dishonesty since. And most importantly, he'd given her something beyond priceless.

Luke.

Her small son. *His* son. The one he knew *nothing* about.

Icy terror destroyed her equilibrium as she realised this man could take *everything*—as quickly and easily as he'd taken her innocence that night. Her heart pounded as the remnants of elation from that unthinking rush of recognition were sucked away by fear and the worst, worst guilt. She should have told him, she *had* to tell him. But not here, not now, not when Luke was due back with Connie at any moment. She needed to get 'Ramon' to leave and she'd tell him later when she'd figured out how…

She should have figured out how already.

'Emmy.' His smile was tight, but still devastating.

She blinked. She didn't want to respond to his looks and charm. Not knowing the truth. Because she'd learned 'Ramon'—her carefree surfer-dude tourist—was really Javier Torres. Billionaire investor. Billionaire playboy. Billionaire *jerk*.

When she'd learned his true identity—a few months

after Luke's birth—she'd never wanted to see him again. Her already bruised heart had broken on finding out he was so lacking in integrity. And not only was Javier Torres a man who lied easily, he was terrifyingly powerful. Initially she'd been too angry to contact him, then she'd grown too scared as she'd realised the implications of his assets and while she knew it was wrong, she'd had no choice. Her childhood had been marred by lie after lie. She'd been deceived before, but, worse, *she'd* also been the liar. And when Javier discovered that last? He'd be furious. She knew well that angry people lashed out in a variety of ways. None of them good. Integrity was everything and trust, once lost, wasn't regained. But she couldn't have another dishonest person wreck her life, even if she had to be dishonest herself to keep him out. Because she wasn't having what had happened to her happen to her son.

Yet even as she mentally rejected Javier, she was hit again by that terrible chemistry. That hidden, secret part of her weakened with want. She'd ached for him for months. He'd starred in her dreams night after night after night—indeed *every* night since then.

Feeling sick with guilt, she was conscious of the empty playpen behind her and the ticking clock on the wall. Protecting her son's future—and her own part in it—was paramount.

'It's been a while…' She forced her parched lips into a smile so he wouldn't suspect anything. As far as he knew, she still thought he was 'Ramon'. 'How may I help? Did you want to buy something?'

He didn't take his intense gaze off her. 'No.'

To her horror he was more stunning than she remembered, with the sort of superhuman good looks that everyone normal couldn't help but stare at. But as she watched him move closer, she realised he'd become sharper. There was a slight shadow beneath his eyes and stubble on his jaw and an edginess about him that was new. Perhaps it was the stress of his business? Were all those wolfish property takeovers designed to amass his personal fortune wearing him out?

The intensity of his gaze strengthened. He'd looked at her this way when he'd seduced her that night—powerfully mesmerising. Yes, there was still that tiny part positively revelling in being in his presence again. Desperately she dragged that wild piece within her back beneath her control. She couldn't let him seduce her again. She couldn't let herself *or* Luke down like that.

'It's been far too long, Emerald,' he said softly. 'Why don't you shut up the shop early?' But his tempting smile didn't quite meet his too attentive eyes. 'Come for a drive with me so we can catch up properly.'

'What?' She froze, shocked by the invitation. Panic tightened her throat. 'I—I can't leave.'

'No? I thought you were a woman of freedom and spontaneity.'

Cold sweat slicked her skin. 'I have work.' And she had Luke. The baby she'd not told him about.

Bile burned the back of her throat, because she was going to have to tell him and she should have already. As soon as she'd discovered his actual identity she should have reached out—there'd been no barrier to finding him *then*. She was, after all, the one determined to live a life of integrity and not follow the path of lies and deceit of her own family. But she'd been too scared of his reaction. Not just to the news he'd had a son, but how he'd react to *her*. She'd been burned before, when people had learned the truth about her background, and she'd been too hurt by his *needless* lie. Why had he needed to fake who he was?

'I never expected to see you here,' he muttered watchfully. 'I imagined you travelling around the world ticking off that bucket list, but have you been in the Galapagos all this time?'

Nervously she swallowed. 'Yes.'

'I didn't realise you worked on the island.'

'It didn't come up in our conversation.' She looked anxiously to the door. Any minute now Connie would arrive with little Luke. 'And I really need to get back to it...'

His smile faded as his whole expression tightened. 'What's the real reason you won't come with me now, Emerald?' he asked quietly.

'What do you mean?' Trepidation slithered over her skin. 'I have work. I'm the only one here, as you can see.'

She felt physically ill at telling half-truths—but what he could do, what he could take...

And then she heard the gurgling chuckle of her beloved little boy. At the next strike of her next hammering heartbeat, Connie appeared in the doorway with Luke in her arms. Emerald's world teetered, about to smash to smithereens and it was entirely her own fault. There was no way to get Connie to turn around, to run and hide Luke. Her only option was to try to fake it through the next few minutes and tell Javier the truth, alone, later, once she'd had a chance to draw breath. She should have come up with a plan months ago. But she'd been too busy caring for Luke. Too busy surviving.

Swallowing the nausea with a fake smile, she tried to act as if nothing horrific was currently happening. 'Thanks, Connie,' she whispered. 'Can you just go upstairs for a moment? I'll be there as soon as I can.'

Connie had stilled. Luke too was abnormally quiet, as if he'd sensed something strange in the atmosphere. The elderly woman glanced curiously at Javier. It was obvious her brain was doing the maths and in this case getting it right. But fortunately she said nothing as she walked past the counter, taking Luke with her.

'Who was that?' Javier asked, the second the elderly woman disappeared up the stairs.

'My boss, Connie.' Emmy could hardly bear to face him, but she forced herself to meet his gaze and her breathing stalled.

Javier was still scrutinising her, his expression sombre. 'I meant the baby,' he explained softly.

Emmy's mind blanked and she stared at him.

'What's his name?' His question was too quiet.

She couldn't think what to answer.

'What is his name, Emmy?' The edge in that repeated question sliced through to her bones.

She gazed up into those achingly familiar brown eyes. She absolutely adored the owner of the smaller set, but these ones held a glint that she couldn't define. A premonition shook her resolve. He'd be steely and unforgiving, but she couldn't lie now. Not to his face. Not the way he had to her.

'His name is Luke.'

'What's his full name?' Javier pressed with unerring precision.

Sweat slicked her skin.

'Didn't you give him a middle name?'

That was when she realised Javier already knew. He *already knew* Luke was his. Terror transfixed her. How long had he known and what had he planned? Because he clearly had something in mind. Him walking into her shop was no moment of chance. She had no idea what to do or say in response—all she knew was that she couldn't trust his handsome visage.

'Lucero Ramon Jones. Isn't that right?' Javier confirmed her fears with dangerously gentle accuracy.

'You've seen his birth certificate?' Her voice barely sounded.

'You left the father's name blank.'

How had he seen that certificate? How long had he been here?

'Emerald?' he prompted.

'For good reason,' she tossed back on a rush of adrenalin and anger. 'I'm not sure who the father is.'

'Are you not?' He cocked his head. 'Emmy, we both know the dates fit. I was your first lover and you've even named him after me.'

Heat surged. 'I named him after the man who *lied* to me. Who didn't even tell me his real name. "Ramon" was nothing but a lie—a fake persona from some entitled sociopath. You're not him.'

He was nothing like the man he'd passed himself off as—funny and charming, carefree yet caring. Javier Torres was none of those things.

For a long moment he was utterly silent, but emotion enlarged his pupils so much that the black-coffee core almost obliterated the cocoa-coloured iris completely.

'What's *my* name, Emmy?' he finally asked in a bloodless, shocked-sounding whisper.

Too late she realised she'd given herself away. Now he knew that *she* knew he'd lied to her. She straightened, determined to hide her fear because surely, in the shades of grey in this mess, *he* was the worst liar between them? And even if he wasn't, she had to be completely honest now. 'Javier Torres.'

He nodded slowly. 'Javier *Ramon* Torres.'

She closed her eyes. That name had been the only tribute she'd been able to offer her son at the time of his birth. She'd felt so betrayed when she'd learned 'Ramon' was really Javier and humiliated that she'd given it to

Luke. But now it was relevant again? It was their common middle name and, while that should be a soothing symmetry, stupidly it hurt her more.

'How long have you known?' His question now had an edge and she couldn't blame him.

'Not long.' She lifted her chin bravely. 'Since the media release about the Flores property.'

The property *she'd* shown him—her most favourite place in the world. Her sanctuary. She'd been naive to share something so special with a stranger. Those moments of lust and excitement had made her brainless. Because he'd bought it and was now transforming it from budget retreat to swanky hotel. He was a brutal, ruthlessly acquisitive businessman. Nothing like the carefree sea god who'd held her spellbound that evening on her precious beach.

'That was months ago.' His mouth compressed. 'Yet you've not got in touch since.'

'You lied to me,' she muttered.

'It seems we're both liars.'

She pushed down her rising panic.

'How could you just try to tell me you didn't know who his father is?' he asked.

'I didn't—not for months anyway and even then I found out little more than your real name.'

'You should have contacted me the second you found that out.'

He was right and yet wrong, because she'd learned more than his real name, she'd discovered his lack of integrity too.

'I don't know *you* at all, nothing other than that you lied to me that night,' she defended herself desperately. 'I couldn't even be completely sure that the jerk written about in the paper was actually the guy from that night.'

Except that was weak of her. She'd glanced at that picture in the paper and known instantly.

'The second I walked in the door just now, you were sure,' he said. 'But you hustled that child upstairs.'

'Maybe that's because I'm *terrified*.' She glared at him, taking a step to widen her stance, wishing she could make a better barrier between him and that stairway.

'Because I present danger to you? To him?' He recoiled. 'Based on what evidence? Was I violent?'

Her throat tightened but she forced the truth to whisper out. 'No.'

'Then what have I done to hurt you? If I remember correctly, *you* were the one who walked out without so much as a goodbye.'

The flash of reproach in his eyes deepened her guilt.

'Why did you leave so early?' he added. 'Why not wake me to say goodbye? Were you *that* full of regret?'

'No,' she muttered, hoarse with burning embarrassment.

'You could have left a note.'

'What was the point? I thought you were a tourist and that we'd never see each other again.' She gazed at him with a hot mix of anger and guilt and sadness. It had been a fantasy experience, she'd not wanted to shatter its perfect illusion with morning-after awkwardness. 'It wasn't like you were planning a second date either. You were passing through.'

'So were you. Or so you led me to believe. You lied as much as I did that night.'

She shook her head. 'I *never* lied.'

He tensed. 'By omission, you definitely did.'

'What about everything you forgot to mention? Like, your real name. Your true intentions for being there. You never said you were looking for something to tear apart.'

'I'm not the one tearing apart valuable things. *You're* the one who's done that—keeping a child from his father.' His voice rose. 'There's no reason you can give that ex- cuses your failure to tell me once you knew who I was.'

'*You* didn't want me to know who you really were. I only discovered that by accident months afterwards. But you were so comfortable to lie, which told me all I needed to know about your integrity.' She snapped at him. She didn't really mean it but emotion had overruled her tongue. 'I never would have said yes if I'd known who you were.'

'You would have said it faster,' he shot back.

'Oh, wow.' She drew in a shocked breath at his sheer arrogance. 'You think you're that amazing?'

He might be six feet three of muscled manly beauty, he might have a brilliant brain and he might have bil- lions in the bank, but he had no integrity. And therefore, no true value.

'The resources I have are amazing.'

'You think I care about money?' she scoffed. She worked as a *volunteer*, the last thing she was interested in was accumulating material wealth. 'If I was a gold- digger, wouldn't I have beaten down your door the second I discovered who you really were?' She flushed angrily. 'I thought you were some chilled-out surfer. I had no rea- son to suspect you were a billionaire bulldozer who buys whatever he wants and then destroys it.'

'Destroys it?' His eyes widened. 'Are we talking about that dilapidated old hostel?'

'It wasn't dilapidated.'

'You showed me a prime piece of land that was in dire need of investment.'

She rejected that notion. Lucero's property had been perfect. Furthermore the old man had been unwaveringly kind to her. But now Javier was ripping apart his legacy. 'And didn't you take that information and use it well?' she raged. 'Well, you're not buying me and you're not buying my son.'

'He's my son too.' His eyes glittered, revealing his own loss of temper. 'It's eighteen months since that night, Emmy. And I've only just discovered he even *exists*. Now he's *nine* months old,' he said. 'I've missed out on almost the full first year of his life. That's unforgivable and you can't keep him from me. You owe me time.' He inhaled sharply and whirled away, clearly struggling to regain his self-control.

Emmy was struck still as her worst fears were realised. Javier was going to fight. He was used to getting his way. Was he going to do whatever it took to get it now? He had everything on his side—resources, power, privilege. She had only intuition and resolve and the fiercest love imaginable.

'Understand this,' she breathed. 'There's nothing I won't do to protect my son.' She would be there at every step. She would never let Javier or anyone else sideline her.

'Nothing? Good to know.' He turned back to face her. His lips curved in a smile full of *bring it on* challenge that fired up that dangerous part of Emerald. 'I consider myself warned. But somehow, I feel confident I can handle whatever you try to throw at me.' He stepped closer. 'You know I can handle you, Emerald.'

His words sent sparks cascading through her—anger, defiance, *attraction*. Unwanted, inappropriate, unstoppable attraction.

And she was furious about it.

CHAPTER TWO

'So, WHAT DO you want to do?'

Javier stared as Emerald Jones squared up to him.

Do? That was the terrible thing. Because the one thing
that he wanted to do right now was the one thing he really, *really* shouldn't. This raw kick of lust was appalling. He decided it was anger, really, fuelling the hit of
ill-timed appetite—his rage tempting him with one way
in which he could assert control. Well, he wasn't going
to let emotion get the better of him. Not *ever*. He very
deliberately took a step back and shoved his hands into
his pockets.

He'd come here today ready to apologise, ready to
take on responsibility for his son, ready to support Emerald once they'd worked out how... But to discover she
knew who he was already? And that she'd found him so
lacking that she'd just 'not bothered' to let him know?

His gut clenched as he strove to think clearly and decide how best to answer her.

Frankly the last twenty-four hours were a blur. He'd
engaged a private investigator to work urgently through
the night the second he'd been driven away from the
store yesterday. Javier had tossed and turned, recalculat-
ing, remembering, reliving. The confirmation had come
mid-morning. Emerald Jones had delivered her son nine

months ago and given him the name Lucero Ramon, Luke for short. Certainty had seared like a white-hot sword cauterising a stomach wound, leaving Javier so breathless he'd almost lost the power to think. He'd had to hurry paperwork to ensure visa requirements were met to get them both on board because he'd wanted to make sure they could have some time to talk—uninterrupted and safe. Although, truthfully, he had no idea where to start the conversation that was more than nine months overdue.

Now he steeled himself against her bone-weakening beauty. The linen shirt dress she wore today closely cupped her curves while the faded blue still brought out the blue of her emotion-laden eyes. But the accusation in them was laughably unjust when it turned out *she* was the one who'd hidden something far more serious. Her glorious hair hung in fiery, loose spirals halfway down her back and that reckless part of him wanted to tangle his fingers into them and pull her close. Instead he finally answered her question. 'Can you close the shop and get rid of that woman so we can talk—?'

'That's Connie,' Emerald interrupted shortly. 'She's amazing.'

'I'm sure, but we need some time alone.'

And he didn't really want to hear about the amazing Connie. Not when she was doing all the things he'd not even been given the chance to attempt—such as spending the afternoon with his son.

He had no real relationship with his own parents and frankly had no idea how to set about building one with a baby. He pushed back the slithering thought that it was too late already, that any relationship he might've fostered with Luke could never be recovered, that, once again, he'd missed out on something fundamental. He didn't have time to squander on that insecurity right now. And at the very least, he could give his son all outward signs of support.

But he couldn't stop himself from questioning her sharply. 'Were you *ever* going to tell me? Or were you hoping to get rid of me quickly and keep your secret? Were you going to deny me and *him* for ever?'

It wasn't the first time Javier had been betrayed, but it was absolutely the worst. An innocent child denied his birthright? How could she claim to love her son yet choose to deny him such a primary relationship? Would she deny him everything Javier *could* offer—his finance alone was outstanding and his son should never have to live in anything less than luxury. His tension coiled tighter with every second that she didn't reply.

'I don't know what I was going to do.'

'Well, we need to figure out things as quickly as possible,' he said, shoving the anger down inside so he could calmly take control of this mess. 'I'd like you to come with me—'

'I can't just walk out—'

'Sure you can,' he muttered in annoyance. 'You've done it before.'

She paled but argued anyway. 'I owe Connie. I need to give her proper notice.'

And she didn't owe *him*? Javier huffed out a tight breath. 'If she's that amazing, she'll understand how important this is.'

Emerald couldn't stall and deny him more time when he'd missed this much already.

'We need to go.' He rocked on his feet, resisting the urge to pace.

He could feel her aggression building, but she turned away. Stiffly she locked the store door and then led him up the narrow stairs to the tiny room above. A swift glance around the bedsit made him grit his teeth.

'Thanks, Connie,' Emerald said, her awkwardness evident in the colour storming her cheeks. 'I'm sorry, I had to close the shop.'

Javier didn't listen to the rest—their voices faded as he gazed in fascination, and frankly in trepidation, at the tiny boy playing on a mat on the floor. He was cherubic—there was no other word for it. A dumpling of a child with dark eyes, dark curls and a beatific smile. Javier felt something in his chest slip, but at the same time his gut tightened. He'd never felt as afraid for anything or anyone in his life. Nor had he felt as uncertain of what to actually do.

Moments later the older woman left. Javier didn't glance or give a damn about her obvious curiosity. He couldn't peel his attention from his son. He had little experience with children. He'd had no intention of having any of his own, but Luke was here and, now that he was, Javier couldn't have him denied his heritage or the opportunities he could offer. Which were a damn sight more than this sparse existence. He had to draw in another cooling breath to stop his temper from flaring again.

The child smiled at Emmy as she crouched and put a soft toy in front of him. Javier's gut twisted again as he watched her with Luke. Given the boy's gurgling gleeful reaction to her, it was obvious she'd cared for him but while he appreciated that, he was also...*jealous*? And there was something else—something worse—bubbling beneath his skin. Another scalding emotion that he didn't want to recognise, let alone release.

'Please start packing, Emerald,' he said bluntly.

She glanced up at him. He saw the nervous lick of her

lips. But it was the widening of the child's eyes that had him instantly regretting how harsh he'd sounded.

'It's not like I can steal him away without you knowing,' he added in a whisper. 'This room is ridiculously small.'

In an almost blinding wave of emotion, he realised he wanted his son to have *everything*. Not just material things, but emotional things—things Javier hadn't had. Security and consistency of care—for one. The trouble was, he didn't know how to begin with that. All he knew was that he needed to get them out of there.

Emerald stood, visibly drawing courage as she walked towards him. 'I thought we could have more of a conversation.'

'About what?' There was nothing to discuss. He could provide a better place for them, there was no question of that.

But as he watched the pulse at the side of her neck flutter, his own accelerated. And she still didn't begin to pack.

'I can't just leave,' she said.

'We need to work this out and we need time and space in which to do that.' He tried to stay reasonable. 'My place is bigger. Or do you want me to stay with you in this shoebox?' He couldn't resist stepping closer to her this time, or taking a Machiavellian delight in the way colour swarmed more boldly in her cheeks. 'Is that what you want? Me to share that narrow bed with you?'

Her lashes dropped, veiling a sudden flare in her eyes.

That other feeling ripped through him. The one he'd desperately wanted to ignore. The one he'd given way to with such glee all those months ago. He gritted his teeth and cursed himself.

This woman had kept the most precious thing from

him and when she'd discovered the truth of who he was, she'd still denied him, yet still all his body wanted was to haul hers beneath his so he could sample her sweet fervour. She'd been so hot that night and he ached to seduce her into that soft, arching slickness once more. He loathed his own weakness.

'I can't spend another night apart from him, Emmy,' he said harshly, curling his hands into fists in his pockets to stop himself from reaching for her and admitting a painful truth in the process. 'I have too much to catch up on.'

'You can't stay here,' she said.

'Then you'd better start packing.' He paced away from her, turning to watch the boy from the safety of the window.

'Where are you staying?' she asked dully.

He didn't feel like answering. He didn't want to waste time or energy on words when the answer would be obvious soon enough. He had too much to process already. Moodily he watched his son. He had no idea how to even approach him.

'Javier.'

He glanced over at the hesitation in her voice.

'Will we be returning here?' Her blue eyes were very wide, very worried.

He steeled himself against the emotion and the effect it had deep inside him. 'What do you think?'

She blinked rapidly. 'You can't just expect us both to move in with you.' She squared her shoulders. 'I have a position here in which Luke can be with me full time. It's the perfect arrangement.'

'Perfect?' He almost choked. 'Living in this tiny room above a store where he's exposed to exhaust fumes and strangers coming in and out all the time? You're busy— he could get into strife when your back is turned.'

She stiffened. 'I would never allow that to happen—'

'But it could.' He was laying it on thick, but he needed to win and he was going with his strongest play—which was her obvious desire to protect her son. 'It's not perfect for *him*. Or *me*.'

She swallowed. 'You expect me to give up everything?'

'You did that to me.' As he gazed at her, the anger and desire within him coalesced. 'So for eighteen months, yeah. You give up everything.' The thought of having her with him, within his power, was appallingly appealing and he couldn't resist demanding it. After all, wasn't it only right and fair?

Not fair. His conscience needled, but the anger drowned out the discord.

'Eighteen months?' Her jaw dropped. 'Luke's only nine months old.'

'I missed every moment of your pregnancy.'

'That wasn't your—that was my…' She trailed off at the look in his eyes.

Eighteen months. Now he'd said it, he'd settle for nothing less.

'I think if you tell Connie the truth, she'll understand completely,' he said crisply. 'I'm sure she'll be pleased to see you both in a better situation and for Luke to have his father in his life.'

He'd never wanted a family on terms like this—a surprise with a woman he barely knew and who'd hidden the truth from him. But he'd do what was right by his son. He'd do better than his own parents had done for him. Somehow. He was determined to.

'How long have you known?' Emerald asked as she fetched a worn striped bag and opened it up. 'Javier?' she prompted when he didn't respond.

He clenched his jaw but knew he had to make an effort and respond even though he hated reliving that moment he'd seen her again. 'I saw you from a distance yesterday afternoon when Connie was returning Luke to you. If I hadn't been there...' That possibility made him see red again. 'So it's only a few hours since I saw his birth certificate.' He broke off, determined to control his surge of anger, purely because of the small piece of innocence cooing on the play mat. 'He deserves the best from both of us.'

Emmy stared at Javier. The remnants of anger and hurt were evident in his eyes but she also saw that, despite his reluctance to speak more, he was trying. And what choice did she have? He was *right*. Luke deserved better and she had failed him. She'd been too scared to reach out once she knew who her 'Ramon' really was.

But the feeling she was fighting hardest? That slithering ripple of desire that had twisted into life the second she'd seen him again. And the moment he'd mentioned sleeping in her small bed? A wave of heat engulfed her again. It was so wrong. So stupid and selfish and wrong.

'It won't take me long to pack.' Her voice cracked and she hurriedly began filling her bag. She didn't have much, nor did Luke, so it wouldn't take long. But as she shoved their belongings together, she couldn't let this continue without trying to explain herself a little more to Javier.

'I left early that morning because I had to get to a project on another island. I've been a volunteer abroad for a while,' she said. 'That night, I'd just wanted an escape and you were...' She trailed off and swallowed uncomfortably. She couldn't explain that bit any more—it was too embarrassing to admit how she'd decided to keep that night as the fantasy it had been. She'd not wanted to spoil the memory of it with an awkward goodbye that next morning.

'When I realised I was pregnant I was worried,' she continued as Javier stood still as still by the window, silently watching. 'I hid it for as long as I could because I couldn't afford to lose my volunteer visa. But then Lucero, the head of the foundation, found out. He was very kind. He helped me, so did others in the community.' She had been so grateful to the elderly man when she'd had nowhere else to go. 'I didn't discover *your* real identity until the property deal was announced after he died. Luke was already a few months old.'

That time had been horrible. She'd been alone, angry, scared, so tired and so broke she was trapped. She'd been grateful and dependent on first Lucero's, then Connie's support. And when she'd finally found out who Javier really was, she'd become terrified that he might find out about their baby. 'I felt betrayed. Lucero was gone, you'd lied. I was hormonal and I had this tiny little boy who'd become the most precious thing in my life and when I learned who you really were I was afraid...' She trailed off again and shook her head hopelessly. How could she ever explain herself to Javier without telling him the rest of her background? But it was too dangerous to do that. She couldn't trust he wouldn't use it against her.

'Afraid of what?' Javier eventually prompted.

She shrugged. 'That you'd swoop in and take him from me.'

She registered the immediate flash of furious hurt in his eyes.

Maybe he'd think she was irrational or over-emotional or something. But the fear of him taking Luke from her *wasn't* irrational in her view. Because that was what happened. Powerful people took away the things she loved most. Powerful people judged and they'd always found her wanting. People had judged her all her life—

slandering her intentions and decisions. Because of her parents, her brother and, yes, the mistakes she'd made herself. People who knew her past didn't trust her. So she didn't trust people in return. Particularly if they had privilege and money and Javier Torres had both.

She had no power with which to fight him, so she'd felt she had no choice but to hide. Luke was too precious. And how could she trust Javier when he'd lied to her from the first?

There was another long moment of silence and she sensed him grappling the emotion, almost as if he were carefully choosing what words he was comfortable to release.

'I'm not a *monster*, Emerald. But make no mistake, I'm no hero either,' he said so expressionlessly that she shivered. 'So I'm swooping in and taking you too.'

His expression was now so fixed it was unreadable— and he was so far from the smiling man she'd met on the beach that evening.

'Is that everything packed?' he asked curtly.

Didn't he want to hear more of her side of the story? Didn't he want to ask more or offer any further explanation of his own actions? Didn't he want to forgive her?

No. Of course he didn't. People who were quick to judge never did. They didn't want to revise their opinions once they'd leapt to their conclusions.

She felt sick. She'd been lost in a fog of desperation, struggling to feed Luke and scared for their future— afraid that exactly *this* would happen. She couldn't risk telling Javier all her truth now, not when he was this remote and disapproving. Her whole background would appal him. But this time she couldn't pack her bag and run away. She had to stay and fight for Luke. She'd escaped her past before, she'd figure out a way to get through this too. And nothing mattered more than Luke's well-being. She'd put up with anything to ensure he was safe and well.

But she wondered if Javier could say the same. Or was this just a powerful man used to being in control venting his anger at being kept in the dark? Was this about him getting control back more than it was about Luke?

'You don't want children,' she said before thinking better of it. 'You couldn't have made it clearer. That night you even said you weren't interested in marriage and kids.'

'Of course I made that clear,' he said frozenly from his spot by the window. 'I always do that to put off women who might think having my baby would set them up for life.' He shot her a pointed look. 'And I needed to be extra clear with an inexperienced woman who'd neglected to mention that she was a virgin until the very moment we were about to have sex. I had to ensure she wasn't hearing wedding bells.'

Her jaw dropped at his outrageous arrogance. 'You think you're some hot catch? No woman who knows what you're really like would *ever* want to marry you.'

His shoulders lifted and dropped dismissively. 'It's amazing what people will put up with when there's a hefty bank balance on offer.'

'Well, it ought to be obvious now that I don't want your money.' She flushed. 'Nor do I want *you*.'

There was such guarded coolness in those cocoa and coffee eyes. 'Legally Luke will be my son and heir,' he countered quietly. 'We don't need to marry to give him my name. That's a simple certificate change.'

'What about my name?' she asked nervously. 'He has that now.'

'No reason why he can't have mine too. Jones-Torres or Torres-Jones.' He shrugged. 'We can flip a coin later.'

So there was to be none of that *you must marry me now* old-fashioned autocratic drama? He was making out as if this were easy. Emotionless.

But it wasn't. Misery swamped her as Javier asserted his paternal authority. But didn't he have every right to do that? She owed. And his calm, apparent reasonableness made her feel worse for having kept quiet these last two months. So now she faced eighteen months of living with him and then what—some shared care arrangement, with Javier offering their son a lifestyle that she could *never* equal or compete with? She almost bent double with despair at the prospect. She'd inevitably be shut out of Luke's life.

'I'll carry the bag, you take Luke,' he said stiffly. 'It might take us a little time to get acquainted.'

Downstairs Connie sent her an anxious look as Javier carried her bags to the big black SUV waiting outside.

'He's Luke's father, isn't he?' Connie swiftly whispered as soon as he was out of earshot.

'It's that obvious?' Emmy asked.

'You don't talk with any man, ever.' Connie smiled. 'And then you bring him upstairs when you're supposed to be working?'

It wasn't as if she'd had much choice. 'Back then, I didn't know who he was…' Her voice faded and she swallowed through the sudden tightness.

'Are you okay?' Connie stepped closer.

Emmy's heart broke at that concern but she quickly nodded, not wanting to get emotional. 'I will be. We will be.'

'Stay in touch. Please let me know how you are…' Connie gave Emmy's arm a gentle squeeze and pressed a quick kiss on Luke's head. 'I'm going to miss you both.'

'I'm going to miss you too.' Emmy's breath caught

and she blinked back sudden tears. 'Thank you so much for everything. We couldn't have survived without you.'

Connie's grip on her arm tightened. 'You're a survivor, don't forget that.'

Her support gave Emmy a much-needed boost. She *was* a survivor and she loved Luke as no one else in the world could. But then she saw the car seat already fixed in the rear of the car and reality hit again. Javier had arrived with no intention of leaving *without* their son. What else had he planned that she didn't know about yet?

'Are you staying at a hotel?' she asked nervously as she sat in the back between Javier and Luke. 'Which one?'

Javier didn't reply as the driver pulled away from the store. Emmy didn't push it. He clearly valued privacy for personal conversations, and that was fair enough.

Less than fifteen minutes later they pulled up, not at a hotel, but rather the marina. Emmy's heart took a knock as she saw a sleek speedboat idling at the dock. A crewman stepped forward when he saw the car pull in.

Emerald put her hand over Luke's tiny one and he gripped her finger. She had no family. Nowhere to go. No one to turn to. Connie was old and had limited resources, she'd helped her the best she could and Emmy couldn't take advantage of her generosity any longer. She had to deal with this alone.

'I don't think that boat is safe for Luke,' she said, desperately searching for a reason to refuse to board.

Javier glanced at her coolly. 'Do you think I would endanger him?' he asked softly.

The tiny hairs rose on the back of Emmy's neck. 'Of course not.'

'Good. We're staying on my yacht.'

Emmy tensed, trying not to let her reaction show because that didn't feel safe for *her*. On a yacht, they'd be isolated and too…*close*. She'd be vulnerable—not because she was physically *afraid* of him, but because she was attracted to him still. She had the feeling he could emotionally devastate her on more than one level and on some small yacht, there'd be no escape.

Javier took the tiny life jacket the waiting crewman now held out for them and turned to where she stood holding their baby. 'This is only for the speedboat. The yacht has been baby-proofed.'

Emmy gritted her teeth and put the jacket on her son; she'd wait and see this yacht for herself to decide what was safe for him.

'I have one for you too,' Javier added.

She glared at him. 'I can swim.'

Javier stared back at her. 'Put it on or I'll put it on for you.'

For a long moment they clashed in silence—the storm of emotion slowly changed the colour of Javier's eyes from that cocoa mix to almost all pure black coffee and Emmy suddenly found herself relenting. 'Will you hold him while I put mine on, then?' she half choked.

To her surprise, Javier's eyes widened uneasily, but he didn't hesitate to reply. 'Of course.'

He held his hands out awkwardly and Emmy placed her son into them.

As Emmy swiftly shrugged the jacket on, Luke contemplated Javier seriously while Javier gazed back at Luke— the wary curiosity in their expressions was identical.

'I can take him now.' Emmy held her hands out the second she was done with her jacket.

Luke babbled at Javier in that exact moment.

'No, that's okay,' Javier said brusquely. 'I've got him.'

A hot wash of discomfort flooded her as she followed them to the speedboat. Was she jealous? Or worse, were her ovaries exploding all over again at the sight of her son and his father assessing each other with such fascination?

The crewman had already stowed her bag, so within two minutes they were moving. The speedboat chugged slower than she suspected it usually did. It was then that she finally paid attention and realised to which vessel they were heading. It had been half hidden beyond a small tour vessel and it wasn't a yacht at all. It was a floating *mansion*. It gleamed as if new—its navy and white trim stylish and the chrome fittings almost blinding in the sun. As they came right alongside she stared, counting the levels up. There were at least four decks she could see. Was there a bunch of other passengers already on there?

'Is this yours?' she asked as she climbed aboard, her arms feeling empty as he still carried Luke.

'You don't like it?'

No one could *not* like it, but Emmy had never felt as uncomfortable in all her life. Was he really this wealthy? 'It's…massive. I thought you were all about environmental eco-tourism.'

'In this instance,' he clipped, 'I'm all about privacy.'

Not even the luxury cruise boats she'd seen arriving here had this detail and comfort. The wooden decks gleamed while the soft furnishings were rich and lavish. There was obviously no expense spared, every fitting and comfort designer. It's opulence and extravagance were staggering.

'Where will Luke and I be staying?'

To her relief he passed Luke back to her. 'Follow me.'

It was going to take her days to find her way around this floating palace. She was hopelessly confused as she followed him up another flight of gleaming steps and along an extraordinarily wide corridor.

'This is your suite,' he said briskly. 'A cabin for Luke has been prepared right next door.'

Emmy barely glanced into her space, but Luke's stunned her. It was huge, with gorgeous curtains dressing the wide windows offering stunning views across the water. There was a cot set up already dressed in beautiful white linen. A mobile hung above it while other baby supplies were stacked neatly in the corner.

Once again the detailed preparation stretched her nerves. What did he want, really?

'You got this ready quickly.' She stepped back out to the corridor, almost bumping into Javier and flushing hotly at the near miss. 'Where's your room?'

'I'm on the deck above.'

Javier sleeping on another level was reassuring, wasn't it? Yet she had a sharp twinge of disappointment. She shook herself and forced her focus onto her little boy. She couldn't believe the size of the cabins or that there could be this much space on a private yacht. She'd be sure to keep both her and Luke's doors open through the night, because she'd never slept in a different room from her son. She tightened her hold on him without thinking and, at the change, Luke wriggled and began to fret.

'He's tired and hungry.' She glanced at Javier defensively.

'I suspect he might not be the only one.' The faintest smile flashed on Javier's face. 'So let's get you both fed.'

Emmy's irritation bloomed. She was *not* some overtired, hungry toddler. 'No, I'd like to unpack his things first.'

Javier drew an audible breath. 'Fine.'

But to her chagrin, Javier didn't leave, rather he went right into Luke's cabin and sat down in the wide armchair.

'Will you hold him while I do it?' she asked.

Again there was that wariness in Javier's eyes, but he answered coolly enough. 'Of course.'

She handed Luke back to Javier, quickly finding Luke's favourite toy so he could clutch it while she swiftly emptied the bag she'd packed.

Javier sat carefully holding Luke while intently watching her unload every item. 'All these things are Luke's. Where are your things?'

'Still in the bag. I'll unload the rest in my room later.'

'That bag is nearly empty.'

She shrugged. 'I don't need much.'

'You spend everything you have on him,' Javier said flatly.

'Of course.' She flushed and concentrated on refolding Luke's few clothes.

'He's bottle-fed?' he asked after a moment.

She swallowed hard, feeling her defensiveness flare again. Was he going to criticise all her choices? 'He's starting solid foods now. I breastfed for as long as I could—'

'I'm not judging,' Javier said calmly. 'I'm just understanding the process. If he takes a bottle, then it doesn't need to be you who feeds him. *I* could do that.' He looked at her. 'You don't think I'd want to feed my own child? Know how to soothe him when he's unwell or unhappy?'

She stared at him. Did he really mean that? Did he want to be that involved? Stupidly the thought terrified her more.

'Does he wake through the night?' Javier asked.

'Sometimes.' She didn't want to admit how demanding Luke could be, but the fact was he was a strong little boy with a healthy appetite and his curious mind was developing rapidly too, which meant he craved more stimulation.

'A nanny could manage him for that.'

'A nanny?' Emmy stiffened. 'I don't need a nanny.'

'You need some help. We both do.'

'I haven't up until this point.' Her hackles lifted instantly as she feared this was the first step towards eliminating her.

'Are you sure you want to argue this now, Emmy?' he asked softly.

But a torrent of bitterness was rising within her. If he wanted to employ a nanny, then he didn't really want to care for his son himself. So did he regard his son simply as an acquisition? Fears coalesced, sending her into a heightened state of confusion and defensiveness, and she lashed out. 'This isn't actually about Luke, is it? This is about you not being in control before. You not knowing he existed. You can't stand that.'

Javier's expression shuttered. 'This is utterly and only about Luke and what's best for him.'

'And you think a nanny is best? Not his own parents?'

Something flickered in his eyes before he blinked it away. 'I think his parents are important. *Both* of them.' He gazed down at Luke's head.

He said that with such fierce conviction Emmy wondered at it, but before she could ask why he felt that so strongly, he lifted his head and fixed her in place with that ruthlessly assessing stare of his.

'But we need to be in the best frame of mind to be the best we can for him,' he added. 'Right now you need food and rest as much as he does. Come on.' He hefted their small son in his arms and stood. 'We'll eat in the dining room.'

He exited the cabin so swiftly Emmy was left staring agape. Seriously? Was he just going to walk away from her concerns? From this conversation?

Her irritation brewing, she ran after him. The stunning

superyacht stole her breath but at the same time stoked her anger. It was ludicrously indulgent. The gleaming marble, backlit gemstones, the polished silverware, the plush sofas and soft cushions and above all sheer size and *space*. Everything was so ornate and over the top it screamed obscene wealth. Even the discretion of the uniformed crew irritated her. They disappeared before she barely caught a glimpse of them—obviously well trained, well paid, well controlled. Had he led her to this formal dining room to intimidate her—to make her painfully aware of everything he had to offer and everything she didn't? There was even a highchair for Luke already. Discomfort and fury mounting, she settled him into it and fastened the small belt.

'I wasn't sure of your tastes, or what time we'd get here, so I requested a small buffet,' Javier said smoothly, preventing her from saying anything more again with sudden 'top host' manners. 'Help yourself.'

She couldn't bring herself to put anything on her plate despite the sudden watering of her mouth at the sumptuous array of freshly prepared, beautiful food. It had been a long time since she'd had anything more than a quick thrown-together comfort eat, but she selected some mashed plantain to put on Luke's tray.

'Stop the stiff-necked pride,' he said, taking the seat next to the one she'd perched on and dispensing with the manners all over again. 'Or I'll feed you myself.'

'I'm not very hungry,' she lied and instantly hated herself for it. Since when was she so shrewish? But as she glanced around the room again, more of the same leaked out. 'You don't scare me with your display of wealth.'

'Emmy.' He calmly served himself a portion of fresh-cooked fish and fragrant rice. 'We're in this room purely for the privacy. I don't want the world staring at us if we're up on deck.'

Her pulse settled fractionally, but she was still tense. Luke, on the other hand, was delightedly experimenting with the snippets of food she'd put in front of him.

Javier was watching Luke with such naked fascination that Emmy felt badly about her exhausted, emotion-clouded judgement of only seconds ago. She wanted to smooth this awkwardness somehow, but before she could speak her stomach rumbled embarrassingly loudly. Javier's eyebrows lifted and his mouth quirked. She shelved her pride and served herself. She almost moaned at her first bite of the seafood. She hadn't had anything as delicious in a long while.

She saw Javier's smile broaden and decided to let him have the win. She did feel better.

'We need to talk—' she finally began, breaking off when she saw him grimace.

'We need time,' he replied after a moment. 'Eighteen months is a good start. We'll work out a permanent arrangement eventually, but by then Luke will likely be ready to spend time mixing with other children in a good preschool.'

'You want to send him to school already?' She gaped at him.

Javier paused. 'Part-time play with other children might be good. I don't want him to be lonely.'

Meaning Javier wasn't about to have any other children? Given that Emmy wasn't either, it shouldn't have mattered, but his pronouncement bothered her all the same. And this wasn't her idea of a conversation, this was him just deciding. She chewed, swallowed and stabbed another forkful of suddenly tasteless food. Her control wasn't just slipping, it was being torn from her. No de-

cisions about Luke would be only hers again. That realisation both discomforted her and made her feel guilty
all over again because it gave her the smallest insight
into how Javier must feel about missing out on everything so far.

'Okay.' She nodded.

But the problem was she didn't want to live with Javier. She could hardly bear to be this close to him. It was
unsettling in ways she didn't want to define, and she
definitely didn't want to *take* anything from him. At the
same time she couldn't deny him what he needed—that
she did owe—time with Luke. And she was too selfish to
give up any time with her son herself. So she had to stay.

'You'll need more than what you've brought on board,'
he murmured.

'No, I won't.' She tried to stay calm.

'You're living under my roof, at my insistence. I'll take
care of your expenses while you're here.'

She shook her head.

'You'll definitely need warmer clothes for winter in
New York.'

She was hardly going to be out and about in the city.
She'd be with Luke. 'I'll figure something out.' She
had almost zero savings, but she was going to have to
make them stretch. And she definitely needed to think
about how she could support herself in the future. She
was used to living a roving existence—volunteering on
various projects for lodging and food as she explored
the world. Even with Luke with her, she'd thought she
might be able to make it work when he was a little older.
But no more. She'd be bound to wherever Javier wanted
Luke—and by extension her—to be. 'I don't need anything from you.'

Javier was watching her closely. 'It doesn't bother me.'

Was that a flicker of amusement in his eyes?

'It bothers me.' She still heard the echo of the insults and insinuations through her pregnancy when a couple of people had whispered about her relationship with the elderly Lucero.

Not to mention Javier's own implied insults when he'd 'explained' why he'd not given her his real name and his arrogant assumption that women wanted a wedding band when they knew who he really was.

While other people might've been able to laugh those things off, she couldn't, because she'd come from a family with no moral boundaries, who wanted nothing more than a free ride at someone else's expense. She never wanted to be anything like them and she'd spent most of her life trying to prove she wasn't.

'I get that you want to provide for our son, that's wonderful,' she said in a low voice. 'But *I* will not touch a cent of your money. I don't want it and I don't need it.'

Javier leaned back in the seat and actually grinned at her. 'Fine. I'll pay you as his carer, then.'

'That's not acceptable to me.' She couldn't even look at him now he was smiling. 'I don't want your money.'

'Well it'll be there,' he replied carelessly. 'It's up to you whether you use it or not.'

That glimpse of good humour recharged the cells of attraction she'd been trying to suppress. He was far too gorgeous and far too close for comfort and this sudden return to affable and easy-going was alarming. Maybe it was wrong of her, but she still couldn't trust him. She couldn't trust anyone. But most of all, she suddenly realised, she couldn't trust *herself.* Because when he smiled at her like that? She was so tempted to lean in and smile back.

Suddenly she actually *appreciated* the size of the superyacht. It was big enough for them to avoid each other. She could have her time with Luke and he could have his.

And that, she realised, was the only way she was going to survive this.

Almost two hours later Javier watched Emmy needlessly adjust the light blanket covering their small son. Luke was fast asleep now, having listened to a story cradled in her arms before she put him into the cot.

'Come on,' he commanded her softly. 'We need to talk.'

It was the last thing he wanted to do. The tension he'd been containing for hours bubbled, seeping out of the lid he'd had shoved on it all day. He knew she'd been scraping an existence as a volunteer for a long time, living above that store, effectively working for free. And now, despite that dinner, she still looked pale and exhausted and terrified. It annoyed him immensely. What was it about him that scared her so? He wanted that fiery woman he'd met on the beach back. Memory surged—she'd looked so liberated and confident and they'd had fun together. More than fun. He remembered the look in her eyes, the sighs she'd released. He *knew* she'd had pleasure with him. And yes, his body tensed, any desire for *conversation* evaporated completely.

'Sit down before you fall down, Emmy,' he growled, mad with himself for remembering the heat of her response. 'And relax.'

'Relax?' She threw him a stunned look as she sank onto the cushions. 'How can I when everything is happening so fast?' She buried her face in her hands. He saw her short-bitten nails, the blister on her knuckle and the tiredness in her slumped shoulders.

Inwardly he cursed again that she'd not contacted him. It was beyond insulting, but it had also hurt *her*. She'd clearly almost been broken trying to survive, despite the little help she'd accepted from those few people. And why had she needed the help of them? Where was her family? She'd said she'd travelled a lot, before stopping here because of Luke, so why had she named her son for an elderly man she'd only known a couple of years?

'Look, just breathe,' he muttered. 'We'll take this one day at a time.'

Her determined independence infuriated him, but he'd overcome it. Oddly he wanted her to feel safe enough to let him take some of the load she'd denied him all these months. And he wanted—

'Why did you lie?' She lifted her head and challenged him again. 'I've tried to explain my actions but you've said almost nothing about yours—offered no *real* reason for why you didn't even tell me your name. Did you want anonymity? To escape the pressure of being a billionaire? Did you just want an ordinary moment with no one watching so you could seduce some stranger without any repercussions?' She shook her head. 'Sorry about that, Javier. But maybe you should try some time on Struggle Street or what it's like to be judged the second someone learns your name.'

He blinked, taken aback by her sudden ferocity. His defences instinctively rose because these kinds of questions were not ones he ever answered. 'You've no idea what I've been through, Emmy,' he muttered in an instinctive unthinking response. 'None of the struggles I've faced.'

'Enlighten me, then,' she dared with a mutinous lift to her chin. 'Tell me something meaningful. Because we have to work through this. We have a child together and we're going to need to get to know each other.'

No, they didn't. He glared at her, rejecting that idea

completely. He and Emerald were Luke's parents, yes. They didn't need to be anything more to each other. They didn't need to 'open up' and reveal all. They only needed to be able to work together.

He saw the blaze in her eyes ignite and struggled to hold back his urge to respond in a far too physical fashion. Yes, the real problem here was he was only interested in getting to know *her* in that one, most carnal way all over again. 'Not tonight.' He gritted his teeth and shut her down, holding back everything else he wanted to *do*.

She was clearly exhausted and beyond the fire, in the shining depths of her blue eyes, he could see a soft entreaty—the desire for something he couldn't offer anyone. She sought emotional intimacy—as if he could build a relationship? *No, thank you, and never.*

'Javier?' she prompted, her temper sparking.

He didn't blame her for getting angry. But he could hardly admit that now he had her alone, and with time on his side, the last thing he wanted to do was talk. He strove to resist the urge to pull her against him, to remind her that they already knew all they needed to make each other feel physically fantastic. 'We have eighteen months to discover whatever we actually need to know,' he growled dismissively. 'Right now I think it's best if you get some rest.'

Her jaw dropped. 'Are you sending me to bed?'

He couldn't tell if the provocation in her eyes and luscious pout was deliberate or not. But it was too powerful for him to stand. He stared at her for a long moment, his inner tension stringing him out.

'No, that's up to you,' he growled, mentally pleading with his hormones for mercy before rising and walking away. 'But *I* need some time out.'

CHAPTER THREE

'HEY.'

'Hey, yourself.'

Cool waves washed over Emmy's feet as she watched the tall hunk of stranger stroll across the white sands towards her as if he'd just walked off the set of an old-school Hepburn movie. He had sandals on and faded red swim shorts finished halfway down muscled thighs—but other than that, he was bare. The waistband of his shorts rode low and a little askew, revealing acres of bronzed skin, smoothly stretched over ridged abs and a wide, well-defined masculine chest. His shoulders were broad and strong. After a couple of moments she had to consciously close her mouth so she wasn't just standing there gaping at him, but it was almost impossible to believe he was real.

She blinked, pleased to discover he was still there. Still smiling. Still walking towards her. As he neared, she saw his face in greater detail—chiselled jaw, lips curved in an open smile—but it was the deep, dark brown eyes that ensnared her—cocoa-ringed black coffee, two of her favourite things and they were impossible to turn away from. She'd encountered a bunch of handsome tourists in her few months on the Galapagos so far, but none like this guy. And it wasn't his jaw-dropping handsome features—each one alone enough to melt any woman—it was the confident, casual manner with which he moved. He had an aura of easy assurance together with an indefinable quality that commanded attention even here, in one of the most untamed, unique places in the world where there were mind-blowing wonders to see in every direction.

Emmy grew conscious of her green bikini—not that it was skimpy, but it hardly hid her curves. Sadly her kaftan was further up the sand in a heap of worn silk, beneath the watchful gaze of one of the many resting sea lions. She'd spent the day combing the beaches for any small pieces of plastic as part of her volunteer placement with the Flores Foundation and had come to the water to cool off and have some quiet time.

'You might want to watch out for my friend there.' She jerked her head towards the nearby sea lion as the man set down the old rucksack he'd had slung over one shoulder. An ancient wetsuit sleeve poked out of the broken zipper opening.

'He's possessive?' The handsome man cast a curious glance at the creature.

'And he has a few friends a few more feet away.'

He nodded and turned back to her with a smile. 'Amazing, isn't it? An incredible beach with beautiful, wild things everywhere.'

'Yes.' But she shied away from the glint of intimacy and double meaning in his eyes. 'There's so much beauty, it's hard to know where to look.'

'Oh, I know exactly where to look.' He watched her intently.

She couldn't break away from his gaze and as she watched, a wicked smile backlit his eyes.

'I've been admiring the boobies,' he added softly.

She rolled her eyes, but he'd said it so lightly, with such a disarming smile, that it didn't sound either sleazy or cheesy when rightfully it ought to have been both. *'Really.'*

'You know, the bluer the feet, the more attractive the bird,' he added conversationally, as if he'd been talking about the birds all along.

The red-and blue-footed boobies were unique to the Galapagos—some curious, some ambivalent, all fascinating.

'And you know it's the males who need to woo their mate,' she said. *'They're* the ones who have to look good and do all the hard work.'

His grin widened to one of pure appreciation. 'Dance well? Strut hard and puff out their chests?'

'Generally look ridiculous, yes.'

'Ridiculous?' He pressed his hand to his very fine chest. 'Ouch.' Laughter crinkled the corners of his eyes.

His smile was the sort that stole hearts at first glance. Her pulse, already thready, sped faster. 'You shouldn't be here, you know.'

'It's private?'

'It's late,' she corrected. 'You might get lost trying to find your way back.'

'Is there a dragon who appears at dusk, to protect its fair maiden?'

Fair maiden? *Really?* She bit back a laugh. 'Perhaps I'm the dragon. My hair only hints at my fire.'

'That I can believe.' He slowly smiled again.

'Yet it doesn't scare you off?'

'Oh, no,' he said breezily. 'I'm not afraid of getting burned.'

She laughed out loud at that. 'Perhaps you should be. You shouldn't be scarred.'

His eyebrows danced upwards. 'Maybe my skin is thick and impenetrable and thus does a very good job of protecting my vital organs.'

'Such as your heart?' She nodded with another little laugh, so not surprised by that idea. 'So if you're so well armoured, then your prey must surely be at greater risk.'

'Risk? From me?' He smiled but there was seriousness in his eyes and he slowly shook his head. 'Dragons are rare and potentially vulnerable, and I don't think beautiful wild creatures should be either tamed or slain. Ideally they're not hurt in any way. I think they should be admired and appreciated and allowed to remain free.'

Of course he did—how safe for him. She suspected he was the wildest of all the beautiful creatures—not *her* at all. But she chuckled at the weak flirtation.

'What's your name?' he asked.

'Emerald.'

'Green?' He frowned slightly. 'You could be Sapphire, for your eyes.'

'I think my parents hoped my eyes might darken that way…'

'But you did your own thing?'

'Always.' It was a bit of bravado, because she hadn't always. But she did now. She'd learned well. Independence was everything. But perhaps, not isolation—not all the time. Not when she was confronted with a temptation like no other. Her heart thudded faster as he smiled.

'You could be Ruby for your hair, Pearl for your smile or Goldie for your skin—'

'Oh, no.' She rolled her eyes at the ridiculousness. 'That's too much of a leap. You can't get past these…' She pointed at the freckles on her arm, an example of the speckles that covered her all over.

'They're beautiful.' He shrugged lightly. 'The sun has kissed where I want to.'

Her jaw dropped that time. 'They're everywhere.'

'Precisely.'

'Oh.' She flushed awkwardly. 'Smooth.'

He laughed, a light teasing dare. 'You're such a treasure, I think I should call you *preciosa*.'

'Sure. You can do that.' She rolled her eyes.

His Spanish flowed and she suspected he was perfectly bilingual, in fact he probably spoke other languages too. He had an air of complete capability—as if he'd be a champion surfer as well, a super-achiever in all areas of life.

'And what should I call you?' she asked.

'Ramon.' There'd been the slightest hesitation before he replied. 'Why are you here?' he asked. 'All alone and looking like you just emerged from the sea like some mythical creature destined to destroy the heart of some poor hapless man?'

'I already told you.' She smiled. 'I'm waiting for the moon to complete my transformation into a dragon. And you're hardly hapless—you have that flame-proof skin, right?'

'So I've always thought.' His gaze dipped before flicking back up to her face.

That frisson travelled along her wiring, electrifying her circuitry. She saw the flash of recognition in his cocoa and coffee eyes. It didn't matter what they were saying—the weak innuendo and frothy banter was amusing but ultimately meaningless. Because it was already there, that connection forged between them at first glance. Absolute and instant attraction, translating to heat and want. And Emmy—who'd never encouraged even the slightest of flirtations, who'd never actually felt the desire

to before—found herself sliding at speed into the ultimate temptation. For the first time, she reached for a moment she truly wanted, a moment with a man for herself.

'Shall I show you something even more beautiful?'
she asked huskily.

His eyes widened. 'Yes, please.'

The bay was stunningly private. A colourful Sally
Lightfoot crab scuttled and under the watchful gaze
of wildlife unafraid of human contact, she trod a path
known only to a few. Emmy didn't trust other people
the way these animals did. It was only a short walk to
another, smaller bay even more private than the first. It
was rarely visited; people didn't get past that other one,
thinking they'd made it to paradise already. But it was
here, hidden and safe. Set back from the sand was an
old wooden boat shed that belonged to her boss, Lucero
Flores. It was his private place, set on the very edge of
his holdings.

'This is incredible,' Ramon muttered as he reached
out to take her hand as naturally and easily as breathing.

Emmy's pulse stumbled.

It was a stunning, magical secret but for the first time
she was happy to share it. 'Isn't it?'

Time stretched as they walked the length of the beach
and explored the shed—laughingly dodging the wildlife
unafraid to make it their home already. And somehow
that invisible connection pulled them together. A languor-
ous heat invaded her limbs, slowing her movements as
he closed the last gap to brush his lips across hers. That
frisson of electricity skated down her spine and radiated
along her limbs.

'Ramon,' she breathed. 'Ramon.'

It was the oddest, most delicious thing. She was melting, while at the same time energy coiled deep within.

With a sigh she let it release, lost in sensations she'd not known she was capable of. All she knew was that she wanted more.

Emmy woke with a start, the soft cotton sheets tangled around her and her own voice echoing in her head. The dream wasn't a dream, it was a *memory*—every word real and she was burning as hot as the moment it had actually happened. Horrified, she clutched the sheet and sat up—she'd been moaning his name!

Or at least, his *other* name.

She gazed at the open door where light gleamed and quickly scrambled from the bed. She was utterly mortified, hoping she hadn't woken her son. Or that anyone *else* had heard her. She ran along the corridor and into Luke's room but froze on the threshold. The sheets were pulled back to reveal his empty cot.

Panic hit like a bucket of iced water. She froze where seconds ago she'd been searing. She hurriedly returned to her room, pulled on her dress. With a push of a button the heavy curtains slid back from the large windows. She stared out in horror. The marina was missing. There was only the vast blue of the pristine Pacific Ocean. They were no longer off the coast of Santa Cruz. In fact, now she'd stopped to think, she realised the yacht was actually moving and she had no idea where they were. Or where Luke was. Not stopping to drag a comb through her curls, she sprinted upstairs, cursing the size of the yacht and all the confusing levels.

'Javier?' she called as she finally found the dining deck. 'Where—?' She broke off, startled to see two suited men seated at the table with a far too relaxed-looking Javier.

Who were they? When had they arrived? Where was Luke?

'Ah, Emmy.' Javier stood before she could ask any of the billion questions flooding her head. 'Come through, Luke will be excited to see you.' He sheltered her from the eyes of those two men. 'He's just through here.'

'You left him alone?' Emmy whispered as she followed him down another corridor.

'Of course not.'

A few feet from the open doorway she could see Luke safely ensconced on a play mat with one of the crew. 'Why didn't you wake me?'

'You were fast asleep, I didn't want to disturb you.'

Emmy froze. He'd seen her sleeping? Fragments of that dream—that memory—assailed her, smothering her with hot embarrassment…and painful yearning.

She shook the weakness off. That evening hadn't been magical, it had been a mistake. He'd had condoms in his bag—more than one—like the carefree casual sex-slayer he was. And they'd used them—reckless yes, but not stupid. But they'd not realised at the time that one had failed.

She blinked and focused on Luke. The best thing to ever hit her life was sitting in the middle of the massive lounge, his worn play mat had been replaced and a vast assortment of new toys were scattered about him— wooden stacking boxes, several soft-looking small balls and some cute carved animals. One of the stewards was kneeling beside him, playing peek-a-boo. At their arrival the steward stood and looked to Javier, who nodded in dismissal, and she swiftly disappeared out of the far door.

'There's a nanny—'

'You've engaged a nanny?' she interrupted him in a fierce whisper. 'Without even meeting her?'

'I'm meeting *him* now,' Javier explained with exaggerated patience. 'He's one of the men back in the dining room.'

'Him?' Emmy's blood pounded loudly in her ears.

'You have a problem with that?'

'I have a problem with not having any input.' She shook her head. 'And I know what you're going to say—you haven't had any in the last nine months.'

'Calm down, Emmy. Yes, I'm angry and, yes, I'm going to need time, but I'm not completely insensitive. You know Luke best, so I was waiting for you to interview the nanny with me, and there are other CVs we can go through if you're not comfortable with how this one checks out.'

'How did you get him here already?'

'I don't sleep as soundly as you,' he muttered. 'I arranged it through the night.'

The truth was she hadn't slept soundly at all—it had taken hours to fall asleep and when she finally had, she'd been tormented by repeats of that dream.

'But before we interview him, there's someone else who'd like to talk to you briefly,' Javier added before disappearing back down the corridor.

Emmy scooped up Luke and watched worriedly as Javier returned with the older of the two men.

'I've spent a lovely half-hour with your son this morning.' The man smiled at her patronisingly. 'I'm Dr Morales, a children's specialist.'

Emmy forced herself to maintain her smile but she was shocked. Javier had had a *paediatrician* look over their son?

'I only had a couple of questions,' he said amiably enough. 'Has Luke ever been on any regular medication?'

'No, never.' She shook her head. 'He's been very

healthy. Only a little grizzly with his first tooth and a small cold once.'

'He's a lovely boy.' The doctor smiled down at her. 'You've cared for him well.'

Emmy was so angry she couldn't think of an adequate response. Fortunately Javier led him away moments later, only to return and tell her it was time to meet the prospective nanny.

That interview process was easy. She sat Luke on her knee and read over the man's résumé while Javier grilled him to the point that Emmy actually felt bad for the guy. His CV was insanely impressive—not only were there papers on child psychology, nutrition and development in his four-year degree, there were courses in defensive driving, cybersecurity and escaping the paparazzi. It took only moments for her to understand that Javier wouldn't allow anyone on board and near Luke who wasn't utterly overqualified and from some elite school. He was used to the best and expected the best from everyone in his life. And he wanted only the best for his son. It was terrifying.

'Emmy?'

She belatedly realised Javier was waiting for her to ask a question.

'Would you mind a probation period, Thomas?' she asked. 'And if you work under observation with Luke initially?'

'Of course.' He smiled.

Javier looked at her and she nodded. She was shamefully glad that there wasn't going to be a pretty nanny staying with them. She knew it was ridiculous of her. She had no right to be jealous of any imaginary nanny being around Javier—she had no hold over *him*. It was Luke she was really concerned about. But she wasn't going to lose time with her son. As she had no job the nanny was going to be virtually redundant most of the time. But that wasn't her problem. Javier wanted to make some decisions here, this was one she wouldn't fight.

An hour later Emmy sat with Thomas, the new nanny, as he met Luke. Through the open doorway she saw Javier casually guide Dr Morales to the helicopter that had appeared on the top rear deck. She had no idea how she'd slept through the arrival of a helicopter. Or through the boat engine firing up and moving them so far from her home.

It scared her that Javier had achieved so much so quickly, but she masked her concerns, staying with Luke and the new nanny until it was time for her son to take a nap. Then she stayed until her son fell asleep, quietly talking Thomas through Luke's routines. Eventually a steward appeared and invited Thomas to follow him so he could get a tour of the yacht.

Emmy took the baby monitor she'd discovered with her so she could hear if Luke woke. Then she walked up the stairs to discover Javier sitting back on the pool deck, looking as if he hadn't a care in the world. As he caught her eye his chin lifted. Something sparked in his expression, as if he'd been waiting for her to find him.

'You know, I don't need your fancy doctor to tell me I've done a good job, like some patronising man…' She inhaled deeply. 'I know I've made mistakes, but I've done the best I could.'

'I know that.' Javier's gaze narrowed on her. 'Maybe the doctor should've checked you over too. You still look tired even though you slept late.'

'It takes more than one night to recover from months of sleep deprivation.' She tried to snatch a breath and calm down, but it was a losing battle. 'I don't need anyone to look me over,' she muttered. 'I'm perfectly healthy.'

'Then it won't be a problem for him to see you. We can recall the chopper—'

'Don't you dare,' she snapped. 'That would be such an invasion of my privacy. I won't have him reporting to you on my well-being.'

'So I'm not to be concerned about you in any way?'

'No. You're not. Stop trying to do the "right" thing all the time.'

'Stop *what*?' He frowned deeply at her. 'You really don't trust my intentions, do you?'

'And you really don't trust me,' she answered. 'I understand it, but to think that Luke might be unwell in some way…? Or that I might have mistreated him…? Or not cared for him properly…? I have put him first in every way I can—' She broke off.

Javier stared at her and slowly shook his head. 'Emerald, I wasn't questioning your capability as a mother.'

'No?' She was so hurt by his action. 'Isn't that exactly what that was?'

'I didn't mean it to be, but I can understand that it might have come across as offensive. I just…' A grim expression tightened his face as he trailed off.

Emmy stared at him impatiently. 'You just what?' She shook her head when he still didn't respond. 'See?' His *so* controlled reticence infuriated her. 'You just don't trust me.'

His expression tightened and he stepped forward. 'I feel compelled to know everything,' he ground out with clear reluctance.

She paused as she heard the raw edge to his admission. 'About Luke?' she clarified softly. 'You can ask me,' she assured him quickly. 'Ask me anything. I want him to have a good relationship with you.'

At that Javier seemed to lose a touch of colour and

Emmy stepped closer—was he worried he wasn't going to be a good father to their son?

'I've missed out on so much,' he muttered so softly. 'What if I can't ever make it up…?'

Her heart ached as she realised how much she'd hurt him. She felt appalled at how close she'd come to denying both Javier and Luke this relationship. She should have contacted him. She should have given him the chance. Instinctively she put her hand on his arm in both apology and reassurance.

'He's so young and he's very loving,' she promised.

She felt Javier's muscles tense beneath her touch and suddenly the atmosphere was charged. Before she could lift her hand away he'd clamped his over the top of hers, pressing her palm against his hot skin. He stepped back and sat on the sofa. By the nature of his hold on her, she had to sit too. Right beside him.

Maybe she should have resisted more. But it flickered between them—that shimmering, powerful thing that sent shivers along her nerve-endings and made her hold her breath. That dangerous, beguiling thing.

His gaze was very dark and deep as he smoothed his hand over the back of hers and then flipped hers over to inspect her palm. 'Why did you work so hard?'

'I owed Connie everything,' she answered, trying to mask the sudden tightness in her lungs. 'Without her, I would've had nowhere to go.'

His grip on her tensed and she sought to make him understand somehow.

'We were in a safe, beautiful place, had a roof over our heads, food on the table,' she tried to explain. 'It might not have been perfect—' She broke off at his snort. 'But it was the best I could do.'

'It didn't have to be like that. You didn't have to work all hours…'

She frowned at him. 'But—'

'I would have helped you,' he growled roughly. 'I would have done everything in my power to help you. You didn't *need* to do this on your own.'

Regret rose, smashing down the last of her defences.

'Don't,' she mumbled as that other emotion spilled, overwhelming her to the point where she had to reject him. 'Don't say nice things to me.'

He stared at her for a second. 'Then what should I do?' he asked with the gentlest of tease in his tone. 'Berate you? Bully you? What am I supposed to do?'

'I don't know.'

His sudden soft chuckle was a torturous reminder of the carefree, humorous man she'd met that night. He'd been playful and kind and she'd instinctively trusted him with so very much. And now something wild and free soared again, enabling her to laugh with him in an effervescent release and for just a moment that terrible tension eased. A split second later tears sprang to her eyes.

'I'm sorry,' she whispered. She was truly sorry she hadn't been able to contact him for so long. And more so that she'd chosen not to when she'd finally found out who he really was.

'I know,' he whispered back, and his beautiful cocoa gaze bored into hers. 'I'm sorry too.'

They'd not meant for this to happen. They'd not meant for a fantasy escape to have such serious repercussions.

'We can move forward,' she breathed.

He stared back at her silently and that charge in the atmosphere strengthened.

But this wasn't what she'd meant. Not this curling heat. She thought they'd just had a breakthrough—but that tiny moment of honesty was now submerged by the need rearing between them again. Intense, unstoppable and inescapable. It was more than a minor itch or low ache. It was a furious hunger and every time she got within five feet of him, it burned. She could barely resist the pull to lean closer still. His hand held hers loosely but she was incarcerated by the spiralling emotions. Flames flickered promise and pleasure. She stared into his eyes and he leaned towards her slowly. Closer, closer still until the conflagration ignited.

'We sh-shouldn't…' She was so breathless now.

But he was so close, his mouth brushed hers even as she tried to speak. 'We sh—'

'Shh,' he commanded and his lips silenced hers.

Her eyes closed and her mouth parted on a sigh of surrender as ecstasy surged through her. She moaned as she felt his answering tremor. His arms went hard and tight around her and she sank against him. In seconds she was utterly breathless, desperate for more. All her cares and concerns—actually all her *brains*—were lost. There was nothing but this touch and the hot fierce temptation that shivered through every cell.

She'd thought she remembered. But she'd not—not the intensity and shimmering raw pleasure to be found right here in his kiss.

She'd never regretted the night she'd spent in his—a stranger's—arms. She'd never questioned her choice to gift him her virginity so swiftly and easily. Because the touch, the pleasure she'd discovered with him, in his body, had been the most ultimate sensation of her life. There'd been no uncertainty, no decision necessary. There'd only been desperation for more. But while swift, it hadn't felt carefree, nothing as easy as that. It had felt *undeniable*.

She'd been overwhelmed then, but the depth of the pleasure now was even sharper. It was as if her body remembered and were starved to the point that it wouldn't allow her to stop this—she literally couldn't pull back until the ultimate release had been gleaned. Her need for his touch was truly shocking—reducing her in this moment to a starving, feral creature, clinging to the source of possible satisfaction.

'Emmy.' With a growl he pulled her closer as if he knew how bad the ache was and he assuaged it only slightly with a powerful press of his body against hers. 'It's okay.'

But it wasn't. She wanted rid of her clothes. She ached for the absolute escape she'd found that night. It was insane that she sought this from the man who posed such a threat to her very soul. Her heart was all and only Luke's, but Javier could take everything else. And it was only that flashing realisation that shocked her from the mists of his seduction.

'No,' she cried—ordering herself to obey more than she was telling him.

Javier released her immediately. Except Emmy was so weakened she swayed after him. He swiftly reached out to grip her shoulders hard to steady her and settle her back from him on the sofa.

'I'm sorry,' she whispered. 'That shouldn't have happened.'

She ached when he released his hold on her a second time—her conflicting desires tearing her apart.

'That was inevitable,' he said roughly. 'You know it as well as I. It's still there, Emmy. As strong as it was the day we met. It's a force neither of us seem equipped to deny.' But there was more than a glimpse of triumph in his eyes.

'Well, we have to.' *She* had to.

Once more she'd all but fallen apart from a single touch—his to explore, to take, to pleasure. She couldn't believe the attraction was so intense and that she'd managed to pull back. She had to find a better defence against it. Because doing this again with him could only lead to trouble.

'Prevent biology?' He glanced at her sceptically. 'Nature wants us to procreate. It seems we're good at it.'

'Well, it's not happening again. That was a mistake.'

His lips twitched but he didn't reply.

'Nothing to say?' She wrapped her arms around her waist, hunching on the sofa.

'We have more important things to argue about.' He shrugged.

That was true, but he was good at avoiding *those* conversations, wasn't he?

'There's no mistake here, Emmy,' he said with that cool confidence. 'There's only what feels good. Why wouldn't you want to feel that again?' He watched her for another moment and his smile faded. 'You're tired.' He reached out and stroked her hair. 'So tired. Right?'

His statement stripped the facade from her and suddenly she couldn't move for exhaustion. All the adrenalin from the last twenty-four hours evaporated, leaving her utterly lacking in energy. He stood and stepped away from her. Regret stabbed but that tiredness swamped it out.

'Look, I'm sorry.' He glanced back at her and sighed. 'Just rest here for a bit. Thomas and I will take care of Luke. I won't...' He trailed off and rubbed in the region of his lowest rib. 'Just relax. You can now.'

CHAPTER FOUR

SHE'D BEEN ASLEEP for *hours*.

Javier paced quietly in the shaded part of the deck, holding Luke close to keep him calm. The child had woken a little while ago and, having had a drink, was now happy to be held and quietly talked to. Though admittedly Javier was running out of things to say. He'd walked around pointing out features of the boat, feeling a fool to think a nine-month-old could ever understand. But he had no clue what else to do and he had to start somewhere.

Javier shot Emmy another worried glance. She was too quiet and still. Protectiveness swept over him. Not just towards the small, sleepy child in his arms, but to that woman lying on the plush sofa. He'd never seen her like this. Peaceful, heart-seizingly beautiful, but vulnerable. She left him breathless.

At least she had more colour in her cheeks now. When he'd first walked into that small shop, she'd paled so quickly he'd wondered if she were about to faint. He'd been stunned that she'd been afraid of him. But of course she'd been terrified, given the massive secret she'd kept from him. And frankly, forgiving her for that was a struggle. He'd missed out on much that he couldn't recover.

Anger mixed with regret and that rush of raw, undeniable lust—the one he was constantly fighting. It had struck him sledgehammer-style all those months ago when she'd walked out of the sea like some siren temptation—all hips and breasts and bold, bold curves, fiery hair and gleaming skin. She'd been irresistible and the desire to make her his had been fierce. He'd busted out every ounce of charm he could muster because he'd wanted her so hard. The flare between them had gone so much further, so much faster than he'd anticipated. But his success had also been certain, because he'd seen it in her eyes too—they'd mirrored his own startled fascination. A flicker of electricity had bound them, drawing them closer together.

It had irked that she'd left before saying goodbye and without leaving him any way of contacting her. But he'd been at fault too, arrogantly failing to tell her his true name.

It hadn't crossed his mind that she'd been working on the islands and that he could've found her again easily. At the time he'd been sure she was a tourist and she'd not said anything to contradict the idea. Truthfully they'd not said all that much of meaning. There'd been flirtation and fun and, beneath, the simmering recognition of mutual attraction and unstoppable desire. Though then there'd been a startling confession—of her inexperience. She'd laughed as she'd admitted it—a bubbling sound of surprise, surrender and pure amusement, and the most primal wave of satisfaction had sunk his reason and he'd vowed to please her. There'd been nothing after that but heated magic—every touch better than the promise they'd both felt. And all he wanted now—the one thought consuming him—was to do it again.

But now it was complicated. He rolled his shoulders, irritated by his own changeability. Seeming to sense Javier's tension, Luke rubbed his face with his little hand, his expression crumpling.

'Mamá's just over there,' Javier awkwardly tried to reassure him with a soft whisper. 'See? She's resting.'

She stirred and Javier stilled, watching as she blinked, then she suddenly sat up, her blue eyes wide.

'It's okay,' Javier said huskily. 'He's here. I've got him.'

Her arms lifted automatically and Javier walked over. Emmy cradled the baby against her soft curves. Her cheeks flushed fractionally more and the gentlest of smiles lit her from within.

Javier stared down at them both, unable to step back. After a moment she looked up at him. Her eyes were dreamy blue now she had her child. But as they regarded each other in solemn silence, wariness stole into them and then that altogether different tension twisted again. All he wanted to do was kiss her again.

'You must be hungry.' He forced himself to speak but it emerged as a hoarse mutter.

She nodded, her gaze dropping. He made himself turn and message the staff, cursing his own weakness.

When he turned back, she'd settled Luke more comfortably on her knee and was looking across the water. 'The engines have stopped. Where are we?'

'Just off the coast of Pinta.'

'This is Pinta?'

He was surprised that she didn't recognise it. 'You've not been here?'

She shook her head.

'But you've been living on the islands for…'

'Just over two years.' She shrugged. 'I've been working.'

'Then perhaps it's time to take a break.' He sat in the

deckchair across from the plush sofa she'd slept on, determinedly maintaining distance and respect.

That wariness returned to her eyes. She was right to be cautious, because he was faking being friendly. As if he were some really good guy who wanted to do right by the woman he'd seduced and the baby she'd then had?

If she only knew what was really going through his mind. Here she was, exhausted from caring for their son for months all by herself and all he could think about was how badly he wanted to tumble her back into bed.

He made himself look at his son and it was a good move, because that awkward feeling returned. He had no clue how to become a father. It was partly why he'd wanted a nanny on board so soon, so he had an expert on hand as well as someone to lift a bit of that load from Emerald. Because he sure as hell couldn't do that yet. He wasn't sure he'd ever be able to.

And he needed to know more about her. Now he'd had a chance to think, he wondered what she'd meant about people judging her the second they learned her name? What was it that had made her afraid to seek him out even for financial support for Luke when she clearly desperately needed it? What was she hiding? Because there had to be something and it had to be big.

'What were you going to tell him when he asked?' he tried to ask mildly.

Emmy shifted on the sofa, startled by the raw edge to Javier's question.

'He would have asked eventually,' he added. 'He'd meet other children with involved fathers. He would've wanted to know about his. So what were you planning to tell him?'

Emmy's heart ached as she read that banked emotion in Javier's eyes and heard the husky edge—as if these were questions he hated having to ask. 'I don't know,' she confessed. 'I was avoiding thinking about it.'

She'd told herself that she could be enough on her own. But not to tell Luke about Javier wouldn't have been fair in the long run. And not finding out if Javier was interested in being involved had been wrong. She should have given him the option, but fear had governed her and somehow she had to explain that to him without telling him everything. Because even though he was trying hard now, she had too much to lose to trust him completely.

'I know I should have contacted you as soon as I knew who you were, but I was so tired and I was just...'

'Furious because you thought I'd lied to you deliberately?' He filled in after her long silence. 'Because I had some bad reason for hiding my identity?'

She had known he'd lied and that had hurt. But it wasn't *only* that that had thrown her. It was the discovery of his status and wealth. A surfing tourist she could have handled. But she couldn't compete with what he could offer. She'd been terrified.

'Actually...' she strove for a measure of truth '... I wanted to succeed on my own,' she admitted awkwardly. 'I didn't want anything—not just from you, but from *anyone*. I was so sick of...' She shook her head, hating having to confess this and unable to articulate it properly. 'I decided I could manage. Luke would be mine and I would be his and we wouldn't need anyone else. I never wanted us to need anyone else. I thought—hoped—that I could be enough for him and that I could do a good job.' To her total mortification, tears spiked on her eyelashes and she furiously blinked them away. 'I didn't want you accusing me of trapping you. Everyone always thinks the worst. The things a couple of people said when they found out I was pregnant... One actually insinuated he was Lucero's baby because I'd named him after him. So I wanted to prove that I could do this on my own. I think I lost perspective.' She drew in a shaking breath. 'But that wasn't fair on Luke and it wasn't fair on you and I'm sorry.'

He was silent for a long moment.

'I accept your apology,' he said formally. 'And I'm sorry I lied that night. I have no real excuse other than I just wanted a night off from being me. I'm sorry I didn't try harder to track you down when I came back. I'm sorry you've been doing this alone all this time.' He stepped closer. 'And I'm sorry I made you feel like you were being judged, or that I was patronising you when I brought in that doctor. But I'm not patronising you now. I'm just being honest. Luke is an amazing little boy and that's all because of you.'

She stared up at him, feeling the fragility of this peace offering and longing to accept it. To believe in it. To hope that perhaps they could make this work. But then she remembered that he knew nothing of who she really was. And when he discovered that shame of her past? She forced her gaze towards the azure water. She couldn't trust that the truth wouldn't be used to take Luke from her.

'Señor Torres?'

Relief and regret hit in equal measure as a steward interrupted them to deliver a platter of fresh fruit, cheese and cold cuts. Emmy snaffled a piece of apple, savouring its juicy freshness and the distraction it provided, and gave Luke one of the baby crackers that had been thoughtfully put on the plate.

'So why were you angry when you learned who I was?' Javier asked after a bit. 'Was it because I'd bought Lucero's property? Or because I'd lied?'

Her nerves tightened. He was so far out of her league—wealthy and powerful—she'd been sure he'd take Luke from her if he knew. He still could.

She needed more time to figure out how she could convince him that she was a good influence on Luke's life. So she diverted her answer. 'I loved Lucero's property how it was—the age of the old hostel, that old boathouse and the value of his foundation for getting volunteers to help keep everything around here pristine. I know it was a little run-down, but I was afraid of what you're going to do with it.'

'But isn't it a good thing for that property to be developed? You must know Lucero wanted it cared for,' he said. 'He didn't have the energy or resources to do it himself. He trusted that to me.'

'To you?' Her stomach dropped. 'You met him?'

'I returned a few months after...' He cleared his throat. 'I was looking for an opportunity here and approached him when I learned he owned that property.'

Javier had been back to the Galapagos before now? And she'd not run into him?

'But I would've known if you'd seen Lucero,' she said, trying to reject the terrible regret rising within her. 'I was his carer round the clock towards the end.'

Javier frowned. 'He told me his carer was called Esme. She was visiting another island when I was there.'

She gasped. 'He called me Esmerelda when he was being grand—Esme for short.'

'Esme. Emerald...' He muttered something indecipherable beneath his breath and then looked at her with a rueful shake of his head.

That shimmering electricity fluttered between them. Fate. It had failed them that time.

'So why did you name our son after him?' he asked quietly.

That question was easy. 'Because he was a good man,' she said simply. 'He gave me a home and I hadn't had one in a while.' She fell silent, realising what she'd just admitted and hoping Javier wouldn't ask why. She rubbed little Luke's back as he sucked on the cracker and quickly thought of a question of her own. 'Why did you want the hostel?' she asked. 'Was it just the location?'

'Mmm.' Now Javier glanced away, his gaze skimming the blue waters. 'Why not go for a swim?' he suggested. 'It's a beautiful afternoon. It'll refresh you after the sleep.'

She shook her head and looked down at Luke in her lap, disappointed by him avoiding directly answering her.

'I'll hold him while you're out there,' Javier offered, and then rolled his eyes at her continued hesitation. 'I promise not to make off with him when you're half a mile from the boat.'

She half chuckled. 'You're not going to turn on the engines and leave me in the middle of the ocean?'

'Of course not,' he said. 'Maybe *you* might try to trust *me*?'

She couldn't hold his gaze for long; the gleam in his eyes threatened to mesmerise her all over again. And the regret she felt?

'I'm not going to hurt him, Emmy.'

'I know,' she muttered with a sad shake of her head. 'I never thought you would.'

She was the one who was going to be hurt. She'd feared it from the moment she'd found out his true identity, and from the second he'd walked back into her life she'd known it would be inevitable.

'Then give him to me and go get changed.'

The water was tempting and she desperately needed to cool down and regain some thinking time. She hadn't taken a proper swim in so long; she'd always had Luke with her. But there was a kind of freedom she only felt in the water. And she knew Javier understood that—they'd bonded over it that night they'd been together.

Down in her cabin, she realised her old green bikini didn't fit as well as it once had. She covered up by draping one of the large, soft towels in her private bathroom around her and then walked out to the rear deck.

Javier was there holding Luke and they were sporting matching floppy-brimmed hats, casting their faces in the shade. Javier's gaze glittered as she dropped the towel and put it on the top step.

'I can't tell you how many times I've thought about that bikini,' he said huskily.

Emmy swallowed hard and she pretended she hadn't heard him. The thinnest tendril of trust was blossoming between them, but that raging physical need threatened to overshadow—or stomp on—that tender shooting stem. She pressed her lips together, holding in the sharp yearning to turn and lean against his body. As crazy, as wrong as it was, she couldn't deny her desire. But she could try to ignore it.

She turned her back, hiding how her heavy breasts had tightened in response to his mere look. They were almost too big for the stretchy fabric encasing them. She stepped down, bracing in the cold water. She struck out strongly, swimming hard, then dived beneath the clear waves. She'd missed this so much—the total liberation as she submerged and let the cold soothe her heated skin.

Animals, as always in this remote, fascinating part of the world, came close. Curious and unafraid and enchanting—

tortoise, sea lions, birds. A weight slipped free, letting her float and enjoy the serene peace of the sea.

Eventually she returned to the boat, climbing up the stairs that made it so easy to get in and out. Physically tired but happy, she wrapped herself in the towel.

Javier had retreated up to the pool deck and was now sprawled with Luke on the shaded sofa. As Emmy walked up to check on Luke, she warily glanced at Javier—had she taken too long? His expression was unreadable behind the sunglasses he'd put on. 'I haven't swum like that in ages, thank you for that,' she said.

Javier didn't answer but Luke gurgled.

'Let me have him.' Impulsively she let her towel fall. 'He loves the water.'

Javier leaned forward. 'He swims already?'

Emmy undressed Luke and lifted him into the warmer water of the onboard pool with her. Luke squawked happily as she swished him through the water. Javier stood at the pool's edge and watched, a smile slowly spreading over his face. Emmy's heart bumped as she heard him laugh. The carefree humour reminded her of that first night. 'You want to hold him?'

She didn't wait for him to answer, she just handed Luke to him.

Javier laughed throatily as Luke bounced excitedly in his arms and wet him completely.

'You mind if I come in with you?' he asked huskily.

'Of course not.' Her mouth dried as she took Luke back from him.

Javier's shirt had got wet from wrestling with their wriggling, giggling, soaked son. She tried not to gape as he peeled it from his body, but it was then impossible not to stare at his rippling muscles as he entered the water and took Luke from her again. The fiercest wave of heat engulfed her at the sight of him engaging with their son. A primal, powerful surge of feminine pride followed— he was the father of her child, he was her *mate*—and her body wanted him again.

Except he *wasn't* hers.

She stepped out of the pool and into the shade, embarrassed by the fierce reaction of her body at the sight of Javier in nothing but swim shorts. That earlier, incendiary kiss lingered on her lips like an illicit sizzle and she wanted another burn.

He laughed lightly again. 'He's a natural,' he called to her. 'No surprise given he's your son.'

Emmy couldn't answer because her heart was in her throat.

Fortunately Javier then called for the nanny. Thomas appeared and capably swept Luke into a massive, soft towel.

'I think he's ready for a tidy-up and a snack,' Javier said smoothly to Thomas and then glanced at Emmy. 'We need time to relax over dinner.'

'Of course.'

Emmy anxiously watched Thomas take Luke inside. But it wasn't that she didn't trust the man with her baby, it was that she didn't trust herself to be alone with her son's father.

CHAPTER FIVE

EMMY WAITED FOR the last page to emerge from the printer and then gathered the leaves of paper together. She'd been in the blindingly well-equipped onboard office for two hours but she was finally done. She stood and stretched in a fruitless attempt to ease the tension from her body.

She'd tried talking to Javier about light things at dinner last night—but the monosyllabic replies she'd got from the most innocuous of questions had swiftly taught her that he wasn't interested in opening up. And perhaps that was good. So she'd then been careful, keeping conversation utterly focused on Luke, and she'd escaped to her suite as soon as they'd put him to bed. She couldn't trust herself around Javier. Not after that kiss. Apparently he was her personal Kryptonite and when she was around him, all rational capacity to think fled, leaving her as little more than a ball of raw desire. To be so undone by hormones was mortifying. The only way to get through it with even a smidge of dignity was to keep her distance.

She knew she needed to let Javier have time with Luke without her hovering as if afraid he were about to make off with him. He needed to forge his own relationship with his son. She'd denied them both that for too long and felt terrible about it.

In the middle of the night—when her stupid brain

wouldn't shut down—she'd thought of one small way she might alleviate some of his loss, but now she'd finished, she was nervous about giving it to him.

She walked through to the pool deck to find Javier alone with Luke. She stopped in the doorway, somewhat stunned to see him engaged in the task of finishing up a nappy change.

He glanced up. 'What?' he sounded defensive.

'You did a good job.' The second she said it she realised she sounded as patronising to him as that doctor had been to her yesterday. But she hadn't meant to be. Javier had said he hadn't meant to either. She was prickly and too defensive and right now so was he.

'The first time I put his nappy on backwards,' she admitted with a shy smile. 'The nurse in the hospital broke it to me so kindly and then showed me how to do it properly.'

Javier sat back and a rueful expression softened the hardness in his eyes. 'I looked up instructions online.'

'Really?' Her grin widened.

'And I checked with Thomas for good measure.' He lifted his son back down to his play mat, where he immediately crawled over to his favourite toy, sat down and stuck it in his mouth.

'You did?' Emmy was surprised. 'You seem so capable, like you're just naturally brilliant at everything you attempt, first time.'

'No.' He laughed softly. 'Definitely not.'

She didn't believe him. He had that aura of surety about him.

'Most people need to try things a couple of times before they get the hang of it,' he said lightly, but his gaze was unwavering and unbearably intense.

Suddenly the most inappropriate recollection ran in

her head. To make it worse, she had the suffocating feeling he sensed exactly what it was that she was remembering.

Their night. Her first times—*all* of them with him. And that intimacy, that sweetness, had turned so hot. She'd adored the muffled laughter that they'd shared before she could only moan. It had been the ultimate seduction.

'I have something for you,' she said, desperately changing the subject so she wouldn't be blinded into brainlessness by that smile. Her face burned as she held out the slim booklet she'd hidden behind her back. He took it from her, his eyebrows lifting in silent query.

'My phone isn't that great, but I took snaps of Luke all the time this year. Like, hundreds of photos,' she babbled nervously. 'I thought you might like some…'

She trailed off as Javier opened the booklet to the first page and then flicked to the next. And suddenly she worried that it would upset him somehow.

'I didn't do it to make you see what you've missed…' She bit her lip anxiously, watching him go through the booklet.

He was too quiet. Did he hate it?

'I hope it's okay I asked the staff if you had a printer on board,' she explained.

It turned out there was an entire office suite that was stocked with all the stationery imaginable, including photo paper. She'd borrowed a computer and loaded the photos, compiling and printing them into a small book using a graphics platform—adding captions beneath to explain how old Luke had been and what the milestone or moment was. It hadn't taken long. The hardest part had been picking which of the many pictures she'd use. She'd even bound it with a piece of ribbon she'd found.

But staring at it now, as Javier went through it page by page, ever so slowly, it looked flimsy and excruciatingly home-made.

Embarrassment burned from her skin, through every vital organ and deep into her bones.

'We can get them printed professionally, of course,' she muttered hopelessly. 'I just wanted you to have the pictures now. There are loads more. I've put them all onto that computer for you, so you have them digitally as well.'

She felt appallingly vulnerable watching him silently turn each page, inspecting each picture she'd selected. Luke having his first bath. His playful smile. On his tummy. Playing in the sand. Javier went all the way through the booklet to the final page and then returned to the first one. It was a black and white shot and it was the only one that featured her as well.

'I just included that because it's the very first picture of him,' she explained in a rushing whisper. 'One of the nurses in the hospital took it moments after he was born.'

A very tiny Luke was lying on her chest. She'd been vain enough to print it in black and white so the ravages of childbirth were less obvious on her face. Not that Javier would want pictures of *her*, of course, but his son. And this pretty much was his son's first moment alive in the world.

'Thank you for this,' he said quietly. 'The photos are beautiful.'

Awkwardly she bent and put together a few of the loose toys, just to avoid looking at him. 'I have an app on my phone to override the usual camera settings and amp up the results a bit.'

'You took these on your phone?' he asked.

She nodded.

'You have a good eye for composition.'

'It helps that I'm completely in love with my subject,' she muttered dryly. Her son was the absolute light and joy of her life. 'I have hundreds—you can have them all. I take them, not to get some stylised perfect shot, but to bring that moment back. The emotions, the story behind that stupid pose, or why I was out looking at the sunset that day…an aide-memoire, you know? Not for anyone else but me.' She realised she was babbling. 'Sorry to be boring.'

'I'm not bored. I want to see the photos. I want you to tell me the stories behind them.'

She glanced down at him and then narrowed her gaze. Her little boy was sitting with a curiously fierce expression on his face. She smothered her spreading smile.

'What is it?' Javier noticed her reaction and turned to survey Luke's stillness on the mat.

'Uh,' she half laughed beneath her breath. 'I think he's testing your nappy skills.'

'Seriously?' Javier looked miffed. 'I just changed it.'

Emmy leaned forward and sniffed delicately. 'Um… well, he needs another change.' She stood.

'I'll do it.' Javier scooped Luke up. 'But I think we need to be in the nursery.'

Emmy hesitated. 'You don't want Thomas to handle this one?' She followed him through to the nursery. 'The poor guy's twiddling his thumbs down on the crew deck.'

'Dream job.' Javier sent her an ironically amused glance. 'I figure, if I can handle this…'

He was determined to learn and be hands-on, not just seeing Luke as 'his' in the sense of a possession. And while that ought to please her and she knew it was best for her baby, it scared her too. What if eventually Luke chose Javier over her? She wouldn't blame him, not when his father could give him so much more than she ever could. She braced against the insecurity eating away at her insides. She had to be better than this—for Luke if nothing else.

'Do you want me to take a photo of you two, when he's decent again?' She bit her lip as she waited for Javier's answer. 'You know, as an aide-memoire for this moment?'

Javier's hands stilled and he glanced her. '*Sí*, thanks.' He bent over Luke and smothered a groan. 'But I hope we have gas masks somewhere.'

She chuckled and went to fetch her phone. With his permission she'd take photos any chance she could... mentally working on part two of his photo book. But when she returned, Javier had finished and he passed Luke to her.

'He needs you. He's starting to fret.'

Luke curled against her, his grizzling instantly silenced. 'He's just tired,' she explained a little guiltily to Javier.

'It's okay, Emmy. I know it's going to take a little time.'

She shifted Luke to her hip and turned away from that look in his eyes. She was a fool for reading double meanings into everything he said. Javier wanted to build a relationship with *Luke*, not with her, yet she couldn't help hoping—and then couldn't help glancing back up to see if there was something to read in his eyes.

But he then stepped back and turned away, shutting her out again. 'I'll go and see if lunch is ready.'

Emmy sank onto the cushions by the pool and cuddled her sleepy son, feeling as if she needed to take another dip to cool off and battle the insane disappointment that Javier had gone inside. But that aching wouldn't seem to stop; it was a tension she couldn't ease no matter how hard she tried.

* * *

Javier tried not to stare at Emmy as they sat in the shade and lunched on ceviche while Luke slept. He wasn't really tasting the fish, he was too consumed by curiosity—unable to stop himself from studying her intently.

She was avoiding looking at him by watching the sea. The longing in her eyes had barely been masked yesterday and it had been the same today. Her love for the water had been the first thing he'd noticed about her. Okay, the second thing. But the sensual pleasure she took in it, he felt too. She was that siren, the mermaid he'd been unable to resist…the fierce dragon woman who'd breathed fire when aroused.

On one level he agreed with her that they shouldn't touch again. That kiss yesterday had burned his brain to ash. There was too much for them to navigate without getting distracted by lust. He'd thought he could put it aside until he'd got to spend some time with his son and figured out how they were going to make their future work. But it turned out that he couldn't concentrate on any of that far more important stuff. The spark they shared was too strong. So now he wondered if he needed to take the opposite strategy. Maybe if they cleared the air of this sexual tension, then they could focus on what was really important?

Not going to lie, it was a far more appealing prospect.

It had been like this that first night too. As inevitable as the setting of the sun. Sheer biology—animal attraction and all that. He didn't think either of them were going to be able to deny their chemistry for too much longer. So why fight it? Why not give in and get it gone? Why not feel good together this one way in which they could?

It was obvious she was struggling with it too, given

she was either avoiding him altogether or gazing at him with that slightly dazed expression. It amused and provoked and made him ache to haul her close and be done with it.

But his intellectual curiosity about her was growing hourly—he had a million questions and she was avoiding answering any of them in any real depth. The only thing he could tell for certain was her love for Luke. He'd seen the anxiety in her eyes when first watching him interact with the baby. And her hovering over Thomas in those first few hours. Not to mention the screeds of information she'd then given both of them about Luke's likes and dislikes and demeanour. She'd taken such good care of him that Javier suspected there was nothing she wouldn't do for their baby. And that was balm on the irritated welts inside him.

The photo book she'd made had rendered him speechless, touching a sensitivity within that he'd not been aware he even had. His first instinct regarding Luke had been to ensure his physical safety, to determine his nearness so that he could give the child all he could offer. Because he knew that what he could offer was mostly material things. But now that the baby was on board, Javier was at a loss where to start in terms of building an actual relationship. He had no idea how to parent a small person. All he knew was that he'd like to do a better job than his parents had—he could only hope he was capable of it.

His father had opted for the straight abandonment approach, walking out when he was only five. While his mother had gone for the outsourcing angle—packing him off to boarding school so she could focus on forming her new family with her new man.

Surely just by being around Javier could screw his

own child up a little less than he'd been? Just by actually being interested?

So he'd studied each photo several times—soaking up details. But always he returned to that first shot of Emerald and Luke together. The image set something twisting alight in his gut. So many conflicting emotions—not just jealousy and anger but pride and awe and absolute regret.

He should've been there. He should've had the chance to share in that amazing moment. He'd not known how much he could want something the way he wanted that. But the underlying lick of doubt about his suitability for parenthood curled and grew larger—was it too late already? Being *absent*, he felt, was the worst way he could have begun.

And despite all that internal chaos, he still couldn't get past his physical desire for her.

His mind circled beyond the reach of his control, returning to his want for her. His body never failed to tighten in response to her presence. He wasn't *vulnerable* to anyone—he'd learned to keep his emotions in check ever since he was a small child packed off to boarding school, scolded for showing emotion, constantly being lectured about how lucky he was, how grateful he should be. But he knew the reality beneath that 'luckiness' of his. His father had left him and then he'd been sent away because he'd not been wanted by his mother either. Because he'd not been wanted, he'd not fitted into the new mould. He'd learned to keep his ambitions his own and his definition of success and fulfilment utterly within his own power and control. No one else would have the power to impact on what *he* wanted and achieved in his life. It was very simple and up till now it had worked.

But his desire for Emmy had kept him awake for so many nights. It had stopped him sleeping with anyone else for over a year. He'd decided he was bored and tired of meaningless one-night stands—that they weren't satisfactory. But that one-night stand with Emmy had been insanely satisfactory. And that was the problem. His recollection of it was amplified, right? It had become too big and was now blown out of all proportion. He needed to slay the dragon it had become.

He needed to get rid of it. They both did. There was really only one way for them to do that. And then it would be gone. Anticipation shot adrenalin into his muscles. They tensed and primed. His whole damn body ached.

'I think I'll have another quick swim.' She avoided his gaze as she stood, as if she somehow sensed his intentions. 'Take advantage while Luke is sleeping.'

'Running away again?' he called softly.

'Pardon?' She turned back to him warily.

'You're running away.'

She faced him squarely. 'We're on a boat in the middle of the ocean. There's nowhere to run to.'

'Yet you're doing it remarkably well.'

'Meaning?'

'Meaning you're very careful not to be alone with me. You're constantly using Luke as your chaperone.'

She stilled, seeming to draw a slow breath before lifting her chin to face him squarely. 'Luke is the only reason we're in the same space again. There's no need for us to spend time together when he's not awake.'

He laughed. 'You actually think that?'

'I actually think that's what's best.' She nodded. 'For all of us.'

'You're that afraid?' he asked softly.

Emmy couldn't deny it—it was the truth after all. She'd managed to avoid being alone with Javier much in these last few hours, sensing her self-control slipping. He devastated her—reducing her to nothing but a wanting, willing piece of woman. It was mortifying.

'You don't think it would be best for Luke if you and I got to know each other better?' he added.

That was the *last* thing she wanted and she suspected it was the last thing he really meant. 'I don't think it's necessary.'

'You said only yesterday that we needed to talk.'

'I've changed my mind. And I don't think *talking* is what you're meaning now, either,' she challenged bravely.

A teasing half-smile lit his eyes and he offered a shrug. 'We're going to be co-parenting that little boy together for the rest of our lives. I think it's imperative we get past platitudes, Emerald.'

'Well, what is it you wish to know?' she asked flippantly—as if she had nothing to hide, nothing to care so deeply about that she couldn't express it. She could pretend she came from a normal family.

'Okay.' He tilted his head and studied her intently. 'Where are your parents?' He watched her steadily. 'Why are you taking care of your child all on your own miles and miles away from your homeland?'

Her heart thudded at the pinpoint accuracy of his questioning.

'Don't you want your own mother to help you out?' he asked.

She couldn't tell him the complete truth, but perhaps she could escape with partial facts. 'We're not close.'

'I got that impression,' he said wryly. 'Why is that?'

She shrugged. 'It's just the way it is. My parents are closer to my brother. I always had itchy feet—a yearning to travel—and when I came here, I fell in love with the islands. You must agree there's something magical about them.'

'Yes, there is.' He watched her, waiting for more. When she said nothing, he frowned. 'When did you first start travelling?'

'As a teenager,' she answered cagily.

'Oh?'

She nodded. 'Always curious, that was me.' But she saw the scepticism in his eyes.

'How did you get the money to travel?'

Her pride was flicked and her defensiveness sparked a more detailed, honest answer. 'I've always had part-time jobs, always paid my own way or worked for bed and board. I've worked on voluntary projects for years. I've got quite good at them.'

'You didn't want to study past school?'

She'd not had the luxury of that choice, but she'd recovered enough equilibrium to know she couldn't tell him that. 'I didn't finish school, let alone get a college degree.'

She sat back, waited for the judgement to begin.

But he too eased back in his seat, a speculative gleam in his eye. 'I dropped out of university.'

'Really?' She was startled.

'Uh-huh.' He nodded. 'I could tell you I didn't have time to waste studying because there was too much money to be made with my entrepreneurial brilliance.' He eased the arrogance with a wink. 'But that's only the braggy bit, not the actual truth.'

She couldn't help smiling. 'Go on, then, what's the actual truth?'

'I was betrayed,' he said simply with a shrug, looking down to veil his eyes. 'Which, I guess, is partly why I was so touchy about you keeping Luke from me. I'd been lied to before about important things and I dislike the feeling immensely.'

Her curiosity bloomed. 'Who—?'

'So, I guess our nanny has more qualifications than the both of us put together.' He overrode her next, most inevitable question with a teasing smile. 'Maybe we made a good choice with him?'

'Maybe, yes.' Emmy gazed at the water again as a sense of intimacy that had swirled for just a second was vaporised by his determined diversion.

That morsel of personal information had only intrigued her more and she'd wanted to ask about his own parents too, but he'd swiftly stopped that conversation from continuing. And perhaps that was a good thing? She was intensely drawn to him, but she still couldn't trust him enough to let her guard down fully. If he knew everything about her—if he knew the criminal history of her parents and her brother, and her own lie? He'd use it all against her in the end. And there *would* be an end to this—in only eighteen months, which suddenly seemed awfully soon. She *had* to step back.

'Am I allowed to go take that swim now?' she asked roughly.

'You need my permission?'

She lifted her chin, determined to put their dealings back to the bargain they'd struck. 'These eighteen months are yours, isn't that correct?'

His cocoa and coffee eyes lit with a challenge she refused to identify—yet she couldn't turn away from it.

'If that's how you want to view it,' he replied roughly. 'For the next eighteen months, your presence is mine.'

CHAPTER SIX

EMMY DIVED BENEATH the water and emerged to take a deep breath but the cool didn't calm her the way she needed it to. That fact was just crazy—she was swimming in a gorgeous lap pool on a luxurious superyacht in the middle of the world's most beautiful destination and she *ought* to be able to relax. Instead she was more tense than ever, and she was angry—with herself and with him—for her curiosity and his reticence and that infernal, eternal wretched desire that couldn't seem to be suffocated successfully by either of them.

She swam a few short lengths, anything to burn off some of her nervous energy. But when she stood to take breath again, she discovered Javier at the end of the pool—wearing nothing but black swimming shorts.

'What are you doing?' She glared at him in surprise. She'd only been away from him for five minutes and it *really* wasn't long enough for her to cool down to safe mode.

'What does it look like?' he challenged. 'Or are you the only one allowed to enjoy swimming in the water?' Something familiar glinted in his eyes. 'This isn't a private beach today, Emmy. This is my boat and it's my pool.'

'And it's your requirement that I'm here,' she tossed

at him. 'So you'll have to put up with me taking up half the space.'

But she knew the pool wasn't big enough for them both. No pool would be big enough. He'd still be too near, with his bared, honed body—all muscle, strength and speed. He was built for physical dominance and endurance and her mouth really ought not to have dried at the sight of him. But it had. She felt tight and too aware, but she stretched her arms out wide along the edge of the pool and let her feet float up in front to pretend she was fabulously relaxed. She refused to curl into something smaller or escape the water entirely as she suddenly felt compelled to do. She couldn't let him chase her away entirely. More precisely, she refused to let her own stupid, treacherous body chase her away. She could control her own urges, couldn't she?

She was going to need to—she had Luke to consider.

Javier lazily walked down the steps into the water, his gaze unerringly on hers, a small smile curving his lips. Emmy's core temperature soared higher with each step he took.

She released a pent-up breath when he finally submerged fully into the water and swam—it took a single stroke to propel him from one end of the pool to another, he was that powerful. But even so, she felt as if there were something leashed about his movements. He emerged with a flick of his head and water sprayed towards her.

Yes, this situation was intolerable. She waded towards the stairs.

'You're a liar.'

His low mutter halted her. She sank back into the water, turning to lean against the wall again. 'What have I lied about?'

Of course he'd think something distrusting. He—like

almost everyone in her life—would think her guilty of anything and everything. Eventually.

He took hold of her shoulders and stared into her eyes for a long time, and then his gaze lowered to her lips. 'When you said this won't happen again.'

He too was tense and the water cast a sheen over his burnished skin, magnifying the magnificence of all the muscles on show. He was a heady feast for every one of her senses. And every one of them clamoured for her to get closer. But the only thing she could actually do was freeze. She had the horrible feeling that if she went to move, it would only be to get closer to him. Not to escape his presence at all.

At that moment the truth slid free. She couldn't resist her desire for him any longer. She didn't ache for his touch, she burned for it. Restless and hot, she was unable to control her thoughts, unable to calm that reckless yearning inside. She couldn't think straight any more.

'Emmy.'

His harsh growl melted her bones. She couldn't swim away from him. Couldn't stop staring at him. Still leaning back against the pool wall, she was barely able to keep herself afloat.

'Will you just come closer?' he muttered heavily. 'Have mercy on me.'

She shook her head, her throat too tight to allow speech. She couldn't seem to catch her breath, couldn't control the pace of her heart, couldn't resist.

And he knew it.

'Have mercy on you?' she echoed, thunderstruck.

'Emmy.' His warning was low and slow and his desire imperative.

Her lips parted but still sound failed to emerge. Instead she wanted something else. Her gaze locked on his mouth—it too was parted as he drew in a deep, steadying breath.

'I'm going to kiss you, Emmy.'

He had to have felt the tremble that shivered through her body at his words.

'Is that okay?' he asked.

She couldn't answer, she could barely nod her assent. But it was enough and his mouth was on hers at last.

'It's been so long,' he groaned.

Because he knew, as well as she, that she wasn't saying 'no' this time. This time, there was no stopping until they were both beyond satisfied. And so she sank into the kiss. Arms entwined, breathless, she pressed against him. He hoisted her up and sat her on the edge of the pool, parting her legs so he could stand close between them, his face now before her breasts.

She looked down in a heated stupor as he glanced back up at her before returning his attention to feast on her body. Her nipples strained tight and hard against her bikini. His shallow breathing teased her as he leaned closer to her neck. Her eyes closed and she fell almost into a delirium as his hot mouth stroked over her skin.

He pressed wide, hot kisses down her neck, across her collarbones briefly before plundering lower, across her décolletage to where her curves were swollen and waiting. Through the wet fabric he sucked her into the hot cavern of his mouth. She cried out, but it wasn't enough for him, or her. He growled as he deftly pulled her bikini top away and her unfettered breasts swayed with newfound freedom. She gasped as he cupped them with wide hands, growling again with feral pleasure as her curves overflowed his hold. He pressed his hands closer, squeezing so her nipples were pushed up even more prominently, lifting them towards his hungry gaze.

'Javier,' she panted as he bent and rasped his tongue across each taut nub. Her hips shifted, her need for this kind of attention further south. For him to ease both their hungers, not by mere tasting, but devouring. But he was focused on the slow, physical worship of her breasts first. He sucked gently at first, then harder—ravenously—until she moaned, almost blindly clutching his head to her body. Desperately needing the damp, low ache to be assuaged. This was too slow. She'd been tipped into the depths of an almost insane desire too soon.

'I'm here,' he muttered, working his hand between them, feeling her slickness as he brushed his fingers intimately against her.

'Oh, no,' she moaned desperately, arching against his hand to give him greater access. Because that instant was all it took for a powerful orgasm to rush her.

'Oh, yes,' he growled with savage triumph.

His rough laugh provided the baseline to her high cry of release. His gaze glittered into hers, magnifying the intensity as tremors of ecstasy racked her body. Dazed, she stared back up at him, locked in the seductive spell he'd cast her into too easily, her mouth parted in sensual supplication as she rode the last of the shudders his fingers had so easily summoned from deep within.

'Please,' she whispered brokenly with a shiver of tender pining.

He answered with a passionate kiss, instinctively understanding what she needed now. His tongue slid against hers with the commanding possession she ached for everywhere. She kissed him back furiously, even as the ebbing orgasm leeched the last of her energy, because she didn't want this to end yet. Her lax legs spread wider and she moaned in the back of her throat as he plundered her mouth. She was hot and slick and soft and so utterly his. But even this achingly gorgeous fulfilment wasn't enough.

She'd wanted it beyond belief, yet was devastated that it was over so soon. She'd come so quickly and they weren't even naked. Now she was limp and forlorn because she'd hit that high too fast and she still wanted more despite her sudden exhaustion. She didn't want it to be over.

'Emmy,' he murmured, his lips gently brushing hers. 'Open your eyes,' he ordered softly with another kiss.

The fluttering feelings deep in her belly resurged. She needed all of him. Tension bracketed his mouth, but he smiled as she finally looked at him.

'You want to see my cabin?' he invited with a teasing look in his eyes.

She welcomed the slide into humour and responded instinctively. 'You want to show me the soft furnishings?'

His smile faded. 'You know, I've thought about it a lot since I found you and Luke. I realise now the condoms in my wallet that day were really, really old.' He shook his head, his gaze sombre. 'That was my responsibility. My fault. I'm sorry.'

'I'm not sorry,' she muttered fiercely. 'I'll never be sorry for having Luke.'

'I know. I'm not either.' He nodded and his lips twisted. 'I've got new ones in my room, okay?'

It was a risk but one she couldn't resist. She ached for that complete intensity. 'Okay.'

He took her hand and walked with her up the short flight of stairs to the master deck. At the top, Emmy paused to stare and take it all in.

'You have your own pool up here?' She glanced at him with a reproachful tease in her eyes.

'It's only a dip pool. I can't actually *swim* in it much.'

He sent her a smile. 'Though there's a spa as well, if you're interested.'

It was insanely luxurious. She licked her dried lips. 'Maybe later.'

The master suite was incredible. Floor-to-ceiling windows offered a view of the ocean, but with the push of a button silk curtains covered them, leaving her feeling as if the rest of the world had vanished and there was only the two of them in this sumptuous, private space. She glanced at the bed—wider than any she'd ever seen and covered with gorgeous soft-looking linen. The photo book she'd made for him was open on the bedside table, displaying that first picture—the one taken moments after Luke's birth where he was swaddled and lying on her chest in the hospital bed. She looked exhausted but was smiling. It had been the most humbling moment of her life.

'You look beautiful in that photo,' he said gruffly.

She turned to face him.

He tugged down his swimming shorts, kicking them aside to stand before her naked, aroused and proud. He gazed at her, his expression hot and hard as his body was. 'Do you want me, Emmy?'

'You know I do,' she muttered.

She didn't need to say it. He could see it, smell it, taste it, feel it. Just as she could in him—in his eyes, his aroused body.

She walked towards him, letting her hands slide from her ribs down her side to her waist and then to her hips. With a confidence she'd never felt around anyone else, she hooked her thumbs into the band of her bikini bottoms and slowly slipped the fabric south.

He stood, transfixed, the passion in his eyes flaring as he watched her bare herself to him completely. 'You have the most lush body.' He groaned as she stopped in front of him. 'So gorgeous.' He reached out to cup her with feral wonderment. 'Just enough woman for me.'

'Just enough?' She shivered with a laugh. She was so far from skinny her breasts were spilling over his hands.

But he nodded with rapacious fervour and stroked his thumbs across her aching peaks. 'Soft and strong and all mine.'

She liked that he appreciated her curves—there were enough of them, after all—and his untamed, possessive hunger stirred her own appetite for all of him.

It shimmered between them. Memories surged, melding with the present as they moved simultaneously towards each other and rediscovered exactly how well they worked together.

She twisted, entwined with him on the glorious bed. It was the first time they'd had such soft luxury. That night on the beach, it had been on the floor of an abandoned boathouse.

'I've never been this aroused,' he muttered hoarsely. 'I'm trying to slow it down, but I don't know if—' He broke off with a sharply inhaled breath, his eyes closing as tension locked his jaw.

She'd thought she remembered this. But the reality was another shift altogether. She slid her hands to his hips, tugging him closer. Arching. Yearning. She couldn't get enough of the passion he poured into kissing her. Breathless she stirred beneath him, aching for him to move closer. She heard his laugh again, hot and hard and ending in a growl as he kissed down her body. She writhed in utter abandonment until he clamped his hands on her hips and held her still for him to savour.

'It's been so damn long,' he muttered with angry passion before he pressed his mouth to her in the most intimate kiss ever. Torturing her with carnal delight until her breathing broke, until she threaded her hands through his hair and clung tightly on as best she could, until her heat rose, steaming her vision.

'Could you please…?' She couldn't finish her sentence. She could only arch her hips towards him again and again.

'Please what?' He paused and teased.

'Not stop!' she cried. 'Please. Not. Stop!'

He laughed at her loss of language. And then he wasn't just kissing her, he was devouring her. Until all she could do was lie there like the willing supplicant she was—hot and wet and his to eat until desperation for everything he had overwhelmed her.

'Please,' she begged, thrashing her head from side to side. 'Please…please…please…'

'Are you ready for me, Emmy?'

'Yes.' She gasped as he rose and pressed powerfully between her soft thighs.

He was big and strong. She'd thought she remembered, but that searing memory was nothing on the deliciously full sensation as he finally thrust, taking his place within her again. With that one fierce push the orgasm he'd held just out of her reach now shattered her instantly. He locked still and deep, allowing her to ride the wave of it while fully anchored on his thick hardness. The pleasure of possessing him was so intense, all she could do was curl her nails into his back and scream.

'Oh, Emmy,' he growled with a satisfied glitter as he watched her go rigid and then crumble about him. 'You're so hot.'

She took a moment to catch her breath, stretching her legs wide to accommodate his size and giving her the leverage to push her hips up and into his—seeking to topple his self-control. 'How hot?' she murmured, daring him to lose it.

She traced his back with pleasure—discovering his strong, taut muscles again as they rippled with the strain he was putting them under as he surged into her again and again.

'More,' she breathed. Pure instinct driving her.

He swore, an earthy, crude celebration of their coming together and all it did was turn her on more. Her energy returned, with manifold intensity until finally they moved ferociously—pounding together in a fierce, passionate dance—pushing closer and closer, each driving action hurtling them both faster into that fantastic tumult of sensation—of white-hot, scalding satisfaction. She screamed it out until she could scream no more and all that fantastic tension snapped.

'We're damn good at this, Emmy,' Javier said a while later as he rested his head on his hand and watched her attempt to recover her breath. 'You do realise that, don't you?'

Sensations were still storming around her body—every drop of blood pulsed with the remnants of ecstasy. She didn't want to answer. She didn't want reality to return. She wanted to remain suspended like this, as if in some dream state of pure bliss.

He chuckled. Her lack of response obviously cluing him in to her wrecked status.

He leaned close again. His kiss was luxuriant and indulgent—slow and lush, as if he had all the time in the world with which to savour and arouse her all over again.

But it didn't take long. As impossible as it was, her hunger returned, strong and powerful, and she shifted instinctively closer.

He met her gaze. His mouth curved. His body moved.

CHAPTER SEVEN

FOR ONLY THE second time in years, Emerald woke late. She stretched, taking the moment to appreciate the pure luxury of the wide bed and pure linen sheets and the delectable stiffness in intimate places.

'Sleeping beauty arises.' Javier grinned from the window as she sat up.

Emmy's heart skittered at his freshness in his bright white tee, black swim shorts and bare feet. His vitality was incredibly magnetic. 'Is Luke—?'

'Up and playing.' Javier lounged one hand against the back of the large armchair at the foot of the massive bed. 'He's had a very messy breakfast and is currently destroying the block towers Thomas's been building with him.'

She relaxed back against the plump pillows. 'That sounds good.'

'It's very good.' Javier inclined his head with a satisfied expression. 'He's very happy. So you can rest a while longer if you need to.'

Something curled in her belly. She didn't want to *rest*. She wanted something else from Javier. Heat built in her cheeks as she realised the truth he'd stripped from her that first night. When it came to Javier Ramon Torres, Emerald was a wanton nymph who couldn't get enough of his kisses. But that madness had been last night. Now the day was bright and she wasn't sure what he wanted—if, indeed, he wanted anything.

'Though I have something for you.' Knowing amusement glinted in his eyes.

She stared as he straightened and held out the package she'd not realised he'd been hiding behind his back. It was gorgeously wrapped in black paper with a white ribbon. Yet her core temperature slipped a few notches. 'When did you get that?' she asked, awkwardness rising.

'The chopper brought it in with some other supplies this morning.'

'This morning?' How had she slept through the sound of the helicopter arriving *again*? The soundproofing in the cabins was astounding and it made her grateful for the monitor Thomas had put into Luke's room even though he had taken the room on just the other side.

As she toyed with the wrapping, her skin chilled too. *This* wasn't what she wanted from Javier—not treats or rewards. She didn't want any things. *All* she actually wanted from him was his touch and even that she didn't *want* to want. 'You don't need to give me anything, Javier.'

He sighed and sat on the edge of the bed. 'Why don't you open it and see what it is? I ordered it after you gave me the book yesterday.'

'Before…'

'Before.' His gaze narrowed on her with mocking humour. 'So don't start thinking poisonous things. I'm not rewarding you because you let me have my wicked way with you again. Why don't you open it before you decide to reject it?'

That he guessed her fears so quickly made her feel ungrateful and overly cautious and appallingly judgy of him. Releasing a wary breath, she unwrapped the gift and discovered a digital camera in a large box.

'I can't accept this,' she murmured as she carefully pulled the camera from the packaging. It was so fancy she wasn't even sure how to turn it on. She set it down on the bed beside her and frowned up at him. 'Javier—'

'I want you to take more pictures of Luke and me. More of your aide-memoires. So it's for Luke as much as anything,' he said matter-of-factly. 'And for me.'

Stilled, she gazed at him. 'Oh, of course. I'd like to do that.'

She appreciated that this request was part of the forgiveness building between them, and part of his relationship building with Luke. And when he was older Luke would see that his father had been around and was there for him from a young age.

'Thank you,' he said.

She smiled wistfully. 'Stop acting so chivalrous. You know *I'm* the one who needs to say thank you.'

'Acting?' he echoed with a gleam in his eye. 'What makes you think I'm acting? Maybe I truly am chivalrous.' He waggled his brows. 'Anyway, I'm betting you want to get up and check in with Luke. Am I right?'

With a swallow she nodded and he left her to dress. Emmy's heart thudded heavily, as if drumming in impending doom. Javier had been right: last night had been inevitable. But *her* newly discovered, awkward truth was that last night hadn't been enough.

After breakfast she curled up on deck, reading the instruction booklet that came with the camera, and experimented with taking shots.

'Why are you taking photos of your hand?' Javier stretched out on the deck, moving toys in and out of Luke's reach.

'I'm experimenting with the light.'

He nodded and rolled to his stomach, looking lithe and gorgeous as he observed his mini-me. Emmy had to fiddle with the camera settings just to stop herself staring at the two of them.

'You've been on your own since you were how old?' Javier asked after a while.

'Sixteen.'

'And travelling the world all that time?'

'For seven years.'

'That's a long time.'

'And a lot of places.' She smiled in reminiscence. 'But I've been on the Galapagos for almost two years of that seven.'

'And how had you not fallen for some guy in all that time?' He lifted his chin and scrutinised her. 'Was there no boyfriend ever?'

She shook her head.

'Girlfriend?'

She kept shaking her head.

'How, Emmy? You're a sensual woman. You're...' He frowned slightly, as if picking his words carefully. 'That night we met...'

Yes, she knew she'd not exactly made it difficult for him. At the time they hadn't discussed it much, they'd been too carried away in the intensity of the moment. She'd been so eager, she knew her enthusiasm had swept away his concern when he'd realised. And then his main response to the discovery of her inexperience had been determination to make it even better for her.

'I don't believe you never had any other opportunity before that night.' He moved another of Luke's toys. 'So why me—why then? What happened to make you choose differently then?'

She didn't know what to say when the plain truth was

that *he* had happened. *He* was the difference. It wasn't as
if she'd decided one day that the next man she met was
going to be the one; it had all been because of him—only
because of him. He'd walked into her life and swept her
away. He still swept her away. And if he'd walked into
her life five years ago or five years from now, she was
afraid he'd still have that same effect on her. He reached
forward, rolling one of the toys in his hand, then squeezing it.

'I'm not going to feed your ego,' she finally answered
with a teasing smile.

But he didn't laugh. 'Has there…?' He cleared his
throat. 'Has there been anyone else since then?'

'I have a *baby*, Javier.' Droll amusement bubbled out
of her. As if she'd had any time or inclination, given her
circumstances. 'What do you think?'

He paused and his answer came slowly. 'I think I
wouldn't blame you if you'd sought a momentary escape…'

Was that what he'd done since then? She stiffened at
the stab of hurt inside. 'Well, I didn't.'

He was staring right into her eyes but he still didn't
smile. 'Me neither.'

She stared back at him as an illicit heat slowly infil-
trated her nether regions. She'd chosen not to think about
the time they'd been apart. Why would she torture herself with the thought of all the women he'd had since
that night with her? But to hear that there'd been *none*?

Now his lips twisted. 'That surprises you?'

'I don't know.' She shot him a look. '*You* weren't a
virgin that night, Javier.'

Amusement crinkled around his eyes as he inclined
his head in an admission. 'No, I wasn't.'

'So why not…?'

'Work,' he answered shortly.

She chuckled at his hasty retreat behind that remote expression he'd perfected. 'Don't worry. I won't take that admission to mean anything other than that you've been as busy as I have. Only you were doing other things, like building billions in the bank and beginning a boutique hotel empire. Just as I know you won't read anything into my not being intimate with anyone else since either.'

His eyes widened and he emitted a sound between a cough and a laugh. 'Emmy...'

'Relax, Javier, I get it. You're curious, but you don't want a long-term relationship with me.'

He had the grace to smile sheepishly but there was a hint of remorse in his eyes that surprised her. 'With anyone, Emmy. Not just you.'

'No marriage?' she asked lightly, not really hoping for an answer given the barriers she expected him to raise any second now. 'Not ever? Why not?'

'I don't believe in it.'

'Really?' She maintained her airy tone and smile. 'As an institution? A construct of the society in which we live?'

He laughed. 'I just don't think it ever works out in anyone's best interests.'

'Not ever? You don't believe there's such a thing as happy ever after?'

He shrugged carelessly. 'I don't believe in fairy tales, no.'

'So you don't really believe there are dragons, either? There's not really any treasure to be found on an island? Okay, good to know.' She mirrored his shrug, only her carelessness was completely feigned.

She'd enjoyed that light, silly talk of dragons and magical creatures that night on the beach. And even though it had been a transient moment, it had meant something—long before she'd learned of Luke's existence within her. She'd been unable to forget Javier. And suddenly she couldn't fake anything any more, there was only plain truth and it slipped out of her in a sad little sigh. 'I haven't felt that chemistry with anyone else.'

For a moment he gazed back into her eyes, his own mix of cocoa and coffee dilating. 'Me neither.'

It was such a low mutter she wasn't sure she'd even heard him properly. She swallowed, trying to ease the sudden constriction in her throat. 'What do you think that means?'

He shook his head slowly and she felt that warning within at his withdrawal. 'Nothing other than what it is, Emmy. Strong chemistry. That's all.' He drew in a breath. 'And it will pass.'

She was sure he was right but there was a tiny fear, buried deep within like a seed about to sprout, that wondered if—for her at least—he was wrong.

'But I don't think it will go away until we deal with it properly,' he added.

And he wanted it to go away? Good, because so did she. It felt like vulnerability.

'And if we deal with it properly?' she asked. 'What happens then?'

'We move forward.' He shifted on the rug.

Her mouth dried as anticipation feathered goosebumps over her skin at the simple glimpse of him. Yes, getting rid of this distraction would make things easier as they worked out how they'd jointly care for Luke. They'd shake their future free from this lust. 'And dealing with it? You mean…like last night?'

'Mmm-hmm.' His eyes told her everything his words didn't.

'How long will it take, do you think?' she asked, shivering at the prospect.

His gaze lingered on her lips. 'I don't know,' he murmured huskily. 'But I'm willing if you are.'

It should have just been a flirty joke, but there was a raw element that chimed a low chord within her. The fact was they'd been drawn to each other on a purely physical level from the moment they'd met and it wasn't going to be exhausted all that quickly.

'We have a few days on board, right?' She looked at him with growing warmth. 'So...'

'We make the most of them?'

She nodded. It could be a huge risk but, given that she couldn't *think* when there was this sensual fog around her, she needed to clear her head to be able to hold her ground with him in the long run.

'So, have you had many girlfriends?' she asked even as she hated herself for her needy curiosity.

His eyes widened at the question.

'You asked me,' she pointed out with a little spirit. 'I don't think it's unfair to expect you to reciprocate.'

'You want full reciprocation?' Now there was a gleam in his eyes that made her think he wasn't thinking about sharing minor confidences, but other more physical things. 'Okay.' He smiled glibly. 'I had a girlfriend at university.'

She bit the edge of her lip because she wasn't sure how seriously he was taking this, but she wanted to ask more. 'Was she the reason why you dropped out?'

'As loath as I am to admit it, she was a big part of that decision.'

'What happened?'

He grimaced wryly. 'We were both extremely driven to succeed—each with our own reasons why. But when it came to it, she didn't believe that I had what it took to get the success that she craved so badly.'

She hadn't believed in him? Emmy was surprised. 'What did she do?'

That teasing light faded from Javier's eyes and for a moment Emmy didn't think he was going to answer.

'She cheated to get ahead,' he said baldly.

'Cheated on exams? Or cheated on you?' She held her breath.

'As she slept with our professor, I'd say both.'

Emmy gaped, shocked. 'I'm sorry.' And she was— both sorry for what had happened and sorry for asking, because he clearly didn't like thinking about it, let alone answering any questions about it.

'I'm not, it was good.' He laughed but it had a bitter edge. 'I got my focus where I needed it to be— which was on work and on doing what I needed to do on my own. But I did have flings, Emmy. A number of nights…'

'But nothing serious?' Emmy muttered. That university girlfriend must have hurt him very badly to put him off marriage so completely—which meant he must've loved her a lot.

He shook his head.

'And what made you so driven to succeed?' she asked, her heart aching a little.

He had that rare combination of ambition and discipline and she suspected he was a complete workaholic. She'd seen him snatching moments every time Luke slept to work on his laptop or phone. He was almost always 'on call' to respond to the chimes of incoming messages.

His eyes veiled and he shrugged. 'I just always was.'

She knew him well enough now to see that those walls had gone right up again—she recognised that expression. And she also recognised his lie—something had happened. He just didn't want to say what. But she let the conversation slide despite her burgeoning curiosity. Because if she asked anything too personal, he might insist on the same from her—especially now she'd been the one to insist on 'reciprocation'.

She had to retreat. There was no need for them to open up too deeply. Not when he'd just said their physical intensity would fade. Once it did, then it would only be necessary for them to make amicable arrangements for sharing Luke's care.

So she swallowed back all the burning questions that filled her brain, on the heartache she feared might follow, and focused on what was right in front of her, right now.

'Will it fade slow or fast, do you think?' she pondered aloud, injecting that lightness back into herself with a cheeky giggle at her own thoughts. 'The chemistry, I mean. Either way, the best is done, now, right? It only goes downhill from here. Every time we're together, it will be a little less awesome than the last.'

'Huh?' He sat up and glared at her; his muscles actually jumped. 'Emerald Jones, that's fighting talk and you know it.'

'Do I?' She blinked at him.

He sat back on his heels. 'Is it time for Luke to have a nap?' Javier didn't even try to hide the sly look in his eyes.

Emmy laughed. 'Luke runs to *his* schedule, not ours.'

'Well…' Javier squeezed another toy in front of Luke's face and sat back as if he weren't at all concerned '… that's fine for now. I can wait.'

'Can you?' she teased, because those bunching muscles of his were telling another story.

'Don't doubt me, Emerald,' he said with downright menacing softness. 'I'll help you realise just how *far* from downhill certain things are about to go.'

CHAPTER EIGHT

'*WHY* ARE YOU awake?' Javier groaned as he watched Emmy slip from the bed and pull on her favourite—okay, *only*—linen dress. 'More to the point, *how* are you awake? We only fell asleep thirty seconds ago.' A slight exaggeration, but it was what it felt like.

'I want to capture the sunrise,' she whispered and came back to press a kiss to his lips. 'You stay here. I suspect Luke is awake anyway.'

'You should come back here and sleep in.' He was only beginning to appreciate how tired she'd been from caring for Luke on her own all these months.

'As if you're making that possible?'

He chuckled and went to tug her back into his arms, but she'd pulled away before he could stop her.

Javier closed his eyes and groaned. He'd unleashed, not a dragon, but a camera-loving demon. These days she caressed that tech more than she caressed him. He laughed inwardly at his jealousy of an inanimate object. And he couldn't get back to sleep now, not without her. That realisation sent a thread of unease down his spine.

What she did—or didn't do—shouldn't matter so much to him. It shouldn't impact on his mood or on his day or on his choices. He tapped his phone and the curtains slid back to reveal that pre-dawn glimmer of light, and he steeled himself to go into the office. There were multiple messages that needed answering, so he spent a few hours on the phone and laptop, exercising the self-control that he was suddenly determined to maintain. Because it could slip, he acknowledged. He could so easily spend all day kissing her. But he wasn't going to. And he wasn't going to listen hard for her voice, or look forward to lunch, or keep an eye on the door in case she went past...

Irritated beyond belief at his failure to *not* do any of those things for hours, he pulled on some swim shorts and went to find his son's mother in the middle of the afternoon.

Luke was napping and Thomas was rearranging the toys and books Javier had ordered. Emmy was curled on the plush sofa. It was her favourite place in the shade, overlooking both the pool and the sea, but she was intently watching something on a tablet. She looked up guiltily as he stepped nearer.

'I hope you don't mind—your assistant said it was okay for me to use this.' She lifted the tablet. 'That it's a spare.'

'You can use anything on board, Emmy. You don't need to ask.' He sat down beside her. 'What are you watching?'

'How-to videos.'

'How to what?' He leaned a little closer to peer at the screen. 'Drive your man wild in bed?'

'Are you saying I need lessons?' she asked archly, but the hint of vulnerability in her eyes scratched a line of discomfort just beneath his skin.

'You know I'm not.' He laughed, leaning closer to steal a kiss. 'Photography skills?'

She nodded and smiled at him. 'That camera is amazing. I want to do it justice.'

'Or you could just have fun with it.' He shrugged, struggling to pull back from her.

'I want to use it properly. I enjoy it.'

That had been obvious in the photos she'd taken of Luke all these months—they showed her eye for framing a good picture. He was pleased he'd found something to give her that she couldn't refuse. Other than his body. He wanted to build more of a bridge between them; it was going to be important for Luke. And this was all about Luke, he reassured himself. He wanted his son to have the security he'd never had. To know that both parents wanted him, loved him, and would be there for him.

Javier watched the shiver ripple down her body as he stroked her arm. She was incredibly responsive to his touch and it spurred him to touch more. He'd discovered there was nothing better than torturing them both with tiny touches. He bent closer to blow softly across the sensitive skin between her shoulder blades. She turned towards him, her lips parted in pure invitation. It was exactly what he'd wanted and everything he couldn't resist.

Yet it still wasn't enough to satisfy the developing ache inside him.

For a few days there'd been nothing but that sensual magic between them as they'd submitted to the sweet, savage desire. And still his curiosity deepened. He didn't want it to deepen. He didn't want to think about her all the time like this. He wanted this all-consuming lust to ease. But it wasn't. Perhaps if he satisfied every element of his curiosity, then it might finally ebb.

He knew she was untrusting and wary of being judged. It seemed she suspected the worst and expected the worst—not just of him, but everyone. He wanted to know why. He wanted her to trust him enough to tell him why.

He knew how hard she'd worked, and he knew better than anyone how inexperienced she really was with men—seemingly with *all* relationships—so what was it that caused her reticence and resentment? Why had she not had a real home for so long? Who had judged her so much? How and why? What had she done—or not done—to deserve it? He needed to know more.

She wasn't this untrusting purely because of him. Sure, he'd been selfish in not telling her his real name that night. And when she'd found out who he was and that he'd invested in Lucero's property, she'd been angry and resentful. But there was real fear within her too. Real fear that he might have taken Luke away from her. He had the horrible feeling she still worried that might happen and he hated that idea. So what was it that had been taken from her in the past? There had to have been loss. Was that why she'd not returned to her homeland in all this time?

He really didn't like the thought of her being hurt that badly.

They couldn't move forward without building some level of trust. Somehow he needed to get her to talk to him about more than her travels, her work. They'd conversed for hours about her voluntary work and the eco-action the Flores Foundation had undertaken to make the former hostel sustainable. He'd known about some from Lucero, of course, but getting the detail from her was fascinating and highly relevant to his own future plans.

But learning more about Emerald *herself* was almost impossible. Tempted as he was, he couldn't go behind her back to discover more about her. But using only his hands to open the puzzle box that was Emerald Jones wasn't working. He was going to use his mouth in more than one way too.

Maybe if he offered her real security she'd open up.

That was one thing he'd felt short of when he was younger and being shoved from boarding school to 'guest bedroom' and back again. But getting his first apartment building had helped and, as far as he could tell, Emmy hadn't had a permanent home in a long time. Maybe she'd like that?

'You know, we can't stay here for ever,' he said idly. 'I'm mostly based in New York. My apartment is in a nice location. There's no reason why I can't buy another in the same building for you.'

He watched closely for her response. She paled fractionally and he saw her struggle to swallow.

'I can't afford an apartment in New York,' she said firmly. 'And I'm not going to let you buy one for me.'

Yeah, he'd known she'd instantly reject the idea of him housing her. She still didn't want to accept anything of consequence from him. But he smiled smugly. 'Well, if you won't let me buy you an apartment, then you'll have to move into mine.'

She stilled. 'I'll live wherever you want me to for the next eighteen months.'

He wasn't rising to her throwing that damn stupid demand in his face this time. 'It makes most sense,' he mulled. 'It'll be more convenient.'

'Convenient for what?' she asked, too calmly.

'It'll give us both best access to Luke and it will be less confusing for him.'

'Confusing? He's nine months old, I don't think he's going to notice where I'm sleeping.'

That she was thinking about where she was sleeping tickled him. 'We'll come back to the islands often though,' he added. 'I want him to understand his heritage more than I ever got to. He needs to know where he comes from.'

She turned to face him. 'You didn't get that?'

He saw the curiosity burning in her eyes and steeled himself to answer at least a couple of the questions he knew she was bound to ask. 'My father left when I was young and I learned nothing of him or his family other than his nationality. I taught myself Spanish as a teenager.' He glanced at her and referred back to their son as quickly as he could. 'I'm glad you use some with Luke.'

She nibbled her lip. 'I'm not great at it, but Connie helped me.'

Javier nodded. 'You know Thomas is fluent.'

'Of course,' she chuckled. 'That's good.'

Javier nodded. 'Usually I have to travel a bit,' he said cautiously. 'I thought you and Luke would travel with me.'

'You want me to travel with you as well?' Her eyes widened.

'I think that's what's best for Luke, don't you?'

Emmy nodded and swallowed back the massive lump in her throat. Of course, it was always about Luke. Javier seemed very keen for their son to have both parents around. Given she'd just learned his father hadn't been there for him, she was beginning to understand why, and she wanted to understand so much more. 'If that's what you think is best.'

'I do, but what do you think?' He watched her, his expressionless game face back on.

'These are your eighteen months,' she reiterated quietly. 'You get to call the shots.'

And if he wasn't going to give much away, she wasn't sure she wanted to either.

He looked at her. As he slowly shook his head and turned away she knew she'd disappointed him somehow.

Later that afternoon, Emmy watched Javier splash

with Luke at the bottom of the stairs at the very back of the boat. The sea was a gorgeous temperature and a stunning blue. The island behind them was a perfect backdrop. Emmy lay on the step just above the water line, her camera strap looped around her neck as she watched the two of them splashing through the viewfinder. Luke giggled as Javier teased him. The baby was at ease now—as was Javier in holding and reaching for him. Emmy played with varying settings to capture every moment because they were so magic.

'Oh,' she breathed and smiled. 'I just took the best photo ever.'

'Hmmm?' Carrying Luke, Javier splashed back up the stairs and she turned the camera so he could see the display on the back.

'You had someone photo-bombing you.' She laughed.

Luke and Javier were smiling at each other, the droplets of water sparkling on their bronzed skin. But in the background was a Galapagos tortoise in the water, his head up, looking as if he was smiling. And beyond him gleamed a snippet of the golden sand of the uninhabited island behind.

'You're right, that's an amazing shot.' Javier glanced up at her. 'Forward it to me?'

'Of course.' She sat back.

She more than liked it. She couldn't stop staring at it. The two most handsome males on the planet—both better looking than any model.

'Put the camera down and join us,' Javier said roughly.

Emmy's heart melted at the invitation and she quickly put the camera away before going to sit on the step beside him. His arm rested across Luke's little belly as they dangled their feet in the water and gazed at the tortoises on the island, who gazed with equal curiosity right back.

'They're just incredible, aren't they?' Javier murmured.

'I never get sick of staring at them. The islands are so remote, so isolated, all the creatures have evolved into something completely unique. So precious, they're fascinating.'

'And beautiful.'

'And undamaged by the rest of the world.' She pondered the rarity before her. 'So lucky.'

She felt him turn his head. 'The rest of the world damaged you?'

'That's what *people* do, isn't it?' she asked lightly.

'And that's why you avoid them now?'

'I don't avoid them.' She scoffed at the suggestion. 'I just choose to live in paradise.'

'This is your definition of paradise?'

'Yes.' She nodded.

'Somewhere remote and isolated and unique?' He echoed her words. 'Like the end of the world or something. Somewhere away from everyone, everything else.' He paused. 'And a place where people don't tend to stay. Visitors come and go. There are no connections for long.'

She stilled at the serious edge to his tone. 'I take it you disagree?'

'I think it's somewhere *safe*.'

'Maybe.' She forced a smile. 'Or maybe you're overthinking it.'

'Or maybe you've just got a little prickly because I've got too close to the truth.' He cocked his head. 'Maybe you're avoiding *life*, Emmy.'

'How do you figure that, really?' She nudged his shoulder and added an eye roll for good measure. 'I have a child—I've been raising him on my own.'

'But that's the point. You've deliberately isolated yourself. And yes, thank goodness for Lucero and Connie for being there to help you to the extent that you'd allow anyone to help you.'

She stared at him.

'There's a compelling difference between you and the Galapagos creatures, though,' he mused quietly. '*They're* not afraid of people. They've not had the predatory experiences that we've had. They've not built the defences—'

'You're looking at a giant tortoise,' she interrupted with a pointed wave of her hand. 'What do you think that shell is for?'

'It's his portable house.' Javier laughed at her. 'Like a little caravan, he has his own roof over his head. But they're friendly, Emmy. That's my point. They're not afraid of people.'

'And I am? Is that what you're ever so unsubtly trying to suggest?'

'Maybe, yes. I think you've got a bit afraid of the rest of the world. I think you've been using your situation with Luke to avoid re-entering a full life.'

'You don't think my life is full?'

'I think it's lonely,' he said quietly. 'I think you've been lonely for a while.'

'And you think that's why I let you seduce me so easily that night?' She felt her defensiveness grow. She wanted Luke to be enough. For her to be enough for him. 'Is *your* life full?' she challenged.

'I'm realising that perhaps it's not, no. I know I focus on work to the detriment of other aspects of my life.' He sighed. 'Certainly recently, I've not...'

'Not what?'

'Taken time for me.'

'Is that what this is now?'

'Partly, perhaps.' Javier reached for her camera and fiddled with it. 'Can we get a selfie with this?'

With dexterity he cuddled Luke and leaned close to her and somehow took a shot. With their wet hair, sun-kissed skin and huge smiles, anyone else looking at it would see a perfect family shot. But the image hurt Emmy's heart—because it wasn't real. They weren't a true family and she was sure he'd only taken the photo as a means to end that conversation.

Yet the moment had been real enough. There'd been pure joy in that instant. But it was only an instant. A permanent reminder of a temporary pleasure. An emotion that wasn't sustainable and that had no real depth behind it.

'That's a good one,' he said.

'You can see the likeness between you and Luke. The resemblance is strong.'

Javier studied the shots. What she said was true. 'I've never looked much like anyone else in my family.'

'Not your father?'

He hesitated. He never discussed his parents, but Emerald wasn't just anyone any more. She was someone he wanted to trust and have trust him. So he answered as briefly as he could. 'I have few memories of him. No pictures. He walked out when I was a child. I thought he'd come back one day and take me with him. But he didn't.' He glanced at her. 'I don't want Luke ever to feel that.'

'That?'

'Being left behind. Being rejected. All that good stuff that sears the soul of a five-year-old, you know.' His lips twisted and his tone was dry as he tried to make light of it, but it wasn't remotely funny.

'Javier—'

'My mother remarried,' he said crisply, finishing the story on his own terms before she could ask him details he didn't want ever to recall. 'She wanted a real fam-

ily with him. They had two sons. Jacob and Joshua.'
He shot her a look and chuckled. 'I didn't quite fit with
that, did I?'

But Emmy didn't laugh with him; she looked deeply
troubled. 'What happened to you when she remarried?'

He grimaced, absently fiddling with the clasp of his
watch. 'I was sent to very good boarding schools. But
despite their often-quoted massive investment in me and
the stellar grades I delivered, it turned out my stepfather
had no intention of bringing me into the fold of the family business. Because I was never part of *his* family.'

Emerald looked pensive. 'What was his business?'

He almost laughed; the question she'd asked wasn't
anything as intrusive as he'd feared. 'Car-parking buildings.'

Emmy stared at him fixedly for a second and he could
see her trying not to smile.

'I know, super sexy, right?' He shook his head. 'But he
made millions. And all I wanted to do was build a business with an even bigger and better bottom line. And one
that was a damn sight sexier than car parking.'

'Financing is sexy?'

'You don't think so?'

She wrinkled her nose. 'I thought you were a surfer.'

'I can surf and finance,' he teased, easing into the detail of his work. That was where he'd found his calling.
'Multi-talented, I am.' He chuckled. 'But you realise that
first up I needed money. Not going to lie, I needed the
capital first and the freedom. So I crashed out of my studies, did the trading and investing and worked around the
clock for years. And when I got enough I began investing
in other things. Other companies and—'

'Property.' She nodded. 'Some hotels. Sustainable.
Well designed. So now you have…'

'Several property investments in various places and I travel between them all.'

'And that includes here.' She frowned. 'When it's almost impossible to invest here.'

'I'm able to do that through my father.' He shrugged. 'That's the one thing he gave me, I guess. Even if he hadn't intended to leave me with anything.'

At the look she shot him, he regretted mentioning him again.

'You don't know why he left?' she asked quietly.

He braced, not at the question, but the gaping void of his own answer, and just shook his head. Javier couldn't either forget or forgive his father, even though he'd tried to do both.

Emmy frowned. 'Had they been unhappy for a while?' she asked.

'She'd met someone else,' he said briefly.

'The man she later married?' Emmy watched as he grimaced, nodded, and the blue in her eyes deepened with concern. 'Maybe he thought you'd have more security with her if he wasn't around? Maybe he did what he thought was best for you both?'

And maybe Javier couldn't bear to think about it because it wasn't something he could ever know. His mother had avoided any discussion of his father from the moment he'd vanished. Javier had only learned where his father had gone and what had happened to him a few years ago. But the reason why he'd left—so abruptly and so finally? That he could never truly know.

'Anyway, I wanted a foothold here and now I've got it.' He sighed. 'Somewhere where I might belong.' He instantly regretted that last slipping out because he saw her expression turn even more caring.

'You don't feel as if you belong anywhere?' she asked.

He couldn't answer honestly—only flip it back on her and try to lighten it. 'Do you?'

'I feel at home in the water,' she said softly. 'I always have.'

He smiled at that. 'Like a redheaded siren.'

'Dragon, a sea dragon,' she corrected with a tilt of her head. 'Have things improved with your mother and stepfather since you've become more successful than the car-parking empire?'

Yeah, he was so done with this conversation. 'There's honestly little but the remnants of festering resentment on both sides,' he drawled through the painful truth. 'I don't bother with family occasions. It's not worth the awkwardness.'

'Perhaps it's not too late for a reconciliation?' She looked so hopeful it almost hurt to answer her honestly.

'No.' He shook his head and half smiled at her naïveté. 'There aren't neatly tied threads and happy endings in life, Emmy. There's just the next phase. It'll have good things and bad, the one true constant is that it will change.'

'So, in your world nothing lasts?'

'In *any* world, nothing ever does.'

'And yet you like to build your beautiful hotels and take care of the environment around them.'

Emmy's eyes were very blue and very steady and as he looked into them Javier's chest tightened painfully.

'Things can last a good while though, right?' she said quietly. 'Like the stars and the moon and the sun. Some things can last long enough.'

He laughed, somehow soothed by her words and the sweet promise of a child's nursery rhyme.

'Some things can last a lifetime.' She seemed to gaze right into his soul. 'Couldn't that be long enough?'

CHAPTER NINE

EMMY WAITED BUT Javier didn't reply. That he'd ever felt unwanted stunned her. 'I'm sorry your parents didn't love you the way they should have.' He should have been utterly adored and she couldn't believe he hadn't been. So no wonder he was protective of Luke.

'It's okay, Emmy,' he said dismissively even as he gazed at her intently. 'I know my worth.'

Did he? Or did he think it was only because of his bank balance? Was that why he was so driven in his business? Why he was so guarded? Because even now he'd barely told her anything and she just *knew* there was more to it. That there was so much more he'd avoided telling her by his swift segue into his work story. She suspected he used work to avoid a lot of things.

As she breathed in, trying to frame her thoughts, he leaned close and pressed a kiss to her mouth. 'But I'm not sure you know yours.'

She shook her head, trying to remain clear-headed and not let him distract her with his seduction. But everything inside her seemed to have softened and she wanted not just to understand him, but for him to understand her. And suddenly she realised the longer she remained reticent, the worse it would be when he learned the truth. And he would find out eventually, somehow.

He'd probably make it his business in the end. Shame crawled over her in a prickling heat with embarrassment and resentment at the thought of some stranger picking over the pitiful facts of her life and telling him behind her back. The fewer people who knew, the better—for Luke's sake as much as anything. So she needed to explain it to Javier herself.

'I know my worth,' she muttered sadly. 'And it's not what it should be.'

He leaned back and studied her sombrely. 'Why do you say that?'

'I don't come from a good family,' she confessed.

'No? What do you mean by good?' He offered an encouraging smile. 'There's no such thing as a perfect family.'

'A law-abiding, honest one would be a start.'

His eyebrows lifted.

'It was petty crime…theft, cars, tech gear, drugs. They're small time but persistent and unhappily married and I have an older brother, Sterling.' She swallowed and gave into the desperate temptation to confide in him completely. 'We were at different schools.' She smiled sadly. 'I'd got a scholarship. You're looking at a former state champion water-polo player.'

'Wow.' He slung his arm across her shoulder and squeezed. 'Go you.'

For just a moment she rested her head on his shoulder. 'My family disagreed. They said school was a waste of time. That I should be less uppity and do the work they needed me to do.'

'And what work was that?'

She pulled away from him and he dropped his arm. 'Sterling had been selling drugs at the school gate.' She stared down at the camera, absently holding it closer. 'I took the fall for him.'

He watched her carefully. 'Why was that?'

'I had to.' She licked her lips, but her mouth remained dry and her throat almost painfully tight. 'He was on his final strike…if he was caught again he was going to prison. My parents said I had to…' She trailed off, hating the horror from that time.

The emotional manipulation had been severe.

'So you said it was you.' He finished it for her with a nod. 'Then what happened?'

'I'd hoped my teachers would see through me. That they'd know I was lying, trying to protect my brother.' She licked her lips again. 'I know it was wrong to lie. It's *always* wrong to lie.'

'It must've been damn hard to make those choices when you're wanting to protect someone you love.'

She nodded, swallowing awkwardly.

'And please your parents.'

She chewed the inside of her cheek, unable to answer.

'I'm guessing your teachers didn't pick up on the truth,' he said softly.

'I guess I convinced them.' But it had hurt. They'd known her for a couple of years. She'd always turned up, she'd always done her best, she'd never let them down. Yet all her past actions had counted for nothing in the face of a few words. Her family history—that assumption—had been used against her. It was as if they'd been waiting for her family blood to seep out. Waiting for her to mess up. Nothing she'd done prior had mattered, in their eyes her downfall was simply inevitable. Just a matter of time. They were so quick to believe the worst, not bothering to try to pick holes in her stupidly flimsy story.

'It was a good school.' She drew a breath. 'I'd worked so hard to get there. I had a part-time job at a fast-food place so I could buy my uniform and supplies and scrape together the travel money for the tournaments...' She swallowed. 'It was my first offence so the police let me off with a warning and some community service. But the principal kicked me off the water-polo team and expelled me from school.'

He waited quietly.

'My brother went to prison less than a month later. He was caught on a breaking and entering job.' She drew breath. 'So my "sacrifice" was all for nothing.'

Javier was very serious. 'And your parents?'

'Didn't care. They were never bothered about my schooling. They wanted me to take on the deliveries he could no longer do. They thought it was good timing that I'd been kicked out.' She lifted her head and stared across the clear water, unable to look at his reaction. 'I knew the only thing to do was leave. I needed a fresh start. I travelled around Australia, working in various cafés, then I went to hotels because often I'd get accommodation thrown in. I'd spend a few months and then move on until I'd saved enough for my passport and a one-way ticket abroad. I've been working or volunteering and travelling ever since.'

'Have you been back home at all?'

'It's no longer my home.' She shrugged. 'And now I have Luke I'd never go back. I don't want him near my family. I can't trust them.'

'You can't trust anyone?' he asked softly.

Silently she looked at him, her throat so constricted an answer was impossible.

'You know you can trust me, Emmy.'

Her heart ached because she really wished that were

the case, but it wasn't. At some point he would judge her. It wasn't his fault, it was human nature. People always did. And she *had* screwed up, hadn't she?

'I'm sorry they all let you down. Your family, your school, your friends. That sucked, Emmy.'

'Car-parking buildings don't seem so bad now, right?' she tried to joke. 'My family business is way worse.'

'Oh…maybe.' He hugged her close and kissed her forehead. 'I'm glad you told me.'

'When I found out I was pregnant…' she murmured softly, releasing the burden of her deepest secrets to him, 'I thought about all my options. I didn't even know your full name. I didn't have any savings and I didn't even have paid employment. No family support. My only friend was an octogenarian on his death bed. What was I doing bringing a baby into that uncertainty? It was nothing short of reckless. But I wanted him for *me*. I wanted someone to love and to love me too. And that was immature and selfish of me because I wasn't in the best place to provide for him and I knew that. So when I found out who you really were? I was afraid you'd go for custody and, with your resources, you'd win easily and you'd be right to.'

She paused, afraid at how vulnerable she'd just allowed herself to be.

But he regarded her steadily and shook his head. 'That never would have happened, Emmy. No judge would have taken him from you. You've given him more than I ever could—love, for one thing. The desire to do whatever is best for him—putting him first and yourself second.' He gazed at her. 'And I would never take him from you. You know, I never thought I wanted children. Ever. But I'm glad he's here.'

She leaned against him. 'I'm glad too.'

And as he lifted her chin and pressed a kiss to her mouth, her last thought—while she could still think—was that perhaps, just perhaps, things were going to be all right.

'I have an event I have to go to in Quito,' Javier said as he left the bed. 'I'd like you to come with me.'

Emmy tensed and lifted her head from the pillow. 'What kind of event?'

'It's business,' he said calmly, but he was watching her too intently with an amused look in his eyes.

'Why do I need to go?'

'You're the mother of my child—the sooner that little fact is out in the world, the better.'

'Why does anyone need to know?'

'I won't have Luke kept a secret. I don't want him to feel that I'm ashamed of him. We show a united front, Emmy. You're the mother of my son and we're friends.'

She swallowed the little hit at that descriptor. 'It just seems a little soon.'

'It's been over nine months already,' he reminded her wryly.

'Won't people be curious? You're wealthy…people are interested in you. They might ask about me, which would be bad.' She swallowed as he looked distinctly unfazed. 'People finding out about my background doesn't worry you?'

'Not in the least,' he said simply.

'You really don't care?'

'I really don't give a damn.' He watched her. 'Why would anyone think any less of you, just because of your family?'

She stared at him. 'They have before.'

'Then they weren't kind people. But you're still reluctant?' He bent over her and cupped her jaw and whispered against her skin. 'Don't you want to accompany me?'

'Are you trying to seduce me into saying yes?' she muttered.

As he pulled back she saw the teasing smile in his eyes. 'Isn't that better than threatening you?'

'I'm not sure.' She wasn't sure that that light teasing wasn't a form of torture all of its own. Because while it was blissful, she was beginning to fear there was nothing real behind it for him. Whereas for her? Something else was brewing. 'Is that what comes next if I say no?'

His amusement faded. 'Do you really think I'd try to order you, Emmy? That I insist on it as part of this eighteen-months thing?' He frowned and a hint of chagrin tightened his gaze. 'I'm actually not that guy. You think I'd leverage some kind of power over you? What would be the joy for me in that?' He shook his head. 'I don't get off on a power trip over you, I get off on *you*.'

Her heart seized, but she still couldn't answer. And that fear—that this was truly, purely physical for him—bloomed.

'Look, if you really don't want to, then I'll accept your answer and go alone.' He gazed at her and suddenly she was wary of the hint of coolness encroaching in his eyes and sensed him starting to withdraw.

She didn't want to lose the fragile intimacy that had built between them yesterday. And suddenly she couldn't say no. She was half afraid that she couldn't say no to him about anything. 'When is it?'

'Tomorrow night.'

'Tomorrow?' she choked. 'You can't be serious. I don't have—'

'Anything to wear? I can arrange—'

'No. *No*, Javier.'

'You can borrow it for the night and give it back to me the second we're home.' He waggled his eyebrows.

'Javier—'

'Let me buy you a damn dress, Emerald.'

'You're not spending stupid money on a dress I'll wear only once.'

'I won't spend stupid money and you can wear it more than once,' he growled. 'Wear it all the time.'

It was impossible not to smile at him. 'Why are you suddenly angry?'

'Because you refuse *anything* I offer.'

She laughed. 'That's *not* true. I've been living with you for the past week. Eating your food. Drinking your water. Learning how to use the camera you gave me. Sleeping in your *bed*. Everything. I've taken *everything*.'

'Not everything, barely the necessities.'

'Necessities?' She waved a hand around the yacht. *'Barely?'*

'You know what I mean.' He glared at her. 'You can't live your life in servitude to your son. You need things of your own as well. Your own life. You're a people person. You're good with them, you like them. You need to let more of them in your life.'

Her eyes widened. Maybe he was right, but somehow that truth saddened her.

'I want you to be happy,' he grumped. 'I want you to meet new people and make friends. Not be alone.'

She was shocked by his vehemence. 'I am happy. I'm *not* alone. I have Luke.'

'He can't even talk back, Emmy.'

'Not yet. But he's getting very close, you know. He can already say mama.'

Emmy shifted uncomfortably as she read the seriousness in Javier's expression. He was being thoughtful and kind, yet stupidly it hurt. Because she wouldn't want or need anyone else if she had Javier, not just as her temporary lover, but as her best friend and mate for life.

But *he* didn't want that from *her*, did he? That was everything he *wasn't* offering.

CHAPTER TEN

EVEN THOUGH SHE'D accepted his invitation, Javier couldn't relax. There was a fleeting quality that made him uneasy—it wasn't just the too rapid sliding of their days on board. It was that the promise they'd made to liberate themselves of this damn chemistry couldn't be fulfilled. Because it wasn't easing. Not yet. So much for the 'downhill slide' she'd predicted. And worse, he had the growing apprehension that Emmy herself was like a mirage—a sylph who'd disappear if he turned his back too long and he'd be left again with this damned raging ache for her. And that if he went alone tonight, he couldn't quite trust she and Luke would still be here when he returned. He hated feeling as if something were about to slip through his fingers.

Because he'd felt it before. He'd come downstairs and the most important person in his life had been missing, never to return. And then he'd been tipped out of his home himself. And he hated even suspecting that he was at risk of something like that happening again.

It was because of Luke, wasn't it? The baby was so vulnerable and so precious...

But he assured himself Emmy wouldn't take him away. Not now he understood her a little more. She thought she needed to be needed and that she needed to *earn* her place—her respect—in people's lives. To earn her place in the world—all those years doing voluntary work? Was she trying to make up for her family's failings? Of course, it was far more complicated than that, but he knew her desire to work so hard for Connie was part of it. The same with Lucero. She'd poured everything into doing the best she could for both of them. And then in being the best mother possible to Luke—even when alone and exhausted. She tried to do her best. So she wasn't about to take her son from what Javier could give him.

But Javier didn't want her to do that with him. To work super hard at being the best possible…what? *Lover?*

She already was that. She didn't need to prove anything to him. And the last thing he wanted was for her to be with him out of any sense of *obligation*. He wanted her with him that way only because she wanted to be— only because she still felt that chemistry the way he did. Because that was all this was and he could still control it, couldn't he? He could spend the day locked in his office, taking time only to see Luke and not needing to set eyes on Emmy for hours. Surely he could do that.

Emmy smoothed the skirt of her dress, appreciating the silk beneath her fingers. It was her first evening out in eons. A snippet of her own time to act like an adult, not a maid, not a mother—but a woman. A whole person—one who'd even had the leisure time to be pampered beforehand to dress up. A beautician had been flown on board and it turned out there was a spa room below deck with a massage table and sauna and she'd very much enjoyed those facilities today.

Her lips felt slick from the rub of colour and her hair was completely loose for once, the curls enhanced—she didn't know how the stylist had worked her magic, but they weren't the usual tumbling tangle of strawberry red, they were actually ringlets.

But suddenly she was nervous. She'd not seen Javier for what felt like years. He'd been in the office, the door sealed shut for hours and now she wondered if she was suitably dressed for this wretched event.

'I can't believe there's a massage and treatment room on board the yacht,' she said dryly to cover her nerves as she walked to where he was waiting.

Javier gaped at her—from her hair, to her eyes, her mouth, her breasts and the flare of her hips, then he visibly hauled his wits together. 'You should definitely wear that dress again,' his voice rasped. 'Like, all the time.'

Yes? Well, he ought to wear suits that sharply tailored as well. She stared at him, drinking in his strong frame, and all that sensual awareness rose and tightened to the point where she couldn't breathe. So much for the chemistry *fading*.

'If we're going to get there at all, we'd better leave now.' Javier swiftly turned on his heel.

But Emmy's nerves fluttered as she strapped herself into the helicopter. She'd never left Luke for more than an hour. And to be flying away and leaving him on a boat in the middle of the sea?

'Stop fretting, he'll be fine,' Javier murmured.

'I know he'll be fine. It's whether *I'll* be fine.'

'I'll do my best to distract you this evening.'

'I thought my mission was to meet new people and make new friends,' she teased archly.

'We can meet people *together*.' He sent her a dark glance that dipped again to her creamy cleavage.

Was that a possessive moment from him? She laughed but she felt it too. In fact she didn't want him talking alone to any other woman. *Ever*.

As the helicopter ascended, she stared down at the superyacht growing more distant by the second.

'Don't worry.' He took hold of her hand. 'We'll fly back for the night. It's only a couple of hours that we're away.'

She laced her fingers through his and squeezed, appreciating that reassurance. 'Thank you.'

He didn't release her hand for the entire flight. He held it again as he walked with her into the banquet hall where the reception was being held. And he was open about their relationship the moment they met the chair of the gala committee on the receiving line.

'Emmy's the mother of my son.'

That was her status. Not his girlfriend. Never to be his wife, but the mother of his son. She knew he meant it respectfully but somehow it hurt, the words wearing a little hole in her heart—the fabric unravelling bit by bit, getting wider with every repetition as he introduced her to other guests. Yet she was proud to be Luke's mother and funnily enough she found she didn't mind the resultant staring of some of the guests. It was refreshing to be somewhere different and she'd dealt with all sorts in her travels. There was little she hadn't encountered and she could manage small talk. All that was involved was asking questions.

In the large reception room she noticed stunning pictures on the walls, promoting the Galapagos. Some of the images were outstanding. Halfway down the length of the vast room, she paused as she caught a glimpse of a familiar smile. That was the picture of Javier, Luke and the tortoise. *Her* picture—massively enlarged and looking gorgeous in the centre of the room.

'I hope you don't mind. I thought it would be a good one to use,' Javier murmured.

As she stared up at it, she noticed a small logo had been added to the bottom left of the print. *Emerald.*

'Do you mind?' he added after a moment.

'Of course not, it looks amazing.' She was bowled over. 'Thanks for the credit.'

'You deserve it. I've actually been approached by a couple of people who want to buy the rights to it.'

'Seriously?' Emmy was amazed. People were offering money to use her photo?

'Do you mind giving me exclusive rights, though?' He turned to face her. 'You'll be recompensed accordingly.'

'*You're* in the picture, Javier.' She laughed as she shook her head. 'And it's a holiday snap, I don't need anything for it.'

'Wrong answer,' he murmured. 'You really need to learn your value, Emmy.'

As they mingled, other guests commented once they learned she'd taken the shot that had become the favourite of the display.

'We have a lot of stunning shots taken on the islands, but that was an extraordinary moment to capture,' one woman said to her.

'I was very lucky.' Feeling a fraud, she smiled. 'Of course, it helps that I'm completely in love with my subject.' Emmy glanced again at the photo. The two males were in such sharp focus—one very young, one very virile. But *both* had her heart.

Her smile slipped as she realised the true extent of her vulnerability. They really did have her. She cared about Javier in a way he didn't and wouldn't ever want. Knowing something of his background, she understood why. His parents had been unhappy and she guessed he'd had a desperately insecure childhood, being sent away. He didn't trust people any more than she did, but then they

differed: while she'd focused on building her tiny surprise family—of Luke—he'd focused on building his
life through his work. And he was still focused on that,
wasn't he? He didn't want more. He still retreated behind
those walls when conversations veered fractionally too
close to the personal, or distracted her with a joke or a
kiss… He'd told her the merest of details and clearly had
no intention of delving deeper or opening up to her more.
But she wanted. So. Much. More.

So how on earth was she going to survive the next
eighteen months? How was she to live the rest of her
life connected and close to Javier, but not in the way she
truly wanted?

'I'd love to be in a photo like that,' the woman continued. 'Most of us would.'

Emmy smiled. 'Yes, I took lots of pictures for passing
tourists when I was out on the beaches.'

'No reason why you shouldn't get paid for that,' Javier chimed in softly.

'For doing someone a favour?' She turned and laughed
at him.

'No, for giving someone a stunning piece of art.' He
contemplated her seriously. 'When our hotel opens, lots
of our guests would like beautiful pictures of them on
the islands. You could take them.'

She paused. Had he said 'our' hotel?

'You have talent,' he said, and she recognised he was
going into his sell mode. 'You have skills and you have
the interest and passion to develop those skills further.
Why wouldn't you?'

Yes, Emmy wanted a job and for it to be something
she could be proud of. But she didn't want to work for
Javier. She *needed* independence—now more than ever.

And she definitely didn't want to benefit from nepotism or charity.

'Emerald,' he said with soft warning and that suffering but amused look in his eyes as he watched the thoughts cross her face. 'You don't like people jumping to conclusions about you, yet you do it to me all the time...'

She paused and gave him a rueful smile. 'But you don't really need a photographer—'

'Don't I? I think it would be an added-value extra for our customers. You'd go on the boat tours with them, take the pictures.' He leaned back thoughtfully. 'In fact, I'm going to have to hire more than one.'

'Well, not me,' she said. 'I can't—'

'Accept any help?' He interrupted with raised eyebrows. 'Why be so determined not to accept any help, any advice, or make use of any contacts?'

'Because I want to make something of myself, *myself*. You of all people must understand that. No car-parking buildings, remember? You wanted to do your own thing. Prove to them that you could.'

'But you've *already* made something of yourself. You've dedicated years to voluntary work. You don't need to prove anything to anyone, Emmy. Not me. And not to yourself.' He huffed a breath. 'Why not do something you'd thrive on and love?'

'Look, it's a good idea,' she admitted. 'A lot of your guests would love it...but I can't be that person.'

He grabbed her hand and stopped her from walking away. 'Don't you think you deserve it?'

She looked at him questioningly.

'Help from someone? Support from someone? *Anything* from someone?'

'It's not that,' she murmured. She'd accepted help before. The problem was that she'd just realised what it was she did want from him. And it wasn't help or support. It was *everything*.

And that included her being able to offer support to him.

His grip on her tightened fractionally before he suddenly released her and stepped back. 'Because it would be for me?'

She said nothing as another guest stepped up to speak to them, but she felt Javier's withdrawal and that ache in her heart intensified.

The evening slipped by in concerted effort of smiles and conversation. Emerald talked and focused so hard, anything to distract herself from her own realisation and that moment with Javier.

So she was tired when they returned to the helicopter and flew fast and low across the water to the waiting yacht. She dozed for most of the trip, her head resting on his shoulder, her hand held in his. Because despite her realisation, she couldn't deny herself his touch.

He gently roused her, then with a laugh half carried her from the 'copter onto the deck and towards his cabin.

'I need to check Luke,' she said softly, properly coming awake.

'I know,' he murmured. 'Already on it.'

The door to their baby's room was ajar. A square of light illuminated the room enough for her to see Luke in his cot. Her son seemed to have inherited her ability to sleep through the sound of a helicopter arriving. Her heart rose into her throat. He was so beautiful.

'I watch him when he's sleeping. I stare at him and I can't believe he's mine,' she confessed in a whisper. 'He's so perfect. It's like magic. And there's nothing I won't do to protect him.' She glanced up at Javier. 'Do you know what I mean?'

In the half-darkness she couldn't tell if he smiled back at her. But she heard the rasp in his whisper.

'I know exactly what you mean.'

That soft answer soothed her anxiety. Javier, she was certain, had fallen in love with Luke. And suddenly, in this midnight hour, having seen Luke, being with Javier…it made her wonder if magic might be real after all. Her heart filled with a bubble of hope. Maybe they just needed more time?

She'd told Javier her truth and he'd still wanted her to come with him tonight. Her family background didn't bother him. So then maybe, *maybe* this could work? Maybe, in time, he would open up to her fully? He would let her really know what it was that had kept him distanced for so long?

Yes, *she* was vulnerable, but she and Javier shared a bond—Luke—and they shared passion. They shared laughter too. Perhaps, in time, something more could grow from those foundations?

'Why are you smiling?' Javier asked when she'd led the way back up to his private deck.

Emmy turned to face him. He was looking at her curiously, his beautiful eyes deep and warm, and she couldn't resist falling into the fantasy.

'You remind me of someone I met once,' she teased him playfully.

His eyebrows arched. 'Who was that?'

'Oh, he was a pirate.'

'A *pirate*?' His grin flashed in the moonlight.

'He came to the islands looking for treasure. His name was Ramon and he was a rogue and I couldn't resist him. He was playful and fun and impossible to say no to.'

'Was he?' A tantalising thread in his voice drew her

nearer. 'Well, you remind me of someone I met once, too,' he said. 'She wasn't like any other woman I'd met before.'

'No?'

'She emerged from the water in this stunning bikini, a voluptuous nymph.'

'That's what caught your eye, huh?' She giggled. 'Always the bikini.'

'What can I say?' He laughed. 'It emphasised her spectacular curves and flaming-red hair. But it was her artless confidence that stopped me in my tracks. She looked so liberated in her wild environment—open and innocent and it turned out she *was* a rare creature in disguise. She was a bona fide fire-breathing dragon and she let me into her secret world.'

'A dragon?'

'The best kind. Beautiful, every inch was a different sort of treasure.'

'Ramon showed me a secret world of his own too,' she whispered huskily. 'Dance with me.'

His gaze flared. 'Dance? There's no music.'

'You know we make our own.' She didn't just dance with him, she danced for him. Teasing her way out of the silk dress.

'You're so damn sexy,' he muttered hoarsely. 'I just want to…'

'To what?' she teased. Because she knew very well and she wanted it every bit as much.

And suddenly this was *her* night. Nothing—no reticence or fear—held her back. It was like that night on the beach when a pirate had appeared and breathed the fierceness within her to life. Only now it was better. Now she understood more what there was to be had with him. And now she understood just what it was she was feeling and how deep it ran and there was no way she could not express it. Not now he was before her again, gazing intently, his jaw slack, his breathing roughened as she danced closer still.

'Emmy...'

It was a cross between a warning and a plea and it only made her burn hotter and her smile more sultry and her heart more loving. And she wanted to love him so very much. She wanted not to hide, not to have to be afraid, not to have to stay silent as she had in other ways for so long.

The truth that had hit her earlier tonight was so huge, there was no hiding it, no denying it and, in this moonlit madness, she didn't even want to try. Instead she let it release—streaming from every pore. Every sweep of her hands, every suck of her mouth, every arch of her hips, spelled out her passion for him. She couldn't stop her own response, her own desire and discovering again the joy of his powerful, guttural response. The need to prove in this one, most basic and instinctive of ways consumed her—that she was utterly his.

CHAPTER ELEVEN

JAVIER STEALTHILY MOVED across the bedroom floor, not wishing to wake her this early. The sun wasn't even a glimmer on the water yet, but his mind was riffing on too many things for him to sleep. Too many uncomfortable things. And suddenly he couldn't stay here…he couldn't float endlessly in the middle of the Pacific Ocean, eating and swimming and sleeping…

Last night had been…*successful*? He should, in theory, be delighted at the way the hotel refurbishment was going and the welcome he'd received from local business leaders. He ought to be delighted at how popular Emmy's photo had been in that line-up celebrating the region—and how touched she'd been he'd used it. And frankly, he ought to be in the recovery position and having extra oxygen tubed in, given how explosively passionate they'd been together last night—how devastating her sexy ministrations on deck had been. She had been pure feminine strength, pure fire and he shook just thinking about it.

So in theory, he ought not to be able to move right now at all.

Instead, the *only* thing he wanted to do was move. The discomfort that had begun as a mere irritating itch beneath his skin had inflamed into a sharp ache that rendered him unable to remain still. He went into the onboard office and focused on a multitude of meaningless tasks. The emails that could wait for replies, he tapped out lengthy responses to at three in the morning. He dictated longer missives for his assistant back in the States to act on later. He listed more things to be done by the rest of his team, brainstormed next developments and new ideas. He checked the global share-price indices, repeatedly, and scanned headlines of online papers and journals. It was all very deliberate and focused—as if by keeping busy again, he could ignore that problematic feeling increasing inside. But though he tried and tried, he couldn't avoid the raging possessiveness emerging within him.

It wasn't a nice feeling. Worse was that it wasn't within his control.

It wasn't regarding Luke—he was different, somehow. There was possessiveness, protectiveness, certainly. But it was embedded within a rock-solid certainty. Javier knew, no matter what, that he would always be there for his son. *That* was a surety.

But the look on Emmy's face last night when she'd risen over his body. The light in her eyes? The tenderness in her touch? That had been too much. Far too much.

And that sense of elusiveness that he couldn't cope with? It was destroying him now.

Instead of being able to breathe easy and just enjoy this passing phase with her, he found himself flexing his fist as if he could hold onto the invisible. Or the impossible. But instead of grasping and getting only air, he knew he needed to push right away. Now.

Because he didn't just like her touch, he ached for her *attention*. And attention, he knew, eventually wandered. It ought not to matter—he assured himself it *didn't* matter. It was just that it hadn't been long enough to burn their chemistry yet. She'd teased him, questioning about how that would fade, but while he'd laughed, he'd been sure it would. It always had before. Perhaps the problem was because he was out of his usual sphere. It was time to return to the real world—not the isolated oasis of unique, protected creatures. The sooner the better.

'I need to go back to New York.' He couldn't even look into her eyes; he didn't want those blues to magnify the nugget of regret lodging in his chest. 'I have work commitments. Some meetings I can't miss.'

'When?' Wariness muted her voice.

'As soon as we're packed.'

'You wouldn't let Luke and I stay here and come back when you're done?'

His gut tightened in instant rebellion at the thought, not just of leaving Luke, but of leaving her. That she'd even asked aggravated the irritation that had been festering for days.

'I'm sorry, that was a stupid thing to ask.' She spoke again swiftly before he had the chance to reply. 'That was just me being...'

Cautious. And Javier could understand it on a rational level. This was her home and Luke's birthplace. But his gut roiled with perceived rejection. *Nowhere* was going to be as good as here for her.

'We'll come back often.' He coughed the rasp from his throat. 'I'll need to for work anyway.'

As always, once Javier set a plan in motion, it was enacted swiftly and precisely. Emmy counted as she breathed, trying to stay calm and not fall to pieces as she left the superyacht that had become 'home' in a shockingly short time period. They used the helicopter again from the boat back to Santa Cruz, where she insisted on seeing Connie to say goodbye and reassure her she'd bring Luke back again soon. Then they'd hopped to Quito and begun the journey to New York. The first-class cabin was luxurious but she couldn't relax. Not even having Thomas to entertain Luke helped, it just gave her more time to ruminate on what was going to happen once they got to Javier's home. And apart from that one query, Javier hadn't bothered her. Hadn't chatted with her. Hadn't shared a laugh with her. It was as if he'd left already—lost in staring at his laptop screen, a frown of concentration and contemplation.

There was no hint—no look, no touch, no murmur—of the magic they'd shared last night. No sign that he'd noticed how much of herself she'd given him then—because, truth be told, she'd given him everything last night. With her arms, her hands, her mouth…her *heart*.

And how could he not have felt that? How could he not know?

Yet it seemed he didn't. Or worse, if he did, he wanted to pretend as if it hadn't happened. Because he was silent and he didn't see her. All he seemed to want was to escape. The problem was they were each to become a permanent pillar in the other's life.

But not in the way she wanted.

So what happened when this 'chemistry' he felt for her finally faded? Where did that leave her? Because it wasn't ever going to fade for her. It was built from something more solid than pheromones now and she knew her heart was about to be broken. Yet because of Luke, she was bound to Javier for the rest of her life. She'd be there, watching like a glued-to-the-pavement passer-by when he found new lovers. And there'd be plenty of them. And when he eventually found a woman he wanted to make his *wife*… She was sure that would happen, despite his declarations to the contrary. He was a fantastic father and an incredible lover and a generous, *all in* kind of person. So when he finally truly fell for someone, he wouldn't hesitate. And he'd never do to Luke what had been done to him. He'd ensure his firstborn child was always kept close, in the very heart of his new family's embrace. While Emerald would be glued in place—on the outside looking in.

'Emmy?'

'Mmm?'

He was frowning at her from across the aisle of the plane. 'What are you thinking about?'

'Nothing.'

'You look like you're about to cry.'

She felt like it. Instead she dragged on a smile. 'I was just drifting…miles away. Sorry.'

'No need to be sorry.' But he looked sombre. 'I promise you'll come back to the islands often.'

It wasn't leaving the islands hurting her heart. Even if they were to stay, the outlook would remain the same. A lonely, heartbroken future.

Javier's residential building in Manhattan was near the financial district. As sophisticated and gleamingly stylish as she'd have expected. Totally the showstopper piece required for a financial *wunderkind* turned property billionaire.

'A room has been partially kitted out as Luke's nursery,' he said as he carried their son in his arms and led her through the spacious apartment. 'But you can do more with it if you'd like.'

She glanced around the timelessly styled suite. Two large frames hung with perfect symmetry on the wall opposite Luke's bed—one held the very first photo of

Luke with her, moments after his birth. The other was the photo she'd taken of Javier with Luke swimming off the coast. There was not, she noted with a dull hit to her heart, a photo of the three of them *together*.

'Thomas has the guest wing,' Javier added. 'And he'll use the apartment I have for my staff on the level two below this during his weekends.'

She rather envied the separate small living room, kitchenette, bedroom and bathroom that was for Thomas's exclusive use.

'There's a computer on the desk for you, also a security card, access code, numbers for a driver if you need one. All the information is in the folder beside it.'

'Thank you.' She glanced and saw the boxes of brand-new things—laptop, phone, watch.

Emotionally fraught, she saw her bags had been put straight into the master suite. Javier's large bed dominated the room and she quickly turned away from it, almost bumping into him behind her.

'I have to go to the office.' Javier stepped back brusquely. 'I'll be a few hours.'

'Of course.'

Yes, his walls were up again and his mind was clearly elsewhere—as it had been the whole trip. It seemed he couldn't wait to get away from them both and she was so hurt. Had he seen what she'd felt last night? Was this why he was rejecting her now? And her anger began to grow—why couldn't he at least talk to her about it? Why not be honest?

She gave Thomas the rest of the day off to organise his things. Finally alone with Luke, she explored the large apartment. It taught her nothing new about Javier—there were no family pictures anywhere other than those two in Luke's room. But given what he'd told her, she wasn't surprised at that. The bookcases were filled with non-fiction on a variety of eclectic subjects. The art hanging in the living area and the sculptures on plinths in the vestibule were probably investments. As was the entire building, of course. It wasn't a home that revealed anything about the inner life or personality of its owner. It was simply pristine and utterly comfortable—as restful and perfect as the hotels he was becoming famous for.

In the gleaming kitchen, the fridge was already filled with organic, nutritious baby food provided by a boutique service Thomas had tracked down. Though, now they were ensconced in their new home, he would prepare most of Luke's meals from scratch. Javier had told her he liked to order food in from any of the numerous restaurants nearby.

So, it seemed she wasn't needed for any kind of house-keeping or cooking support... or anything much else.

Emmy took Luke for a walk around the neighbour-hood to familiarise herself with the area. Then, while her son napped, she swallowed her pride and set up the new laptop Javier had had delivered. She would search online for possible work. Truthfully Javier's thoughts had been helpful and she loved the idea of doing something with her photography. She had several skills and she'd figure something out; she always had in the past. But she got side-tracked looking at an online article about Javier. It referenced his staff—personal assistants, lawyers, accountants. He oversaw a whole empire she knew little about. Yet he'd talked to her about his plans earlier in the week on the boat when they'd both been distracting themselves from their own lust. He'd taken the time to answer her questions about what he did and why. He'd asked for her own experiences and advice on how to continue the legacy of the Flores Foundation. They'd debated the need and meaning of the voluntary programmes, the importance of sustainability. And she'd enjoyed every moment of those discussions.

She refocused and searched online for possible jobs, brainstorming ideas on paper as she went. Hours passed and she fed and bathed Luke, reading to him. Then dined herself.

Javier still didn't return.

She curled up in one of the large cosy armchairs in the library and chose a movie to watch. She was behind on all the latest releases and Javier had subscriptions to all the streaming services.

'Emmy?'

She stirred. The room was in darkness; the sound on the television had been lowered. She must've fallen asleep in front of the movie. Javier was standing a short distance away. Wearing only boxers and a tee, he'd apparently just showered. She sat up, embarrassed that he'd caught her. But at the same time, her mouth dried. He was so gorgeous.

'Have you eaten?' he asked.

'Thanks, yes.' She unfolded her legs and ran her hands down her thighs. 'I got a delivery from the Italian on that list you left. It was delicious.'

'Good.' His reply seemed distant. 'Look—' he ran his hand through his hair, his expression grim '—I know we've only been back one day, but I have to take an overnight trip to Miami tomorrow. I thought we'd all go.'

Emmy stilled. His work schedule was going to be challenging for her to find something of her own. Did he really want her to go too? 'If that's what you want.'

Silence stretched. In the semi-darkness she couldn't read his eyes.

'I'm sorry I was home later than I'd wanted to be.' He

rubbed his arm and took a step closer to her. 'I've checked on Luke. He's fast asleep.' His lips suddenly curved, softening the seriousness in his stance. 'You were too. But you need to be somewhere more comfortable.'

She didn't reply as he took her hands in his and tugged her to her feet. He didn't say anything more as he led her to his bedroom and that huge bed. He'd turned the covers down already. She sank into the soft linen, too tired to resist her own desires. She wanted the pleasure he gave her. She couldn't deny herself, despite that growing warning within. And in seconds that alarm was silenced anyway—drowned in the physical delight washing through her. And Javier's mouth and hands were as hungry and as desperate as her own. It was as if they were both determined to keep too busy and keep mouths too full to let secrets slip.

CHAPTER TWELVE

'THOMAS HAS LUKE,' Javier muttered when she stirred as he left the bed early the next morning. 'Sleep in while you can. I'll be back this afternoon to take us to the airport.'

Sleeping in was an impossibility but Emmy didn't reply. When he'd gone she rolled onto her back and stared at the ceiling, hardening her resolve. They'd spent the night attempting to satiate that physical desire with a lengthy, wordless expression of pure lust. But the playful, passionate element of that night at the gala had gotten lost somewhere along the way. Last night had felt more desperate, more frantic—to her at least. And she *had* been desperate to hold back how she really felt. Her heart ached, but she knew she couldn't hold back the truth in those moments of intimacy again. She *would* end up telling him how she felt.

And that would be terrible. That would be an exposure worse than any. Worse than the fear of people finding out and judging her for her family's actions. She would be so vulnerable. Because she knew—absolutely—that what she felt for Javier was not reciprocated by him.

He'd told her, quite openly, right from the start—even that first night on the beach—he didn't want a long-term lover. He didn't want a wife. He didn't want a real relationship with her. He believed, not in love, but in chemistry. And in his world, that chemistry would all be used up soon enough.

But he'd not really told her why. He'd mentioned his father, his mother's remarriage. But he'd not talked to her about how that had all really felt. He'd been almost glib and joked it off before changing the subject as quickly as possible. He'd not wanted to open up to her.

And wasn't that fair enough?

Except she'd opened up to him. She'd told him of her shame of her family, of her own mistakes, of her own choices. And he'd accepted her.

But he wouldn't allow her to do the same for him. He didn't want to the same way she did.

So she now had to accept that.

Suddenly this Miami trip was a saviour. It was her opportunity to take the time she needed to clear her head and make the move she needed to make. She knew Javier could offer Luke everything and he'd begun to love Luke as much as anyone could. He'd become a wonderful father who wanted to be there for his son.

Emmy couldn't ask anything more of him than that. He didn't have to love *her* too.

Her problem was *she* was in love with him. It had snuck up on her so quickly and it was so much more than that wickedly wonderful passion they shared. He was gorgeous—strong and fit. But he was also funny and loyal and intelligent and special. But it was her problem and hers alone. She couldn't let it negatively impact on Luke. Or on Javier.

But she needed time to process and move past her disappointment and heartbreak. She could work out a plan that she could live with long term given the time and space to do that. Because she couldn't continue this as it currently was. She couldn't live this close with him not actually wanting her in the same way. She couldn't keep giving of herself, couldn't fall deeper and deeper still with every kiss, with every conversation...

And she needed to face the reality of her future with Javier as a loving, active parent in Luke's life. She needed to let Javier take him, to face time apart from them both and get used to being on her own for periods of time. Because even if she and Javier were really together as a couple, that would happen at times. They wouldn't all be able to travel together always. So she needed to start now and deal with it. And she could do that. For Luke. For Javier. And for herself.

Fortunately Javier Torres wasn't the only one who could make swift plans. Emmy too knew how to get things done. She had years of survival behind her. She could handle this.

'Can you take Luke down to the car, please, Thomas?' Emmy asked the nanny when Javier arrived in the early afternoon as he'd said he would. 'Javier and I just need a moment first.'

She saw the questioning look Javier shot her, but he said nothing while Thomas and Luke were still present. Emmy kissed her son's head and indulged in a tiny extra-tight squeeze before handing her most precious bundle to the hyper-efficient, affable nanny.

'What's up?' Javier asked once the elevator door had slid shut.

Emmy locked her knees to try to combat the stupidly nervous tremble within. 'I'm not coming with you.'

Javier cocked his head, his gaze sharpening. 'You what?'

'I'm not coming with you to Miami.' She cleared her throat and spoke more forcefully. 'I don't want to.'

'And you decide to announce this now, when we're all packed and Thomas and Luke are already in the car?'

'It makes no difference to you whether I come or not.'

'On the contrary, it makes a very great difference to me.' He actually smiled at her.

Seriously? Was he reducing this moment to *sex*? Another distraction in the form of a joke? She stared back at him sombrely; well, that would be right—that was all this was to him.

His smile faded. 'Emmy—'

'I'm not going,' she said in a low voice. 'You go. Take Luke.' She blinked back the appalling storm of hot tears that threatened to spill.

For a split second his jaw slackened. 'Why? What's wrong?' He lifted his head sharply. 'What are you going to do while we're gone? Will you be here when we get back?'

With one doubting question he sliced away the last stable ground from beneath her feet.

'Did you really need to ask that?' She stared at him, hurt. 'And you say *I* expect the worst from people?' She crossed her arms in front of her chest, holding herself tightly. 'You do too, Javier. You expect it from me. You don't trust me. I don't think you ever have.'

'That's not what I meant.' He jerked his arm to the side and drew in a deep breath. 'Is it because you're tired?' he asked in a determinedly reasonable tone. 'Because I can reschedule. I'll fly early in the morning and back late tomorrow night. Then neither of you need accompany me.'

His offer of an alternative hurt her even more. Because he was *trying*, he wanted to do what was 'right'. But that wasn't enough for *her* needs. Because he was still holding his own truths out on her.

'That's unsustainable in the long run.' She shook her

head firmly. 'The travel you need to do is hard enough—you need to be at your best for your business. And for Luke. You need to take him and stay overnight tonight. Come back when you're done.'

He stood very still. 'In the long run?'

'We need to start as we're going to carry on. This is one night. I know you'll care for him,' she said.

He watched her with an intent frown as if trying to parse some other meaning to her words.

'Look, you're taking Thomas.' She tried to lighten her tone so she didn't sound as if this were some death knell. Even though it felt like it. 'You know, the nanny with all the amazing qualifications. And he'll be with you, his father. Who loves him.'

'You're happy to let Luke go, just like that?'

She pressed her lips together for a moment to bite back the pain. 'One night away is nothing compared to what you've already missed out on. And I'm not asking you to miss out on another night with him now I know how much it matters to you. I wouldn't do that to you. Go.' She was angry with him for not moving already—for making this harder than she wanted it to be. 'I know you'll care for him. I know you'll bring him back safe and well and happy.'

'So you're doing this for my benefit?' he queried quietly. 'But what is it that *you're* going to do?'

She didn't want to discuss her plans with him; she wasn't ready to yet. 'I just need some time.' She still tried to play it lightly.

'Not away from Luke,' he said with annoying perceptiveness. 'You're nearly in tears at the thought of being apart from him for one night.'

She stiffened, trying to stem the emotion from leaking out of every pore.

'So, no need to offer any more clues.' He stepped right in front of her. 'It's *me* you need some time from.'

His insistence broke her.

'Yes,' she gritted. 'It's you.'

He stiffened but he didn't step back. 'Why?' He folded his arms and stared right into her eyes. 'What have I done?'

She shook her head at his continued push. 'Don't be cruel.'

'Cruel?' Shock—and accusation—crackled in his voice. 'All I'm asking for is honesty. I want to understand, Emmy. Have I done something wrong? It shouldn't be that difficult to tell me.'

The face that he had no idea how difficult it was for her to even face him right now was so very telling. He had no idea of how she really felt. Of how he was hurting her. She glanced away from him.

'I can't do this—' she muttered.

'Be honest?'

'That is so very you, Javier.' She inhaled sharply. 'You seek *answers*. But not intimacy.'

'What does that even mean?'

'You want to know things, so that way you can provide a neat solution and keep everything in your control. So you can pat yourself on the back, satisfied you've ticked all the boxes and done all you could. But you never make *yourself* vulnerable. You never offer all the answers of your own.' She broke off. She didn't want to slam him. She didn't want to debate this when she was still figuring it out for herself. 'Look, by inviting me to travel, you're trying to include me in everything with Luke, I get that. And I appreciate it, especially when I wasn't as fair at the start. But I'm just an added extra you don't really want or need. And I don't want to be that extra burden on you.

Right now the financial aspect is too much already. I'm trying to work on that.'

'You don't need to—'

'I do. For my own dignity I need independence.'

'I have enough resources to support—'

'Don't you understand? That's *not* what I want from you.'

'Then what is?'

She stared at him. 'You don't want me to say what I really want. You won't want to give it to me.'

'Why not tell me and let me decide? Instead you're throwing a grenade out the door with me and not being brave enough to deal with the fallout. I'm trying to do what's right for *all* of us. Most especially for Luke.'

'As am I,' she tossed back hotly, her handle on her emotions slipping further still.

'Really? *You're* the one who won't stick around anywhere long enough to establish real relationships. Who ran away to one of the world's most remote places where other people pretty much only passed through. And you only stayed there because having Luke anchored you. You're terrified to trust anyone. The second you think you're at risk, you run—only this time you can't, you're stuck, so you're pushing back on me. Why not be brave enough to be honest about what the damn problem is? Why not fight for yourself, Emmy?'

'What do you think I've just done?' She glared at him. 'I've just told you...' She trailed off in shock as everything rippled upwards from the depths in which she'd long suppressed it and she could no longer hold a word of it back. 'I've been afraid for so long. Afraid of my family. Afraid of losing my place. Afraid people would find out about everything and they'd then reject me—because they have before. I lived on a knife edge all the time, just waiting for everything to go wrong, and that was a horrible way to live—'

'How many times do I have to tell you I don't care that half your family are criminals? It doesn't bother—'

'I know you don't care, Javier,' she snapped harshly. 'I know that. *That's* the point. *That's* the problem here.'

He froze, his eyes wide and his face whitening.

'You know what?' she questioned, losing her control entirely. 'You were right—I did seal myself away in a safe sanctuary. I'd not realised the extent to which I'd hidden away on the edge of the world, avoiding mostly everyone so I didn't have to fear that judgement. But while it was paradise, I was missing so much. Then I met you and I had Luke and opened my world right up. Because I can't deny him what I denied myself. I can't keep him hidden away in some sanctuary where he doesn't get everything he deserves. You were so right about that. But *I* deserve more too.' She shook inside as every emotion, every yearning poured forth. 'You want me to carve open my wounds and expose my bleeding heart, Javier? Fine. I'll do that. Here's my honesty. I can't continue with the uncertainty of you "fading" on me, while I *know* the feelings I have for you won't. Because I don't just feel lust, Javier. I've fallen in love with you. But you don't want to love me.'

He stared at her, an arrested—and appalled—expression in his eyes.

'I know you believe you don't want marriage or a long-term relationship—because it always ends in divorce, right?' she barrelled along despite that horror in his face. 'You tell yourself *nothing* lasts. Which means you don't have to make the *effort*. It lets you off the hook. You don't have to try. *Why bother? It won't last anyway*. It's lazy, Javier. And it's cowardly.' She glared at him. 'Yet here you are, determinedly building beautiful buildings to last longer than your own lifetime. And even though you know there might be some seismic shift in the earth that breaks it apart anyway—you still go ahead and build it. But in your personal life, you can't accept that some things might be beyond all your control but it's worth braving it anyway. That it's worth the risk…but you won't open yourself to the threat of that chaos. *I'm* not worth that risk to you. You're happy to sleep with me. You're happy to foot all my bills…but you're not happy to truly commit to me, because this is just "chemistry", right?' Hurt ignited rage and every emotion poured from her in a torrent of sadness and regret. 'But it isn't—not for me. And I can't live with that uncertainty and insecurity.'

Concern tightened his features and that expression-less—*dead*—look in his eyes that she'd grown to *loathe* emerged.

'And you keep holding out on me,' she cried bitterly when he didn't respond. 'You won't open up to me. You use sex, or a laugh or your work or just this…just silence. You won't ever say what you're really, actually *feeling*.'

'Emmy…'

It was the pity in his voice that did her in and destroyed the last of her hope. 'No, don't—' She held up a hand, warding him off. Warning him not to step nearer. 'Don't try to tell me that it's not just me, that it's any woman. Any one. Because here's the thing. I know you're capable of love. I've seen it—you love Luke. But that's different. That's snuck up on you in a primal way that you have no choice over. You can't deny it. And that *is* love. It is too big for someone to contain it, or conceal it…it leaks out. Like it's leaking out of me right now. But you can deny it for me, because you don't love *me*. So I can't let things go on as they are knowing you can't give me what I want. You don't feel the same. And I get it. I'm not…what you really want. Fine. But you don't get to monopolise the best of me. Not all of my time in this part of my life. I deserve more. I've missed out on so much and I can't let myself settle for not good enough again. So I can't… I can't stay in this…undefined…sleeping-together arrangement. It's tearing me apart. It's destroying everything I've built for myself.'

'You're saying I'm destroying you?'

'My sleeping with you is. My living with you like a lover is.' She made herself lift her voice and finish this. 'I know we need to deal with each other. And I'm sorry because I'm not in a position to be fully independent from you yet—not in Manhattan. Not where you need Luke to be. So you and I both have to compromise. I hate it, but I have to accept your offer of living space, only for as long as it takes to set myself up independently. But I won't travel with you. I want you to take Luke. I don't want you to miss out on any more time with him.'

'Wow, that's so generous of you.' His eyes flashed like shining black stones. 'You're afraid of judgement, but you're not afraid to dish it out as far as I'm concerned. I made one mistake when I didn't tell you my full name, and you've never wanted to forgive me—'

'No. It isn't about that. I'm long over that. It's not about forgiving, but what you can't—won't—give me. You offer everything material, but nothing precious. Yes, I might have hidden away in some ways on the islands, but *you're* the one keeping safe. You're the one refusing to open up emotionally. You won't tell me so much more than your name…you can't even tell me properly *why* you even needed to do that. Why did you want a break from being you, Javier? Why didn't you like your own company that night?' She flung her head back as he stood there, pale and silent. 'We're different people, with different needs. And we had this wonderful night together, but that was supposed to be it. With Luke, we've been brought back together and we succumbed to that attraction again. But ultimately we want different things. And that's okay. I just need some space to work through how this is going to be.'

'So when I get back?'

'I won't be in your bed waiting for you. I'm not sleeping with you any more. We're co-parents. And that's it.'

'You think it can just end between us—just like that? Emmy.' He shook his head in rampant disbelief. 'Last night we—'

'It's *over*,' she snapped fiercely. 'That part has to be over. Please don't try to change my mind. Please respect my choice. Please don't make a joke of what I'm trying to tell you. Or I *will* have to leave.'

He stared at her.

'We both want what's best for Luke, but I also need to do what's best for *me* in this. And that is not to be with you.' She gazed at him, so hurt but still unable to let go of the last remnants of hope. 'And the worst thing is the fact that I'm *always* going to want more from you. I'm going to want more than you can *ever* give me,' she said. 'I don't want the *things*. I don't want the fancy boat or amazing bling or designer dresses. But *you* can only give me the things.' She looked up at him. 'You can't give me the love and trust and intimacy I want from you. It's not there.'

He said nothing. He didn't argue with her. Didn't deny the truth. Didn't tell her any of the words her foolish heart ached to hear.

'I didn't want to *say* any of this,' she groaned sadly. 'Why did you push? Why couldn't you just leave me? Why did you have to be so mean?' She hated that she'd lost control and revealed everything of herself. It was humiliating. But worse, it was painful because it only proved what she'd already known. He didn't love her. He didn't want her the way she wanted him. 'This is why I need time away from *you*.' She was furious with him and herself. 'Please go now. I promise I'll be here when you get back. I would never leave my son.'

'But you'd leave me.'

'*Yes.*' A million times *yes*. She could barely see him through the tearful haze in her eyes. Right now she wanted to run away from him faster than she'd ever run from anything in her life.

CHAPTER THIRTEEN

JAVIER STALKED OUT of the building, his stomach tight.

'Let's go.' He jerked his head at his driver and chose to sit in the front passenger seat and not engage with his son, safely tucked in the back with the nanny. He needed to cool down and process before he could speak to anyone. Right now he was raging inside.

Emmy's rejection of their physical relationship was a rejection of *him*. Her refusal to travel with him on this, the shortest of trips, was a rejection of *him*. If she had complete freedom of choice—no small son to think of—then she would utterly reject him. She would walk out and not look back and never return. He knew it. He'd seen it before.

Her words? Her passion? Telling him she was in love with him in one breath and asking him to avoid her altogether in the next? She didn't want him. She didn't love him. If she did, why would she instantly do the one thing that would hurt him the most? Why would she shut him out?

So he didn't believe her declaration. Not for a second. She had been isolated for too long. She'd been lonely. She'd been inexperienced. She'd hit some sort of high from the companionship and closeness that she'd never really had before and confused that with...what she thought was love. In fact, he raged inwardly, it wasn't actually *him* she thought she was in love with. It was the change in circumstances. It was—he hated to realise—a kind of gratitude, or, worse, some sort of sick Stockholm syndrome, because they were bound to each other because of their baby. Trapped together, so her hormones were helping her make the best of it by believing her to be…in love with him, the father of her child.

He flew to Miami. On the flight he calmed down enough to read to Luke, the same little story over and over, softly murmuring the rhyme for the entire journey. Anything to avoid the thoughts—the echo of her words—circling over and over in his head instead.

But then his little son slept and he decided to work late in the hotel, only it was impossible to concentrate. So, late at night, he abandoned the effort and tried to sleep. But then, in his dreams he was transfixed by the vision of Emerald Jones, fire-breathing beauty—promising everything in one instant and stealing it back the next.

And her words kept echoing. Her accusations. Her truths.

Because what she'd said was right, was it not? He didn't want a relationship. And maybe they'd been over-complicating things by continuing to sleep together even though they'd left the islands. Maybe this was the right time to end that side of things. It was only sex, after all. And getting clarification, boundaries, back would be good. That was what he'd wanted all along, wasn't it? But more phrases she'd thrown at him kept echoing in his mind.

You don't get to monopolise the best of me. Not all of my time…

Did that mean she wanted to be free to meet someone else? Rationally he knew that she should. Of course.

And she *would*. She was a stunningly vibrant woman who ought to be scooped up by some guy and adored for all eternity.

He flinched and had to shift position in his suddenly uncomfortable bed. He couldn't stand the idea of some other jerk adoring her. He winced at his dog-in-the-manger attitude. He didn't want her but didn't want anyone else to have her either?

Things—okay, yes, relationships—*didn't* last. He'd seen it time and time again. He'd borne the brunt of the fallout. And it was his own fault for reigniting that passion with her. Except there was no way he could have resisted at the time. And nor had she been able to. He'd been right about that 'chemistry' at least. It was uncontainable.

But he also knew that now she'd made her decision, she would stick to it. Emmy had determination and strength and this choice of hers would last. *She* was one person who could remain constant and true.

And that sudden realisation? That made his whole chest ache all over again.

He doggedly forced focus in the meetings the next day. He refused to let his staff down or his business slide because of his personal life. But he concluded the schedule as quickly as he could, returning to Luke. To hold and quietly vow to his son that he would never, ever leave him. Because being left—being rejected—*sucked*. And it hurt. And it *damaged*.

And it had happened to Javier before. More than once.

Only he'd never really told her that, had he? And he'd certainly never really stopped to consider just how it had damaged *him*.

He paused, making himself reflect on those moments in his past that he'd chosen to forget for so long. Those most painful ones—what kinds of warped lessons had they taught him?

Was what she'd said fair? Had he held back from her?

He couldn't sit still to consider the answer; he knew it already. But at the time she'd said it, he'd been too busy being hurt—too busy feeling that horror of rejection again—to be able to think clearly enough to respond.

Only now he had the time to think. And it wasn't pleasant.

Was he going to let the scars from the past stop him from seeing the future that might be possible? The chance that was right in front of him?

On the flight back to New York Luke slept again and Javier closed his eyes too—trying to figure out what to say to her when he saw her next. But he didn't see her. She'd moved her few clothes from his room to that last spare bedroom on the far side of Luke's. So Javier did the decent thing and went to work again late at night—giving her time to reunite with their baby without him watching.

An hour later he stared at the list she'd messaged through, barely biting back the urge to sprint back to the apartment and storm into her new room and tell her exactly what he thought of her 'timetable'—an appalling co-parenting arrangement in which they completely avoided each other. He pushed away that instinctive wound—his own petulant assumption that it was a rejection of him. That *he* wasn't enough. He was overreacting. But she'd struck a nerve. And how was it her hit could hurt this hard?

He got home late and the apartment was too quiet. He stole into Luke's room and watched him sleep a while. Inexorably his attention was drawn to the photo he'd ordered hung on Luke's nursery wall. The portrait of Emmy and Luke, moments after Luke's arrival, had struck him the second he'd seen it. All the emotions rose every time he looked at it—protectiveness, possessiveness. They overwhelmed him. He lifted the picture from Luke's wall and put it in his own room. He went to sleep looking at them and they were the first things he saw when he woke. But the misery rose, the rage blurred and slowly the truth settled. He needed that picture—it was his own aide-memoire—because they were the two most precious things in his life.

But now he knew the picture alone wasn't enough. He wanted the real things—*both* of them with him, all of the time. And it was only now that she'd pushed him away that he realised that he, too, struggled with secrets, and struggled without certainty. He'd thought he had it all sorted—had offered her 'everything' he could in a half-assed, cowardly way. He'd suggested she stay with him, offering her no security. He was a jerk. But he'd not realised it himself—not until now. So his ineptitude, his silence of the other day when she'd opened up and hurled all her thoughts and feelings at his head, appealing to his heart…that had hurt her. It had hurt him too. Because he'd kept his heart buried away for so very long he'd just about forgotten it was there.

He'd *never* had emotional security. But he wanted his son to have it—to give it to him. He wanted to do that for Emmy too—so very differently and so very much. And she, more than anyone except perhaps himself, needed that certainty. She needed to hear the truth. She needed absolute honesty before she would believe. And he needed her to forgive him and to believe in him. This separation—he realised far too late—was the antithesis of what he wanted. He wanted *everything* with her.

He'd been so self-defensive, so focused on building his walls, he'd become blind to his own emotions. All the things he'd done—not just providing for her, but listening to her, laughing with her, wanting to bring her out, making love to her—they'd all been the actions of a man falling deeply in love.

He just hadn't seen it in himself. And she'd not seen it either and that was on him. Because he'd been so damn defensive he'd hidden it too well from her. She'd opened up to him—she'd been so brave, so vulnerable, so trusting in him. But he'd *hurt* her.

So while he'd long been decisive, he knew whatever action he took now, whatever gesture he tried to think of, it wasn't going to be enough. Because it was the *words* that were required. Words—or lack of—could hurt, but words could also heal. Sometimes stupid words could be forgiven. And honest words would be believed. He hoped so, anyway. He had to think that it might be possible in this case.

Because Emerald Jones, he finally realised, was his gorgeous dragon—she'd made him believe in something he'd thought was mere myth or fairy tale. But it was magic and real—it was hot and wonderful and scary as hell. She'd made him believe in the existence of love.

CHAPTER FOURTEEN

'THOMAS?' EMMY WALKED into the apartment. 'Luke?'

She listened but heard no reply. It was four days since her blow-up with Javier. He'd taken Luke and gone for the night. She'd indulged in a horrendous crying jag. Then she'd wiped a cold flannel over her face and moved her stuff into the spare bedroom farthest from Javier's. She'd spent the night alternately wiping her eyes with that cold flannel and giving herself a pep talk and desperately trying to find a distraction for herself. Find work. Study. Survive.

She'd managed to avoid him mostly since their return. He'd been gracious enough to stay away for her reunion with Luke.

He'd apparently agreed to her suggestion of him leaving for work later, so he had time with Luke in the mornings. She lay on her bed and pretended to read or sleep or do something—anything—until she heard the front door close and was certain he'd left for the day.

She had dinner early, with Luke, and retreated to her room again when Javier returned home for the night. She'd booked onto an online course to improve her photography skills and researched some courses on management for charitable entities. She had a strong idea of what she wanted.

Thomas was the epitome of discretion and kindly courteous, leaving her with Luke as she needed the time to hold her baby and express love to him. But right now her baby wasn't here. There was nothing to distract her again from the heartache and hopelessness of loving Javier or the anger within that she'd missed out.

Why couldn't she have more? Why couldn't she have it all?

She walked towards the lounge, absorbing the emptiness of the apartment like a hit to the side of the head. But an achingly familiar, tall figure turned at the window. Her heart leapt into her throat. Not from fear, but worse—joy. The bubble of rapture burst a split second later as she remembered.

'Javier.' She stopped on the threshold. 'I'm sorry. I didn't realise you were home early.'

He looked cold and tired. His powerful form was half hidden by a loose black turtleneck and jeans. He hadn't shaved, and his hair stood in tufts as if he'd been tugging on it or had just not bothered with it for the day because he had other things on his mind.

'Don't apologise.' He watched her steadily but didn't step closer. 'Thomas's taken Luke to the park for an hour or so. I cancelled my meetings.'

Warily she waited in the doorway. It was obvious he had something to say and she could hardly walk away before he'd had the chance. But it was too soon for her—that aching wish inside her threatened to leak out all over again.

'We can't go on like this, Emmy. We can't keep avoiding each other.'

Her heart pounded. 'Actually, I think it's working well,' she argued stiffly, striving to retain self-control. Seeing him as little as possible was absolutely for the best. Because just seeing him like this, now, made parts of her ache in ways she wanted to avoid for ever.

His jaw tightened and his teeth clamped. 'I'm not well and I don't believe for a second you are either.'

She flinched.

'I was a jerk to you.' His voice was low and didn't sound like him at all.

She shook her head. She didn't want him to apologise, to be nice to her. She didn't want any sort of sympathy or pretence of caring because they'd happened to create a child together. She wanted to forget what she'd said, forget their physical intimacy and just move forward with new distance between them. It was the *only* way she could survive it.

'I shouldn't have said what I said,' she said hurriedly. 'It wasn't fair. Please forget it. We've just…we need to move on.'

'I'm never going to forget what you said, Emmy. Not ever.' He stepped closer but stopped as he saw her reaction to his words. 'And I don't want to move on.'

Emmy put her hand on the doorjamb for support. Caught in that doorway, she couldn't step either forward or back. It was as if she were trapped in a kind of purgatory.

'You told me you're in love with me,' he said quietly.

Her heart ruptured. This wasn't purgatory. This was pure *hell*.

She didn't need him to remind her. Didn't need her secrets ripped open for scrutiny again. The exposure burned.

'I keep replaying it in my mind—keep trying to recapture that moment. I want to keep it for ever.'

She shook her head and tried to step back but he lunged forward and caught her hands. Just the very tips of her fingers. She could've easily slipped free, except the look in his eyes fixed her to the spot. He'd always floored her with that infinite deep brown gaze, but the emotions swirling made that cocoa mix more magnetic than ever.

And for once, he stood as still as she. All that dynamism and energy of his was directed intensely at her.

'Please, Emmy. Stay. Listen.'

She blinked, absorbing the hit of emotion in that husky request, and she knew there was no way of escaping this now. So a moment hung—a beat for breath, for fear to bloom but for courage to be sought.

But then he spoke again.

'I thought about all sorts of… I don't know, ways to try… I thought about whisking you someplace amazing… but I don't want to do that—to use props or places to try to…' He frowned and muttered a curse against himself. 'I just want to ask for a few moments of your time. To listen just to me. Then decide for yourself what you want to do.' He swallowed. 'And whatever you want to do, I'll accept. I won't stop you or stand in your way.'

Was he saying he was letting her go? That he wanted her to go?

His cheekbones sharpened as he suddenly sucked in a breath. 'The day my father left wasn't anything extraordinary. He didn't give me a special hug. Didn't give me a photo or a medallion or a book or even a few words of explanation to remember him by. He just left in the afternoon for work like usual…' He trailed off and she felt the sudden trembling in his hands and realised just how painful this was for him to relive.

'Javier, you don't have to—'

'I do have to,' Javier argued hoarsely. 'Not just because you need me to, but because *I* need to. I know I need to and I want to. But I just hope you can be patient with me because…' He ground his teeth together. But then he drew another breath. 'It was days before I realised he wasn't coming back. Months before it sank in that he didn't want to see me any more and that he was never going to make contact. I couldn't believe he hadn't taken me with him. I'd thought we were close— I have these memories of him carrying me, playing… I'd adored him, Emmy…he was my papa…' He closed his eyes suddenly and his skin seemed to tighten more as every muscle flexed. 'But he just left me. I never saw him or heard from him again. I found out only a couple of years ago that he'd died in a car accident when I was almost twenty.' He released a sigh that was almost a groan. 'I was pretty small when he left, Emmy, but I think it might've left a big scar.'

The hurt in Emmy's already aching heart deepened.

'And then I remember when my mother left me at that school the week after she'd married a man I barely knew, and frankly was a bit afraid of, and it was only a month after my father had disappeared. She told me it was best for me. That I needed to get a good education. That I was to work hard. And I did. I worked so hard because I wanted to please her enough for her to want me to come home. But she never did. I was always sent away. All year, every year. And I remember finally going there for brief holidays and seeing the family photos of her and him with their two sons and not me. Never me.' He drew in another harsh breath. 'It was never me, Emmy.'

Emerald almost couldn't stand to see him in such devastating pain. Because recalling this, saying this, was pure pain for him. 'Javier—'

'I remember when I found out Beatrice had cheated,' he rushed to override her. 'You know, I'd thought I had someone on my team for once. That I had someone I could trust. But I didn't.'

She twisted her hands so she could hold him and stop him slipping his free. But he didn't try to; he looked into her eyes and laced his fingers through hers and visibly forced himself to keep speaking.

'So maybe I got bad at trusting people. Maybe I got used to never saying what I really wanted or how I really felt because, for a long, long time, there wasn't anyone who really wanted to listen. And because I didn't want to feel that badly again. I think I thought I had it nailed. It was easy not to open up to people, Emmy. It was easy to work and make money and be successful and buy all the things and enjoy casual sex and not ever really give a damn, because no one had really given a damn about me…' He drew in another shuddering breath. 'Until then there was you.'

Her heart stuttered, then stopped.

'It was easier than anything ever, to spend time with you, Emerald. And it was so good right from the start that I didn't want to be me, I wanted to be free of all that, to just enjoy being with you,' he whispered brokenly. 'And it was still the easiest when we were on the yacht until it became the hardest. Because I didn't realise what was happening until it was too late and then I didn't even know how scared I'd got. So when you said you didn't want to go with me to Miami and that you didn't want to sleep with me any more… it hurt a part of me that I thought had been numbed long, long ago. I lashed out. I instantly leapt to the conclusion that you'd leave while my back was turned. Not because I think the worst of *you*, but because I feared the worst had happened to me. Because it's happened before, Emmy. It's happened too much before and, honestly, there's a scared bit of me that will probably *always* worry that one day I'll wake up and you'll be gone.'

In this moment, time stopped. She couldn't hear for the thud of her pulse in her ears, yet somehow his words landed right on her lacerated heart.

'*That* is my worst nightmare, Emerald, and the horror of it is, I've been living it these last few days. Because there is *nothing* worse than waking without you beside me. Not even talking to you like this now—and talking about my father and my mother is hideous. But I'll do it because I need you to understand why I couldn't before…' He broke off and shook his head again. 'There's *nothing* worse than realising I could have had everything with you only I then threw it away because you were right. But I wasn't just lazy, Emmy. I was a coward too.'

'No, you weren't.' Because she understood. She knew. And now she couldn't stop the trembling invading her limbs. Her fingers shook, her legs, her lips. She blinked again and again but there was no stopping the torrent of emotion wrecking her body. Tears torn from despair to hope, from devastation to desire, tracked down her cheeks.

'Don't cry, *preciosa*. I'm trying to tell you how sorry I am. And I need to tell you. I need to talk before I touch too much, because if I touch too much I won't be able to talk any more and I know I need to talk more, but it's hard and I'm so very sorry I hurt you.' He bent his head, his voice the lowest, broken whisper. 'I want to give you what you need. I want to open up and be there for you. You're beautiful and special and you saying that to me was brave and I was such a coward back to you. I couldn't hear you properly because the anxiety was raging inside and not letting me accept your words.' His voice shook and she leaned closer still to hear him. 'I wanted it so much it scared the hell out of me and I pushed it away. I pushed you away. I denied your feelings and I shouldn't have. But I'm not now, and I hope you can listen to mine. I love you, Emerald. I've fallen for you—so hard, so completely. I love you and I want to do whatever you need me to do.'

'You don't have to,' she muttered. 'Please don't feel like you have to.'

He smothered a growl and stepped closer. 'Believe me, Emmy. Please believe me.'

She wanted to so very much, and seeing him like this? So emotional, so vulnerable, and so very determined... Her heart swelled so fast it simply burst.

'Hell, Emmy, you know it's hard for me to talk about this...so please believe me when I do,' he swore hoarsely and abandoned his resolve to touch little and talk lots. 'Or let me *show* you.'

She leaned in to meet his kiss, meshing with him in a seal that she never wanted released. The passion of the kiss sank all reason. Certainty slowly settled into her skin as the kiss deepened and lengthened. There was *only* this kiss and this kiss was *everything.*

All words were lost as touch took over—and that need to express beyond words. They stripped right there, in the hallway, hasty and quick and stumbling; they were too lost in each other to care where they were. There was only the desperation to reveal everything, to be bared, to connect as intimately, as completely as possible. All the while returning to that kiss.

She melted as he caressed her and then groaned. She understood his haste and confusion as to where to touch first because she felt it too. Clumsily perfect, they slid clothes from skin, and then there was nothing but searing heat as they finally coupled.

Locked deep inside her, he finally tore his lips from hers and bore his cocoa and coffee gaze straight into her soul. 'Love you. Love you. Love you.'

With every echo he pushed—a surge deeper, a thrust more powerful than the last. An almost savage declaration of the sweetest of things.

She saw it, felt it, believed it. Whispered it back, over and over until passion and pleasure coalesced and meant words would no longer form. All that could escape were sighs of delight—and then, with a final tight arch of her body and a fierce push of his, there was only the scream of ecstasy.

She stroked her fingers over his sweat-slicked back as he lay slumped over her. She loved their shared loss of power and she lay contently pillowing him.

Eventually he rolled, pulling her close to cradle her head on his chest.

'I'm sorry I ripped up at you. I just lost it. I'm sorry I couldn't figure this out sooner.' He groaned. 'But you believe me now?'

She nodded. 'I want to believe you so much.'

He kissed away her tears. 'It'll happen. The heartache will ease.' He swallowed. 'But I know now how it lingers, doesn't it? The fear.'

She nodded. 'It lurks, yes, hiding away, ready to strike. But we blast it away with the heat, right?'

'We do.' He rolled to his feet with a growl. 'But we'd better move for now. Luke will be back soon.'

Her heart soared all over again. She couldn't wait to cradle their baby together.

'I would do anything I thought was best for him, wouldn't you?' She grabbed Javier's hand and turned him to face her.

He nodded. 'Of course.'

'So maybe they really did think they were doing what was best for you?' She reached up and wrapped her arms around his shoulders. 'Maybe your father didn't want to stand in the way of your mother's happiness, and maybe he thought you really would be better with her or that you were young enough to forget him. And maybe...' She sighed. 'Maybe your mother really believed the boarding school would be better for you—that it would stretch you academically and give you space to adjust to a new man in her life? Or that it may even protect you a little?'

His smile was both tender and a touch distressed. 'You really do want to believe the best in people, don't you?'

'But isn't it possible? Don't you look at Luke and know that you would sacrifice whatever you thought was necessary to give him the best possible chances?'

Javier looked thoughtful. 'Perhaps you're right. I'd like to think you're right. But I can never know for sure that's what my father was thinking, Emmy.'

She nodded sadly. 'Then know this: *I* love you. And I will *never* leave you.'

His kiss was so passionate it was almost violent but she melted into it, marvelling as she felt him shuddering with need and emotion.

'Shower,' he choked.

She held his hand and led him into the large bathroom suite. Javier swiftly flicked various levers in the massive shower space and, once satisfied with the temperature blasting from the several heads, he turned and led her under the warm streams of water. They leaned together beneath the fall. It was heavenly—as if all their old hurts were washing away. He lathered soap and rubbed her down and kissed her sweetly until it wasn't just her skin that felt radiant and fresh and happy, it was her soul.

'I was wrong when I said I didn't care about what your

family did. I care about the effect they had on *you*. How they made you feel. I'm sorry I didn't listen well enough before.' He held her tightly in his arms. 'You know, if you ever want to go back and face them or challenge them or anything—even if you just want to return there for a while—I'll go with you. I'll always go with you—wherever you want or need to go. I'll be there too.'

'Right now I just want to be with you.' She shook. 'I need you.'

'I need you too,' he muttered. 'I spent every second of these last few days wondering—what you're thinking, whether you were still here, whether you missed me as much as I did you. Wishing you were right beside me so I could share something that just happened with Luke… missing *this*.' He caressed her curves the way he knew made her tremble. But he didn't stop talking, didn't let the desire take over before he'd said what he needed to say. 'I see now I didn't want to let anyone get close. But Luke has my heart in his little fist and I'm a hostage to fortune where he's concerned. But I'll always be there for him.' He held her hips and breathed right against her mouth. 'But you have a power to hurt me like no one *ever* has. You annihilate me, Emerald.'

'I wouldn't ever want to hurt you.'

'I know. Because I feel the same about you. I hurt you and it's the worst. Trust me, Emerald. I won't make that mistake again.'

Finally, finally she was beginning to believe it.

He must've read it in her eyes because he suddenly smiled—a light lifting his expression and making him more rakishly gorgeous than ever. 'You know, you had me from that very first night.'

She chuckled. 'I know I had a particular part of your attention.'

He framed the side of her face with his palm. 'You had all of it, it's just that neither of us was willing to recognise or accept it at the time.' He drew in a breath and leaned closer. 'But why do you think I went back to the island?'

'For the same reason you went there in the first place. The same reason as anyone—to explore paradise.'

He shook his head. 'Why do you think I invested in that particular property? Why that hotel?'

'Because you wanted to refurbish it—you like building beautiful things in beautiful places.'

'Why else?'

'Because it's in a place that's part of your heritage. And you wanted to feel connected to the land?'

'That answer is the one I've given to others as the most personal I could bear to utter before now. But why most of all?'

She didn't speak; there was another lump in her throat making it impossible to.

'You didn't think that it was because I had the best night of my life there and I wanted to remember it? Because I wanted to make the property as beautiful as my memory of it was? Because it was the one thing from that night that I *could* capture? Because I'd lost you.' He shuddered in her arms. 'But it brought you back to me. You take photographs…but that place was my aide-memoire for *you*.' He gazed down at her. 'This is my home.' He put his hand over her heart. 'Right here. Wherever you are. With you and with Luke.'

'He's our treasure.'

'Sure is.' He breathed against her skin, his lips gifting little kisses as he told her his truth again. 'And the beautiful dragon wasn't protecting the treasure, she *is* the treasure. You've given me the greatest joy in my life and

I know that there's more to be had with you. I don't want to miss out on you, *preciosa*. *You're* the magic in my life.'

When he let go and dropped his defences, he *really* dropped them. And Emerald flew right into his embrace—right into his heart. She poured her soul into his kiss until he staggered and spun her back to the wall so he could brace them both.

'I got hung up on things lasting—not lasting,' he panted. 'Forgetting that anything can happen at any time. And you were right, it was an excuse to be lazy. To avoid commitment. There's only the now—the snap of *this* moment,' he growled and thrust hard, claiming her again completely. 'And I don't want to have just this one. But *all* the moments I'm given, I want to share every one of them with you.'

Emmy fell deeper into the well of his warmth. Shivers of delight—of certainty—wracked her body as she realised the absolute pleasure of loving and of being loved was finally theirs together. It was the sweetest relief ever. She'd never imagined life could be so very wonderful. But it was—and it *would* be, for every moment to come.

CHAPTER FIFTEEN

Three years later

EMMY HOISTED THE strap more firmly over her shoulder and walked down the corridor to the pool deck, pausing the second the occupants of the shaded sofa came into view. Her bones melted and she only just scraped enough energy to stealthily fish the camera from her bag to snap the moment.

Javier Torres and his mini-me, Luke, were sprawled across the soft navy cushions. Both wore swim shorts, their tanned, slightly sandy limbs akimbo, their dark lashes long, their breathing deep. The two of them were breathtakingly gorgeous in their own ways and causing serious damage to the regularity of Emmy's heart. But she had time to take only the one picture before Javier stirred, somehow sensing he and Luke were no longer alone.

'Hey.' She lowered the lens and smiled at him.

The light that ignited in his eyes swelled her already full heart to bursting.

'You're back already?' he whispered and carefully sat up so as not to disturb their sleeping son. 'Did I sleep through the helicopter?'

Emmy nodded. 'Shows how tired you are when you can sleep through that racket.'

'Hell, yes.' Javier stretched his back and gestured for her to lie with them. 'It's been busy. We swam for hours this morning.'

Luke had just turned four and he was a little sponge, soaking up the experiences they were so lucky to be able to give him.

'Mamá?' Luke stirred and blinked. 'I saw a land iguana. There aren't as many of those as the marine ones.' He earnestly told her the most important things the second he realised she was there. 'And there were *lots* of sea lions.'

'Were there?' She hugged him. 'That's wonderful.'

Where other children his age had an encyclopaedic knowledge of dinosaurs, Luke had an insatiable appetite for information about the unique creatures of the Galapagos. This trip they were working their way around a couple of the outer islands, stopping often to swim at the stunning bays.

'Hopefully we'll see some more later.' She kissed his forehead.

'Are you staying now?'

'Yes.'

She'd hopped to Santa Cruz just for the night to welcome the new intake of Flores Foundation volunteers she'd recruited. Nowadays she worked part-time in that capacity, fitting in some photography when she could, depending on where they were travelling to next.

Javier had taken out his phone briefly and a moment later Thomas appeared on the back deck below.

'Luke?' the nanny called cheerily. 'Would you like to come to the galley so we can make something for afternoon tea?'

'I'm going to make *milhojas*. With peaches.' Luke beamed at her. 'It's your favourite.'

'It is and I would love to have some when you've finished.' The peach and pastry treat was delicious.

Luke toddled off with serious enthusiasm. From her vantage point on the deck overlooking the rear of the boat she watched him meet up with Thomas and the two of them disappeared inside. As Emmy turned back she caught her husband's intense gaze on her.

'Are you feeling okay, *preciosa*?' he whispered.

'I'm a bit tired too. This baby dragon of ours didn't let me sleep much last night.' She was six months pregnant and starting to feel it.

Javier placed his hand on her round belly and gently rubbed—gorgeously attentive. Well, just gorgeous. 'Then we should take advantage of Luke's industrious moment and have some quiet time ourselves.'

'Quiet time?' She chuckled, but she was melting already.

His answering smile flooded her with that warmth and security.

In the privacy of the master suite he turned to her—all remnants of sleepiness banished from his eyes by the dark burn of desire.

'I missed you.' He pulled her to him, sweeping his broad hands over her body. 'Missed every inch, every minute.'

She pressed closer against him, seeking his heat and hard welcome. She adored his strength and passion. 'So you're saying you missed my body?' she teased.

'God, yes.' He kissed her—teasing her lips with his tongue before taking full possession of her mouth. Only when she moaned with reciprocal need did he lift his head to gaze into her eyes. 'And your sass. And your spirit...*preciosa*.'

'It was only one night.'

'It was an eternity.'

He took his time to tease her, touching every way he knew that drove her crazy—tormenting her with playful, loving fervour until she was gasping for air and restlessly seeking to drive him as wild as he made her.

'Javier—'

'I want this too much to have it over too soon.' He tantalised with playful authority that only ignited her more.

For she wanted it too—this sweet, hot slide of happiness encapsulated in movement and murmurings. In moments like these—so many moments—of vitality and humour and joy.

'It's not ever going to be over,' she vowed, switching to rise above him and ride them both to that infinite source of pleasure.

'No,' he agreed, reaching up to cup her face and give her the source of balance she needed. 'Because I love you, I love this with you, and I love what we've created…right here. Right *now*.' He shuddered as he powerfully thrust up beneath her and drove his message home—deep into her heart. 'And the beautiful thing is, it's *always* now.'

'So you'll love me for a lifetime?'

'You know it.'

As they soared together and then finally rested in tender completion, his whispers soothed the fiery old scars on her soul. She was no longer alone and isolated and afraid of someone seeing her truth. He loved her as she was. He saw and celebrated her, as she did him.

She held his hand and pressed it to her chest so he could feel the regular beat of her heart. 'You know you're locked in here with me.'

'Good.' He kissed her again. 'There's nowhere else I'd want to be.'

On the edge of the earth, she found the safest of places—in the magic of his heart.

* * * * *

COMING SOON!

We really hope you enjoyed reading this book.
If you're looking for more romance, be sure to
head to the shops when new books are
available on

Thursday 3rd
September

To see which titles are coming soon, please visit
millsandboon.co.uk/nextmonth

MILLS & BOON

Coming next month

CHRISTMAS IN THE KING'S BED
Caitlin Crews

"Your Majesty. Really." Calista moistened her lip and he found himself drawn to that, too. What was the matter with him? "You can't possibly think that we would suit for anything more than a temporary arrangement to appease my father's worst impulses."

"I need to marry, Lady Calista. I need to produce heirs, and quickly, to prove to my people the kingdom is at last in safe hands. There will be no divorce." Orion smiled more than he should have, perhaps, when she looked stricken. "We are stuck. In each other's pockets, it seems."

She blanched at that, but he had no pity for her. Or nothing so simple as pity, anyway.

He moved toward her, taking stock of the way she lifted her head too quickly—very much as if she was beating back the urge to leap backward. To scramble away from him, as if he was some kind of predator.

The truth was, something in him roared its approval at that notion. He, who had always prided himself on how civilized he was, did not dislike the idea that here, with her, he was as much a man as any other.

Surely that had to be a good sign for their marriage.

Whether it was or wasn't, he stopped when he reached her. Then he stood before her and took her hand in his.

And the contact, skin on skin, floored him.

It was so...*tactile*.

It made him remember the images that had been dancing in his head ever since he'd brought up sex in her presence. It made him imagine it all in intricate detail.

It made him hard and needy, but better yet, it made her tremble.

Very solemnly, he took the ring—the glorious ring that in many ways was Idylla's standard to wave proudly before the world—and slid it onto one of her slender fingers.

And because he was a gentleman and a king, did not point out that she was shaking while he did it.

"And now," he said, in a low voice that should have been smooth, or less harshly possessive, but wasn't, "you are truly my betrothed. The woman who will be my bride. My queen. Your name will be bound to mine for eternity."

Continue reading
CHRISTMAS IN THE KING'S BED
Caitlin Crews

Available next month
www.millsandboon.co.uk

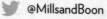

MILLS & BOON

THE HEART OF ROMANCE

A ROMANCE FOR EVERY KIND OF READER

MODERN

Prepare to be swept off your feet by sophisticated, sexy and seductive heroes, in some of the world's most glamourous and romantic locations, where power and passion collide.
8 stories per month.

HISTORICAL

Escape with historical heroes from time gone by. Whether your passion is for wicked Regency Rakes, muscled Vikings or rugged Highlanders, awaken the romance of the past.
6 stories per month.

MEDICAL

Set your pulse racing with dedicated, delectable doctors in the high-pressure world of medicine, where emotions run high and passion, comfort and love are the best medicine.
6 stories per month.

True Love

Celebrate true love with tender stories of heartfelt romance, from the rush of falling in love to the joy a new baby can bring, and a focus on the emotional heart of a relationship.
8 stories per month.

Desire

Indulge in secrets and scandal, intense drama and plenty of sizzling hot action with powerful and passionate heroes who have it all: wealth, status, good looks…everything but the right woman.
6 stories per month.

HEROES

Experience all the excitement of a gripping thriller, with an intense romance at its heart. Resourceful, true-to-life women and strong, fearless men face danger and desire - a killer combination!
8 stories per month.

DARE

Sensual love stories featuring smart, sassy heroines you'd want as a best friend, and compelling intense heroes who are worthy of them.
4 stories per month.

To see which titles are coming soon, please visit

millsandboon.co.uk/nextmonth

JOIN US ON SOCIAL MEDIA!

Stay up to date with our latest releases, author news and gossip, special offers and discounts, and all the behind-the-scenes action from Mills & Boon...

 millsandboon

 millsandboonuk

 millsandboon

It might just be true love...